Nora Roberts published her first novel using the pseudonym J.D. Robb in 1995, introducing to readers the tough as nails but emotionally damaged homicide cop Eve Dallas and billionaire Irish rogue Roarke.

With the In Death series, Robb has become one of the biggest thriller writers on earth, with each new novel reaching number one on bestseller charts the world over.

For more information, become a fan on Facebook at /norarobertsjdrobb

Titles by J. D. Robb

Naked in Death
Glory in Death
Immortal in Death
Rapture in Death
Ceremony in Death
Vengeance in Death
Holiday in Death
Conspiracy in Death
Loyalty in Death
Witness in Death
Judgment in Death
Betrayal in Death
Seduction in Death
Reunion in Death
Purity in Death
Portrait in Death
Imitation in Death
Divided in Death
Visions in Death
Survivor in Death
Origin in Death
Memory in Death
Born in Death
Innocent in Death
Creation in Death
Strangers in Death
Salvation in Death
Promises in Death
Kindred in Death
Fantasy in Death
Indulgence in Death

Treachery in Death
New York to Dallas
Celebrity in Death
Delusion in Death
Calculated in Death
Thankless in Death
Concealed in Death
Festive in Death
Obsession in Death
Devoted in Death
Brotherhood in Death
Apprentice in Death
Echoes in Death
Secrets in Death
Dark in Death
Leverage in Death
Connections in Death
Vendetta in Death
Golden in Death
Shadows in Death
Faithless in Death
Forgotten in Death
Abandoned in Death
Desperation in Death
Encore in Death
Payback in Death
Random in Death
Passions in Death
Bonded in Death
Framed in Death
Stolen in Death

J. D. ROBB

STOLEN
IN DEATH

PIATKUS

PIATKUS

First published in the United States in 2026 by St Martin's Press,
An imprint of St Martin's Publishing Group
Published in Great Britain in 2026 by Piatkus

1 3 5 7 9 10 8 6 4 2

Copyright © 2026 by Nora Roberts

The moral right of the author has been asserted.

*All characters and events in this publication, other than those
clearly in the public domain, are fictitious and any resemblance
to real persons, living or dead, is purely coincidental.*

All rights reserved.
No part of this publication may be reproduced, stored in a
retrieval system, or transmitted in any form or by any means, without
the prior permission in writing of the publisher, nor be otherwise circulated
in any form of binding or cover other than that in which it is published
and without a similar condition including this condition being
imposed on the subsequent purchaser.

A CIP catalogue record for this book
is available from the British Library.

Hardback ISBN 978-0-349-44623-3
Trade Paperback ISBN 978-0-349-44624-0

Printed and bound in Great Britain by Clays Ltd, Elcograf S.p.A.

Papers used by Piatkus are from well-managed forests
and other responsible sources.

Piatkus	The authorised representative
An imprint of	in the EEA is
Little, Brown Book Group	Hachette Ireland
Carmelite House	8 Castlecourt Centre
50 Victoria Embankment	Dublin 15, D15 XTP3, Ireland
London EC4Y 0DZ	(email: info@hbgi.ie)

An Hachette UK Company
www.hachette.co.uk

www.littlebrown.co.uk

Ordinary riches can be stolen from a man. Real riches cannot.
In the treasury-house of your soul, there are infinitely precious
things, that may not be taken from you.
—Oscar Wilde

Love is not a product of reasonings and statistics.
It just *comes*—none knows whence—
and cannot explain itself.
—Mark Twain

Chapter One

As she stood in skinny-heeled shoes instead of boots, a gown instead of trousers, Eve Dallas thought whoever invented the gala should be brutally murdered.

Maybe they had been, and their body fed to wild dogs.

Since that would've happened decades, maybe centuries before this September night in 2061, she considered the case closed.

Regardless, the strange institution of the gala remained a part of society's fabric. At least it did if you happened to be a murder cop married to a billionaire.

The Marriage Rules demanded it.

The whole deal supported Sarah's Song, a worthy charity, a national network for victims of domestic abuse founded around the turn of the century. While she couldn't argue with the cause, she wondered why people needed to wear fancy clothes in a big, fancy ballroom, stand or sit around making small talk, spend buckets on drinks and dinner instead of staying home, comfortably, and sending those buckets.

But that was just her, obviously, because people packed the big-ass ballroom and the big-ass space outside of it where various bars served various drinks.

In the rosy light and flower-drenched air of the ballroom, hardly anyone sat at the swankily decorated tables yet. She'd learned the gala had a specific order to things.

You had your arrival time, where you had to walk a kind of media gauntlet while society-type reporters took photos or videos so they could tell people who didn't rate an invite what you were wearing.

Then it was for-God's-sake-get-me-a-drink time, where you hit one of the various bars.

Fortunately, she'd crossed both those off the list.

Now it was mill-around time, where you stood in those skinny heels and talked to people you didn't actually know, and likely wouldn't have any further business with unless they ended up in the morgue.

After mill-around time came sit-around time, while servers served some sort of salad, and people went up onstage to thank everybody, to make their speeches.

Blah blah blah.

Then a meal, but you had to keep talking around the table, or to people who decided to come by and talk while you were trying to eat the fancily plated whatever they served you.

She had no doubt the food and the service would be top-notch. After all, the ballroom and the whole damn hotel belonged to Roarke. Which probably meant the gala people hadn't paid buckets for the space.

Once the servers whisked away those plates, brought out dessert, someone would make another speech—applause, applause.

Then the entertainment. Which, since Roarke had connections, would be Avenue A, with a guest appearance from Mavis.

Bright spot, she admitted, except she'd probably have to dance, and in these damn torture shoes. Dancing with Roarke, okay, fine, but dancing with whoever?

Marriage Rules, she reminded herself, and took another sip of very nice wine.

And even after all that, when it was finally socially acceptable to get the hell out, there was departure time, where you had to have yet more conversations before the mercifully short drive home.

Maybe the gala inventor should've been thrown to those wild dogs while still breathing.

Then Roarke, gorgeous in his tux, as comfortable in the formal wear as she imagined he'd once been in cat-burglar black, smiled at her.

"It's only a few hours," he murmured with the Irish flowing through it like harp song over green, mist-soaked hills. "And for a cause that matters, in so many ways, to both of us."

"You say that, but you're not standing on stilts."

"Fashion's a killer even you can't toss in a cage, Lieutenant. You're stunning." He took her free hand, kissed her fingers while those impossibly blue eyes looked into hers.

"All right now, time to share this beautiful woman."

Eve recognized the man who approached and the woman at his side as the heads of Sarah's Song. She knew the story—he'd been eight when his widowed mother had remarried. The abuse began shortly after the I-do's. Eventually, she'd taken her little boy and run, but not far enough or fast enough.

Now, some sixty years later, the boy who—on his mother's orders—had run for help that had come too late, held out a hand to Roarke.

"It's lovely to see you both. Eve, Martin and Sylvia Ellison, the brains, brawn, and heart behind Sarah's Song."

Martin caught Eve's hand in both of his. He had hair the color of old pewter that shot out in the same kind of electric shock bush sported by her former partner and current captain of EDD, Feeney. He had a ruddy, lived-in face and a toned-up, lightweight boxer's build.

His deep, dark brown eyes smiled into hers as if she were the only person in the room. Inside a streaky silver-and-white goatee, his lips curved.

"It's wonderful to meet you at last. Sylvia and I are big fans. That's probably not the right word," he said with a laugh she could only describe as jolly.

"Admirers of the work you do, and how well you do it." Sylvia nudged at Martin so she could shake Eve's hand. "Fair warning, we'll probably ask a thousand questions about that work before the night's over."

She smiled, a tall woman, thin as a whippet in a gown the color of her husband's hair. She wore her own in a cap of black curls, and had eyes of molten green.

Martin winked. "We've used our status for the privilege of sharing your table. Lots of schmoozing to do, but we'll enjoy sharing the meal with you, Roarke, Nadine Furst, your friends Louise and Charles, and, when they're not performing, Jake and Mavis."

"Not to mention Leonardo. That's one of his designs, I'm sure, and just gorgeous."

Eve glanced down at the gown. Roarke had called the deep purple bleeding and blending lighter and lighter as it rose up her body ombre. All she knew was it fit, had pockets—and a slash up one leg nearly to her damn waist.

"Ah—"

Roarke laid a hand on Eve's shoulder, bare but for the skinny strap that went back to the deep purple. "Leonardo's not only a good friend and Mavis's husband, but he understands just what the lieutenant needs in wardrobe."

"It has pockets."

Sylvia just beamed. "Shouldn't everything?"

"We won't keep you now," Martin said. "We want you to know how much we appreciate all you do. Dochas . . ."

He trailed off as he mentioned the women's shelter Roarke had built, and Eve saw clearly that some grieving lasts forever.

"It represents," he continued, "what my grandmother hoped for when she founded Sarah's Song. Not just safety, but hands outstretched to help, to renew, to rebuild. I hope you enjoy the evening."

Eve gave a little sigh when they walked away. "They're nice."

"They're exactly what they seem. Generous, intelligent, caring people. They're also interesting. You won't be bored. Let's get you another glass of wine."

Because she figured it made her a moving target, she went along. It didn't stop people from waylaying them. She blamed it on Roarke. People recognized him. And if they didn't, who wouldn't be attracted to the tall and gorgeous? All that black silk hair, the wild blue eyes, the mouth sculpted by a particularly artistic angel?

She saw plenty giving him a second look, a third, murmuring behind their hands as they did.

When she said just that to him, he laughed.

"And no one notices the long, lanky woman with the cap of deer-hide hair, the eyes like aged whiskey that take in every detail she sees. The chin that looks like it could take a punch. And has," he added, brushing a finger down its shallow dent.

"There's a group of three women at your two o'clock. Every one of them's mind-fucked you, a couple times each."

"Ah, is that why I feel so used yet oddly unsatisfied?" Deliberately, he touched his lips to hers. "There, that's better."

She had to smile, especially since one of the three women heaved a sigh and laid a hand on her heart.

"Enough of the milling. It's got to be sit-down time by now."

"Then we'll find our table and do just that."

They not only found their table—after the gauntlet of stop, talk, go, stop, talk—but Nadine and Mavis were already seated there.

They huddled together, giggling over something. Or Mavis giggled. Nadine, Eve considered, had more of a snicker.

They couldn't have looked more different, less like two women who would be not only friends, but great, good friends.

Mavis Freestone, former grifter, current rock star, mother of one with another on the way, had her hair in a spilling fountain of twisty curls tinted electric blue. A tiny woman, at least from Eve's stance of five-ten (without the stilts), she wore glittery, gleaming gold that hugged her impressive baby mountain like loving arms.

Eve figured she could've put her fist through the hoops dangling from her ears.

Beside her, Nadine Furst, ace on-camera reporter, bestselling crime writer, Oscar winner, and cohab of Avenue A's front man, wore a gown of smoky red. A sophisticated hue in a sophisticated cut that left one well-toned shoulder bare. She'd rolled her streaky blond hair into some sort of twist. A couple of jeweled pins sparkled in it.

Mavis spotted them first. Her face, already glowing, lit like the sun. "You're here! No dead bodies!"

"Night's young," Eve said, and put a hand on Mavis's shoulder before her oldest friend tried to haul her baby mountain out of the chair.

Roarke bent down to kiss her cheek, then Nadine's. "Breathtaking, both of you. How fortunate am I to share a table with three stunning women? Ah, and here's yet another," he added when Louise and Charles approached the table.

Dr. Dimatto did stun, Eve supposed, in a pale lavender gown that looked delicate enough air might tear it. And somehow added the faintest lavender tint to her gray eyes. Beside her, tall and lean, Charles Monroe looked as if he'd been born in a tux.

The doctor who'd turned her wealthy upbringing on its ear by opening and running a free clinic, and the former licensed companion, now sex therapist, made a solid couple, a solid marriage.

So hug time postponed sit-down time.

"Get a load of us," Mavis said with another giggle. "We're all mag to the ex. You ever figure it, Dallas, you and me, duded to the mega max and doing the totally uptown gala thing?"

"No."

"And she'd still rather be chasing a psycho down a dark alley."

Eve looked at Nadine, and thought it was good to have friends who knew you.

"Yes."

"Ah, let it chill, Dallas. Lap up the moment. This is my last gig before Number Two makes an entrance."

"I don't have to ask how you're feeling," Louise said as she took her seat. "I can see it. Not much longer now."

"How do you perform carting all that around?"

Mavis's eyes twinkled at Eve. "Wait and see. The guys'll be here soon. Leonardo just stepped out to tag August, make sure everything's aces at home with Bella. He's spending the night because it'll be a long one."

Since she'd run August, the nanny, former military, solid, Eve didn't worry there. Plus, Peabody and McNab shared the big, rambling, sort of fascinating house.

"Jake's with us," Nadine said. "They've spread the band around the tables before they take the stage."

Leonardo swept in wearing what Eve imagined he considered a tux with a long, billowing coat that reminded her of dusters in old Western vids. His hair didn't fountain like Mavis's, but it did spill in curls around his wide, copper-hued face.

He shook Roarke's hand, bent to kiss Eve, then repeated with Charles and Louise.

"And how is the beautiful Bella?" Charles asked.

"Perfect. Just perfect. They're having a dance party. August said Bella claimed since Mama and Daddy went to a party, she should have one, too. So Peabody and McNab came over and they're having a dance party before bedtime."

"You've made a happy home."

Leonardo beamed at Charles as his big hand covered Mavis's.

People began to take their seats at their tables when Jake came in from a door to the left of the stage. Then several of them jumped up again. So Eve watched as he did the walk, stop, talk, and in his case, pose for a selfie or sign the evening's program.

A good guy, she thought. He handled it all smooth as silk, patient and easy, but still making progress. Rather than a tux, he wore rock star black—jeans, shirt, leather jacket, and boots that suited his tall, lean frame.

No colorful streaks in the black mane tonight, she noted.

When he finally got to the table, Nadine poured him a glass of wine. "You earned it."

"Did. Hey, everybody." He grinned at Eve. "Hardly ever see you without the badge and weapon."

She tapped the evening bag—the one just big enough to hold her essentials. "You're still not."

"Oh. Okay then. Feel safer already."

They served the salad; they started the speeches. The first, fresh and pretty, the second, mercifully short and heartfelt enough she noted several people dabbing at their eyes.

As the main course came out, Mavis sighed. "Gotta waddle."

Eve gave her a blank look. "What?"

"Ladies' room."

As Leonardo helped her out of the chair, Nadine rose. Louise rose. Eve started to cut into what looked like some sort of actual beef. And Nadine tapped her shoulder.

"What? Really?"

"You're security. Bring your weapon bag."

"Security, my ass." But Eve grabbed her bag and rose. "You couldn't have had to waddle during the speeches?"

"Number Two was sleeping, but now? Sometimes they sit on your bladder. Sometimes they dance on it." Rolling her eyes, Mavis rubbed at the mound. "Someone else is having a dance party."

Since Eve didn't want that image stuck in her brain, she said nothing more. And didn't have to pull her weapon on the trip to the restroom.

She didn't mind the dinner portion, in fact enjoyed it. Maybe it wasn't pizza and beer with friends, but it was still sharing a meal with friends. And the Ellisons had stories to tell or conversational gambits that pulled stories out of others.

"I read," Sylvia began, "that you and Lieutenant Dallas met when she arrested you. That can't be true."

"Solid fact." Mavis lifted her glass of sparkling water, toasted Eve before drinking. "I had an off day that turned out to be the best day because Dallas busted me."

"What did you do?" Martin asked. "If you don't mind telling us."

"What'd I do, Dallas?"

"Fumbled a wallet lift. You got the wallet—some tourist—but you'd been trailing him, and I caught the lift."

"Caught me, too. I was better at the grift than the lift. Short cons, I ruled short cons back in the ago."

Then she put a hand over Martin's. "The street was better to me, for me, than where I ran from. What you're doing tonight? What you and Sylvia do, what Dallas and Roarke do? I'm all in. Anytime I can help."

Martin brought her hand to his lips. "You're a beautiful soul. It shines right out of you." He gave her hand an extra squeeze before turning to Eve. "And do you often make lifelong friends with former grifters and thieves?"

"Mavis was the first."

He laughed. "And the last as well?"

Eve thought of the man sitting beside her, so obviously amused. "Not exactly."

As dessert came out, Jake turned Nadine's face to his, kissed her. "Gotta rock."

And rock they did.

After an enthusiastic introduction from Martin, Avenue A took the stage to the thunder of applause. And with the blast of the opening riff, people poured onto the dance floor. They shook it in their tuxes, designer gowns, sparkling jewels. Some—more than some, by Eve's estimate—held up their 'links to capture the moment.

Halfway through the first set, Mavis wiggled. "Gotta waddle."

"Again?"

"Not that way. Gotta waddle up there. Haul me up, moonpie."

"Just how," Eve murmured to Roarke, "is she going to do whatever she does up there when somebody has to haul her out of a chair?"

He just smiled. "Wait and see."

She waited, and she saw.

The drums went to a pulsing beat, like a heart quickening. Jake held his hands over his head, clapped in a steady rhythm along with his other bandmates. And so, Eve noted, did people on the dance floor, at tables.

"How do we rock tonight?" he shouted.

And in call and response, the ballroom shouted back, "Loud!"

"How do we rock tonight?"

"Hard!"

"How do we rock tonight?"

"Wild!"

He did something on the guitar that sounded like a primal scream. Mavis, dancing onto the stage, managed to do the same with her voice.

The crowd roared.

As the music roared back, Mavis twirled around the bass player. The dozens of glittery strips that formed her skirt spun as she did.

Then she and Jake, eyes locked, moved together.

"Down went the sun, so the waiting's done. You and me, baby, gonna have some fun. Rock me. Loud. Rock me. Hard. Rock me. Wild."

Leonardo gripped Eve's hand. She'd have sworn his irises went from round to heart shaped. "Isn't she . . . Isn't she . . ."

"Yeah. She's all that."

During the next song, Mavis hip-bumped the keyboardist aside, and took over herself.

"When did *that* happen?"

Leonardo grinned at Eve. "She's been practicing."

"She's good." Beside Eve, Charles let out a half laugh. "She's really good."

"The band's been teaching her," Nadine said. "They're crazy about her. Well, who isn't? Jake says she's got a lot of untapped, and she's thirsty. So he's into helping her tap and drink it up."

Eve turned to Roarke. "Did you know she could do that?"

"I didn't, no."

"She wanted to surprise you." Leonardo just kept beaming. "She really hoped you wouldn't have to work tonight so you'd be here, see her play in public for the first time."

She did three numbers, the last in the set of her own composition. When the band took their break, Mavis came back to the table.

She sat with a *Whew!*, shook back her curly fountain.

"You astound me," Roarke told her.

"Aw." Then she looked at Eve.

"Wow."

"Really?"

"Serious wow, and I don't give up my serious wows lightly. You were great."

"I love gigging with Avenue A now and then. They're all just mag. Just mega mag."

Leonardo urged a glass of water on her. "Hydrate, my moon and stars."

"Yeah. Whew."

"Did you know," Eve wondered, "that Number Two sometimes moves one way when you move another?"

Now Mavis grinned. "Yeah. Number Two knows how to rock it. Loud, hard, and wild."

"Duty calls." Roarke took Eve's hand.

"Did someone get dead?"

"No." He shook his head at Mavis. "Part of the duty for me and mine tonight is socializing."

"Right." Marriage Rules, Eve reminded herself. "We'll be back."

"You gotta. The second set slays."

She did her duty, shook hands, made the small talk—or listened to it, when she had a choice. She watched women, and more than a few men, look at Roarke as though they wanted to lap him up like ice cream.

The second set slayed. She had to spend some time on the dance floor—part of the duty. She didn't mind that part when it was Roarke on a slow one.

"You're enjoying yourself."

"More than I figured, yeah."

"It's nice, darling Eve, to have an evening like this with you now and again."

She looked at him as they swayed on the crowded dance floor, as Mavis's bright voice blended with Avenue A's on lyrics about forever love.

"But unlike me, unlike Mavis, you always imagined yourself here—in a place like this. Owning a place like this."

"It helped me escape to believe it." He touched his lips to hers. "I didn't imagine you. That was beyond my ken. But here we are."

"Here we are," she repeated, and laid her head on his shoulder.

When the music stopped, and the ballroom thinned out to staff and a few stragglers, Mavis rubbed a hand on her belly.

"I'm not ready to call it. The bar's open, right, Roarke?"

"It is, of course."

"Are we up for it? I'm pulling the pregnant card. In a few weeks I won't be up for sitting in a bar with friends after midnight. It'll be rocking-chair time. It's Friday night, and we've got an overnight babysitter."

"Up for it, Lois?" Jake asked Nadine.

"Why not? It's Friday night. We're young, we're beautiful."

"Absolutely true." Charles turned to Louise.

"Nobody says no to a pregnant woman."

"Come on, Dallas," Nadine urged. "If you can work half the night on a case, you can have a drink in a bar after a gala."

"The first one's my job," Eve began. And Mavis gave her the puppy eyes and kept circling her hand over her belly.

Ten minutes later, it occurred to her here was something else she'd never imagined.

That she'd all but take over a fancy bar in a fancy hotel with a rock band, a pregnant rock star, a fashion designer, a reporter with an Oscar under her fancy belt, a doctor, a former LC, and an Irish gazillionaire who happened to be her husband.

Or that she'd have fun doing it.

Maybe it was the wine—damn good wine—or the bar snacks, the spicy little nuts, the fat olives, the crunchy something or other.

But no, she had to admit, it came down to the company.

Nadine shifted to her. "Jake and I got the full tour of the house."

"It's something."

"It is. It's so frigging happy. Not just the colors, the things, the style. It's in the damn air. Peabody and McNab's section, so different from Mavis and Leonardo's, but the same vibe. Happy-as-shit vibe. That blown-glass chandelier Peabody's mother made? Jesus! I want one for my own. Mavis says they're coming to the housewarming. I'm going to try to talk her into making me something."

Nadine reached for some crunchy stuff while Mavis had the band doubling over with laughter.

"Don't call me crazy."

"I don't think I ever have. Called you a lot of other things."

"True. Jake and I are looking to buy a vacation place. Together."

"Okay."

"It's not crazy?"

"I don't know. Maybe. Where's crazy?"

"Tropical, that's what we want. Beaches, privacy. We're going to talk to Roarke about where. Why not tap somebody who knows about all of it?"

"Okay." So she turned to Roarke. "Best place for Nadine and Jake to buy a vacation home. Tropical, beaches, privacy."

He leaned around Eve to speak to Nadine. "Investment property or a second home?"

"Second home."

"Villa or condo?"

"Villa. We want a house. Ah, something big enough to have guests when we want. With a pool, beach access, close enough, but not too close to restaurants and shops, some nightlife. He'd need a music space, I'd need an office space. We'd want at least four bedrooms, maybe a guesthouse. It's crazy."

"Not at all. You might want to explore Saint Lucia or Turks and Caicos."

"We've been looking at both of those. And Saint Bart's. And, well, too many others. It gets overwhelming."

"Why don't I send you a list of what I think may suit you?"

"Really? I'd appreciate that so much. We're both turning in circles about it. You found my condo, and it's exactly right. Then when we did the tour of the new house, saw how right it is for all of them, I thought, well, maybe Roarke can find what's right for us on this wild idea."

"I'll send a list, but you'll be the judge of it."

"Jake? I'm going to kiss Roarke."

"Okay."

Nadine nudged Eve back, leaned over, gave Roarke a smacking kiss.

Louise let out a peal of laughter and rubbed Mavis's baby mountain. Charles signaled for another round.

And Eve's communicator sounded.

"Uh-oh," Nadine said.

Eve pulled it out of her purse. "Dallas."

Dispatch, Dallas, Lieutenant Eve. See the officers at 1120 York Avenue. Possible homicide.

"Acknowledged. Contact Peabody, Detective Delia. I'm on my way. Dallas out."

Conversation had stopped, and eyes had turned to her.

Mavis lifted her shoulders, gave Eve a sympathetic smile.

"Well, hey, at least they waited to kill somebody until after we got to party."

"Yeah, some murderers are considerate that way. Gotta go."

"Drinks on the house," Roarke said as he rose. "Stay as long as you like."

Nadine looked up from her 'link. "That's the Barrister House. Owned until his death last winter by Henry J. Barrister, founder of Zip—global and off-planet shipping. Current residents his son, Nathan—current head of Zip—and his spouse, Aileen, two college-age daughters. Nathan has a sister, also in New York, divorced, no kids."

"Only you, Lois," Jake murmured.

"Good to know. Later. I would be dressed like this," Eve muttered as they walked out.

"We can stop at home on the way."

She wanted to, but . . . "Better to get there. Swing back after, change, get my ride if I have to go into Central. Except I'll need a field kit."

"In the car."

She glanced up at him. "You're always handy. Anyway, this is more my version of Friday night."

"It is, but, Lieutenant, it's now Saturday morning."

Chapter Two

Because she'd spent a large part of the evening sipping from an apparently bottomless glass of wine, Eve popped a Sober-Up before she got in the car.

It wasn't a long drive, and after one in the morning, a quick one. Still, Eve had time, since Nadine had given her the springboard, to do a quick run on the residents of Barrister House.

"Nathan Barrister, white male, fifty, looks clean from a quick pass. Married to Aileen Carville, mixed-race female, age fifty, for twenty-five years as of next month. Also looks clean. Daughter Chloe—age twenty-one—Harvard, business major. No bumps at this point. Daughter Anya, age nineteen—also Harvard, law student. Sister, Joy Barrister, age fifty-two, fifty-three in November—divorced, no offspring, resides Third Avenue. Also looks clean.

"He's CEO of Zip Global—founded in 1995 by his now-deceased father—who was married, and divorced, four times."

"An optimist then."

"Ha! Both his offspring come from the third marriage to Tina Glenn Barrister Carlyle Nance. So optimistic enough there for three tries. The old man was worth about a hundred and twenty-five billion at TOD."

She glanced over. "Doesn't hold a candle to you. And what does that mean? Why hold a candle? Sure, if it's dark and that's all you've got, or okay, romantic ambience."

"I'd say the Sober-Up hasn't kicked in, but you'd ask that if you hadn't had a drink for a week."

"Anyway. They've probably got live-in staff, so whoever's dead might be family, might be staff, might be somebody else altogether."

"I suppose it's wait and see again. But not for long."

He turned toward a gate.

"Gated. Should've figured."

"I know this place—the history, in any case."

Eve leaned past him to hold up her badge to the security cam. "NYPSD. Lieutenant Dallas and expert consultant Roarke."

She watched the red light scan her badge, then a human voice responded.

"Officer McNee, Lieutenant. Passing you through."

And silent as the grave, the gates opened.

The three-story house of faded, rosy brick stood tall and square. A detached garage connected to the main house with a glass-enclosed breezeway. Shrubs and leafy trees scattered artistically over the manicured lawn.

"Big place," Eve said, "but there's that candle thing again."

Roarke laughed.

"It was built during New York's Gilded Age for what you'd call a tycoon. Unfortunately for him, his son, who inherited, lost the bulk of the wealth gambling. At the tables, on the horses, in the market. And so the house sold and was for a time a museum. It was ransacked and damaged during the Urban Wars, after which, it seems, Henry Barrister bought it for a song. Likely it cost him more to have it repaired, refurbished."

"How do you know all this? You know the Barristers?"

"I don't, no." He shot her a glance. "I know all this because it's my business to know, and in fact, when I'd made up my mind to base in New York, I looked at homes like this, buildings like this."

"Then built yourself something completely different."

"Built what suited me, and what I'd built in my head as a child. Again, I don't know the Barristers personally. But I do know Zip as a solid, successful, well-run company."

They got out of the car, and while Roarke went around to the trunk for a field kit, Eve approached the uniform standing in the wide, covered portico.

Both the double doors behind him had lion's heads with rings clutched in their jaws. To her eye, they looked pissed off.

"Officer McNee."

"Lieutenant."

He stood as straight as a poker. Young and green, Eve thought, and his polished shoes, spotless uniform, and squared-on cap reminded her of her first look at the then–Officer Peabody.

"Give me the rundown."

"Sir. My partner, Officer Lawrence, and I responded to the nine-one-one at one hundred hours, two minutes. We arrived on scene at one hundred hours, eight minutes, approximately two minutes after the arrival of the medical techs."

When Roarke joined her, McNee stopped, swallowed.

"And?" Eve prompted.

"Sir. A woman identifying herself as Uma Acker, the housekeeper, gave us entry and took us back through to where the MTs attempted to treat the victim, a male the housekeeper identified as Nathan Barrister. They pronounced him as deceased at one hundred hours, nine minutes."

"Were others on scene?"

"Sir, yes, sir. Two women. Aileen Carville, the victim's spouse. The MTs administered a mild sedative, as she was very distressed. Um . . . Joy Barrister, the victim's sister, who placed the nine-one-one. Two more individuals arrived from another section of the house and were held back by my partner and myself. Staff members, Lieutenant, who live on the premises.

"Sir, my partner, Officer Lawrence, has all the individuals in the kitchen area, and posted me here when you announced your arrival."

"All right. Stand by, Officer. My partner should be on her way. Inform your partner I'm taking the body first. Where's the body?"

"Sir, the victim was killed in an office area on the main level, two rooms back from the central stairs."

"And you know he was killed there because you were there at that time?"

"I . . ."

"You know he was killed rather than suffered an accident of some nature, as you saw the killing?"

"I— No, sir, I . . ."

"Correct response? The DB is in an office area on the main level, two rooms back from the central stairs."

"Yes, sir."

"How long have you been in uniform, Officer?"

"It's my third day, Lieutenant."

"First DB?"

"Yes, sir."

"You gave a decent report. You'll need to do better. Next time, leave out the conclusions. Focus on facts known and any relevant observations."

"Yes, sir. Thank you."

"Stand by," she repeated, and went inside.

"He's very young," Roarke commented.

"And has a ways to go."

She scanned the enormous entrance, the grand staircase with its carved newel posts in the shape of sitting lions.

They didn't look real happy, either.

The marble floors, white as the Swiss Alps, looked just as cold to her. The room to the right held an elaborate fireplace. Its face—white marble again—was framed by white pillars, topped by a thick, white mantel.

A glossy white grand piano dominated one corner. A couple of long, high-backed couches in gold, a few chairs in white-and-gold stripes, tables—white or gold—sat in an arranged formality that made her back itch.

The smaller room to the left sent out the same stiff and formal vibe with its white sofa, little slant-top desk in gold.

"Nobody lives in either of these rooms," she decided, and walked on.

She found the office, and the victim.

And knew immediately the MTs had compromised the scene. Though it irritated, she had to assume they'd felt they had no choice.

The victim lay on his back, his head and hair drenched in blood that had yet to congeal. His eyes had begun to film, so the blue had a dull and glassy stare. He wore what had been a gray, long-sleeved tee—soaked red at the shoulders—and a pair of gray sleep or lounge pants. One gray house skid lay beside his right foot, the other near the big desk of glossy black.

He wore a gold wedding ring and some sort of medallion on a gold chain.

As she sealed up, took her recorder out of her purse, and clipped it on, Eve glanced around the office. A few paintings that were likely good ones hung on muted gray walls. A chair rail in deeper gray ran about three feet up the walls. A couple of black leather chairs, a gel sofa in a quiet blue gave the room some style.

The desk held a large comp monitor, a data and communication unit, framed photos that faced whoever sat at the desk. To the right, a door that would have blended into the wall if it were closed stood a few inches open.

Though she'd check it, she considered it a storage area, as to the left the door to a half bath stood open.

For now, she focused on the body.

"Record on. Victim is a Caucasian male, pronounced dead by medical techs at one hundred hours, nine minutes. The scene has been compromised by same. Though the victim is now on his back, the blood pattern on the floor indicates he was turned. Visible evidence of a head wound, probable weapon a large rock—looks like a decorative piece, about eighteen inches long, ah . . . eight inches wide at one end, descending down to about three at the tip."

"I believe that's a piece of amethyst, Lieutenant."

"Yeah?" She glanced up at Roarke. "Expert consultant IDs said rock as amethyst, lab to confirm. Said piece, situated on the floor by the right side of the desk, has blood and gray matter on the head."

She took out her Identi-pad, pressed the victim's finger to it. "Victim is identified as Nathan Barrister, age fifty, of this address. No visible defensive wounds. Victim wears a gold ring on the third finger of his left hand and a gold chain with . . ." She tipped the medallion up with a sealed finger. "Yeah, a Saint Christopher medal."

She turned the head, huffed out a breath at the severity of the wound on the back of the victim's head. "No wonder they pronounced so quickly. With this? If he wasn't dead when they got here, he sure as hell was by the time they tried working on him."

She sat back on her heels. "Close to one in the morning. He's dressed for bed or lounging around. Maybe he's working late, or came down to work.

"The way this looks? He's bashed from behind as he's walking back from that door over there. Check that out, will you? Probably office storage. You sealed?"

"I am, yes."

As she continued her examination, Roarke, avoiding splatters and pools of blood, moved to the door.

"Not office storage, no, it's not that." He had to put his back into it to fully open the door. "It's a vault."

"A vault?" She looked up from her gauges that told her TOD was about ten, maybe eleven minutes before the MTs arrived.

"And it holds some very interesting treasures."

She stood, walked over. It changed things, she thought. Changed everything.

She saw paintings that even her novice eye recognized as important. Jewelry sparkling behind individual glass displays. Sculptures, statues, what she assumed were artifacts, and more.

"What you have here, Lieutenant, is a small, exclusive, private, and ill-gotten collection."

"I get the first three. How do you conclude the ill-gotten?"

"For one? That exquisite Renoir? Stolen from the Smithsonian about, oh, maybe twenty-five years ago. The ruby necklace there? Stolen again, from—if I recall correctly—a countess, from her manor house in . . . it might've been Sussex."

He caught the look she slanted him, shook his head.

"There's an empty display there."

"There is indeed. And also a tablet on the built-in desk. I'd wager you might find the inventory."

"Yeah. Yeah." She looked back at the victim. "He maybe hears something, comes down to check. Bam, bash. Killer grabs one thing? That's a question. Maybe only has time for it. I'm going to want that tablet checked, but I need you to check the house security first. I'm going to tag the morgue, the sweepers, then start interviews."

She turned back to the closet. "It doesn't look like whatever was in that display would've been the handiest to grab if you were in a hurry. If somebody found the vic like this? Look at the timing. It had to be practically on top of TOD.

"Security," she said again. "Security feed. Any sign of a break-in."

"I know the drill well enough."

"Peabody should be here soon. If she brings McNab along, put him to work."

She made her way through the house, taking her time, as she wanted a sense of the whole. That sense turned a one-eighty when she saw the kitchen/lounge area.

She wouldn't have called it casual, but the entire area read warm, welcoming, comfortable. Not stark white, no I'm-crazy-rich gold. Instead, the soft green walls—with an entire one taken down to what might've been the original brick—added a kind of calm.

In a nook with padded benches, a trio—two women, one man—sat with their faces shocked, their eyes damp.

A pot of what smelled like tea sat on the table along with cups and saucers. Wide windows let in the wash of security lights that shined over a garden area going into its fall fade.

The appliances gleamed, the acres of counters spread in slate gray while the cabinets, glass fronted and lit, had frames of dark forest green.

In the lounge area, two women sat, huddled together on a long, L-shaped couch in that same forest green. The wide entertainment screen showed a painting of a dreamy landscape in its off mode.

People lived in this room, Eve thought as the female officer got to her feet. Some lines fanned out over the light brown skin at her eyes. The eyes themselves were a deep brown and sharp.

"Officer Lawrence."

"Yes, sir." She head-gestured and walked Eve back a few feet. "Ms. Carville, the victim's wife, found the body. The MTs gave her a light sedative, as she was hysterical. She states she came down looking for him, and found him. Ms. Barrister, the victim's sister, heard her screaming, rushed downstairs. She made the nine-one-one. At the table there, we have Uma Acker, the housekeeper, live-in, who also heard the commotion, came out of her room in the staff quarters downstairs. She woke the butler, John Tyler, and he woke the cook, Divine Fortigue, also live-in staff.

"Ms. Carville compromised the scene, as she tried to lift the victim, had him cradled in her lap when the MTs arrived. My partner and I did what we could to preserve the scene when we arrived, and moved all residents into this area."

She cleared her throat, glanced back toward the couch. "Carville has his blood all over her, Lieutenant. The sister has some, too."

"Understood. I'll take the wife first. My consultant is checking security. Did you notice a door on the left side of the crime scene?"

"Yes, sir. Slightly open. We didn't touch it or go any farther into the room than necessary so as to not further compromise the scene."

"Okay. I expect my partner shortly. Any assistance you can give to the consultant is appreciated."

"I'll do what I can."

Eve walked over to the trio at the nook. "I'm Lieutenant Dallas with the NYPSD. Either I or my partner when she arrives will be with you shortly to take your statements. In the meantime, I'd like a chair so I can speak with Ms. Carville and Ms. Barrister."

"Of course, Lieutenant." John Tyler rose immediately. Average height, on the beefy side, he moved with as much dignity as possible in a navy robe over pale blue pajama bottoms. Eve pegged him as late forties with his low crown of salted black hair over a square, dark-complected face.

His eyes, darker still, showed signs of recent weeping.

He carried a ladder-back chair from the dining room, through the kitchen, and into the lounge.

"Ms. Carville." He spoke quietly, gently. "Lieutenant Dallas is going to speak with you now. May I refresh your tea?"

"What? I don't know." She looked blankly from Tyler to Eve. "I don't know what to do."

He picked up the tea that had obviously gone cold, then lifted the second cup as well. "I'll just bring you fresh. Lieutenant, may I offer you tea or coffee?"

"Coffee, thanks. Just black."

Taking her seat, Eve faced Aileen Carville.

"Ms. Carville, I'm very sorry for your loss."

"Nate" was all she said. She looked down at her hands, hands still smeared with blood, as were her arms. The cotton top and pants she wore were soaked with it.

"I know this is a difficult time."

"Do you?" Joy Barrister snapped out the words as her eyes welled.

"Yes, ma'am, I do. We're going to do everything possible to find out what happened and who's responsible. Ms. Carville, I need to ask you some questions."

"Can't you see the state she's in?"

"Ms. Barrister, I need to speak with Ms. Carville. I'll also have questions for you. The sooner I begin, the sooner we'll have some answers. Ms. Carville, can you tell me what happened?"

"I don't know. I don't know." Tears slid out of liquid eyes the color of faded denim, down cheeks more gray than the dusted gold caramel in the ID photo Eve had studied.

"Mr. Barrister was downstairs," Eve prompted. "Where were you?"

"You won't treat Aileen like a suspect!" Joy Barrister gripped her sister-in-law's hand. "You come in here, wearing an evening gown, for God's sake, and interrogate her when someone's just murdered her husband. My brother!"

"Ms. Barrister, I'm sure Ms. Carville would like your comfort at this time, but if you continue to interrupt, I'll have you taken to another room."

"Of all the—" Joy broke off when Eve shot her a single, hard warning look.

"I apologize for the dress." Eve addressed it to Aileen. "I was at an event."

"It's a lovely dress. You look lovely." Aileen glanced up as the cook, with a wavering smile and teary green eyes, brought the tea and coffee on a tray.

"Excuse me," she said to Eve, and handed Eve her coffee. "Now, you drink some of this tea this time, missus. You, too, Ms. Barrister. Won't you let me clean her up?" she asked Eve.

"No." Aileen hugged herself. "No. It's Nate's. It's Nate's blood. I couldn't stop the bleeding. I couldn't wake him up."

"Do you know why he was in his office?"

Aileen turned, finally focused on Eve. "Are you a policewoman?"

"I'm Lieutenant Dallas, yes. I'm in charge of finding out what happened to your husband."

"He wasn't feeling well. A headache, a little wheezy, a little cough. He had a fever, too. Just ninety-nine-point-one, but he didn't feel well. He said he'd sleep in one of the guest rooms, go to bed early, but I said no, he should sleep in our room, in our bed. You always feel better in your own. I'd take a guest room."

She rubbed bloody fingers on her temple. "We always go around like that when one of us isn't feeling well."

"Can you tell me what time he went to bed?"

"It was not long after eight. Divine made him chicken soup for dinner, and tea for bedtime. He took some cold medicine, and I told him if he wasn't feeling better, I'd call our doctor tomorrow and cancel my trip."

"Your trip?"

Once again, she looked around with eyes dazed and blank.

"Oh. I was going for the weekend with some friends to a spa resort in, ah." She rubbed fingers on her temple again.

"Rhode Island," Joy said, gently now.

"Yes, that's right." She smiled. "Nate said not to worry. Divine's chicken soup would do the trick. I took the guest room. I had a new book, so I read awhile. There was a show I wanted to see, so I watched . . . I can't remember."

She put a hand to her brow, then brushed it through her hair. "Funny, I wanted to see it . . . I checked on Nate a couple of times. He sounded a little raspy, but he was sound asleep. Then . . . I'm not sure what time it was. I'd gone back to my book, but I couldn't read any more. It was late, I think. Late. I got up to check on Nate one more time before I went to sleep, but he wasn't in bed. The bathroom door was open, and he wasn't in there."

When she seemed to go blank again, Eve picked up the tea, handed it to her.

"Oh, thank you."

"What did you do then?"

"Then? Oh, I thought he may have gone downstairs to the kitchen for more tea, or fresh water, or . . . something. I thought I heard something. Um, I thought I heard something as I came downstairs."

"Something like?"

"Like something had fallen, and I thought, oh, for God's sake, that's Nate walking around in the dark when he's not feeling well, bumping into things, knocking something over. I thought that, and I called out to him, but he didn't answer me."

She set the tea down, let out a long breath. "He didn't answer when I called out to him. I went back to the kitchen, and turned on the lights, but he wasn't there. I called out again, and walked to his office. It would be like him to wake up and think of work.

"I saw him. I saw him, and he was on the floor. Blood, and he was lying there, in the blood."

She looked at her hands.

"I was screaming. I can hear myself screaming as I ran over to him. I tried to stop the bleeding, to wake him up, but I couldn't stop screaming. And—and Joy came."

"She had his head in her lap, if you want to know." Joy swiped a tear off her cheek. "I could see—I called nine-one-one, for an ambulance, for the police. When Uma rushed in, I told her to let them in the gate, in the house. I couldn't help Nate. I tried to pull Aileen away, but she wouldn't—" Her voice cracked, and she pressed her lips together.

"Where were you, Ms. Barrister, before you entered the office?"

"In bed. Sleeping. It was around one in the morning, I think."

"You're living here?"

"No. I'm having some updating done on my condo. I'm staying here while that's going on." She lifted her fingers to her eyes, inhaled long and slow. "I apologize for being rude. This is . . . this doesn't seem real."

Eve saw Peabody coming. "No apology necessary. Excuse me one minute."

"Max-ex dress," Peabody said, and spoke again quickly to avoid the snarl. "Roarke filled us in. McNab's with me, and now with Roarke. I can tell you right off, the security jammed from zero hours, seventeen, blipped for a few seconds at zero hours, forty-two, then fully off again until zero hours, fifty-nine."

Eve's brows drew together at the timeline. "Okay, that's tight. I've got TOD at zero hundred, fifty-five hours, nine-one-one logged at zero-one-oh-two hundred. That's damn tight. Nook there. Butler, housekeeper, cook. All live-in. Start with them while I finish with the wife and the sister. Get us as accurate a timeline as possible."

Peabody, her red-streaked black hair in a high, bouncy tail, and wearing what looked like comfortable and professional brown trousers and a navy jacket Eve currently envied, walked to the nook and introduced herself.

Eve went back to the lounge. "I'm sorry. I needed to update my partner. Ms. Carville, are you aware there's a vault in your husband's office?"

"Henry's vault? Nate's father. Yes. We—Nate—the painters—stumbled over it during some remodeling."

"Stumbled over it?"

Aileen looked helplessly at her sister-in-law.

"Nate had the office painted," Joy said. "During the process, as Nate told me, the painters tripped a mechanism, and the panel over the vault slid open."

"You were unaware it existed?"

"Henry never told us." Aileen spoke again. "I don't know if we'd have ever found it ourselves. When we decided, after Nate inherited the house, to live here . . . We considered selling at first. It's such a big house, and our girls are already in college, but it's where Nate and Joy grew up, and such an historic building.

"Once we decided to stay, we wanted to make it more ours. It's a big job. We started back here, where we all spend so much time. The kitchen, lounge, dining room, the powder room. The staff wing needed some updating, too. Then we did our suite, and a couple of guest rooms. Nate wanted to make the office more his. He works very hard. We had my office done at the same time."

"So you found the vault when?"

"Last month. No, no, I'm sorry. It was in July. The girls were back for the summer."

"And you opened the vault."

"Not right away—we didn't know how. We thought we'd have to hire someone to open it, but Nate finally found the combination in his father's files."

"I don't know why you're wasting time over something like this when my brother's been murdered in his own home. Anyone with eyes could see he didn't suffer that terrible injury from a stumble or fall, so . . ."

Joy trailed off. Her mouth opened slowly; her eyes, a deep blue, widened. She set down the teacup she'd lifted with a rattle.

"The vault," she murmured. "Oh my God."

Chapter Three

"Did you leave the vault unlocked?"

Even as Joy shook her head, Aileen answered. Between the shock and the sedative, she'd gone into a dreamy state.

"Oh, no. Never. When we opened it, we were just stunned. It's like Aladdin's cave. Nate said none of what was in there was on the estate inventory. He was sure of it. We were going to call the lawyer about it all, then I told him to let me do a little research first. It's what I do. I'm a freelance researcher. Honestly, all I did to start was take a picture of the Renoir. Neither Nate nor I believed it was real, but as it turned out, it was! And it had been stolen . . ."

She rubbed a hand on her temple again. "I can't remember where or when now. It's in the file—actually, there's a tablet in the vault that has everything listed. It took some time for us to get through the passcode. Anya finally did. Our youngest."

"Everything in there was stolen goods," Joy continued, then pressed her lips together. "My father kept excellent records on the tablet in the vault. When and where acquired, how much he paid, the worth of the piece—obviously he updated that regularly. It was shocking, and mortifying."

"And yet those stolen items remain in the vault."

"I know it's taken more time than it should," Aileen admitted. "We were so dumbfounded and, well, horrified. We weren't sure whether to go to the lawyer. We didn't want to involve the police."

"Because?"

"My father's reputation." Sitting stiffly now, Joy locked her fingers together. "Our company's reputation, and the public trust. Call us selfish, but we didn't want the company, our employees, and certainly not our family to suffer for something Henry Barrister had done. We wanted to plan out a way to return all of it, somehow, and anonymously if at all possible."

For the first time she picked up the tea, drank as if to soothe her throat.

"Alternatively, we tried working on a statement—but what could we say? Our father, the founder of Zip Global, was a thief, a man who paid to have paintings, jewels, objets d'art stolen, then hoarded it for his own personal, private enjoyment."

"Our poor girls," Aileen mumbled. "They'd be smeared by this. They'd rise above it, but they'd bear the weight. I asked Nate to let me research every piece—some had been stolen from individuals. We could find out the heirs. Maybe it would be possible to contact each one, separately, work out a return, explain we hadn't known, but now we did, and wanted to do what's right. We could ask to have our names kept out of it."

"But in case we couldn't guarantee that—and how can you?" Joy asked. "We worked on a statement, and on the best way to deliver that statement, if necessary. We would put our PR team on alert to help us handle any fallout."

"And when did you intend to do all this?"

"Nate talked to the lawyers—the estate attorney, Garrett Beyer—last Monday. We thought we should start there. We felt it was best to have legal advice and representation before we made contact with the list of owners I compiled."

"Who else knew about the contents of the vault?"

"Oh, just the family. Nate, me, the girls, Joy. We didn't even tell the staff."

She looked down at the tea she still held in her hand, but didn't drink.

"I have to confess we lied to the crew working on the house. We told them the vault held Henry's old files, newspaper clippings, magazines with articles on him or the company, that sort of thing. I mean to say, it had all been in that vault for so long, some of it for a couple of decades, even more, we didn't see the harm in taking our time, making sure it all went as smoothly as possible."

"We never intended to keep any of it."

"Oh, no! Absolutely not!" Aileen set down her cup, held out her blood-smeared hands to Eve. "You can ask Nate. We . . ."

And she looked at her hands. Eve watched the entire night fall around her again. The hands trembled, and she threw back her head and wailed.

Uma Acker, a tall bony woman with hair the red of a fading sunset twisted into a clip at the back of her head, got up quickly, strode over.

"Please, let me take her. She can't sit here covered in his blood this way. Please, let me take her upstairs."

"Go ahead. I need her clothes." Eve took out an evidence bag. "Please put them in here, close the seal."

"All right. Come on now, Ms. Carville, come with me. We'll go upstairs, we'll get you freshened up, get you clean clothes."

"No, no. It's Nate."

"He wouldn't want this for you, sweetheart. He'd want you to let me help you."

"I don't know what to do, Uma." She let Uma help her up. "I always know what to do, don't I?"

"You'll know in the morning. That's soon enough."

"They fell in love in college." Joy watched them go, swiped at another tear. "They never fell out of it."

"You heard your sister-in-law scream?"

"What? Yes. Or I wasn't sure it was Aileen. I just heard screams—I think I thought it was a show at first, turned up too loud. Then I realized it was real, and came running."

"Is the house soundproofed?"

"No. I'm a light sleeper, especially when I'm not in my own place. I think—I can't be sure now, as it just blurs—but I think I was half awake before the screaming started. I think I might have heard Aileen go by my room. She'd have to pass my door to get to the stairs. But I might be imagining that.

"Lieutenant, we have to tell their daughters. Aileen's not thinking straight yet. We need to get them home. I can arrange for a company shuttle to bring them here from Cambridge. Aileen and her girls will need each other now."

She pressed a hand to her face. "We'll have to make some sort of statement, but I can do that, as his sister."

"The office, at least, will need to be sealed off until fully processed. If there was a break-in—"

"What else? That damn vault," she muttered. "How did whoever did this learn about it, about what was in it? We were so careful. But . . . maybe my father wasn't. He wasn't as sharp as he'd been. The last couple of years, he hadn't been as sharp."

"Who might he have told?"

"I can't tell you. Maybe he had a second snifter of brandy and bragged to someone at his club. Maybe he wanted to impress a woman. His age didn't preclude him from wanting to impress women."

Now she shoved her hands through her dark blond hair. "Or I suppose it could have leaked through the lawyer's office. The house has good security. Not the best, in my opinion, but good security. I wish Nate had upgraded the system before doing the work on the interior."

"Your brother inherited the house."

"Yes. Our father had very traditional ideas. The son inherits the family home. Which was and is no problem for me. I'm more than happy with my condo. There were multiple bequests, for Nate, for me, for Aileen, for his granddaughters, for his staff."

"The same staff?"

"Yes, Nate and Aileen kept everyone. No reason not to."

"Any friction between you and your brother?"

Joy gave her a sour look. "I'd hardly admit it if there were, but others would be happy to tell you. So I can truthfully say no. Nate and I always got along. We needed each other—as our father was either focused on the company or on his current wife or female interest. And we liked each other. He was an easy man to like, so no, before you ask, I don't know if he had enemies. None he told me of.

"Lieutenant, I really want to lie down for a while. Just lie down in the quiet. If there's more, can we get to it later?"

"Sure, but we'll need your clothes."

"My clothes?"

"They also have blood on them."

She looked down, shuddered. "Oh. Of course."

Eve handed her an evidence bag. "Thank you for your help. And I'm very sorry for your loss."

"I appreciate that." She rose. "Can you tell me where they'll take my brother?"

"I've asked the chief medical examiner to take care of him. I'll leave his card if you or another family member wants to contact him."

With a nod, she started out, then stopped. She turned back with a hint of fear in her eyes.

"Will you post a guard? If whoever did this comes back, gets in again. I don't know where or how security was breached, but until we know and fix . . . We can hire private, but tonight."

"We'll have someone on the premises."

"Thank you."

Eve rose, walked over to where Peabody sat with the cook and the butler.

"I've got everyone's statements, Lieutenant."

"I don't know if it's early or late for you, but I'd be happy to fix breakfast for you and the rest of the police here."

"I appreciate that, but we're fine. Could I ask you, Ms. Fortigue, and you, Mr. Tyler, how long each of you have worked in the household?"

"Fifteen years," Divine said. "I started the year after I lost my husband. John—Mr. Tyler—came, what was it—two or three years after me."

"Two, and close to three. So over twelve years. Mr. Henry Barrister was a good employer. Mr. Nathan and Ms. Carville have been the same. Their daughters are delightful."

"Uma—Ms. Acker. It's about twenty-two years now, as she told Detective Peabody. Nearly half her life. She worked for the cleaning service before that."

"Thank you both for your help."

"I don't understand what could've happened." Tears blurred the cook's eyes again.

"It's our job to find that out. The office will be sealed off for the time being, and at Ms. Barrister's request, there will be uniformed officers on the premises tonight."

Before they left, the butler retrieved the chair from the lounge, carried it back to the dining room.

"What have you got?" Eve asked Peabody.

"None of them are sure of the time they woke up. Acker—the housekeeper—heard screaming, or thought she did. She said it took her a minute or two to realize it really was screaming, then she jumped out of bed. Their rooms are downstairs. She says she banged on the butler's door first, then ran up, and found the wife on the floor, cradling the victim, still screaming. The victim's sister had her 'link out, contacting nine-one-one.

"The butler came onto the scene, then the cook. They all corroborate. Tyler says he heard Acker bang on his door, shout something was wrong. That's when he heard the screams. Fortigue, the cook, said she heard banging and running, then the screaming."

"And leading up to all that?"

"Barrister wasn't feeling well. The cook made him chicken soup, and he went up to bed not long after dinner. The butler and housekeeper were already in their quarters by then. Fortigue states Aileen Carville was concerned about Barrister, that he tended to get a respiratory deal late summer, early fall. The sister said something about he'd always done that, it wouldn't be serious. She went down to her quarters about eight-thirty."

"Any sense of conflict in the household?"

"Nothing. The sister's been here for about ten days, and plans to stay for about another week or two, or however long it takes the crews to finish the work on her condo. Both the victim and his sister go into work through the week, generally leaving by eight-thirty. Carville generally works at home."

Peabody finished off the last of the coffee Divine had made her.

"The victim and his family moved in the second week of May. There were some worries—with the staff—whether they'd sell. All three state they've come to consider this home as much as employment, so they've been grateful the victim and his family kept the house, and kept them on."

Peabody glanced around. "They're also happy about the changes they've made. My impression? They respected and admired Henry Barrister, but they really liked Nathan Barrister. Liked the whole family."

McNab pranced in, blond tail of hair with its red tip swinging. His bony ass was covered with baggies the color Eve thought you'd get if you mated an orange with an eggplant. Since his shirt screamed in orange and purple zigzags, she assumed that was deliberate.

His usual forest of hoops and studs curved up both ears.

"Wild digs. And holy shit, that vault. It's like the high of high-class pawn shops. And the actual vault? It's like way last century. Classic. If it hadn't been open, I could've cracked that baby in about fifteen minutes."

Then he grinned. "I figure Roarke for under half of that. But still."

"Security?" Eve said.

"Right. Definite breach. The system's dated, too. Solid enough, but an easy decade or more behind. Broke in right through the office window. What they did? Unlocked it electronically, then just opened it, came through. Didn't bother to lock it on the way out. Slick enough," he added, "but it didn't take that much with this system."

Eve started out for the office. "Did the morgue pick up the body?"

"Yeah. The sweepers just got here. We opened the tablet—just a standard password deal. It's got everything in there listed. Plus what the dude paid for it, when he got whatever, what it's worth, all of it."

She stopped in the office doorway, watched sweepers taking samples of blood, others bagging the amethyst or dusting surfaces.

"Where's Roarke?"

"He wanted to check something outside. We've been through the place—a lot of place to go through. Just surface right now. But going by surface, it doesn't look like anything's out of place except in here. I took a look through the desk 'link—nothing hinky. Same on the one in the second office."

"I'm going to talk to the sweepers, do a pass through the main level. From the tablet, do we know what's missing?"

"Yeah, it's jewelry, emeralds and diamonds. Big-ass emeralds, a shitload of diamonds. Something called the Royal Suite, and worth like a quarter of a freaking billion. The expert says some more than that. Extreme wow on that. Anyway, we made you a copy of the data. Roarke's got it."

"Maybe that explains why they only took one thing. Grab that and leave. Except, the victim interrupted."

She turned as the housekeeper stepped out, both evidence bags of bloody clothes in her hands.

"Ms. Carville's nightclothes, Lieutenant." She handed her the one in her right hand. "And Ms. Barrister's. Do you want mine? Some blood transferred when I . . ."

"No. You didn't have any on you before you went upstairs."

Despite looking weary to the bone, despite the more recent signs of tears, the woman seemed rock steady.

"Ms. Carville?"

"She contacted her daughters. It was . . . difficult. Ms. Barrister's arranging a shuttle for them for the trip to New York. After, I convinced her to drink a soother. I was afraid to try anything stronger, since they'd given her a sedative. I think she'll sleep awhile. I hope she will. Is there anything more I can do?"

"I'd like to see downstairs."

"Of course. If you'll come with me."

"McNab, stick with the sweepers unless Roarke needs you. I want security locks on the crime scene windows, and monitors in place. See if Roarke can change the combo of the vault."

"Copy that."

"Peabody, with me."

Uma took them back into the kitchen, into a mudroom area and the back stairs. Stairs, Eve noted, that led both down and up.

"Should I call for John and Divine?"

"No, no need."

"Originally, the downstairs area held more bedrooms for staff. Men's quarters on one side, women's on the other. The kitchen, the servants' hall. When the house served as a museum, much of this area was for storage, repair, cleaning, authenticating, and so on."

The stairs opened into a good-sized lounge with entertainment screen, a couple of sofas, a few comfortable-looking chairs.

"During the Urbans, the museum was ransacked, damaged, then abandoned as others were during that period and for a time after. Mr. Henry Barrister purchased it, and did extensive repairs. This is now our shared lounge. Divine enjoys jigsaw puzzles."

She gestured to a table where one was in progress. "John and I may add a piece or two now and then. We have an eat-in kitchen, our rooms with en suites. There are two other bedrooms, but since I came to Barrister House, only three live-in staff.

"Occasionally, other temporary staff may be housed for large events."

She broke off, closed her eyes. "Did he suffer? Do you think he suffered?"

"I don't think so."

Uma nodded, pressed her lips together. "We share an office. Though Divine prefers to work on her menus, food orders, and so on in the main kitchen or her own room. I generally use the desk in my room, but John and I have no issues on sharing the office space."

"In all the years you've worked here, you've never been inside the vault?"

"I didn't know there was a vault until I heard you talk about it tonight. Until I saw, just now . . . I don't understand it."

"Who cleaned the office?"

"When the first Mr. Barrister occupied it, he used a droid. Since then, I've done the daily cleaning, and our cleaning service would clean once a month."

"I've got the name and contact for the service, Lieutenant."

Eve just nodded at Peabody as she roamed the space. "Any outside egress?"

"Yes." She led the way into the kitchen, white and spotless, and through it to a walk-in pantry with steps leading up to slanted doors.

"For emergencies, and I've never used them in the two decades I've lived and worked here."

Eve climbed up, examined the locks, the security pad, and put it on her list for the sweepers.

"Did you have plans if Mr. Barrister had decided to sell the house?"

"As I said, this has been my place for half my life. I think I might have taken some time to decide, to plan. Henry Barrister remembered us in his will. He was a generous man, so I could have afforded to take time. We were allowed to stay, that was Nathan Barrister's generosity, while they considered their options."

"Okay. I'll be upstairs. When we leave, the office will be sealed, and we'll have officers stay on the premises."

"You must find who did this, Lieutenant. He was a good man. A good son, a good husband and father."

"Finding who did this is our priority. We'll be in touch. If anything occurs to you, however trivial, contact me."

"Believe me, I will." The first hint of anger broke through the shock and grief. "Someone came into our home and took a life. Believe me, I will. Good night, Lieutenant, Detective."

Eve head-gestured to Peabody and started for the stairs. As they went up, Peabody glanced back.

"It's a really nice, comfortable space. It's like sharing a big, three-bedroom apartment. And no commute to work."

"Roarke and McNab probably took a look at that lock. I want the sweepers to dust it anyway. No commute to work," she repeated as Peabody closed the door behind them. "Easy to get out of the office, back downstairs. If you're smart—and why wouldn't you be?—you'd stage it to look like a break-in. Murder of the moment, most likely, but the theft had to be planned."

She walked back out and into the entrance hall.

"Quick trip up and down the stairs this way, too."

"You don't really think it's an inside job?"

"Not discounting it. It's as easy to believe the staff knew about the vault as it is to believe they didn't. It's been there a long time."

One of the white-suited sweepers came in, shoved up her goggles. "We're about done in there, Lieutenant. Want us to seal it?"

"No. I'll take care of that. There's a lock and security pad downstairs, behind the kitchen area—outside doors, up a ladder. Process that. Inside and out."

"Will do. Some vault, huh?"

"Yeah, some vault. Peabody, arrange for a couple of uniforms, one to patrol the property, the other to sit on the crime scene. Rotate them out, another pair in at oh-nine-hundred. Then you and McNab can go get some sleep."

"I can write this up."

"No, just get me your reports. I need to think about it. Meet me at the morgue tomorrow. We'll say ten."

"The vic's wife, Dallas? I can't see it."

"Nobody knows the inside of a marriage unless they're inside it. Staff, yeah, they'd have a good sense, but nobody knows the full story except the people in it. She's low on the list, but nobody's crossed off, not yet.

"Find McNab, take off. If you see Roarke, tell him I'm almost done."

Eve stood where she was a moment. She let the quiet take over. But for some murmurs, some shuffling from the sweepers as they spread out to process other areas, that quiet held.

In it, she walked to the office, skirted the blood, moved to the window. Electronic lock, disengaged.

She used a single finger to lift the glass. Smooth and easy. And soundless.

Twelve-seventeen, she thought, jam the security system. A minute or two, a couple more if you're cautious, careful to reach the window, disengage lock. You're inside by, at a guess, twelve-twenty-one, twenty-two.

She moved over to the vault.

"Have to know where it is," she muttered. "Already know it's here and at least some of what's inside. How long to open it?"

McNab said fifteen minutes, less for Roarke, but she wouldn't take that as fact until she'd spoken with Roarke.

"Let's figure you've got it open by twelve-thirty-five, maybe a few minutes longer. What the hell are you doing from then until you bash Barrister? Take what's in that empty display, lots of big shiny emeralds. Maybe gloat over them."

Wandering inside the vault, she frowned.

"Did you hear something? Hear Barrister coming down? Oops. Maybe you hide, don't figure you can get back out unseen yet. Wait, wait. Maybe."

She didn't much like it, but maybe. And maybe the whole process took longer from the jam.

"What about the blip? That's a problem. Your jammer signals the security flipped back on. Oh shit. Have to fix that. Everybody's asleep, don't panic. Just get it down again."

She closed her eyes, tried to see it.

"Napping on your feet, Lieutenant?"

She snapped back, found Roarke right in front of her.

"What, did you come in the damn window?"

"Well now, it was open, wasn't it?" He ran a finger down her chin. "I'm told you're about done."

"About. Trying to get the timing so it makes sense. Start at the top. How long after the jam to get to the window? I figured you were out there doing a test or two."

"And so I was."

As he spoke, he crossed to the window to add the security lock. "After the jam, you wouldn't wait long, but it's a quiet neighborhood, so likely wait a minute, make sure the jam held, be certain no lights suddenly come on. No alarms sound. And so they did, as I can tell you the gates opened enough for a man to slide through at twelve-eighteen, and closed again."

"One minute from jam to gate, okay."

"Someone good enough for all that would, I suspect, be smart enough to take time making his way to this window."

He turned from it to set up the monitor she'd ordered.

"Be sure no one's out for a walk to help them sleep. Be sure they haven't suddenly gotten a dog."

"How long, most likely?"

"Exactly, as this window lock disengaged at twelve-twenty and forty-two seconds. So there you have three minutes and forty-two seconds."

Since her recorder remained on, she thought but didn't say: You're the B and E expert.

"Then?"

"Listen. Listen to the house, to the tones of the quiet. Rushing equals mistakes, so you don't. Make certain, then hit the mechanism that slides the panel open, and there she is. An old beauty, and one that takes a different skill to seduce than what you'd find more usually today. It's math and listening again, patience, nimble mind and fingers."

Because he sounded nostalgic, she rolled her eyes. "How long to open it?"

"As it's not connected to the system—she's an old beauty, remember—I can't tell you exactly. I'd wager between ten and twelve minutes, if you're experienced, so you'd approximate half-midnight and add a minute or two. I'd add a bit more, as after coming in, he may have taken that time to listen, feel the house, assure himself he's alone. So, give it, ah, twelve-thirty-five, a minute or two on either side, to enter the vault.

"Now, it may be he stood here, a moment or two, basked in it all. Foolish, but understandable, as it's an impressive array, and you don't just dump something like the Royal Suite in a sack. Too precious. You've got separate bags or cases for each piece."

"How many pieces?"

"Five if you're counting the earrings as one. And you'd take a bit of care. Add another five or six minutes, more if—and who wouldn't?—he wanted to hold those beauties in his hands for just a bit."

"Still a time lag before TOD." But not as much of one as she'd calculated. "Why only take the emeralds?"

He smiled at her. "You've theorized that already."

"Because that's what someone hired him to take. But still, all that? Tempting. So a pro, a pro for hire. Or a pro who already had a buyer lined up for the emeralds."

She circled back to the door.

"She said she came down looking for him. She's in a guest room because he's feeling off and went to bed early. She checked on him a few times, and the last time, he's not in bed, so she came down looking. She said she heard a thump, like he'd knocked something over. She's back in the kitchen, according to her statement, so it should've been a loud thump."

"Like a man falling after being coshed."

"Yeah, like that. She walked down this way. It would take her a minute, maybe two if she went the other way around the central stairs. Finds him, starts screaming. So the killer's out by the time she gets to the office. But it's damn close."

"Ninety seconds, perhaps a little more, from that spot, through the window, and at a run—and you'd run, wouldn't you then? Bolt away from the house, and over the wall, as the gates didn't open again until the medicals and cops arrived."

"The killer could've gotten past her in that minute or so, but . . . doesn't hit the logic button they'd go for the door. Why go that way, when the window's there?"

She took another look around. "Locks and monitors set and activated?"

"They are."

"Then I'm going to seal up the room. I need that copy of what's in the vault. That's a whole other thing to deal with."

"I have that for you."

"He was the variable." Eve studied the blood on the floor. "Otherwise, probably in and out again, way under an hour. Slick. But he wasn't feeling well, wheezy, a cough, little fever. Maybe woke up, came down to make something hot to drink, or decided to work to take his mind off feeling like crap.

"No sign of a struggle. Attacked from behind."

Roarke said nothing as she sealed the room, until they'd walked out and she disengaged her recorder.

"You run," he said now. "There's a reason you don't bring a weapon to a job like this. Caught? It's more time in a cage even if you never use it. So you don't bring one."

Eve heard it in his voice, the lightest touch of anger.

"A job goes wrong, you run, as nothing's worth your life or anyone else's. But this one didn't run. So it's panic at best, or it's just being willing to take a life at worst. The rest was well-thought-out, I'm figuring. And as you say, the victim was a variable not considered.

"It should've been. You always consider the variables. If his wife heard him fall, the thief had the Suite in hand. No need, no need to kill when you can run. The victim had no weapon, you'd have found it."

Eve slid into the passenger seat as Roarke got behind the wheel. "Killer could've taken it."

"That would be as foolish as it comes, and I don't see foolish in this setup."

As he drove, he sighed. "And now I'm going to add to your troubles. There's an ivory statue, sixteenth century, in the vault. Exquisite work. A sculpture of the goddess Venus. Some—as I recall—seventeen, eighteen years back, I lifted that from a museum in Florence."

"Shit. Just shit. You said you didn't know the Barristers."

"And don't. I took a job—for that specific item—through a broker. As I did, darling Eve, when I stole the Royal Suite from the Tate Gallery in London a year or so before."

Now she just stared at him. "Well, fuck me."

"Ah well, I've a strong feeling you won't be in the mood for that. Not in the least."

Chapter Four

Since pulling out her hair wouldn't change a thing, Eve let her head drop back and stared through the sky roof of Roarke's fancy car.

"I need to know everything."

"And you will. I didn't note the Venus straight off, you see. Then McNab and I got into the tablet, the inventory. Well, that was a bit of a jolt, I admit."

"Oh, really?"

Understanding, he patted a hand on hers. "I could hardly say: 'Why, look here, Ian, that ivory piece the old man paid sixteen million for? Well, I had that in my hands one lovely spring night.' Then there was the bigger jolt when I saw the Royal Suite on that list, and not in the vault. So what I'd had in my hands on a damp and windy night in London had ended here. And been taken again, in blood."

She sat in silence a moment.

"How did you hook up with the broker?"

"One earns a reputation in certain circles. And the broker was also known to handle deals such as this professionally. He offered me the job because he believed I could manage it, and because he knew he could pay me less than others who could, as I was hungry. Not that Summerset didn't keep my belly full, but hungry in other ways."

She knew what it was to be hungry, in all kinds of ways.

"And you said—how long ago?"

"I'd have been about eighteen."

Now she had to just sit there a minute. Just sit there.

"You broke into the Tate Gallery in London and stole a bunch of jewelry worth a quarter billion when you were a teenager?"

He smiled a little as he turned to their own gates. "I was precocious. It was worth that, or about that, and it's worth more now—today's money—and more yet to a collector, due to history and notoriety."

She lapsed into silence again as they drove toward the castle of a house with its scatter of lights on to guide their way into welcome. The house with towers, turrets, more rooms than she could count.

A house he'd built, very likely aided in that with some of his take from stealing the emeralds.

"How much did you get?"

"I remember very well. Ten million. Enough, more than, to change my life. I'd had solid takes before that, but nothing near as exciting, or as profitable. I did some other jobs for the broker, like the Venus, but still, for the most part, preferred finding work on my own."

Once he pulled up, stopped the car, he shifted to her. "I can't change who I was or am, Eve, and wouldn't. Because here I am, with you. But I can be sorry this complicates things for you."

He'd complicated things for her since the first instant she'd locked eyes with him.

And she couldn't be sorry for it.

"I have to think my way through it. I've got to get out of this dress and these damn shoes, and think."

Then she made herself breathe. "I knew who and what you were and are when I married you. It didn't stop me, did it?"

"That's a fact I'm grateful for every day."

"But I have to think."

She got out of the car, shoved at her hair. "There's no reason to think what happened tonight has anything to do with . . ." She stopped at the door. "The broker."

"Dead, some seven, maybe eight years now. And far too professional to steal from a client when he lived."

"He'd have known the client."

Roarke opened the door. "Ah, there? Maybe yes, maybe no. But as a careful man who ran his business for a few decades, I'd say he would've done his due diligence. Now, the client might not be aware the broker knew, as the typical deal would be a down payment—wired from account to account, a portion of which would go to the person or the team doing the job, as down payment. Nonrefundable on all sides, that."

He paused as she pulled off her shoes before walking up the stairs.

"When the job was done, the piece verified as authentic, another portion of the payments would be transferred. It would be up to the broker and client how to deliver the piece, and once done and authenticated, the remainder of the fees wired. And so, done."

"The broker was in Dublin?"

"I'll say he floated, though he came from Mayo. An international business he had. I want to say I never probed too deeply there, as he treated me fair throughout our . . . association. I never heard he treated anyone less than fair."

"A sterling character."

Roarke shrugged off the sarcasm. "In his way."

The minute they hit the bedroom where the cat sprawled across the acre of bed, she pulled the dress over her head.

And made a sound like a woman having a very satisfying orgasm.

Then stood, lean and limber, in the tiniest excuse for a bra and briefs nearly the same color as her skin.

His lips curved. "Yet another reason to be grateful every day."

She flicked him a look before pulling out a nightshirt. She peeled out of the underwear, then yanked on the nightshirt.

"I have to think."

"You'll think in your sleep, no doubt of it. And let me add something to your thinking. I'll be of help here. I know what it takes to plan a job like this, and there's no planning such a job without a client at the ready or a way to put the Suite on auction, in the underground with those who'd not only covet it but have the wherewithal to pay what I believe would rise up beyond half a billion USD."

"Half a fucking billion."

"The notoriety, Eve. It's been lost for nearly two decades. More, it's recognizable. It's famed. It couldn't be fenced in ordinary ways. And it would be undeniably stupid to break it up, to pop any of the stones. The value would plummet."

She followed all that—simple logic. But couldn't quite just slide over the half a billion.

"He knew it was in there. He knew about the vault and he knew the emeralds were in it. How?"

"That I don't know. But I'll be thinking about it myself. And I've a few lines I can tug you can't."

"Other thieves."

"And former associates. So to speak."

He'd already removed his jacket, loosened his tie.

He came to her now, took her hands. "I never put a fistful of jewels, a painting, a piece of art however exquisite over a human life."

"I know that. I couldn't be here if I didn't know that. I need to find someone who did."

"And I'll help in any way I can. You need some sleep, and I could do with some. I'll wake you. Tell me when."

He would, she thought, whatever time she said.

"Seven-thirty will do it. Enough time to write this up, set up my board, think, then get downtown to the morgue. Saturday morning, traffic shouldn't suck too hard."

"Half-seven then."

She got into bed. The cat stirred himself to belly up, then curl at her back. When Roarke joined her, he drew her close, kissed her brow, her lips.

"They say it takes a thief to catch one."

"In my world it takes a cop."

He brushed his lips over hers again. "We'll blend our worlds on this. We're good at it."

She couldn't argue with that. Even as her mind circled, she dropped into sleep.

The next thing she knew was coffee.

The scent of it, rich and dark, sliding into her senses. And when she blinked open her eyes, there it was, strong and black, the seductive steam rising over a tall white mug.

And there he was, sitting on the side of the bed, holding it out to her.

She pulled herself up to sit, reached for the mug with both hands. The fact he wore jeans and a T-shirt threw her off.

"Where's your suit?"

"Which one?"

"The one you're not wearing."

"It's Saturday, darling."

"It's—right." The first, life-altering sip woke up her brain. The second was just luxury. "We were going to sleep in, hit the gym, take a swim. We talked about maybe wandering around the street fair."

"And seeing how many street thieves we could spot between us. Murder plays hell with even the best-laid plans."

"Especially the victim's. Anyway, thanks for the coffee."

When she'd gulped it down, she handed the mug back to him, then headed into the shower to complete the process of waking up.

She'd never know how Roarke did it. Whether he bagged eight hours of sleep—rare—or two, he could get up, dress, buy a small planet, hold a virtual meeting with somebody in Mumbai, then sell the small planet he'd just bought at a profit, all before breakfast.

That alone was likely one of the reasons he'd been such a successful thief. Now, of course, she had to deal with the fact he'd been successful enough to steal a bunch of emeralds that ended up in the secret vault of a dead man.

No reason, she thought as she stepped into the drying tube, no reason at all to think that long-ago theft had any connection to last night's theft and murder.

And still.

She grabbed a robe, this one the color of the wine she'd enjoyed the night before, and stepped out.

Roarke sat, tablet in hand, cat sprawled across his lap. Domed plates and a pot of coffee waited on the table. He glanced up, smiled at her in a way that made her regret duty called.

"Off you go now, mate." He nudged the cat down. Galahad slid himself to the floor, stretched, stalled, then stalked away to sprawl again in a patch of sunlight.

As Eve walked over to join him, Roarke poured her more coffee.

"Okay, let's just get this out of the way."

"Fully awake now, are you, Lieutenant?"

"Yeah. While it's unlikely something you stole when you were eighteen connects to the case other than the fact you're the reason it was in the damn vault, it's tricky."

"It is a bit, isn't it then?" He lifted the domes off a full Irish breakfast.

"A bit? Roarke—"

"The only person who can connect me to the Royal Suite died seven years ago in March, at the age of a hundred and six, from natural causes. I checked. Well, there's Summerset," Roarke added with an elegant shrug. "But I think we can be confident in his discretion."

Since Summerset was more than Roarke's majordomo, but the man who'd taken him in, a brutally beaten boy, and given him a home, had stood as a father, Eve couldn't argue that one.

"The point is," she began as she sampled the Irish bacon—so damn good—"part of the investigation has to probe into the original theft. How those jewels—all the contents of the vault, but those jewels particularly—came into the victim's possession. Who knew about the vault, about the contents?"

"Understood. It would be difficult, even for you, Lieutenant, to find any crumbs to follow back to that brilliant night. You'll contact Scotland Yard, Interpol, Tate security, their insurance investigators. And you'll find I left not a single crumb for them to follow."

She ate some eggs. "Now you're bragging."

"I can't deny it's a fond memory for me. Near to six months of preparation as I recall, the mental and physical challenge of it, perfecting the timing, creating the tools, learning how to, in a way, dance under, over, around the beams."

He smiled in memory. "A kind of ballet, or kata. A combination of both."

She had to admit, it didn't annoy her as much as it should that she would have loved to have seen him do it.

He buttered a slice of toast, offered it to her. "I was young, Eve, but never reckless. I knew if I could succeed with this, I could do anything I needed to do."

"What about Brian, your other friends in Dublin back then? The people you ran with?"

"Not a word to any of them, no. If I'd failed, it would pull them down into it, wouldn't it? There's a reason Brian punched me in the face when we walked into the Penny Pig a few years ago. I pulled back from my mates, slowly, gradually, then all at once.

"The jobs I took, or the ones I aimed for on my own? Bigger, riskier. They were my family, and I trusted them. But."

"It only takes one slip."

"Yes, only one. So I made sure not to slip."

"How did you handle the money? The fee?"

"As with all. Wired into an account I'd set up, and from there into another, and into a company I used as a front until I could dissolve that. Investing it, you see, as we lived as we always did. I had the hotel, the first building I bought, so you—well, it's just a matter of washing the funds clean, then building them. Invest in another property, keep your sidelines, we'll say, well to the side."

"Basically, buried accounts, two sets of books."

"Well now, more than two for certain before you. I've closed that door, and you'll have to trust me. There's no key to be found."

"I just don't want to find some . . . awkward surprise while I'm digging."

"I'm doing some digging of my own. I made some contacts this morning."

"Who? Where?"

"I'm going to skip over the who, as we'd be back to awkward there for those I spoke with who may still be in the game. And the where's here and there. But none I spoke with knew—or admitted to knowing—about this job. If it was brokered, none I've reached as yet know the who there."

"What about the original broker? Did anyone take over his business?"

"His grandson, who's now retired and living in Italy."

"Where?"

"I'll find out if you like. The broker's legitimate businesses—which of course he financed through his brokerage—passed down to his wife and children. He had but one wife through his life, and six children. He left plenty to share—properties, a pub, a restaurant, and so on. But to the grandson of his youngest son, he left what he used to build his comfortable fortune."

"Since he's dead, why don't you say his name?"

"Lifelong habit. In any case, how would it help you now? And how would you explain knowing any of it?"

He gave her hand a pat, topped off her coffee, then his.

"I know the man I worked with kept both his clients' and his, I suppose *agents'* would do, names out of his records. He had a kind of code. Such as, for this? It was . . . let me think."

Frowning, he sipped coffee.

"I believe it was something like Yank Scut—*scut* meaning he didn't much care for Barrister—for the Five Green Pieces—those being the jewels—through the Jammy Jackeen. That would be me."

"What the hell does that mean?"

"The broker came to Dublin from the west counties, and *jackeen*'s a Dubliner—in an insulting way. *Jammy*? It's lucky. And he had—you can't hold me to the exact of it except my own take, which I remember very well. He had, I'm thinking he had ninety-point-ten. That would be—"

"I get it. Ninety's his take, ten's yours."

"There you have it."

"And how do you know he kept his records that way?"

He gave her one of his easy shrugs. "Because after I turned over the jewels, I made it a point to slip into where he kept his office one night and see for myself. I made sure nothing but his word against mine could tie me to them."

As she ate, she twisted it one way, wrapped it around another, turned it upside down, then back again. She just couldn't manipulate it all to pull his eighteen-year-old self into it.

"What about the other piece? The statue."

"Ah, the magnificent Venus." He finished his eggs. "The Bargello in Florence."

"I don't want the details, at least not now. My head might explode. Just, first, is that the only other thing you stole that's in that vault? And second, did it all work the same as the emeralds?"

"Yes and yes."

"Okay. For now anyway, we're going to put that aside. Not away, Roarke, aside. If I hit on something that feels like it could flip in that direction, in your direction, we'll figure out what's next."

"And if I do, I'll tell you. I'll share with you anything I find out. This will make a splash in the media, but it will also have a considerable impact in other circles."

"You need to be careful with your own shovel, pal." She rose. "Whoever did this didn't hesitate to kill."

"And whoever did this has very likely already turned over the goods, collected the fee, and enjoyed a lovely afterglow."

"Not everyone's as slick as you."

She went into her closet. Because she refused to think about clothes, she grabbed black trousers, a black tee, a black jacket, belt, and boots. And the weapon harness she'd hung in her closet the evening before.

"No cracks about funerals," she said as she came out. "I need easy today."

Now he rose, stepped to her, drew her in. "And I've made it harder than it has to be."

"Not you, not really. It just is harder than it has to be. Or *stickier*'s the better word.

"I need to write it up, set up my board and book. Structure makes it easier, too."

"I'll set up your board. You." He pointed at the cat wandering innocently toward the plates. "Out." To make sure of it, he hauled the gray pudge up in one arm, and after stepping out with Eve, closed the bedroom door.

"And I know, yes, he might just figure out a way to open the door and get what he wants." He used a thumb to scratch under Galahad's chin and made him purr. "He might've been a grand associate back in my before."

"You did have associates in your before."

"I did, yes, now and then. But none in the jobs that apply here."

She really did need to put it aside, Eve reminded herself. She needed to focus on this time, this investigation.

When they turned into her office, Roarke put the cat down, and she went straight to her command center.

"I haven't downloaded the scene from my recorder."

"I'll handle it. I know what you'll want on the board. If I miss anything, you won't."

After she opened operations, he worked on the auxiliary.

It gave her time to write up her report, to start the murder book, and then to do a full run on the victim.

Nathan Barrister had done well for himself—up until a few minutes before one that morning. The only son of a wealthy man, he'd had the best education money could buy—and from the looks of it, brains and application had carried. He got his MBA from Harvard—so his oldest daughter continued that university tradition.

He'd joined the business as a VP at twenty-four—after spending the best part of a year traveling after grad school.

He'd cohabbed with his future wife in the same condo his sister now owned. Married at twenty-five. They'd moved to a house in Brooklyn—if her math was on target—when they expected their first child.

They owned a second home in the Hamptons, a flat in Prague, and some sort of cabin in Maine.

Before the bequests in his father's will added to it.

His wife's business, launched while they lived on the Upper East, had earned a solid rep by the time they'd moved to Brooklyn and started a family.

He'd been COO of Zip Global by forty.

No criminal, no addictions that showed.

On his father's death, he'd taken over as CEO, had inherited the Barrister House, its contents but for some specific bequests, a villa in Tuscany, its contents, some commercial properties—including Zip's Manhattan headquarters—a yacht, two vehicles, a private shuttle. Not to mention several billion.

She checked the time, calculated she didn't have quite enough to do deeper runs on the spouse, the sister, the staff.

She glanced over, saw her board complete, and Roarke sitting on the sofa talking on his 'link.

She left him to it and walked over to the board. Hands in pockets, she studied it. Yeah, he knew how she liked it done, and saw nothing left out.

The position of the body at the crime scene. Not where and how he'd fallen, but she could extrapolate, within reason, by calculating how and why it had been moved.

The wife comes in, turns him, ends up cradling him. The medicals move her back, lay the body down to attempt a miracle.

No reason in either case to reverse the direction of the fall, or to change by any substantial amount the distance from the vault, the desk, the door, from where she'd found it.

"Walking away from the vault and toward the desk." She circled the board. "Had to be. Check with the MTs, make sure they didn't move him, but had to be."

When Roarke joined her, she continued to think out loud. "He doesn't close the vault—not trying to hide it or the contents—but starts toward his desk when he's hit from behind. That clear kind of tray thing there on that stand. The same size and shape as the murder weapon."

"A lighted display," Roarke told her. "It would shine from below, show the amethyst off."

"On the office door side of the vault. There's no sign of struggle, scuffle, fight. Maybe the killer slides behind the office door. 'Oops, gotta hide.'"

She circled, hissed out a breath.

"But shit, didn't he have ears? Didn't he hear somebody coming? Maybe not until too late to take a dive out the window. He grabs that big purple chunk of rock. Barrister sees the vault open, walks over, looks in. 'Well, shit, we've been robbed.' Turns, starts for the desk. Killer steps out."

Eve joined her hands together to mime holding a bat.

"Swings. Barrister goes down. Drop the rock, then dive out the window."

"Sloppy," Roarke said. "In the end, sloppy. Panicked and sloppy."

"What would you've done? You can't get to the window and out in time."

"That would've been a mistake, but they happen."

He studied the board, the crime scene as she did. And very easily imagined himself there, in the dark with a fortune in his hands.

"Better to slide behind the office door as you said. Wait. He comes in, goes to the vault, you slip around the door while his attention's fixed there. If you've done your job, you know how to get out another way, as that's a basic thing to know. The security's still off. Into the next room I'd go, and out that window. Out and over the wall before he'd finished telling the cops he's had a break-in."

"No panic?"

"Panic gets you nicked," he said simply. "And murder? Beyond taking a life, it gets you life instead of the five to ten you'd deal down."

"You'd get more than that five to ten if you'd been busted before."

He acknowledged that. "True enough. Added to it, you'd do the time empty-handed after having those sparkling baubles in hand. There's no word about the theft as yet. Not from the sources I've tapped. A take like this? There'll be some talk soon enough."

He ran a hand down her back. "It could be some of the sources might hear something that cracks the door a bit. Brian's doing a bit of poking."

"Brian."

"He's not in the game, and hasn't been, really, since we were barely more than lads. He's a publican, but he hears things, and knows how to prime a pump. Added, he's not one who'll hold back because I'm married to a Garda."

Smiling, Roarke patted her ass. "He's very fond of you, Lieutenant Darling."

"Right. I've got to get going." She walked back to her desk, picked up her recorder, and fixed it on. "Morgue first. Then I'll go into Central. It should be quiet, so I'll work there for a few hours. I want to stop back by the Barristers' on the way home. Do a follow-up, talk to the daughters."

"I'll do what I can from here."

She paused by the board again. "I'm speculating Barrister left the vault door open because he was going to report the break-in, and if the wife and sister are telling the truth, he intended to return everything. Took too long to figure out how and when, whatever, but they weren't keeping the stuff. I believe that—or lean toward it—because there's nothing to indicate otherwise."

"But you'll talk to the lawyer, the daughters."

"Yeah, I will. So I get why he didn't close the vault. But why didn't the thief? Maybe ran out of time again, but why not?"

"The vault could've given him more trouble than he'd anticipated. Or his popper on the electronic window lock needed finessing. Or he spent far too much time playing about in the vault. Or."

"What's this *or*?"

"He followed instructions, and they were to leave it open."

Intrigued, she angled her head. "Why?"

"Bragging rights for the client, if the client's an eejit. More likely, if it's that *or*? The client wanted it known quickly the Suite had been stolen—even if just by the owner of the vault."

"Like a smug factor?"

Laughing, he nodded. "Could be that simple and petty, yes. And likely figuring no one's going to report the break-in, as they'd have to explain how it was they had possession not only of the emeralds but of all the rest in the first place."

"I buy that *or*. Not just the smug factor, but figuring no cops involved. And I've got one more *or*. Knowing this Barrister will bring in the cops."

The way he nodded, she knew he'd reached that *or* himself. "So the theft makes a splash, a public one. Adds excitement for a potential auction."

"And boosts up that smug factor. I've got to get started, and I'll be back when I'm back. Go on, get that workout, take that swim."

"I may." He took her by the shoulders, kissed her, lingered. "Take care of my cop."

"Always the plan."

He watched her go, and decided not to think about those best-laid plans.

Chapter Five

She'd been right about the traffic. It glided along relatively smoothly as she headed downtown. Pedestrians, on the other hand, swarmed. Joggers bounded down the sidewalks or pumped in place at crosswalks. Others strolled, walked dogs, pushed a variety of baby carriages. Still more streamed in and out of bakeries, delis, cafés or huddled at carts.

The air through her open window smelled of cart coffee, yeasty things, sidewalk flowers, and the occasional out-of-order recycler.

The sound was movement—the rolling traffic, the crowd, the bass beat through another open window, or the blat of a maxibus pulling up to a stop.

She made it nearly halfway before the first ad blimp lumbered overhead and blared out its morning hype for fall sales.

SNUGGLE INTO SWEATER WEATHER AT THE SKY MALL!
KICK UP YOUR HEELS IN BOOTS, BOOTS, BOOTS!

It seemed to her that marketing, one way or the other, tried to shove the current season aside like it was the enemy.

Ignoring the sales pitch, she watched an airboarder complete a pretty good reverse flip. In the next block a couple embraced beside a waiting Rapid Cab as if one of them was going off to war. As she braked for a red light, an old man with a streaming white ponytail ran huffing across the intersection.

The front of his shirt read: THREE MILES A DAY.

And the back: KEEPS THE REAPER AT BAY.

Beneath his baggy red shorts he had knobs for knees, toothpicks for ankles. His stringy arms pumped as he hit the sidewalk and kept jogging east.

Barring a cardiac incident, Eve figured he'd do the three miles in decent time.

Saturday morning New York City kept her entertained all the way to the morgue.

Her bootsteps echoed along the tiled white tunnel that smelled of death and bleached lemons. Inside the break room, she spotted a woman in scrubs who studied Vending without joy and muttered to herself.

"Shit coffee or shit tea. Maybe shit cocoa."

Eve continued on and pushed through the doors of Morris's home away from home.

Like Roarke, he didn't wear one of his sharp suits today, and again, it threw her for a moment. Instead, under his clear protective cape he wore a green T-shirt with jeans and black kicks. He'd wound his dark hair into a single thick braid.

Today's choice of music as he stood over the dead ran to something jazzy with a lot of complicated piano.

"Sorry to pull you in on a Saturday."

He just smiled. "The dead may, we hope, rest in peace, but the work for them never rests."

"I hear you. His wife states he wasn't feeling well, turned in early. Wheezy, slight fever, so she slept in the guest room."

With a nod, Morris gestured toward Barrister's open body cavity. "Upper respiratory infection. Not serious, but enough to make him feel, in medical terms, like crap, and warrant an early night.

"Otherwise, I'm finding a healthy male, one in good physical shape. Muscle tone indicates regular exercise. Last meal, chicken soup, eaten at about seven last night. He'd taken OTC cold meds, had some valerian tea with lemon. I'd say closer to eight last night."

"Which is worse?" She stepped up to the slab. "Murdered when you're feeling great, or murdered when you feel, in those medical terms, like crap? Kind of a toss-up, but I think I'd rather go out feeling great."

"I'd have to agree. Who wants their last moments dominated by a raw throat or gastronomical distress?"

"Yeah." She shrugged. "Either way, you're on a slab. No sleep meds then?"

"Nothing more than what's in the cold tabs, but the lab will confirm with the tox report. He shows no sign of addiction, illegals, alcohol, tobacco, herbals."

"Mild injuries to the face, knees. Hit from behind, fell forward, knees hit, face hit."

"That's accurate. A blow to the back of the head with a heavy object. In your prelim notes last night you indicated a rock. I didn't see your updated report before I left this morning."

"Yeah, sorry, I didn't write it up until shortly before I left."

"Understandable. Given his TOD, I imagine you didn't get home until near to four this morning."

"That's about right. Big rock." She held her hands apart. "Sort of club-shaped. Roarke ID'd it as an amethyst."

"An amethyst."

"Yeah, big purple rock." She pulled out her 'link, brought up the crime scene photo as Peabody walked in.

"Sorry, sorry. Delay with the subway, so I hiked it. Whew."

"I just read that three miles a day keeps the Reaper at bay."

"Yeah?"

"I read it on a T-shirt, so it must be true."

"Nothing keeps the Reaper at bay forever, but you'll die in better shape." Morris studied the image. "That's a beautiful stone. A pity to use it for taking a life."

"It'll need to be cleansed," Peabody said.

"Seeing as it's got blood and brains on it, yeah, they'll need to clean it up."

Smiling, Morris stepped back to the body. "I believe Peabody means a spiritual cleansing. Still, if his family loved him, they won't want it back. Your notes indicated a break-in."

"That's also accurate."

Eve filled him in while he worked, and Peabody found something—anything—else to focus on.

"Fascinating. What joy does someone gain by hoarding the precious only for themselves?" He shook his head.

"Considering the OTC meds, round about eight, is it likely he'd have woken, gone down sometime after twelve-thirty, heading toward one?"

"With the infection at this stage, it's very likely he'd have slept poorly, even with the meds, and after four hours or so, very likely been restless."

With his microgoggles in place, he opened Barrister's mouth, shined a light. "His throat's inflamed. Again, it's not serious, but would be very uncomfortable."

"So he gets up." Eve began to pace. "Goes down. Maybe going to get more tea, take more meds. But he didn't. He goes into the office. Did he hear something, see something? Maybe just glanced in, saw the vault open. Possible."

"No defensive wounds," Morris told her. "Nothing to indicate a struggle."

"Bashed from behind. Never saw it coming. A couple minutes, maybe three minutes later, because she's looking for him, because she hears something fall, his wife walks in and finds him. Just him. Killer's gone, that fast."

She frowned. "The window's closed. He closed the window behind him. But not the vault."

"The window's the escape route," Peabody pointed out. "Takes a second to close it, and then nobody's going over to look out and see you running away."

"And it would take longer to close the vault, close the panel. Yeah."

She slid her hands into her pockets. "His daughters are coming in from college. They may want to see him. I'm going to do a follow-up with the family later today."

"I'll have him ready for their goodbyes by noon. If they want to visit later than one, Cicero will be on duty. I'm scheduled to meet Garnet and her daughter about that time. We're going to the street fair."

Garnet DeWinter, Eve thought, scientist, bone expert, and fashion plate.

"That'll be fun. McNab and I were going but, you know, dead guy. But Mavis, Leonardo, and Bella are. You should tag them, maybe meet up."

"I'll do that."

"We'll get out of your way." Eve took a last look at the body. "If he hadn't had a cold, he'd probably be alive."

As they walked out, Eve ran through the timing again in her head. "It's all so damn close. If the wife checks on him after he wakes up, but before he goes down, she's likely the one who goes for tea or whatever.

Or gets him more meds. Need to check if they've got an AutoChef in the bedroom, because why not program tea there if that's what he wanted?"

"The cook kept loose valerian tea leaves in the pantry. He didn't want any at dinner, but she suggested he have some before bed. Since they keep it for a kind of sleep aid, and nobody actually likes it, it's not programmed. She always makes it at the time, a cup when needed, and adds fresh lemon because he prefers that when he's not feeling well."

"That covers that. I want you to contact the MTs who worked on him, get the position of the body when they arrived—in relation to the vault, the door, the desk, the window. How much they had to move it to examine and pronounce."

"Okay."

"It won't be much. The uniforms were right behind them."

Outside, Eve got behind the wheel. "We'll work at Central. I've done a deeper run on the victim, and I'll copy you. We need one on the wife, sister, daughters, staff, and the dead father.

"Probably at some point the dead father's four ex-wives."

She pushed back into traffic, already thickening, and headed downtown.

"We're going to split the list of stolen items in the vault. Since it's Saturday, we might not reach anyone with real authority. But I'm betting when we say, 'Hey, we found your priceless painting of an unripe pear,' they perk up and get us somebody."

"How about telling somebody at the Tate, 'Hey, we found out where your bunch of emeralds and diamonds were, but oops, they're gone again'?"

"Yeah, that'll be a knee-slapper."

She had to be careful, had to be guarded in what she told Peabody and how. And she hated it.

"Roarke's reaching out to some contacts. So far there's no talk about any of this. The theft, the murder, or the fact that Barrister had a load of stolen art and jewelry in a vault in New York."

Peabody gave her the side-eye—Eve felt it. "Okay. I guess there will be talk about it all pretty soon."

"That may be to our advantage. He thinks, and I agree, this Royal Suite is too recognizable, too famous, for a fence—even a high-end one."

"So somebody wants to do what Barrister did—the father anyway—keep them all locked away just for him."

"Maybe. Or, and what feels more likely, or at least worth pursuing: auction. Exclusive, underground. Then somebody with piles of money locks them away and gloats over them."

"It's stupid, you know?" Shaking her head, Peabody looked down at her cowboy boots. "Somebody with that kind of money could buy whatever the hell they wanted."

"The *David* thing. The big-ass *David* statue thing. He has a big ass, all tight and toned, and in proportion, but big."

"Okay, not that. But you want to wear emeralds as big as my fist, you buy them. But someone like the vic's father—his type—that's not enough. They want the shine. It's really a smear, but they see it as a shine, of taking it, hoarding it."

When they turned into the garage at Central, Peabody shifted. "Is it really, really frosty? The *David*. I mean seeing it for real, is it frost extreme?"

"I didn't think it would be. Okay, so a giant statue of a naked boy with a slingshot. So?"

She pulled into her slot, parked, sat a moment. "It doesn't seem possible. It's taking your breath, dropping your jaw, and you're thinking that can't be real, and why is it so beautiful, this giant naked boy with a slingshot? How did anyone create that level of detail out of a giant slab of marble anyway? So take frost extreme up however many more notches are left, then double that."

Peabody sighed. "One of these days I'm going to see it for myself. That and all the other really frosty extremes."

They got out of the car, walked to the elevator.

"All somebody like Henry Barrister can do is gloat," Peabody added. "They can't really admire or look in wonder. It's just stupid."

"If he wasn't dead, it'd be a pleasure to lock him up instead of all his loot. But since he is, and we've got murder attached to this theft, Roarke's going to keep his ear to the ground. And we're going to have EDD looking for chatter on the underground. We're going to see if we can pull in Detective Willowby. Underground shit's her specialty."

"That's a good call. Do you want me to reach out?"

"No, I'll do it. Talk to the medicals, start your half of the loot list."

They walked into a mercifully empty elevator.

"Get what you can get done by one, then take off. Hit the street fair."

"Oh, but you said you were doing a follow-up at Barrister House."

"And I can handle it. You can push on the rest of the list tomorrow. But Sundays are worse than Saturdays."

When the elevator opened and two annoyed-looking uniforms hauled in an even more annoyed-looking man of about twenty-five—trench coat, baggies, well-worn kicks—she resigned herself to the company of a busted street thief.

"I found that stuff. You can't prove otherwise. I told you, I found it, picked it up. Finders keepers."

The uniform on the right cast her eyes up. "Right, dipshit, you just happened to find three wallets, two 'links, and a wrist unit while strolling down Broadway."

"That's right! You can't prove otherwise. It's my fault they're just lying there?"

The second cop slanted a look back at Eve and Peabody. "Yeah, like all the stuff you got busted for strolling along with last time was just lying there."

"That's right."

"You're really bad at this," the first cop decided as they muscled him off again.

"Some people," Eve considered, "should just get a regular job. It may suck to bus tables or ring up sales at a twenty-four/seven, but it's got to be better than cooling it in a cell for thirty or sixty days a couple times a year."

They got off, walked down to Homicide to find Baxter and Trueheart at their desks. The young, earnest Detective Trueheart worked his comp. The slick-dressed Baxter had his fancy Italian shoes on his desk, his chair kicked back, his eyes closed.

"Since you caught the weekend roll, shouldn't you actually do something to earn the pay?"

Baxter opened his eyes. He touched a finger to the side of his head in casual salute. "Been quiet, and we caught up on paperwork so pulled a cold one. My boy's doing some research on it. I'm giving it some thinking time."

Since she often took her thinking time in the same position, she couldn't bitch.

"Saw you caught one," he continued, "so we put it on the board."

She glanced over, saw Trueheart's precise printing.

"B and E gone south. If you need extra hands or brain cells, we can put the cold one back on ice."

"What's the cold one?"

"Eight years cold. Woman mugged to death in Central Park. Looks like a mugging—struggle, she falls, cracks her head open on a rock. Looks that way, until you squint."

"Keep on it."

She went to her office, hit the AC for coffee, and drank some of it looking out her single, skinny window. Another position she favored for thinking time.

First question: How did the thief and/or whoever hired him, if hired, know about the vault and contents?

First answer: As a general rule, a secret's only a secret if everybody who knows about it is dead.

Conclusion: Someone in the family let it slip to someone else. Maybe the estate lawyer knew about the vault all along. Or he just found out as stated, and someone in his office let it slip. The dead father confessed/bragged/let it slip on his deathbed. Or he told one of his several wives along the way. Or a fuck buddy. Or the staff knew more than they admitted.

Alternate conclusion: Someone in the household set it up so they could pocket a whole bunch of money. Or start their own secret collection.

Hire the thief—maybe through a broker. It would take time to set it all up for the break-in.

"And they'd need that," Eve mused. "Can't just go in, pocket a bunch of stuff. Gotta have the break-in, and it has to be real to pass the cop sniff test."

Drinking coffee, she paced.

But why not schedule it when the family's out? On a holiday, out for dinner and a show, something? No way, of course, to predict Barrister would come down with a cold, feel crappy, get up, and find the vault open.

Bad luck, she thought, and tight timing.

She sat to open the murder book, added what she'd learned from Morris. Then set up her board.

Before she started on her portion of the list, she mimicked Baxter, but kept her eyes open and on the board.

If the wife were involved, the timing shouldn't have been so tight. If she knew the break-in would happen at that time, wouldn't she have made damn sure her husband didn't go anywhere near the office? Slip him a stronger sleep aid—simple enough—and keep an eye out in case.

If the murder was part of it, the timing hit wrong again. Leave him lying there until morning, or at least another hour or so. Then scream your ass off.

"Doesn't work. Doesn't fit, not really. And her story holds, right down the line."

It wouldn't stop Eve from doing a deeper run, then working her way through the rest of the family.

But she had to deal with a vault full of stolen property. And she had an idea on that.

She reached out, across the Atlantic, to Inspector Abernathy of Interpol.

When his face came on-screen, she thought he looked as pinched and snooty as ever, with a layer of the smooth over it. But she noticed he wore a casual shirt, and behind him some sort of bush with a bunch of little blue flowers bloomed.

"Lieutenant. There's nothing you can say that will move me from my garden and into a train, a plane, or a car going anywhere."

"Okay. Then I guess you wouldn't be interested hearing about a vault full of stolen art and jewelry, much of which came from various points in Europe. Have a great weekend! Bye."

"Wait. What vault?"

"The vault inherited by a guy currently on a slab in the morgue. He earned his place there by, apparently, interrupting a thief. The thief did manage to get away with something for his trouble. Just a little something called the Royal Suite. Maybe you've heard of it."

He straightened in his chair as if electrocuted. "You have the thief? You have the Royal Suite?"

"No, I have a dead man, and a lot of other stolen property nicely displayed and carefully cataloged in a vault on the Upper East Side. But I'm interrupting your Saturday."

"Shut up. I need the details."

"Which is it? I shut up, or give you the details?"

He sniffed, then he hissed. "You can stop winding me up now."

"I'm sort of enjoying it. Nathan Barrister, son of Henry Barrister, who founded Zip Global, the shipping and delivery giant, was murdered last night."

Since she'd—mostly—finished winding him up, she ran through those details, cop to cop.

"We will, of course, keep the property safely secured. We will, of course, have each item authenticated. And we will, of course, begin the process of having each item returned to its rightful owner. I assumed, correct me if I'm wrong, Interpol would have an interest in assisting in that, I expect, complicated process."

He was up now, pacing. "I need a list, a description, and a photo of every item."

"I have that for you."

"I'll contact my superiors immediately. We will, naturally, take over possession and security for the property."

"No. That property is connected to a murder in my city. Just throttle back," she ordered before he could speak. "I'm inviting you in, I'm giving you a big, shiny gift because we both know the light's going to blast all over this. Billions of dollars of stolen art, artifacts, and jewelry, recovered after—in some cases—several decades. But my priority is Nathan Barrister, is finding the person responsible for caving his head in. Next in line, recovering the emeralds. And finally, seeing that everything goes back where it belongs."

He didn't look snooty now, but frustrated and anxious.

"You fail to understand that the Royal Suite is far too valuable and far too well-known to be treated like an ordinary theft. In the hours since it's been taken it's very likely found a place in yet another vault, and may very well be held there until it can be put up for auction exclusive to those who not only can afford its worth but care nothing for how it was acquired."

She waited a long, slow beat. "Do I look like this is my first round in the ring, Abernathy? We're taking steps to monitor for underground auctions on this level. Feel free to add Interpol's experts in that area. They can coordinate with our EDD."

"Be sure we will."

"Look, I'm not just bringing you into this because it saves me the time and frustration of talking to a few dozen museum people, insurance people, collectors and juggling their particular priorities. I'm bringing you in because I know you'll stick till it's done, and done right."

Now he looked, at least slightly, mollified. "I believe that's a compliment."

"It's a fact, take it any way you want. I'll send you the data on the contents of the vault."

"And we will contact the rightful owners, insurance agents, and so forth."

"Good. On the monitoring and fishing, you'll want to coordinate with Captain Feeney of EDD."

"Yes, I remember Captain Feeney. Is Roarke . . . consulting on this matter?"

"He is." At Abernathy's twisted smile, Eve's face went to stone. "Careful where you walk, Inspector. You could get something very nasty on your shoe."

"I'd comment that perhaps he has some contacts who may be able to ferret out some helpful information."

"If he does, and they can, it'll go in the pile. I'll send you the data, along with my more current report. Now, I've got a murder investigation to run."

"I have no doubt you'll find the responsible party. You'll stick until it's done, and done right. Another fact. I'll be in touch."

Satisfied, Eve walked out to the bullpen. "Forget the list for now."

"Best news of the day. I'm getting a lot of runarounds in a lot of languages. Why?"

"I pulled Inspector Abernathy into it. He'll deal with the contacts."

"That's brilliant. That's why you're the LT."

"Run the daughters, will you?" She glanced around at the empty desks. "Baxter and Trueheart?"

"They're talking to people—friends of the vic in the cold case. They're looped in if a call comes through."

"All right. I'm tagging Feeney, and Detective Willowby. Run the daughters." She checked her wrist unit. "You've got time to run Henry Barrister, and the estate lawyer. Then go. Unless something breaks, I'll work from home tomorrow. I'll keep you plugged in."

"I can run the sister, too, or the staff."

Eve weighed the time. "Take the cook for now. If I get bogged down otherwise, I'll toss the others at you."

As she turned, she pulled out her 'link to contact Feeney.

His hangdog face and mini-explosion of wiry ginger hair threaded with silver came on. Like Abernathy he wore a casual shirt—his choice of industrial beige.

She recognized the background as his office, stopped, turned on her heel. "You're in Central."

"Yeah. You, too."

"I'm heading up."

"You got better coffee. I'm coming to you."

She pocketed her 'link. "Feeney's in EDD. He's coming down."

"Protect and serve, twenty-four/seven, three-sixty-five. We need T-shirts."

"Yeah, that's really what we need."

Eve went back to her office, programmed coffee for two.

Her 'link signaled. When she pulled it out, she saw Commander Whitney on the readout. She'd been expecting this.

"Commander."

"Lieutenant. Nothing like a quiet weekend."

"No, sir, nothing like it."

It started to shock her system to see men she knew best in suits and ties in the casual. In Whitney's case, it included a Giants cap over his close-cropped salt-and-pepper hair.

It just didn't seem right.

"We had some of the grandchildren over last night. I've just read your report after some morning touch football. They're ruthless," he said with some pride. "Forty-two stolen objets d'art, which included the now-missing-again Royal Suite."

"Yes, sir. I've just spoken with Inspector Abernathy of Interpol about contacting the various authorities regarding same."

"Correct move. This property will have to be removed, today, from the crime scene to a high-security location, then authenticated."

"Yes, sir. On my schedule to arrange that. I intend to return to the scene this afternoon and conduct follow-up interviews, and also interview the victim's daughters, who have traveled back from college."

He puffed out his cheeks. "I'll handle the transfer arrangements, and the initial media release. The second can wait another day or until Monday. We want the valuables secured first."

She'd hoped he'd say just that.

"Yes, sir. I have the room sealed, with police locks on all entrances, and uniforms on the property. The alarms have been reset, with Roarke and McNab adding another layer. I have those codes."

"Give them to me now."

As she relayed them, she nodded, gestured to the coffee when Feeney came in.

"The murder weapon. A club-like rock of amethyst."

"That's correct."

"On the job you start thinking you've heard it all. Then you hear something else. We need to set up monitoring for chatter about the emeralds, any potential sales or auctions, coordinate that with Interpol."

"Captain Feeney's with me now, Commander. I planned to request Detective Willowby of Special Victims to assist."

"Yes, this is in her wheelhouse. I'll talk to her captain, make it so. I'll be in touch. It's a hell of a list, Dallas. Ask Feeney if he remembers the Corot."

When Whitney clicked off, she waited while Feeney sipped at his coffee and studied her board. With his shirt he wore shit-brown baggies and kicks that looked older than she was.

"So this asshole had a bunch of stolen art and jewelry all locked up in this vault—and that's an old beauty. Making billions from Zip wasn't enough for him."

"Apparently not. And his son paid for it. Both the wife and sister state they didn't know about the vault, or its contents, until after the old man died and the son and his wife started doing some painting and redoing shit. It actually plays."

"Whitney wants to know if you remember the Corot."

"This painting here?" He tapped her board. "Bunch of trees and rocks. I don't get it. Me? If you're putting something on the wall, it oughta have color. Anyway, yeah, it got boosted right out of the Metropolitan, back in the thirties. Slick job. Not our case, but I remember. Said it was worth about ten million. Bunch of trees and rocks."

He turned to her. "I remember hearing about those emerald pieces getting boosted. That was big fucking news. Out of London, and worth a lot more than the trees and rocks."

"Roarke says maybe over half a bil today."

Feeney whistled through his teeth. "That's all they took?"

"Either that's what they came for—most likely—or all they had time for. First, why are you here at Central on Saturday?"

"We're having a family thing tonight, and Sheila wanted me out of the way while she's fussing around. Figured I'd deal with some paperwork."

He gulped more coffee. "Looks like you're saving me from that."

"Take the desk chair," she told him. "I'll bring you up to speed."

Chapter Six

They had a rhythm going back to her uniform days when he'd taken her off the beat to train in Homicide. That rhythm made briefing him easy and quick.

"So the old man collected like this for decades. Probably easier and cheaper to pull it off during the Urbans and the right after. Then he ends up buying the place that used to be a damn museum. Bet he got a chuckle out of that one."

"You gotta figure."

"You looking at his exes?"

She eased a hip on the corner of the desk. "You gotta figure," she repeated. "Maybe he lets one—or more—of them in on it. I don't weigh that one heavy. Maybe something slips out, or one of them sees something that puts her onto it. But she waits—and that's kind of shaky—until he's dead to go after something. The biggest something in there."

"Victim show up clean on the run?"

"Yeah, near to squeaky, so there's that. If they know him at all, they'd figure he'd do just what he planned to do. Return everything."

"'Might as well get a little something for my trouble. I married the bastard, and what'd I get out of it?'"

"I'm going to look into that, but no matter what, it didn't add up to half a billion in emeralds. The mother of the victim and his sister remarried—twice. She currently lives in the South of France with her number three. The first wife just celebrated her centennial. Two other marriages, two other divorces. No offspring. She has an apartment—the pied-à-terre deal on Madison—but her base is Kauai. Second ex, an actress—Barrister was also her second ex—lives in Malibu, second home in Aruba, with her number three. The other ex—that's number four—lives in Bozeman, Montana, with her second husband and two kids from that marriage."

Once again, she had to tread carefully. Once again, she didn't like it.

"Roarke thinks it's likely a theft like this—something of this value and fame—would be contracted. Like through an intermediary, a kind of broker. So the thief might not know who's paying him to steal it. He can't sell it himself, not on the open market, I mean. And it would bottom out the value to bust it apart, reset the stones."

He just nodded along with her. Because they had that rhythm, she knew he understood she had to tread carefully.

"Makes sense to me. I knew about it because it was a bfd at the time it got plucked. We'll set up the sneak, keep tabs on any chatter. You get Willowby in, and she's got plenty of aces up her sleeve."

He pointed at the board, at the murder weapon. "That's what bashed him? Hell of a thing. Just sitting around?"

"In the office, on a kind of tray that lit up."

"Weapon of opportunity then. Victim wanders in before you're done. Grab, bash, go. But he had to know—or if a hire, that one had to know—about the vault."

"That's number one. Who knew and how. It wasn't that tricky a job,

Feeney. Their security hadn't been updated. Decent but not tough to undermine. The vault—old. Some skill required, sure, but it doesn't strike me any of it took a master. Not like plucking a Corot out of the Met, or emeralds out of the Tate."

He scratched through his wiry hair. "Yeah, I'm with you there. Add in somebody who panics easy enough to kill. Or doesn't care about adding murder to the mix. Well."

He got to his feet. "How about you top this off, and I go up and arrange the sneak before I head home?"

She got him more coffee. "Interpol's going to contact you."

"No problem. I'll get back to you when I've got something to get back to you about."

"Appreciate it."

When he left, Eve took the desk and started the run on Joy Barrister while she looked over Peabody's data on the housekeeper.

Uma Acker grew up in Yonkers, where her mother still lived. Her parents divorced when she was twelve and her younger sister eight. Her father lived in Wyoming and listed himself as a lieutenant colonel in the True Patriots militia.

Because Peabody was thorough, she'd listed Lloyd Acker's numerous arrests, including a spousal battery charge a few months before the divorce.

Uma Acker got in a couple years of community college while working for the cleaning service the Barristers still used. Then began her employment—first as an assistant housekeeper—at Barrister House.

No marriages, no offspring. No criminal.

Eve made a note to have Roarke dig into the financials.

She heard Peabody's boot-clomping approach, glanced over.

"I just sent you Henry Barrister's data. It's a lot. Baxter and Trueheart are still in the field. I can do another run, stick until they get back."

"No, take off. I'm going to keep at it awhile, then I'm taking it home. I'm running the sister now."

"Anything hits, tag me."

With a nod, Eve turned back to her screen.

Joy Barrister, age fifty-two—fancy private schools like her brother. Harvard MBA like her brother. At thirty-one she married Anton Sampson. The marriage lasted three years. No offspring.

Sampson, age fifty-two, part of the Sampson-Burnett family who made their fortune with Burnett Wine and Spirits, remarried two years after the divorce, remained married, had three offspring.

Joy lived in Barrister House until her marriage, and during the separation moved into the Barrister-owned condo, which she'd inherited in full upon her father's death.

After college, she'd officially joined the family firm, full-time as a VP in accounts, domestic, and now stood as chief financial officer.

To the tune of one-point-eight million a year, plus bonuses.

She toggled back to check Nathan Barrister's annual salary. Two-point-six.

And made a note to consult Roarke on the pay gap.

She was on the board of a couple of charities, served as treasurer for the Barrister Family Foundation—and that one brought in another eight hundred K a year.

The victim had served as president, same salary.

Interesting.

The divorce had netted her a town house, which she'd promptly sold. He'd bagged the house in Isle of Palms, which he still owned. He got a boat; she got a car. And blah blah, Eve thought, pretty standard rich people settlement.

No criminal.

She turned to the board, frowned.

"Plenty of money to hire a thief, but why? No handling the whole thing quietly that way."

She heard a bark of laughter from the bullpen. Baxter and Trueheart were back. She'd take all this home, bounce a few things off Roarke, update her board there. Swing by Barrister House on the way.

Maybe shake something loose.

Before she could shut down, her 'link signaled.

"Dallas."

"Lieutenant Dallas, I'm Chloe Barrister. My dad . . ."

"Yes. I'm very sorry for your loss."

Her eyes, a strong blue, were swollen from weeping. She'd pulled her dark, curly hair back in a tail that left her face unframed and accented knife-edge cheekbones.

"We went — we went to the place to see my father. I don't understand how . . . I need to know how. Why. What are you doing to find out who did this?"

"Everything we can. Finding out who took your father's life is my priority. If you and your family are available, I'd like to come speak to you again. I'll try to answer some of your questions."

"Yes. Please. Yes."

"I'll be there within the hour."

Eve shut down, shoved at her hair, then walked out to the bullpen. This time both detectives worked their comps.

"I'm in the field, then I'm home. Any thawing on the cold case?"

Baxter kicked back. "We talked to the vic's sort of boyfriend at the time. Casual, not exclusive, but amiable with benefits. He's married now with a kid on the way. Stuck to his story. They were going to meet up for dinner, but he had to cancel—a work thing. And that checks out now like it did back then."

"Stuck in the office, with witnesses," Trueheart put in. "Until after nine. Went out for a couple of drinks with some office pals, shared a cab with one of them, and got home about quarter to eleven."

"TOD?"

"Twenty-three-fifteen. And yeah"—Baxter shrugged—"gives him about a little room, if he moved fast, to meet up with her, take a walk in the park, and kill her. But there's no buzz, no vibe, no nothing."

"Add one of his apartment neighbors saw him come in. They both bitched about the elevator being out again, and walked upstairs together." Trueheart shook his head. "It came off he really liked her, but neither one of them were thinking about the long haul."

"She liked to walk at night," Baxter added. "That's in the file, and both he and the best pal corroborated. But both of them said then, and now, they didn't get why she'd have been in the park. She sometimes cut through there during the day, but never at night."

When Trueheart picked it up again, Eve thought they'd developed that easy rhythm partners needed.

"The best friend vouched for the boyfriend. Said they all liked to just hang when they could get together. That's the vic, the boyfriend, the best friend, and the guy she was seeing."

"Married to him now, and got twin toddlers. Cute kids. And she had cake." Baxter smiled with the memory. "Really good spice cake."

"She's taking a baking class for fun."

"Yeah, go figure. She was adamant the vic wouldn't have cut through the park at night, not alone. If she went through, she'd been with someone. Nobody ever turned up. So we're going to turn them up. Right, partner?"

Trueheart lifted a fist to bump. "You got that."

"They weren't serious or exclusive, so."

"Yeah. Somebody else she went out with. Nobody popped." Baxter rubbed his hands together. "We're going to make 'em pop."

"Keep pushing on it."

She took the glides down. She had to make something pop, she thought. The straight line led to a break-in and theft ending in murder. But who hired the thief? Who knew about the vault?

The family. Potentially the staff—though they denied it. Also potentially four ex-wives, and if she lumped them in, she had to accept any one of them might have told someone else.

Secrets were generally bollocks.

She waited until she'd driven out of the garage to contact Roarke.

"Hey. I'm leaving Central, going by Barrister House for a follow-up and to talk to the daughters."

"Why don't I meet you?"

"There's no need for that."

"It's a lovely day for a walk. I'd enjoy one."

And he had a cop's sense with people. Plus, he should have had that lovely walk on a Saturday afternoon.

"All right. Traffic's not too bad. I'm heading up the East Side to avoid the blockades for the street fair, but so are a lot of other people."

"I'll stroll. See you shortly."

It would help to have him, she couldn't deny it. A second pair of ears and eyes. More, she'd hit an emotional storm at Barrister House, and he had an innate knack for soothing emotional storms.

Though thick, traffic moved smoothly enough, and still gave her time to note the crowds taking advantage of the damn near perfect weather.

Fashionably dressed women carried bags from high-end shops, and others took a break from that to nibble on a salad and sip wine at a sidewalk table. Tourists craned their heads up to gawk at airtrams, skyscrapers. Alternately they gawked at the display windows of those fashionable shops and carried their own bags holding their tangible memories of a trip to the city.

Kids screamed in a playground as if they were charging into battle.

Parents and nannies watched with such complacency she wondered what they'd spiked their go-cups with.

She watched a delivery woman with the goofy Zip logo on her uniform cart packages to a building.

A man had made a fortune on that service, she thought. A man whose greed or obsession to hoard what wasn't his had led to the death of his only son.

For paintings of rocks and trees, for shiny stones, for sleek statues.

Was it just the having—and by nefarious means? Was it a kind of twisted love and admiration for the precious?

Maybe both.

Every indication led her to believe the son hadn't shared his father's need, that obsession. Henry Barrister must have known that, seen that. Even on his deathbed he hadn't told his family about the vault, the contents.

Clearly, he'd created a detailed will, arranged for his property, his company, his money. But not the vault.

Why?

"Because it was still his. Just his. He took it with him. No one else could have it."

That fit for now. But she decided she'd run it all by Mira, for a shrink and profiler's analysis.

It would matter in the way everything mattered.

As she pulled up to the gates, Roarke did actually stroll over to her car. He'd added a jacket—thin, soft black leather—and a pair of sunshades.

She wondered how many people along the lovely walk had had to wipe a little drool off after a glance at him.

He slid into the car, leaned over, kissed her.

"Not-quite-autumn in New York puts on a hell of a show."

She had to agree. "I saw a woman wearing see-through pants as wide as the East River sashaying up First Avenue. She beat the indecency law by a skinny pink thong."

"As I said, a hell of a show."

Eve held up her badge for the scanner. "Lieutenant Dallas and consultant Roarke."

As the gates opened, her 'link signaled. She answered on her wrist unit. "Dallas."

"Lieutenant," Whitney began. "An armored police vehicle and security team will arrive at Barrister House in about twenty. The items will be secured in a vault at the Metropolitan Museum of Art. I'll send you the particulars."

"Yes, sir. I'm just pulling up to that location now. I can help coordinate the transfer."

"Do that. Detective Willowby has contacted Feeney, and will be at your disposal."

"Thank you, Commander. I'll have an updated report for you by this evening."

"I'll be looking for it."

When she pulled up, she turned to Roarke. "How secure is the Met?"

"As good as they come." When she continued to study him, he smiled. "Once or twice."

"Once or twice," she muttered, and got out of the car.

John Tyler opened the door. The butler looked like a man who hadn't slept in days.

"Thank you both for coming. The family is in the lounge."

"Mr. Tyler." She turned to the uniform who stepped up behind him. "Officer. An armored police vehicle and security escort will arrive shortly to transfer the contents of the vault to a secure location. Please verify their identification and give them entry."

"Of course."

"Officer, anything to report?"

"No, sir. Officers Upton, Harvet, and I have patrolled the grounds while one of us remains posted outside the crime scene door."

"Continue that. When the transfer is complete, you're all relieved."

From there, she followed the butler, and paused again at the office door. The uniform rose from his chair to stand.

She looked past him, examined the door. Seal intact, locks engaged.

"Stand by, Officer. You'll be relieved shortly."

The family spread out in the big space. Anya, the younger daughter, blond-streaked brown hair as straight as her sister's was curly, stood in the kitchen. The cook's arms wrapped around her as Divine swayed and murmured.

The widow sat on the sofa with her older daughter, their hands clasped. Joy Barrister paced.

"We could hire our own investigators."

"You're certainly free to do that, Ms. Barrister," Eve said as she came in.

Pressing a hand to her face, Joy stopped pacing. "I don't mean to disparage you, it's just . . . We need answers. And—and we need to make a statement. Soon. The media—it won't stay contained much longer."

"We're going to ask for privacy." Chloe spoke up and shifted yet closer to her mother. "We're going to keep it brief."

"I'm sorry, sweetheart. I'm struggling with this. I want to do what's best for everyone."

"Lieutenant, can I get you a chair?"

Eve shook her head at Tyler. "No, this one's fine."

She took one of the oversized chairs angled between the sofa and the screen as Roarke did the same. Today, she thought, she could give the widow a little space.

"Ms. Carville."

Aileen looked up. "He doesn't belong in that place. Nate doesn't belong there. It's so cold."

"It won't be for long. Ms. Carville, we're arranging to have the contents of the vault transported to a secure location."

"All right. We don't care. We don't care about those things. Without those things, Nate would still be here." Her voice rose. "I don't want those things in our house."

"Mom."

"I'm sorry. I'm sorry, baby." She pressed her lips together as Anya rushed over, all but threw herself into her mother's arms. "We'll be all right." She kissed Anya's hair. "I need to find my strength. It just keeps slipping away."

"I'll be strong for you." Chloe looked directly at Eve. "We need some answers."

"While the investigation is in its early stages, there is movement. The NYPSD is coordinating with Interpol."

"Interpol." Joy dropped down on the end of the sofa.

"Many of the items in the vault were stolen from museums and private collections throughout Europe. It's possible whoever broke in here last night has a connection to one or more of those previous thefts."

"My grandfather stole those things—paid to have them stolen."

"Oh, Chloe." Anya pressed her face to her mother's shoulder.

"We can't pretend, Anya. We have to face it."

"People will think Dad helped."

"They won't. They won't because we won't let them. Because he didn't." Once again, Chloe looked at Eve. "He didn't and he wouldn't."

"There's no evidence that your father conspired in those original thefts. And all indications are that he learned of the existence of the vault and its contents after his own father's death.

"Mr. Tyler, where is Ms. Acker?"

"Seeing to some household tasks. Do you want her?"

"It would be helpful, yes."

As Tyler took out his 'link, Divine carried over a tray.

"Now, you'll have some tea, and some of these little sandwiches. You need your strength. You won't find it, missus, if you don't eat. Your girls need to eat."

She looked at Eve, smiled at Roarke, then back to Eve. "You both help yourself here. You look tired to the bone, Lieutenant."

"I'm fine. Ms. Carville, I know this is very difficult, but details can be missed. I'd like to go over exactly what you remember from last night. Your husband wasn't feeling well."

"He wasn't. He came home early."

"From work?"

"What? Oh, yes, he came home around three, I think. I was working, but I stopped when I could to see why he'd come home early. He was in his office, and I could see right away he wasn't feeling his best. He said he was feeling a little off, that's all, so he'd work from home, take it easy.

"I thought it might be the start of that cold he tends to get this time of year. I mentioned it to Divine, and she made chicken soup. When I finished work—a little after five, I think—he was wheezy, and he said his throat was sore. I said I could call the doctor, or we could just run to the neighborhood clinic, but he didn't want to."

Crossing her arms, she squeezed her daughters' hands. "You know how Dad is about doctors."

"A big baby," Anya said, struggling to smile as tears rolled.

"A great big baby. I took his temperature, and he was running a little hot. I said he should go up, lie down. I'd bring him the soup and some tea in bed, but he told me not to fuss. Just one of his stupid colds. He'd sleep in the guest room."

Eve saw Uma come in, walk over to stand by Tyler and Divine.

"I put my foot down on that. He sleeps better in his own bed, so I'd take the guest room, and if he wasn't better in the morning, I was calling the doctor and staying home. He agreed to the doctor but insisted I go on my weekend trip. I decided to wait until morning, see how he was, then cancel if that was best."

She shifted to look back at Divine. "He ate well. I felt better about that. He ate a full bowl, and said your soup was a miracle. A tasty miracle."

"He did. Then you talked about your girls, if you don't mind me saying, and that you wondered how they were settling in back at college. And if Chloe was serious about the boy she's been seeing. Mister worried a little she was, but you said she wasn't, not very much as yet."

"That's right." She sighed, opened her other arm so Chloe moved into it. "And I reminded him we'd met in college, and that worked out just fine. He seemed a little bit better, but so tired. And the cough hurt his throat. I could see it. He went up, and I took him the tea you'd made to help him sleep. Oh, I forgot, Joy came home."

"About six," Joy agreed. "I got in on the soup, and it was wonderful. I'd gone by after work to check on the progress at my condo. Nate looked lousy, a little worse than when I saw him right before he left the office. He always seemed to get that same respiratory deal this time of year. And resisted the doctor, as Aileen said. I went up not long after both of you did."

"Yes, that's right. I spoke to you after I tucked him in—gave him cold meds, the tea. You said you'd help me in the morning, pushing him to the doctor, if I needed it."

Aileen smiled a little. "You told me to take my getaway, you'd be here to look after your baby brother. We laughed a little, said good night. I read for a while, watched a show I'd wanted to see, read a little more. I checked on him intermittently, and he seemed to be sleeping well. Then I realized I was falling asleep over my book. I think I had dozed off for a while. I went to check on him one last time, but he wasn't there. He wasn't there."

"Do you remember the time?"

"Not exactly. I know after midnight. I did glance at the time, a few minutes after midnight, and thought I could sleep in a little, so one more chapter. That's when I think I dozed off for a bit. I know I felt a little groggy when I got up, the way you do when you've dozed off. But he wasn't there."

"You went downstairs."

"Yes. I looked for him first. He wasn't in the bathroom, or in the little den upstairs where he liked to sit sometimes. I thought he might have gone down to the kitchen, for more tea, or more soup."

"Were the lights on downstairs?"

"No, not in the foyer. We keep a light on there if someone's coming home late, but everyone was home. I called—not loud—the way you do when everyone's sleeping. And I walked back to the kitchen."

"Which way? You have central stairs. Did you go right or left?"

"Oh, I must've gone left. That's habit. My office is on the left. He wasn't in the kitchen. We keep a low light on in there at night, but he wasn't in there. I heard something. Like something fell. A kind of thud? Then another thud."

"Two thuds?"

"Yes. Ah, yes." She closed her eyes. "One, then the other, and I thought Nate had knocked something over, or tripped in the dark. So I called out again, louder, I think, and walked down to his office."

"Was the light on?"

She shook her head. "No, no. Moonlight. I saw him in the moonlight, and the security lights. I saw him on the floor. Nate. I didn't think. I thought he fell, and I ran to him, and dropped down."

"Ms. Carville, can you tell me: Was he on his back?"

"On his back? No. No. I . . . I turned him over, and the blood. All over my hands. His blood. I started screaming, and couldn't stop."

"Isn't that enough?" Chloe murmured when Aileen began to tremble. "Isn't it? Drink some of this, Mom. Drink it for me. Please."

Eve shifted to Joy.

"Run your evening through for me."

"After I went up, spoke with Aileen, I checked on some work, watched part of a vid. It had been a long day. I was asleep by ten or so. I thought I heard someone walking down the hall. I sleep light. And it's not my home, so probably lighter yet. But I'd drifted back to sleep when Aileen's screams woke me. I ran out, and I ran downstairs. I heard her screaming from Nate's office, and I saw Nate. I saw Aileen trying to hold him. I turned on the lights, and I ran over to them first to try to see if I . . . Then I called nine-one-one."

"You had your 'link with you?"

"She was screaming. Yes, I grabbed it on the run. I got down on the floor with her, tried to see if Nate . . . Uma came rushing in, then John and Divine at some point. It's mixed up a bit. The MTs got here, then the police."

"You know all of this," Chloe said. "Why make them relive it?"

"I know more now," Eve said simply.

One of the uniforms came in. "Excuse me, Lieutenant. The transport and security team are here."

"I'll be right there. You need to excuse me for now."

"Just get those goddamn things out of our house." Aileen laid her head back, closed her eyes. "Get them out of my husband's house."

Chapter Seven

When Eve stepped out, Roarke turned his attention to Aileen.

"Ms. Carville, is there anything I can do for you? Is there anyone I can contact for you?"

"I—no. We tried to reach Nate's mother, but . . ."

"She's on one of her retreats," Joy supplied. "Don't worry, Aileen. I'll track her down. We're going to take a little time before we let anyone else outside the household know."

"I know who you are."

Roarke shifted his gaze to Chloe's. "I'm here to assist the lieutenant and the NYPSD, and your family, in any way I can."

"Why?"

"Chloe."

"It's a reasonable question," he said to Aileen. "A few years ago, I would have heard about your father's death through business associates or the media. I would have been sorry, but unless we had had a personal relationship, I would have moved on. But I've come to see the intimacies and cruelties of the willful taking of a life, what it does to those left in its wake. I've certainly seen that finding those responsible for the taking of a life isn't simply a job for Lieutenant Dallas or those she works with. It's a calling.

"She won't stop," he added, and with such quiet surety it rang in the room. "I hope it's some small comfort to you at this horrible time to know she won't stop until she finds the person who took your father from you."

"It won't bring Nate back," Aileen murmured.

"No, she can't do that. But she'll do everything she can do, and more if more's needed, to find who took him away. Why am I here?" He looked back at Chloe. "I have a great need to help her."

Outside, Eve waited for the armored truck and its escort. Just a few billion being transported across Manhattan, she thought. No big deal.

Then her shoulders relaxed. She saw SWAT commander Lieutenant Lowenbaum get out of an escort vehicle.

"Good to see you, Lieutenant. Sorry about the weekend duty."

He shrugged, a good-looking fair-haired man with an easy attitude and nerves of steel. "Happens. Doesn't much happen we guard a shitload of art and so on. We've got museum security tagging on."

He gestured to another group wearing Kevlar and sidearms with their dark suits.

"More meeting us at the drop-off. You sure pull some interesting jobs, Dallas."

"Yeah, I'm lucky that way. Let me take you in."

"Let me introduce you to Morbelli. Head of Met security. She thinks she's in charge."

"Doesn't hurt to let her think it."

She walked over with him to a group of six where a Black woman of about fifty with a tough build, hard eyes, and dark hair cropped close to her skull stepped forward.

"Security head Morbelli, Lieutenant Dallas."

"Dallas."

"Morbelli."

"Museum security will take charge of the property." Like her hair, her voice was clipped tight. "Each item will be recorded, cataloged, security packed, and labeled prior to transport. On the other end, each item will again be recorded, cross-checked, unpacked for authentication. You will receive a copy of the recording and ensuing report, as will the agents and inspectors in charge at Interpol, as will the proper authorities connected to each item secured by us."

"That'll work. If you'll come with me."

"Packing will be done by a team authorized by the Metropolitan Museum."

Morbelli didn't bother to introduce them, but Eve noted they dressed not in black suits but more like sweepers. She led the way.

She went straight to the office. "Record on."

"Record on," Lowenbaum echoed.

"All records on," Morbelli ordered.

"Lieutenant Dallas unsealing the crime scene door, accompanied by SWAT commander Lieutenant Lowenbaum and Metropolitan Museum Security head Morbelli and team."

She unsealed the door, disengaged the locks, and opened the door to a room that smelled of blood, death, and sweepers' dust.

"The scene's been processed, the electronics are with EDD. The windows are also sealed and locked and monitors installed."

Before entering, she took out her 'link, shut down the monitors.

"Clear there." Moving in, she skirted the blood, went to the panel, tripped the mechanism, then slid open the panel. "I personally relocked the vault after my consultant changed the combination. Reopening now."

She turned the dial, ordered herself not to be embarrassed or sentimental that Roarke had used their wedding anniversary.

After depressing the thick brass lever, she used it to pull—with some effort—the vault door.

Beside her, Lowenbaum let out a low whistle. Beneath it, she heard Morbelli's involuntary gasp.

"That's a hell of a thing," Morbelli murmured. "A hell of a thing." She stepped in, took a long, slow look, then seemed to pull back into her spit and polish. "All right, let's get started. Lieutenant Dallas." She inclined her head. "Thank you for your assistance."

Eve gave her the same head gesture. "Thank you for yours. I'm going to remove the monitors, the seals, and the police guards on the windows."

"If Lieutenant Lowenbaum has the property secured, you might open them."

"You're covered."

As the team in sanitized white trooped in, Eve went to the windows. As she unsealed, removed guards, she saw through them members of SWAT stationed.

She opened the windows, breathed in the blissfully fresh air.

This part was off her hands, she thought, and the boot of stress on her neck lifted.

Morbelli stood, arms folded, watching the activity in the vault like a hawk. After they exchanged another brief nod, Eve started out.

Chloe stood outside, arms also folded, blocked by security.

"I want to go in. I have a right to see where my father died."

"He's not in there, Chloe."

"I have a right to see where he was murdered."

Eve held up a hand to security, then took Chloe's arm. "That's far enough," she said at the doorway.

She felt the girl jerk, felt her tremble. But she didn't cry out. Instead, she made a low, keening sound, then sucked in her breath and stopped it.

"How did they kill him? What did they use to kill him? I didn't want to ask the medical examiner in front of my mother."

"There was a display piece in the office. An amethyst."

"The magic crystal?" Another keening sound escaped again, and she swallowed it. "We called it that, Anya and I. Granddad told us he won it from a wizard in a poker game."

When she clutched at her belly, Eve grabbed her arm again. "If you're going to be sick—"

"I'm not. I won't." She'd gone pale as glass, still trembled, but fought to stiffen her shoulders.

"Let's walk outside. You could use the air."

When Chloe only nodded, Eve guided her out.

"I'm okay. I have to be. My mom . . . she's not weak, but she's shattered. She's just . . . lost right now. They really loved each other. Not everybody does who stays married. But they really loved each other. They liked each other. This is all going to come out now, isn't it? The things my grandfather stole."

"Yes."

"I loved him. We always had so much fun when we visited here. My dad used to say how Granddad liked us better than he did his own kids, and Granddad would say, why wouldn't he? He didn't have to raise us, clothe us, educate us. He only had to enjoy us."

Pressing a hand over her mouth, she breathed through her fingers. "But he was a selfish man. Only a selfish man could have all that stolen and locked away. Now my dad's gone, and he'll be smeared with that. And he didn't do anything wrong. He was working on the best way to give it all back."

"I know that. I believe that."

"It's what everyone cares about. His blood's all over the floor. My mom's broken, our family's broken, but all everyone cares about are those things. All these guards and weapons, for the things, and my father's dead."

That keening sound. Eve didn't have to hear it to know it lived inside a dead man's daughter.

"I have to care about the things. They were my responsibility, and now they're not, or soon won't be. I have to care about the things because they're the reason your father's dead. And he's mine now. Not the same way he's yours, but he's mine now and deserves the best I've got."

"You don't know him."

"I know he fell for your mother in college and never quit. I know he maybe got a boost at Zip, but he worked to earn his place. I know his cook made him chicken soup and valerian tea not just because it's her job but because she cared about him.

"I know he ran track in high school—pretty good sprinter," she added as Chloe stared at her.

"I know he liked to read science fiction novels, played tennis. His best man at the wedding was a childhood friend, and a few years later, he was best man at that friend's wedding."

"How do you know all that?"

"I know all that, and more, because he belongs to me now."

Chloe looked away. "The guy I'm seeing, he was really into the Furst books, the vid. And I thought, right. They cashed in because she's married to a guy who's got more money than ten gods, and she's probably playing at the cop thing while thinking about her next trip to Paris. Then my aunt said when you came last night he was in a tux and you were wearing a designer gown."

"That part's true. We were at this charity thing when I got the call."

"Why didn't you pass it off? Why didn't you just hand it off and go on dancing?"

"Because I'm a cop, and someone was dead. I work Homicide because the dead can't speak or stand for themselves, so I speak and stand for them. That's it."

With a nod, Chloe wiped at her eyes. "I had to be pissed at someone. Had to blame someone or I'd just fall to pieces. But that's a stupid way to get through this. I'm sorry I used you for it."

"No need to apologize."

"Please. There is, for me. I'm sorry."

"Accepted."

"He said—Roarke said you wouldn't stop. He said this was your calling, and you wouldn't stop until you found who killed my father. Is that true?"

"Yes."

"Okay. Holding on to that's a better way not to fall to pieces."

"Chloe, did you tell anyone about the vault?"

Her tear-filled eyes widened in something like horror.

"God no! It's—it's just shameful. Who wants to tell people your grandfather stole priceless art, historic jewelry, and worse, did it just to lock it away like—like some finger-tapping miser. Plus, we promised, all of us. We take promises seriously. You don't make one unless you know absolutely you can keep it.

"Not even some casual thing," she added with a little smile. "Like, 'Hey, Dad, will you bring home some ice cream?' He'd always say he'd try, or he'd make a note of that. Because what if he fell and broke his ankle, or had to help deliver a baby?"

At Eve's expression, she laughed. "Honestly, that's the sort of thing he'd point out. So when you promised, you had to mean it all the way. And we promised, no one said anything about it to anyone until we figured out how to make it all right again. And it hurt him, Lieutenant, because he knew we had to make it right again, and it would stain his father's name. The father he'd just lost. It hurt, but he was going to do it."

She took a breath. "Before you ask, Anya wouldn't, either. We barely talked about it when we were alone because it's painful." She looked back out to where security loaded packed items in the armored truck. "It's going to hurt. I worried about that, about how I'd handle the talk around campus when it came out. Now? It's nothing. The sooner it hits, the better."

"Can you think of anyone who your grandfather might have told?"

"I don't know. I know he didn't tell my father or Aunt Joy." She let out a sigh. "He liked women—you probably know that. Dad called it Henry Barrister's 'Asinine' Heel. Kind of a joke, a play on Achilles' heel."

"I get it."

"I wouldn't say it's impossible he might've said something when he was, you know, caught up. But if he did, I don't know who, I don't know when."

"Did you ever meet any of his friends or his 'Asinine' Heels?"

That got another little smile. "Now and then. Once he decided we were old enough to behave at a dinner party, we got to come sometimes. He liked entertaining, especially if he had a new beauty to show off. Always young. I think thirty-five to forty was the cutoff. It was the money. Not that he wasn't charming, interesting, even dynamic nearly to the end. But no thirty-year-old's going to get naked with a man seventy years older unless he's rich."

She shrugged. "He knew it, Granddad wasn't stupid. But it didn't bother him. In fact, he got a charge out of it. He loved us, Anya and me especially. That was real. He was always so good to us. But he was a selfish, dishonest man. I know that now. We all have to live with that now."

She looked back toward the house. "I need to get back to my mother. If you come up with more questions, or if you get any answers, we'll be here. I'm going to have what Anya and I need sent from college."

"You're not going back?"

"Not now. We'll take a pass this semester. Mom will fight that, so we'll compromise and take some classes remotely. But we're moving back for now. She needs us. God, we need her. So we'll be here."

"All right. I'll be in shortly."

"Did I help at all?"

Eve met her eyes. "Yes."

"Something else to hold on to."

When she went back in, Eve tracked down Lowenbaum.

"It seems to be moving along faster than I figured once I saw the vault. There's a frigging Cézanne in there."

She'd started to speak, but now just stared at him.

"What? I know stuff. The jewelry? I can tell you it's really shiny. The statues and that? Either hey, pretty, or wow, weird. But the paintings? I know stuff. He's got a Cézanne in there, a Degas, a Renoir, a Corot, I think an early Picasso, and that was just at that initial scan."

"I sense unplumbed depths."

He grinned at her. "I got some that are plumbed, too. Anyway, Morbelli runs a tight, efficient ship."

"Good to know. I'm going to take another run at the household. If she's not done when I am, I'm leaving it in your hands."

"We got it covered."

"I wouldn't leave otherwise. You could tag me when everything's moved and secured."

"Can do. What the hell was that guy thinking? Locking all that away?"

"Mine," Eve said. "All mine."

When she went back in, Roarke met her in the foyer.

"The widow went up to lie down, her youngest with her. The older daughter just went up to check on them. The sister's using the widow's office to draft a statement."

"The staff?"

"About their duties. I asked that they stay available to you."

"That works. I'll take the sister now. Listen, you don't have to hang around for the rest of this."

"It's rather fascinating." He glanced back toward the crime scene. "I'll go when you go." Despite the recorder, he touched her cheek. "Haven't eaten since breakfast, have you then?"

"I'll get something when we're done here. If you're staying, maybe pick the best spot for me to talk to the staff, separately, housekeeper first."

She walked to the second office, where Joy Barrister sat at the desk, staring at the monitor. She'd done her makeup, Eve noted, and carefully, but the strain showed through.

"I have to interrupt you."

"It's fine. I can't get my head around it. I can't ask Aileen to help. She's just not up to it. And I don't want to call the PR team who'd usually . . . it's too personal. But we have to have something. It's going to hit the media soon. We have to be ready."

"I'm going to give you the name of our media liaison."

"Roarke's?"

"No, NYPSD's media liaison. He's very good, and it's best if you coordinate with him anyway. On the statement, on the time and the place to give it."

"Oh yes. Of course." She lifted her hands. "I need to do something, but I'm not doing very well at this. Do I need to go over everything about last night again?"

"No, unless you remember something else."

"I wish I did." On a sigh, she pressed her fingers to her eyes. "I wish I'd gotten up. If it had been Nate I heard walking down the hall, I wish I'd gotten up, gone down with him. Maybe . . . Well, maybe doesn't count."

"Ms. Barrister, someone knew about the vault, at least some of the contents."

"Yes, that's painfully obvious."

"Your brother told you."

"Yes. He asked me to come over, and said it was important. When I got here, he took me into the office, shut the door. When he locked it, I was not just surprised but a bit anxious. He looked upset. Then he opened the panel."

She pushed at her hair. "Honestly, I was delighted. A secret vault! What fun, I thought. He told me our father had done something criminal, something we had to deal with."

She rose, began to pace. "I said something about don't tell me he has bodies of ex-wives we don't know about, but he didn't laugh. Nate loved a joke, but he didn't laugh. He opened the vault."

Joy stopped, stared out of the window.

"At first, I was just stunned. I didn't understand. I couldn't understand why our father had all those beautiful things locked away. Why weren't they on display? And Nate told me they were stolen. That when he found them, he looked up every item, and every one had been stolen, and over the course of decades."

She shook her head, rubbed her arms, paced again. "I didn't want to believe it. But he showed me the tablet. It was all there. Now, I was horrified, and I admit my first instinct was to lock it away again. Lock it all away and forget it was there. I thought of our name, our reputation, the business. I thought of all that first. Nate didn't, and of course, he was right."

She stared down at her hands, then pressed her fingers to her eyes again. "I did ask—begged—for time. We needed to find a way to return everything discreetly. Even, if possible, anonymously. We needed to research how it could be done. Find the best way, then work through the lawyer. If I hadn't pushed for that time, that discretion, it might have been done quickly. This would never have happened."

"You were shocked, upset."

"I was. God, I was."

"Did you tell anyone? A trusted friend, a confidant?"

On a half laugh, Joy shook her head. "I don't trust anyone that much. What my father did was shameful, and that shame could fall on us if we didn't handle it all perfectly. No, I told no one."

"Did your brother? Is there anyone he'd have trusted enough?"

"Not for this. We swore, as a family—the girls, too—that we wouldn't speak of it to anyone until it was time to contact the lawyer, or whatever intermediary we'd chosen."

"It had to be hard to live with."

"When something's that hard, you find ways to put it away, to compartmentalize. Otherwise, you'd go crazy. Nate and Aileen did talk about it, in private."

"Here, with three live-in staff?"

"In the office, or in here, with the door closed. Or at my condo, just the three of us. Aileen started to research the laws in every country where something was taken. I don't think it was overreacting to want to be sure we wouldn't be charged, to want to protect ourselves. We all agreed it was worth the time, that these pieces had been in there, some for decades. What would a few weeks matter?"

She closed her eyes. "In the end, it mattered far too much."

When Eve stepped out again, Roarke waited.

"Uma's ready whenever you are. The small sitting room off the entrance would do. There are pocket doors you could close if you needed to."

"Okay. Would you mind sending her in?"

"Why don't I send her in with coffee?"

"Even better."

As she walked down to the sitting room, her 'link signaled. One glance at the readout had the slow beat of a headache pulsing in her temples.

"Nadine, I'm busy."

"Investigating Nathan Barrister's murder. I'm aware. I'm at the gates. SWAT and armored vehicles aren't usually deployed post-homicide. What's the story?"

"I'm not at liberty to discuss the particulars of the investigation at this stage."

"So you want me to go on air with the report of SWAT and security swarming the Barrister estate, the armored vehicle?"

"No, I don't."

"I have to do my job, Dallas."

Eve turned, started back toward the office. "Why are you at the gates?"

"I have very good sources. I may be the first here, but that won't last."

"I'm putting you on hold."

"Dal—"

Eve cut her off, then stepped to the doorway. "Morbelli, I need an estimate. How much longer before you're packed, loaded, and on the way?"

"This isn't a process that can be rushed, Lieutenant."

"Not asking you to rush, asking for an estimate. Certain elements have leaked. I need to stall."

Morbelli's hard eyes narrowed to sharp shards of steel. "This is a very efficient team. Another twenty minutes."

"All right." Eve started back to the sitting room, took Nadine off hold. "I'm going to ask you for a solid."

"All right."

"Hold off until the armored vehicle heads out. About twenty minutes. Do that, and I'll give you a one-on-one when I'm done here or can break."

"All right. Did you get any sleep?"

"Couple hours."

Uma walked in with a small tray holding a fancy cup and saucer. "Gotta go. Have a seat, Ms. Acker."

"It's Uma." She set down the tray, sat, folded her hands. "How can I help?"

"You stated at least since Henry Barrister's death, you cleaned the office."

"That's correct."

"And you never happened upon the panel over the vault?"

"No. I want to say, if I had, and had seen the vault, I wouldn't have been surprised. This is an old and important house, it was a museum in part of its history. I don't think I'd have been surprised. Though I would have assumed he knew, I would have told Mr. Barrister—Mr. Nathan."

"And your coworkers?"

"Yes, I believe I would have mentioned it. It would've been so interesting."

"And finding it interesting, you might have mentioned it to a friend, a relative."

"Absolutely not. Lieutenant, you can't keep a trusted position for more than two decades if you tend toward gossip. I understand whoever broke in, whoever did this horrible thing had to know about the vault and what was in it. They didn't just stumble onto it, that's implausible. But I didn't know about it, and if I had, that knowledge wouldn't have gone outside this house."

"In your statement early this morning, you indicated that Henry Barrister had approached you regarding a personal relationship with him."

"You mean sexual relationship, and yes, he did broach the subject when I began working at Barrister House. I demurred; he accepted that. It never came up again."

"How did you demur?"

She sighed first, then let out a half laugh. "All right. I'm not sure how it matters after all these years. I gave him three reasons, all carrying—as I told him—about the same weight. First, I wanted to keep my job, and felt such a relationship could compromise my position. Second, he was old enough to be my grandfather. Third, when I considered an intimate relationship, I preferred women."

Uma lifted her shoulders. "He took it very well, and we had a very pleasant, professional, and friendly relationship until his death."

"Okay then. You would've worked here through a couple of ex-wives, some romantic partners."

"Mr. Barrister was between wives when he hired me."

"Which ones?"

The faintest hint of a smile touched Uma's mouth. "His third and fourth. Since this is a police investigation, I will say, yes, he had some romantic partners before he married again. I believe the fourth marriage lasted about five years. Possibly six—I'm not sure."

"Not important."

"Mr. Barrister, the senior, certainly enjoyed a number of other intimate relationships after his final divorce. He also traveled extensively and, I believe, enjoyed brief relationships while doing so."

"You knew him fairly well. His habits, his likes, his dislikes."

"Yes, or I thought I did."

"Would he have told any of the women he was intimate with about the vault?"

"I've asked myself that over and over. I can't say absolutely not. Lieutenant, in the last year or two, he wasn't as vigorous, physically or mentally, as he had been. A bit—sometimes more than a bit—forgetful, occasionally confused. He recognized it, and it frustrated him. The physical limits of his age frustrated him. But recognizing those limits is a reason he began to turn over more and more of the business to his children. Or so I believe.

"He was proud of what he'd built, had every right to be proud. I don't know why he filled that vault with what didn't belong to him, could never really belong to him. I don't know."

Chapter Eight

Eve had Uma go over the movements and timing again, then asked her to send Tyler in.

He sat stiffly, and worry covered him like his dark suit.

"Tell me about your relationship with Henry Barrister."

"He was my employer, and provided a very pleasant work atmosphere."

When Eve said nothing, Tyler cleared his throat. "I liked and respected him, and believe that was mutual. He enjoyed backgammon, and would invite me to play on occasion. In fact, he left me his set, his prized backgammon set, an Asian antique of jade and bone, along with the more usual one we often played on."

"You must have had conversations."

"We did, of course. On some of those occasions he would share his concerns and opinions with me."

"What sort of concerns and opinions?"

"A wealthy man's, Lieutenant. The market, politics, business. He might speak of whatever woman or women he had an interest in."

"But never about the vault or its contents?"

"No, never. But . . ."

"But?"

"The current situation has caused me to think back, to try to, I suppose, reinterpret some of those conversations. He did admire the finer things, Lieutenant, and owned many. Art, of course, jewelry. He would say—I've thought about this in depth since this morning. He would say a man's possessions prove his worth. What he can obtain and hold lift him above those who can only admire."

Tyler's eyes clouded as he looked away. "I was very fond of him, Lieutenant, and it's very distressing to realize not just what he'd done but that he measured his own worth by what he hid in that vault. He'd built a business that spans the globe, he had two children, two lovely granddaughters. He sat with presidents and kings, but he measured himself by what he'd taken from others. It breaks my heart."

She ran him through the rest, including some nudges on his personal life. Then decided to take the cook in her own domain. The kitchen.

"We should be on our way in about five minutes. Ten at the most," Morbelli told her.

"I've got one more interview. The story's going to break within the hour." Less, Eve thought. "Let whoever needs to know on your end know."

She walked to the kitchen, where Roarke sat comfortably at the island as the cook took a tray of cookies out of an oven.

The smell convinced Eve that heaven was a bakery.

"Sit down right there," Divine told her. "I'll get you some coffee to go with these. The girls favor these, and I hope they'll help a little."

"Ms. Fortigue."

"When someone's given the name Divine, why wouldn't she like to be called by it?"

She slid another baking tray in the oven. "Last batch," she said as she went to get the coffee. "I like watching the crime shows—the real ones and the made-up ones. I think I know what you're going to ask me. You'll want me to go over this horrible morning again to make sure it all lines up. And you'll wonder how I could've worked here all these years and not known Mr. Henry's secret. Who I might've told about it if I had known."

She put cookies on a plate, set it on the island. "You try one of these. You've had a long day, as we all have. I'm going to make beef bourguignon, as the family needs something hearty and filling. Is it all right if I start on that while we talk?"

"Yes, fine. Did Henry Barrister ever suggest you do more than cook for him?"

"Meaning warm his bed now and then? No, he didn't, but then I was too old for his tastes when I came to work here. I was fond of Mr. Henry. He liked my cooking, and never failed to tell me. Whenever he had one of his fancy dinner parties, he always saw I had good help."

She got out a big pot, poured some sort of oil in it.

"I was fond of him, but most of my time's spent in the kitchen, or at the market, at the island here planning menus. He wasn't one to sit where you are and have a chat."

She got out bacon, began dicing it. "Mr. Nathan was, and so is Ms. Aileen, the girls. Now, I took Mr. Henry coffee or a snack or what have you into his office more than plenty of times. But he never said: 'Look here, Divine,' and opened up that wall."

Because they were right there, Eve reached for a cookie. Took a bite.

Her entire system rolled over and begged for more.

"Oh, man."

Divine shot out a smile before putting the bacon in the pot, giving it a stir. "It's my magic power. It's why I took this job after I lost my husband. Our kids were grown, and I didn't want to live where we'd lived and face the loss every day. I made my home here."

She took out a slab of meat, began to cube it with a knife that looked deadly.

"Mr. Barrister senior had begun to slow down. Maybe wasn't as sharp as he had been."

"That's true." Divine took the tray of cookies from the oven, set them aside, gave the pot another stir, then returned to her cubing. As if they were all dance steps in a well-choreographed routine.

"He'd forget things, get annoyed with himself for it. He said to me once, not long before he passed, that old age was life's biggest and coldest bitch. I think that's why, at his age, he was still chasing women, and liked them young. He feared death, I believe, but feared losing his . . . abilities even more."

She got out a slotted spoon, took the bacon out of the pot and onto a plate. Then, to Eve's puzzlement, began to dry the cubed meat with a towel.

"He wasn't a fool, Lieutenant, Mr. Roarke, not even at the end. He knew a woman your age, or younger yet, looked past his age to his money, and what he could give them. But he got what he wanted, and had plenty of money to spare."

"It seems to me that what was in that vault would be even more incentive."

Lips pursed, Divine paused, nodded at Eve. "That hadn't crossed my mind. I must be tired. I can't tell you if he did such a thing, but I can see how you'd wonder if he might have."

"Do you know any of the women he entertained, let's say, over the last year or two?"

"Young, beautiful." Divine lifted her hands. "I'll say the parade slowed a bit in the last year or so, but it still marched. I never paid much attention. He had to tell someone, didn't he? I know he didn't tell his children. But he had to tell someone or how would this murdering thief know? If I had to guess, I'd guess a woman. Women were his weakness."

When Eve and Roarke walked out of the kitchen, Uma waited.

"Lieutenant, sir, they've just finished in the office. Can you tell me when I can clean it?"

"It's been processed, and if all items in the vault have been removed, it's clear. I can give you the names of some cleaning services that handle crime scenes."

"Thank you, but I worked for Mr. Barrister. I work for his widow, for the family. This is my home, and tending to it my job. I'll do the cleaning."

"Would they want you to?" Roarke asked gently.

"Right now, his family can't be worried about this. They've already had plenty, and there will be more to come. And they've had enough strangers in the house."

Eve remembered seeing her friend Crack cleaning up blood after a murder. His place, his job.

"I'm going to ask you to look up the process, to protect yourself and the family."

"I will."

"You may want to prepare the family that Mr. Barrister's death, and at least some of the circumstances, has leaked to the media. I'll address some of that when I leave, so they need to be prepared."

Uma closed her eyes briefly. "Yes, thank you. We've expected this."

"I'm going to advise you to screen any incoming communication, at least until the family has released a statement."

"I'll speak to Ms. Carville and Ms. Barrister."

"If you or any of the household remember anything else, have questions, contact me or Detective Peabody. At any time. Thanks for your cooperation."

"Of course. I'll see you out."

When they stepped outside, Eve hissed out a breath. "Nadine's at the gate."

"Ah, so that's what you're addressing."

"I have to let Whitney know the storm's coming. Give me a couple minutes."

"Why don't I walk down to the gate, keep Nadine occupied until you're ready."

"Yeah, do that. Only take the car through so we can leave from there. I'll walk. It'll give me a little more time."

After rolling some of the tension out of her shoulders, she took out her 'link. It signaled a text, one from Lowenbaum telling her they'd arrived at the secure location.

A little more tension drained.

Whitney picked up quickly.

"Commander, Lieutenant Lowenbaum advises that they've arrived at the museum."

"Yes, I have that information."

"Commander, Nathan Barrister's murder has leaked. Nadine Furst is at the gates of the Barrister House. She arrived when SWAT and security and the armored truck were here."

He let out a long exhale. "Well, hell. Not unexpected. Kyung is working with the victim's sister on a statement from the family, but we won't be able to head this off."

"No, sir. I traded her holding off for a one-on-one after the truck was secure. How do you want me to handle this?"

Once through the gates, Roarke pulled over, parked. He walked to where Nadine was getting ready for on-air reporting in a suit the color of port wine. He gave the woman holding the camera a quick smile.

"Just you and your camera then. How's Jake?"

"Enjoying a quiet Saturday."

"Ah, well."

"So, you're standing in for Peabody?"

"She put in a long night. The lieutenant sent her off."

"Any chance you'll go on record, on camera?"

"Not a one." He said it cheerfully, gave her shoulder a light pat. "I know your patience here is appreciated."

Nadine looked past him to where Eve started her walk to the gates. "That's great, but in my line, patience isn't its own reward."

Eve opened the gates, strode through. They closed quietly behind her.

"That was a little longer than twenty."

"Couldn't be helped."

"Full disclosure. We got roll of the truck and security leaving the residence."

Eve just nodded. "No problem. Let's get this done, Nadine."

"All right."

Nadine signaled to the camera, and as she tapped her earpiece, Roarke stepped out of range.

"Trace. We're ready here. They're breaking into current programming, the in-studio will toss it to me. We're live in five, four, three." She held up two fingers, then one.

"Thank you, Evan. I'm standing outside the gates of the Barrister House, the home of Nathan Barrister, where tragedy struck in the early hours this morning. Nathan Barrister, the son of Henry, who founded Zip Global Shipping and Delivery, served as CEO of the monolithic company after his father's death. While Henry died peacefully last February at the age of a hundred and two, his son was struck down early this morning, apparently by an intruder.

"I have with me Lieutenant Eve Dallas of the NYPSD, who leads the investigation into Nathan Barrister's death. Lieutenant, what can you tell us regarding the circumstances?"

"At approximately one this morning, officers and medical technicians responded to a nine-one-one call from this residence. The medicals pronounced Nathan Barrister as deceased, and the officers secured the scene."

"How was Mr. Barrister killed?"

"He suffered a blow to the back of the head. Evidence indicates an intruder or intruders compromised the Barrister House security, gained access to the property. This individual or individuals entered via a window of the home office on the main floor used by Mr. Barrister. At this time, evidence indicates Mr. Barrister entered the office and was struck down by the intruder, who then exited via the same window and fled the scene."

"Was anything taken?"

"Certain items are missing from the residence. I'm unable to report details of those items at this time."

"Who else was in the house at the time of the attack?"

"The victim's wife and his sister and three live-in staff."

"You've eliminated them as suspects?"

"We're in the very early stages of the investigation, and have no reason, at this time, to suspect any member of the household. However, we have solid evidence of the break-in."

"Lieutenant, my information is the nine-one-one call and the time of death were within minutes. Did one of the household witness the murder?"

"Statements from members of the household corroborate that Mr. Barrister was unwell yesterday. The ME confirms the victim had a respiratory infection at the time of his death. As a result, Barrister retired early, and his wife used a guest room. She checked on his status several times, and when he wasn't in their room, she went downstairs to look for him. She subsequently found him on the floor of the office. Her screams woke the rest of the household."

"She didn't see the intruder?"

"She did not. Evidence indicates the intruder fled very shortly before she discovered her husband's body. The evidence, the statements, the circumstances all verify this."

"Lieutenant, when I arrived here, I observed an armored vehicle inside the gates, along with members of the SWAT team and other security personnel. While my view was somewhat obstructed, I did observe items being removed from the house, loaded into the armored vehicle, which left the property, accompanied by SWAT and security, and traveled to the Metropolitan Museum of Art."

When Eve's eyes narrowed, Nadine returned a look that said clearly: I do my job, too.

"Can you tell us what was removed, why, and what bearing this has on Nathan Barrister's murder?"

Here it comes, Eve thought.

"Shortly after the Nathan Barrister family inherited the residence and relocated here, during some remodeling, redecorating, a crew member discovered a mechanism that opened a wall panel. The panel concealed a vault, one that dates back to when the house was first constructed. The surviving members of the household all state none were aware of the panel, the vault, the contents. Eventually, Nathan Barrister found the combination to the vault among his father's personal papers."

"And opened it?"

"That's correct."

"Don't keep us in suspense."

"The vault contained paintings, jewelry, other objects of art and artifacts, all stolen over a period of more than three decades from various museums and private collections."

For maybe the first time since they'd met, Eve observed Nadine speechless.

It didn't last.

"Have you identified this art, jewelry, ascertained how it came to be in what appears to be a secret vault?"

"The items removed from the vault and now secured will be officially identified, authenticated, and, with the cooperation of Interpol and any local authorities, returned to their rightful owners, as the Barrister family had planned when they made the discovery."

"Are you saying that Henry Barrister stole or obtained by other means numerous and valuable items of art and jewelry over the course of decades and kept them in a hidden vault, in his home, and his family was unaware?"

"Evidence indicates Henry Barrister facilitated the thefts, and when his surviving family discovered their location, they began the process to, again, facilitate their return. I have no reason, at this time, to believe otherwise."

"Were the items missing from the residence taken from the vault?"

"Evidence indicates affirmative. That's all the information I can give you at this time. The family will release a statement. The NYPSD will conduct a media conference. My priority is to identify and apprehend the individual who murdered Nathan Barrister. That's it."

"Thank you, Lieutenant. These stunning revelations bring more questions," Nadine said to the camera. "As we gather more answers, more information, we'll keep you informed. This is Nadine Furst reporting from the gates of Barrister House."

Nadine signaled cut to the camera, then, since Eve had already started toward the car, rushed after her.

"Wait a minute!"

Eve turned back. "How do you run in those?" She pointed at Nadine's sky-high heels. "Do you start running around in them at like twelve, thirteen?"

"It's an inherent skill. Dallas, Jesus! Henry Barrister, secret vault, stolen art and jewelry. This is a huge story."

"Somebody bashed Nathan Barrister's head in. That's my story."

"Look, I get it. You know I do. I had plenty of time waiting for you to do some research there. He comes off as a good man, a good husband, father, businessman, citizen. I want you to find who killed him, and any help I can give there, I will. But I can't ignore the billion-pound elephant in the room. How much are we talking? I won't use it from you—I'll find out otherwise. But off the record, how much?"

"The museum guys have to authenticate and value. But I'd say make that billion-pound elephant plural."

"Jesus. The man had a rep—a hound-dog-with-women rep—but this? A supersecret private collection, one his family didn't know existed. You're buying that?"

"Yeah, I'm buying that."

"Okay. Tell me what they got, what they took. I'll hold it, you know I'll hold it until you give me the go. I'll do my own research, no sharing with my team."

Nadine, Eve knew, kept her word. No matter how big the story, integrity came first.

"The Royal Suite."

"What is that?"

"Do your research. I've gotta go."

"Dallas—"

"Nadine." Roarke put a hand on her arm. "She's barely slept, barely eaten. And here come your colleagues."

Nadine looked around, saw the vans pulling up, the reporters hotfooting it down the sidewalk.

"Go."

"Give the family a break," Eve said as she got into the car. "The house is full of grief."

As the shouts for *Lieutenant Dallas!* rang out, Roarke pulled away.

Eve put her head back, closed her eyes. "And I have to do a media conference either tomorrow or Monday, depending."

"You shouldn't be so good at them. You are," he insisted when she just gave a quick snort. "You're clear, you're brisk, and the obvious impatience adds to it. So does your emphasis on the victim. You gave Nadine more than I thought you would."

"Whitney cleared it. We agreed she'd find out anyway, and she doesn't sensationalize. Well, she doesn't have to sensationalize the vault thing. It'll have a life of its own."

Eyes still closed, she thought out loud. "Why didn't he run? Didn't he hear Barrister coming down the steps, moving around? Why didn't he? If he did, why not take what he had in hand and go? It's a lot, right there. And for all he knew, the Barristers would just swallow the loss. But you add murder, it's going down just like it's going down. Instead of a stretch in a cage, it's life."

"He may have killed before."

"Yeah, I'm going to look at that."

"After you've had a meal."

"I need an hour down first. My brain's going numb. Just an hour."

"All right then. It's still pleasant out. After you rest a bit, why don't I grill some burgers? We'll retire the grill for the season soon enough."

"Peabody says her dad grills the whole year. Goes out even in the snow to grill the veg burgers or whatever."

"I don't believe I'm that dedicated."

"Yeah, I wouldn't be, either. I gotta look at the wife, because you've gotta. Dig down, see if she's got gambling shit, or a side piece, something she could be blackmailed for. She didn't want him dead, but the rest . . . I don't see it, but I have to clear it. Same with the sister, the daughters, the staff."

"Why don't I look into their financials?"

"Yeah, that's why you're the expert consultant. You can't fake that kind of grief," she murmured. "The wife. I see grief all the time. Some can fake it, and damn well. Others feel it even if they did the killing. Those can throw you off the scent, for a while at least. But you can't fake what I saw. She loved him, depended on him, enjoyed him. She didn't want him dead. But it doesn't mean she didn't have some part in the theft."

"You have to look," he agreed. "But I don't see it, either. As you said before, why take a guest room?"

"He insisted on taking one, so she did instead. She said she drifted off awhile. Maybe she was keeping watch, but did just that. Drifted off."

Like I'm doing right now, Eve thought as he drove through the gates.

"Wakes up. 'Oh shit, where'd he go?' Goes down, finds him. Last thing she wanted. Pile some guilt on grief." She sighed as he parked. "Doesn't ring for me, but I'm looking anyway."

She walked to the door, turned to Roarke. "If Summerset snoots at me, I may just bite him in the throat."

"Fortunately for all of us, he's at the street fair. He enjoys them."

"Right." So she walked into a blissfully empty house.

Before she could take the stairs, Roarke scooped her up.

"I'm not that tired."

"Yes, you are."

"Yeah." She let her head drop on his shoulder. "I am. I need to get a consult with Mira."

"Mmm."

"Henry Barrister's a big factor in this. I want her take. Have to talk to the ex-wives. Any of the sex mates he had most recently. Somebody knew about the goddamn vault."

"No question of it."

The cat came out from wherever he'd occupied himself and jogged along beside Roarke. Intuiting the direction, he bounded ahead, and was sprawled across the bed when Roarke carried Eve in.

"You'll make room, mate."

He set Eve down, took off her jacket, her weapon harness.

"Just an hour. I just need an hour."

"Then turn off your numb brain and take it."

When he pulled off her boots, she flipped around to her stomach. The cat made room; Roarke tucked a throw around her.

"You're on duty," he told the cat.

And he would engage the monitor to watch over her in case nightmares chased her while she slept.

In his office, he started on Aileen Carville's financials first. After he initiated the search, he contacted his old friend Brian in Dublin.

"And how's it all going then?"

"About how it was," Roarke told him. "And you?"

"It's Saturday night in the pub. We've Rory's group doing a *seisiún*. Lots of tourists joining the locals for a pint. I'll not complain."

"And are you hearing anything that might be of interest to me and my cop?"

"Well now, there wasn't a peep when last we spoke. Then the Yanks broke the story, and there's plenty of talk. I'll be using the snug for a moment or two, Mary darling. Take over for me."

"Speculative sort of talk," Brian continued, as he went into the snug behind the bar and, closing the door, closed off the pub noise. "Plenty of interest in what might've been taken, and what's left. I've a few names, potentials you could say, of who might try for such a job across the pond, as they've had previous success."

"I wouldn't mind having the names."

"I'll give you those, and add it's the murder that throws them off. There's one or two who might fit there as well, but again, speculative."

"Understood, and appreciated, Brian."

Roarke noted down the names, recognized most.

"Thanks for this. I won't keep you away from the stick on a Saturday night. Why don't you come for Thanksgiving? Come over with the family, stay a few days."

"Well now, I wouldn't mind that a bit. How's our Lieutenant Darling?"

"Taking a bit of a nap at the moment. She wears herself out."

"You give her a kiss for me when she wakes. If I hear more, I'll pass it to you." He laughed. "And here we are, street rats that were, helping out the coppers. What a world."

"It's all what we make it, Brian. I'll be talking to you."

He ended the call, glanced at the monitor.

She hadn't moved a muscle, though the cat had draped himself over her ass as he tended to do when she slept face down.

Satisfied, he got a bottle of sparkling water from his office friggie. And settled into helping his cop.

Chapter Nine

She couldn't have slept deeper if she'd been laid out in a drawer in the morgue. He gave her the hour, then stretched it another thirty minutes. When she began to stir, he set aside the work.

When he got to the bedroom, she sat up, tangled in the throw, one hand absently stroking the cat.

Her face looked warm from sleep, her eyes still heavy with it.

He went to the AutoChef for coffee.

As she had that morning, she took the mug in both hands.

"Twice in one day. Right? It's still today? I feel like I slept a week."

"It's the very same day."

As she drank coffee, he could all but see her mind wake up. And she smiled at him.

"Maybe I could take another hour."

He leaned in, kissed her. "You'll have a meal first. We'll take another hour later on."

"Huh. Well, if you don't want to get me naked, I need to update my board and—"

"A meal, Eve. That's first for you. And while you have it, I'll tell you about the financials I've been through."

"Did you find—"

"While we eat. I'll handle the burgers. You can deal with the chips—fries," he corrected, "you'll want with it. As I do, come to think of it. And I'm in the mood for a pint."

"I wouldn't mind a beer."

"Good. You'll want your jacket and boots."

She reached for her boots. "It's not the wife. I have to look into the whole gambling, addiction, blackmail, sex-on-the-side thing, but it's not going to be the wife."

"I'll agree with you." He handed her jacket to her. "Let's start the grill and have a pint."

"I've lost track of the time."

"It's half past I'm bloody hungry."

Amused and awake, she went down with him. While he did whatever he did to get the grill going—she stayed out of that one—she sipped a beer.

Cooler, she thought, than the last time they'd done the sit-outside deal. But pleasant. Before long, the scent of grilling meat joined the perfume of flowers. For her contribution, she went into the kitchen—definitely not her domain—and programmed the AutoChef for a basket of fries.

Glancing around, she thought of the Barrister cook. She figured Divine would approve of this—enormous—space. Slick, sleek, efficient, but still, like the air outside, pleasant.

It smelled a little like vanilla, a little like lemons. In fact, she spotted a glass bowl of lemons on a counter. One of the windows had a glass bump-out thing where green plants thrived. She knew they were herbs—she wasn't a complete idiot—but had no idea what Summerset did with them.

She took the fries out as Roarke put the plates with their burgers on the patio table.

"It's a pretty nice kitchen."

At her comment, his eyebrow winged up. "Do you think so then?"

"I see a lot of kitchens." She sat, scooped fries onto her plate, and gave them a good snow shower of salt. "This one has the same sort of feel as the Barristers'. I mean that someone who enjoys it uses it."

"Summerset does enjoy it, but won't be using it this evening. He just let me know he ran into Mavis and company at the street fair. They invited him back to the house for dinner."

"That's somebody else who likes a kitchen. Peabody probably gets a nice little orgasm every time she walks into hers now. And Mavis is getting into the whole thing, too."

She took a bite of burger. "That's never going to happen with me."

"I believe I'd worry a bit if it did."

"But we're good, right?" She gestured with a fry. "We put this together. It's not like we'd starve."

"We're fine and good."

"Since we're fine and good, how about that update? The financials?"

"Before that, I'll tell you I spoke with Brian. Since the story broke, there's been considerable talk. Speculation, as he put it. And he gave me a few names of people in the business of thievery who might pull off a job such as this."

"How many names?"

"Eight to start, and I imagine your friends at Interpol know most of them."

"I'll run them."

"To save you some time, I eliminated four of them, as I confirmed they were nowhere in or near New York at the time of the murder."

"How can you be sure?"

"Because." He gestured with a fry back at her. "I'm the expert consultant. The other four's whereabouts are more nebulous, so might warrant a look."

"They'll get one. Do you know any of them?"

"A few, by reputation. None personally." He smiled at her as he ate. "We don't have conventions or monthly meetings, darling. Not even a secret handshake."

"But you never worked with any on this particular list."

"I didn't, no. If and when I worked with others, each would have a specific area."

She gestured again. "Such as?"

"Well now, say you wanted to hit a bank. Not with the bursting in with weapons, all the shouting, and people huddled on the floor. That's messy and too often violent. But you might want to find your way into a vault or some particular safe-deposit boxes. You might put together a team where everyone has their own area of expertise."

Eve decided her best response was a grunt.

"If it helps? If I were to have planned the Barrister House job, I'd have worked alone, and I'd give you a probability of ninety that's what happened here. It's a basic job. The take's staggering, but the work's basic."

"A man's dead."

"And shouldn't be. Not only for human reasons, Eve, but because it was a basic, step-by-step job. Jam the security—and that wouldn't be especially tricky—get inside—again, simple enough. Open the vault, which would take a bit of time but only rudimentary skill and some practice. Get the take, get out. But you'd prepare for contingencies. I don't think you'll find your killer on the list Brian gave me."

"Because?"

"They're experienced, and good at what they do. It's the panic that doesn't fit for me, not with this bunch. So I'm thinking, if I want to hire someone for a rich take but simple execution, why not someone I can get on the cheap? Someone good enough who'd do the job for a fraction of what someone—we'll say like me—would demand."

She sat back. "That's a good angle. Damn it."

"Might be they didn't mean to kill Barrister. Just grabbed something to put him down so they could get out. That doesn't matter," he said before she could. "But it's plausible."

"Okay, yeah. It's plausible. I'll still look at the list."

"Of course."

Thinking it through, she ate another fry. "Someone less experienced might brag about pulling it off, dead man or not."

"The quickest way to end up in the nick, but yes. Ears are out for such a thing."

"Appreciated."

He sat back with his beer. "As to the financials. The widow has her own business account where she deposits her fees, pays any business expenses for more than twenty years. She does quite well. The majority of their properties, stocks, accounts are held jointly. When he inherited the house, he had it put in both their names. He does—did—have an account in his name only, but that appears to be for his personal expenses, wardrobe, tailoring, grooming."

He sipped his beer. "It's all tediously aboveboard. We actually have the same accounting firm and estate attorney. But it's not surprising, as they deal with wealth."

"She inherits the lot?"

"He—and she—have provided very well for their daughters. He's split his interest in Zip between his wife, his girls. His affairs, and his widow's, are in meticulous order, as best I can tell. There's nothing in either to indicate a gambling problem, an addiction to be fed, a side piece, or blackmail payments."

"What I figured."

"I ran through the daughters'—and that didn't take long. I can give you the particulars, but it's quicker to say they're wealthy, responsible young women who haven't, so far, abused their privilege."

"Also figured."

"Joy Barrister, I haven't quite completed. But at this point, I can say she's a careful investor. The divorce didn't cost her, unless you count the fact her ex is also quite well-off, and their combined wealth put them both on another level."

"I can count that."

"With her father's death and his bequests, she now owns the condo outright, and like her brother with Barrister House, is having considerable work done to, I imagine, make it more to her taste. She spends lavishly, but well within her means, which are also lavish. She does have one small, in comparison, questionable account."

"Really?"

"It's not unusual for someone with great wealth to work the system to try to protect some of that wealth. She has some rental properties scattered here and there and holds them under an LLC. And more or less adjacent to that, this other account. Technically questionable. She might get a rap on the knuckles for it, but no more than that. She opened it after the divorce."

"Okay, you could look a little more there, since that's the first out-of-bounds on any of them."

"I'll do that, and the staff. I could have a conversation with our estate attorney."

"Why is it *our* estate attorney?"

Eyes sober, he reached over and took her hand. "I know it's a burden to you, and I'm forever grateful you bear it, and so gracefully. But our marriage, our partnership, our enduring love and excellent sex has made you a wealthy woman."

She looked into those wildly blue eyes, where humor danced under the sobriety. And said, "Bite me."

"There's that excellent sex again. You met with the estate attorney in regards to your will."

"I'm dumping it all back on you."

"And," he continued, "asked me to deal with other eventualities, then—though I'm painfully aware you didn't read the prenup document thoroughly or comprehensively—you signed it."

"Yeah, yeah, but—"

"But. Garrett remains both my estate attorney and yours. So if you want, I can have a conversation with him. Or open the door so you can do so."

"I'd rather the first, but it has to be the second."

"All right then."

"Somebody spilled the vault thing to somebody else. That's the only way this happened. If they did it for gain, it's somewhere in the financials. If they did it to brag? That's harder to pin down. If revenge plays in? That's why I have to look at the ex-wives and bed rompers. Since it doesn't look like either the vic or his wife played around, I look at the sister, the daughters, the staff for that angle.

"Anyway. I'd better get to it. I guess we need to clean this up."

Once they had, simple enough in the slick, sleek, and efficient kitchen, they started upstairs.

"You hang with Summerset sometimes in there."

"In the kitchen? Yes, now and again."

"So why do they call that other space a butler's pantry? He's not a butler. He's more . . . a castle manager."

"He'd enjoy that distinction."

"And people have what they call a butler's pantry who don't have anything or anyone remotely like a butler. It's just another one of those terms that make no sense. Maybe I'll change my will and leave everything to Galahad."

"Your mind is a constant fascination to me."

"There's a lot on it right now."

"Including butler's pantries and inherited wealth for cats."

"They're handy distractions." She stepped into her office. "Done with them now. I'm going to update the board, write up this last round of interviews, a report on the transfer from the vault. Then I'll start looking at the thieves. The exes are scattered all over the place, so because of the planet's damn rotation, that'll have to wait until tomorrow."

"You'll be busy enough without that. I'll contact Garrett, and get back to the financials."

She took his hand before he turned away.

"It lifts the burden a little. The excellent sex, and the coffee. They lighten the load some. The fact you not only get the job but are willing to put in time? It does a lot to counteract the whole money thing."

"Whatever I can do to ease your pain, darling Eve."

"I don't even mind you being a smart-ass."

"Well now, in that area I can't begin to compete with you."

"You're competitive, but yeah, I win."

Fueled with some load-lightening coffee, she updated her board, wrote up her reports. She killed a few brain cells doing the calculations on reasonable times to contact Henry Barrister's ex-wives.

Then she dug into thieves.

It shouldn't have surprised her how clean their data was. When she'd first run Roarke, she'd found only the bare minimum in his official record. No arrests.

She imagined he'd had more than a few knocks when he'd run the streets of Dublin as a kid, but he'd wiped the slate clean.

She suspected the group she'd studied had done the same, or paid someone to do so. Maybe not quite as clean, but nearly.

She focused in on the arrests—charges dropped—for assault by one Ignatious Clapp. Two arrests, one in Killarney, Ireland, one in a hotel in Spain, where he now lived.

She dug down to the police reports, hit the translator for Spanish. Then after reading, sat back and frowned.

In Ireland, Clapp had gone after some man when he learned that said individual had smacked a kid around—age eleven. In Spain, a second individual had gotten physical with a woman server in the hotel bar.

In both cases Clapp had pummeled said individuals, then had surrendered to the authorities without incident. Witnesses corroborated, charges dropped.

But, Eve thought, it showed he had a capacity for violence—and she suspected there may have been other altercations that hadn't involved local cops.

So Clapp went to the top of her list.

When Roarke came in, she looked over.

"I've finished the sister and the housekeeper," he told her. "I've started on the butler."

"Hold that a minute. Ignatious Clapp."

"Ah, yes. I've heard of him. Definitely experienced. I believe he focuses on jewelry, and lives now in semiretirement in . . . I'm not sure."

"Barcelona. He's got some assaults—charges dropped—on his record. Went after a guy who smacked a kid around one night on the street in Killarney. Then took on another who'd harassed and gotten physical with a waitress in, as it happens, Barcelona."

"Well now."

"Yeah, well now. But it shows he'll use violence. He busted up the first guy's hand, in addition to knocking out a couple teeth, realigning his nose. He broke the second guy's jaw, among other things."

"I'll wager the hand he broke's the one that smacked the child, and the jaw? Likely used to insult the woman."

"You'd win the bet, and still. I'm going to pass his name along."

"You'll do what you must, as it's murder. Clapp would be past seventy, wouldn't he?"

"Seventy-seven."

"I think, when you find who you're after, he'll be younger, less seasoned."

"Because you were, when you stole them?"

"Not just that." Frowning, he shrugged. "It's one of those gut feelings, as you're prone to. This is, and we can't deny it, an area I know something about. I put myself there, Eve, in that room, at that vault, overloaded with the sensation of seeing it all. I take them, hold them in my hands."

He held them out, palms up. "For a moment, just one moment of indulgence, I let myself feel the weight, admire the beauty, because for that one moment, that one moment only, they're mine. That's a thrill I can't explain to you, it has to be felt."

As he often did, he picked up her coffee, took a sip.

"But then I'm out and gone. Say while I'm having that moment of indulgence, I hear something. And no matter how indulgent, Eve, my ears are pricked for any sound. And it's more."

He set down the coffee, wandered to her board, back again.

"It's a sense you have. You're alone, or you're not. When you feel you're not, you go. If somehow that sense failed you long enough for someone to come along, you make yourself slippery and you run.

"It's not cowardice. It's practicality. It's survival. Even if you lose what you'd come for, well, there's another night, another place, another treasure to hold in your hands."

She didn't speak for a minute.

"How hard was it to give up?"

He brushed a hand over her hair. "I haven't a single regret on that score."

"That's not what I asked. How hard was it to give it all up?"

"Brutal, that's the pure truth, but without a single regret. You're my treasure, Eve, and not for only a moment of indulgence. I'd rather hold you than any other."

"Does this, consulting, working in your way on investigations, make it any easier?"

"Surprisingly, it does, yes."

"Anything I can do to ease your pain."

He laughed, leaned his hip on the leg of her command center. "On to Joy Barrister then."

Before he could continue, her 'link signaled.

"It's Inspector Abernathy."

"Do what you must."

"Dallas," she said. "Doesn't the planet revolve in your location?"

"My location at this time is New York."

"Is that right?" And no casual shirt now, she noted. A Brit copper's black suit and tie.

"I'm here to monitor the authentication process and aid in the methods of return. At this point, the experts in such matters have authenticated a Cézanne, a Picasso, an ivory statue of Venus, the Gardelli ruby ring, the Blue Moon sapphire necklace and earrings, a Ming dynasty vase, and a Mayan artifact."

"That's progress."

"It is. It will likely take another day or two, perhaps three, to authenticate and document the rest. We're also investigating the theft of the Royal Suite. I've spoken to your commander."

"In investigating the murder of Nathan Barrister, the NYPSD will also investigate the theft."

"Understood. We intend to coordinate and cooperate with you on that matter."

"In that spirit, I have a couple of names you might want to look into."

She read him in, waited.

"I appreciate this, Lieutenant. I'm not holding back. My focus has been, to this point, on what has been recovered. I know Interpol is working in conjunction with your EDD on monitoring underground auctions and chatter. As far as I know, there's nothing yet to report there."

"When there is."

"When there is. My word on it. If any of the names you gave me lead to more, you'll hear from me. The recovery of so much stolen property may ring loudest, but Interpol doesn't take murder lightly. Nor do I. I'll be in touch."

Eve replaced the 'link, then ran her hands up over her face, into her hair. "That's done."

"You're starting to fade again."

"Not that much. Joy Barrister."

"Nothing that shows. She's made money from her money—smart investing, good property purchases, well maintained from what I can see. It's clear to me why she's CFO. Her records there? Again, from a cursory look, meticulous and clean. I'd say she's a woman who takes her position very seriously."

"Likes to travel?"

"She does. Europe and the tropics seem favored, though she travels to Asia, South America, and so forth. Sometimes on the company dime, sometimes on her own."

"Companions?"

"Company staff when it's business. Occasionally a travel companion when it's personal. No one there who seems of particular importance, in that the travel companion rarely repeats. She appears to be a woman who enjoys her position, her wealth, and her freedom to choose her companions."

"Okay, staff."

"Not much there. Nothing—what's that word you use?—hinky. Again, wise investing, and I wouldn't be surprised if they got advice from the Barristers there. They use the same investment firm as Henry Barrister, though a different financial adviser, as none of them are in the Barrister bracket.

"In college—before she took the job at Barrister House—Uma Acker was seriously involved with another woman."

"How'd you get that from her financials?"

"If you go back, and I did, there was a shared bank account, and two names on an apartment lease. When I checked the other woman, I found she'd been killed in a vehicular accident—about six months before the start of Uma's employment. Which explains why, every year on the date of death, Uma purchases flowers—always white roses."

"To take to the gravesite. Okay."

"The butler. John Tyler owns a share in some beach property in North Carolina. His parents also own shares and have retired there. Travel-wise, he visits them two or three times a year. His financials are in good order, nothing in the hinky area. He does, occasionally, play the horses. Small bets, and he wins more than loses. I assume he's seeing someone, or someones, as two or three times a month he charges what would add up to dinner for two at a nice restaurant. He also buys flowers on occasion.

"He lives within his means, with sporadic indulgences—such as orchestra seats, generally for two, a few times a year. Broadway. He enjoys musical theater."

"I think we'll dig up his dinner/theater companions. You never know."

"Until you do. And last, the divine Divine. A widow—she married Jasper Fortigue when she was but twenty-two, and lost him in a construction accident—work-related—when she was thirty-eight. Two children, boys who were sixteen and fourteen at the time of their father's death. She received a lump sum payment, both from insurance and from the construction company.

"From what I can tell, she used it to pay her bills, raise her children, start college funds, and take classes. Culinary classes.

"She's also been careful with her money. Small investments, but she banks the bulk. She doesn't own any property, but helped both her sons buy homes. She lives simply. Her travel is almost exclusively limited to a two-week trip—with her family—to various locations. They rent a house, a big one, at the beach, in the mountains. From a financial standpoint, she is what she seems. Someone who loves her work, loves her family, and gives her best to both."

"Any romantic or sexual companions?"

"None that show."

"Loves her family, vacations with them. Maybe she knew about the vault, just mentioned it to them."

"Do you really think so?"

"No, but it's best to cover it. I'm going to talk to the guy who found the wall panel, see what that turns up. This thief? He didn't just wake up one day and think: You know, I bet there's a vault full of good stuff in that office in that house. I'm going to go grab something."

"No."

"Go over it with me one more time. The process."

"Unless the thief is a complete idiot, this was a brokered job."

"What if he is?" She rose, circled the board. "He's an idiot. You said the job itself was simple, basic. So lack of experience could be a factor. Hell, maybe it was his first job."

"You can't discount it, I suppose. That's considerable and fantastic luck on his part."

"Not if someone told him how to do it. Someone told him about the vault, maybe helped him gain access."

"Someone in the household again."

"Going back to dead Henry, yeah."

She saw the steps and how the steps could work.

"Somebody lets it slip, and somebody else decides they want a piece of that. Can't wait long, either, not if they know the Barristers are making arrangements to give it all back."

Hands in pockets, she studied the board. "Something to play with. Take me through the broker angle again."

"The client engages the broker. Alternately, the broker learns of something worth moving on. Either way, he then selects the thief, offers him a fee. This is sometimes a percentage of the resale value, or a flat fee."

"And the thief wouldn't know who the client is, or if the broker himself is the client."

"He wouldn't, no. Unless the broker is a complete idiot. For a take of this scope, it feels highly doubtful."

"Most criminals have a wide stupid streak." She glanced at him. "With some noted exceptions. But okay."

"With this scope, it's also very possible the broker doesn't know the identity of the client. That's risky, but this take? So tempting. Arrangements are made. Fees, payment schedule, drop-off details. The thief, barring idiots, takes the time to study, research, case it out, practice and so on. Once the job's complete, drop-off, authentication, payment.

"For something like this, as I said, you're not going to pop out the stones, reset them or sell them loose, and bottom out the value. So the client either has a private collection or intends to go to private auction."

"Let's hope it's the second."

She rubbed her eyes, blinked them open to stare at the board. "Need to talk to the exes."

"And that's for tomorrow. Come now, shut it down. Some solid sleep will give you a better start on it."

"Yeah, yeah." She blew out a breath. "Yeah. Thieves and emeralds and Interpol."

"Oh my."

Laughing, she rubbed her eyes again. "I know that one."

So saying, she went back to her command center to shut down.

Chapter Ten

He saw the tension in the way she rolled her shoulders, circled her neck.

"Knotted up, aren't you then?"

"Yeah, some."

After cupping a hand on the back of her neck, he judged it more than some. He knew ways to untie those knots.

"How about a swim?"

"Ah . . . yeah, actually. I could use it." As they walked to the elevator, she looked at him. "Even if you just want me wet and naked."

"Well, of course, but I also enjoy you dry and dressed. For example," he said, and when they stepped into the elevator, turned her back to the wall and covered her mouth with his.

He loosened several knots, along with her shirt.

"You could wait on that until we actually get to the pool."

"No time like the present."

As his mouth took hers again, he unbuckled her belt. He felt her heart pounding against his, heard the hum in her throat, felt the give in her body. He changed the angle of the kiss. Deeper, just a little deeper.

His fingers slid down, over her breast, over her belly, over her center, then in.

She came in one quick burst. Before she could draw the next breath, he was inside her.

Pinned to the wall, she could do nothing more than feel. The rush, the heat, the shattering pleasure. Her body pulsed and pumped, greedy for more, on fire now for this fast, fierce mating.

He knew she was lost, felt her trembling surrender to him, to herself, to this dark, drowning need they could bring to each other time after time after time.

When her trousers, her shirt, slid to the elevator floor, his hunger spiked. In a sudden frenzy, he pulled the support tank over her head, tossed it, so she wore only the teardrop diamond on a chain, and her boots.

Eyes on hers, he cupped his hands under her thighs, lifted her. Now she chained around him, arms, legs. Now her lips fused to his as they whipped each other to the edge of madness, and over.

She might have slid bonelessly to the floor, but his body, pressed to hers, kept her upright. Breathless, skin slick with sweat, they held there until he turned his head to brush his lips under her ear.

"More relaxed now, I'll wager."

"Did you say something? It's hard to hear with all these bells ringing. Jesus, we're still in the elevator. I'm naked in the elevator."

"Not altogether. You're still wearing your boots. It's a fascinating look."

"Right. I'm going to take them off. And we have to pick up all this stuff."

"As otherwise, Summerset might come across the scattered clothes and suspect we've had sex in the elevator."

"Well. Yeah."

She pulled off her boots, gathered them and the clothes in her arms. "I still want a swim."

"Then we'll have one."

He walked with her through the tropical paradise of plants and vines and flowers to the blue sparkle of the pool.

She dumped the clothes on a chair. "I need to reboot my brain after that."

"I can help with that as well."

He scooped her up, kissed her. Then he tossed her, high over that sparkling blue. The sound she made caught somewhere between a scream and a squeal before she hit the water.

She surfaced, shoved her wet hair out of her face. "What are you, twelve?"

"I'll just have to prove, after we've had our swim, I've more skill and experience than that."

Stripping off the rest of his clothes, he dived in after her.

After some laps, some lazy floating, a bout of underwater wrestling, he proved his skill and experience.

She slept, and deeply. Until she dreamed.

Dreaming, she stood at the crime scene that smelled of blood and death. The vault stood open and held its treasures.

As she stood, Roarke, in cat-burglar black, came through the window. "You can't be here."

"Now then, I have a job to finish, just as you."

He walked past her, gave her a wink, then stepped into the vault.

He opened a satchel and drew from a velvet bag the ivory Venus.

"Lovely, isn't she?"

"It doesn't belong here."

"It wasn't for me to decide that. A man has a living to make, after all."

With care, he removed the tiara from the Royal Suite from another bag, placed it, then the necklace, the bracelet, the earrings, and finally the ring.

"I held those," he said, "held them as my own for a brief moment of time. Ah, and the thrill of it, beyond words. But it was the ready I needed, not the sparkle."

He turned, smiled at her. "Though you'd look like a queen wearing them. A goddess."

"That's not what I want."

"I know it, my darling Eve, or why would I have stopped looking for that thrill? I found more in you than ever that. You brought me the joy, the comfort, the ease—and who would've thought I needed the ease of belonging?"

He stepped out, gave her arm an affectionate rub.

"The precious and the priceless," he said, "but nothing in there is worth more than the life of the man you stand over and for. I believed that before you, and know it only more strongly since. I might have risked my own life for the precious and priceless, but that's a different thing than the taking of one.

"You know that very well."

"Yes. I know that."

"I'd best be off now, as you've work to do."

"Who took everything else?" she murmured.

As he stepped through the window, Roarke sent her a smile. "There's a question."

And he was gone, like a shadow in the dark.

On the floor, Nathan Barrister sat up. His face, his clothes were wet with blood. His eyes looked dull and full of sorrow.

"I didn't take any of those things. I didn't know about them until after my father died."

"I believe that. But you kept them, for weeks after you did know."

"It's not the same, is it?"

"The possession of stolen property . . . No, not the same."

"I loved my father. I thought I knew and accepted his flaws. He wasn't what you'd call a great dad. I know because I've tried to be. But he was a good father. He built an important business, ran it well. He treated his employees fairly, even generously."

With those sorrowful eyes, Nathan looked into the vault. "I don't know why he did this, why he needed this."

He turned to Eve. "We wouldn't have kept all this. Is it so wrong I wanted to find a way to fix this and still protect my family? Our business? My father's reputation? What harm did it do to take some time to find the best way?"

"It harmed you, Nate. It killed you."

"I didn't know."

"Who did?"

He only shook his head, lay back on the bloody floor. "I didn't know."

"Somebody did."

She woke to find Roarke sitting on the sofa. No suit—black jeans, a light sweater nearly as blue as his eyes—which reminded her it was still the weekend.

Instead of lying on Roarke's lap, the cat stretched across the back of the sofa as if reading whatever Roarke did on his tablet over Roarke's shoulder.

"Did you dream then, before you woke?" he asked her.

"I guess. Yeah." She sat up, realized she felt—body and mind—like a woman who'd been sexed into reviving sleep.

"I'm going to get a workout in."

"All right. I've done one myself already. We'll have Sunday breakfast when you're done."

She saw the fire simmered, and the sky window over the bed ran with wet.

"It's raining."

"Buckets. You'll be working at home, at least for the most part, I'm thinking."

"Yeah. Unless." She pulled on gym pants, a tank, running shoes. "I'll be about an hour."

"Then you'll tell me what's on your mind, won't you?"

She got coffee, nodded. "Once I figure out what's on it, I'll tell you."

When she went down, he checked the time, then rose. He'd get some work of his own done while she figured it out.

In the gym, she programmed a three-mile run, selected a tropical beach because she didn't need a challenge. Just movement.

While her body worked, so did her brain.

She polished off the run with weights until her muscles said enough already. She rounded that out with a short session in the dojo with the master, and finished with five strong laps in the pool.

When she came up, Roarke and the cat had deserted the field.

She pulled out an old NYPSD sweatshirt, sweatpants. If she had to go out, she'd change, but she'd work at home in comfort.

She took them into the bathroom, set them aside to grab a quick shower. Because of where her mind had traveled, she thought of the cold shower, the frigid tub of water she'd been subjected to as a child. The meanness in it.

She set the water hot, let the pulsing jets pummel her with heat.

When she came out, Roarke sat as he had before. The table held a pot of coffee and two domed plates.

"You look rested and ready."

"I feel rested and ready. Galahad?"

"Decided he preferred Summerset's company. And Summerset enjoyed the company last night. He also told me he expects Number Two's arrival within a couple of weeks. Three at the most."

"How would he know?"

"I have no idea, and didn't ask, as I know what we'll be expected to witness yet again. Unless we plan a holiday and find ourselves in Australia, for instance, when the day comes."

"She'd wait until we got back. I swear, she'd find a way."

"Ah well."

He removed the domes. Pancakes, bacon, berries.

He thought of her, Eve mused. He always thought of her.

"That's what I call Sunday breakfast." She topped off his coffee, then poured her own.

After drenching the pancakes in syrup, she cut into them.

"I dreamed about the vault, all the stuff, you, coming in—through the window—putting the Venus and the Royal Suite in there."

"As, in a way, I did."

"Yeah, in a way, you did."

She ate some bacon, shifted to him. "You were in that . . . line of work most of your life."

"If you don't count the last few years, all of it. They used me as part of a con, or a ploy, a distraction to a lift when I was, what, three, four, five? I don't clearly remember. Then I was out on my own, and expected to bring home a decent take. I learned to do just that to avoid the boot or the fist. But got them often enough in any case. You know this."

"I know this. Brian, your other friends, were part of it."

"We did what we had to do." He spoke simply, but she heard the mild annoyance under the tone. "It was a different world, Eve."

She put a hand on his arm. "I know that, too. Can you tell me the first thing you stole?"

"I couldn't, no. Something plucked from a pocket, I'd expect."

"How about the last?"

"The last? That would've been a few months—near to a year—before I turned and saw you at the funeral. While I was easing off that line of work, I didn't know it was my last."

He smiled now, in memory. "I'm pleased it was a worthy last."

"And was?"

"Cartier had a shipment of stones coming in, to be selected for commissioned pieces. Diamonds—blues, whites, pinks, reds, greens, canary. The client wanted a kind of diamond rainbow, colorful and unique. It's not so easy to trace loose stones, you see, so I gathered them up, sold them off here and there, taking my time about it."

"I remember that." She jabbed a finger at him. "I remember that heist. That was you? Who did you work with?"

"No one at all. I'd be disinclined to name names for you, but no one at all."

"They figured it was a team. Had to be."

"It wasn't. I will say, I had another job in the planning. I'd worked on the ins and outs quite a while. Then there was you, so I let it go."

"You didn't need the money anymore. It wasn't for that. It was for that thrill you can't describe."

"It was."

She put down her fork, then took his face in her hands. Looking into his eyes, she kissed him. "Okay," she said, and picked up her fork again.

"Who's saying that? My wife or the cop?"

"Right now, both. And both are going to ask you for a favor."

"What might that be?"

"I want you to look at the list of stolen property again, at the dates, the locations. Then give me your best shot at who took those items. On their own, part of a team. Working with a broker or not."

"It would be a guess."

"An educated one. And in return—though it sticks—I'm not going to go after or send anyone after those names. Just the one, if it pops, who did this."

He drank coffee as he considered. "I'll look, but—"

"I'm going to push on who the cops looked at in each case. Compare.

I've given Interpol a couple names, and maybe it'll play out. The loot, however major, only comes into this for me if and when it leads to the person who killed Barrister.

"It's all going back where it belongs, and that's enough for me. Barrister's father put that stuff in there, and it might help to know who made that possible."

"I made it possible for him to put the emeralds in there. That leads to making it possible for someone to take them out again."

"The person responsible for Nathan Barrister's death is the person who picked up that rock and caved in his skull. I'm not saying that because I love you. I'm saying that because it's a fact."

She ate more pancakes. "If you don't have something else going on, you could take a look while I'm talking to Interpol and, hopefully, interviewing ex-wives."

"It's Sunday, I can do what I like. I like working with my cop."

"I like working with my former thief. I killed my father."

"Eve."

She shook her head. "I was eight, he was raping me again, beating me again. I thought he'd kill me. So I killed him, and kept killing him after he was dead because I couldn't stop. I did what I had to do. So did you. And now, here we are."

He picked up her hand, kissed her fingers. "Here we are."

They went to work. At her command center, Eve started with Inspector Abernathy.

He reported four more pieces had been authenticated.

"The media's beating the jungle drums. Not just here," he told her. "Everywhere."

"They'll have to keep beating them for a while."

"Actually, I'm to answer some questions, along with a museum representative, your mayor, and your chief of police in another two hours."

"You're welcome to it."

"I'm told there's to be a more extensive media conference tomorrow, at Cop Central, which will include you and your partner."

"Great. Can't wait. Meanwhile, I'm working on a homicide. In the spirit of cooperation, I need you to get me some information. Who the authorities looked at, interviewed, suspected in each theft."

"That's no small amount of cooperation."

"I'm aware. If this particular angle leads me to Barrister's killer, you'd certainly be welcome to interview them regarding any and all of the previous thefts. Which may lead to closing some open cases."

A hint of satisfaction came into his eyes. "I can tell you your husband was looked at in any number of those open cases."

"Abernathy, do you believe Roarke murdered Nathan Barrister?"

"No, I don't."

"If you could get me that information, I'd like to work this angle."

"I'll see what I can do."

"Appreciate it."

She ended the call, cast her eyes to the ceiling.

She got up, walked around her board, and shook off the simmering annoyance.

And sitting again, she decided to go in chronological order with the ex-wives of Henry Barrister.

Angelica Frank Barrister LeVoy Gruber enjoyed a mimosa by the pool on a sunny day in Hawaii. To Eve's eye, the hundred-year-old first wife had undergone enough work to tighten every inch of her skin to the point it might split apart in a dozen places at any sudden movement.

It took Eve about five minutes to deduce she'd get nothing out of the woman beyond a grudge held for nearly three-quarters of a century.

"I'm not surprised to learn Henry was a thief. He cheated on me with that redheaded slut, among others. I made him pay for it. If I hadn't found it too much trouble, I'd have attended his memorial. I'd have worn a red dress and danced the cha-cha."

She kept that one short, reasonably certain if the woman had known anything, she'd have been happy to spill it. As long as it smeared shit on her first ex-husband.

She tried wife number two, the redheaded slut. Darla Starling, actress, still had red hair. She'd also had work done, but Eve thought the woman looked a lot more human than number one.

She had big blue eyes, and a single tear slid down her left cheek with what Eve saw as beautiful and practiced grace.

"It's still hard to accept Henry's gone. And now his son! I didn't really know Nathaniel."

"Nathan."

"Of course. Henry and I weren't blessed with any children during our time together. We had a fiery relationship. It just burned itself out."

"Before that happened, did he tell you about or show you the vault?"

"No, and I refuse to believe Henry had any part of all that."

Like the graceful tear, the look of umbrage seemed well practiced.

"He can't defend himself, so I will. He loved art, and had a brilliant collection, right out in the open! He loved buying jewelry. I have a lovely collection from our time together. He'd never do this. I didn't know his son well, or his daughter, but I'm inclined to believe they're responsible."

"That's unlikely, Ms. Starling, as some of the items in the vault were stolen when they were, literally, children."

"Well. I'll never believe it of Henry. He was honest, hardworking, generous. We had a wild and burning love. He would have told me."

"He was involved with other women during your marriage."

"As the flame began to die. He had a weakness, and that blond bitch seduced him. He cast her off, didn't he? Her and the others. We even tried to rekindle the flame, but it was done. Only quiet embers remained."

She tossed back her hair. "Trust me. He didn't have any part of this, but if he had? If he didn't tell me, he didn't tell any of those who followed me."

When she finished that conversation, Eve took a tour of her office, then stopped by Roarke's.

"If you cheat on me with a redheaded slut or a blond bitch, I'm going with wife number one's method. Number two's making him out to be a hero, one with whom she shared a fiery passion, and who had a weakness for women who seduced him. Poor Henry. The first couldn't drum up the energy to attend his funeral, but if she had, she'd have worn a red dress and danced the cha-cha."

Sitting back, he swiveled in his big leather chair. "You're always dancing at my funeral."

"Steer clear of redheads."

"Noted."

"Abernathy's going to get me the information I want. He let me know, straight off, that they looked at you for a lot of the thefts."

"Well, you had to expect that."

"I did. I'm going to tackle wife number three. The first two didn't know anything."

"Number three would be the victim's mother."

"Yeah. Look, when I get the investigators' reports, I'm going to copy you."

"On the data from the thefts?" Sitting back again, he sipped from his tube of water. "Well, that, at least, will be fun."

"Yeah, Ferris wheels and merry-go-rounds. All my fun comes tomorrow when I have to do another damn media conference on this whole mess."

"You'll get through it. Eve, I've started with the first thefts, and have a couple names in mind. But, well, one's dead, one retired to Barbados a decade ago, and the last, he's into his eighties, and I can't see any of the three would apply here."

"Flip it around," she suggested. "Start at the other end. Somebody who stole for him forty, fifty years ago is less likely to have waited so long to take this job, if he knew about the vault in the first place. Five, ten years ago? Barrister could've started slipping—more likely at that age. And his death opens more of an opportunity."

"Ah." He gave her a nod and a smile. "Well now, that's why you're the cop."

"You don't really want to do this. That blocks some thinking angles."

"I have some qualms, yes. But a man's dead. You've the right of that. I'll work from the other end."

"How about we put in a few hours here, and if nothing breaks, we take a walk out to the pond and hang awhile, watch a vid later."

"I'd like that."

"Me, too. I'm hitting the next ex. When Abernathy comes through, I'll copy you."

Chapter Eleven

Eve reached Tina Glenn Barrister Carlyle Nance, wife number three and the mother of the victim, while she lounged on a balcony overlooking the Mediterranean Sea.

Plenty of work here, too, Eve deduced. That, and the perfectly applied makeup, helped the seventy-four-year-old pass for closer to fifty.

Her blond hair fell in long, luxurious waves to her shoulders. She wore enormous sunshades over eyes her ID termed violet-blue. She'd dyed her lips—full and pouty after their last treatment—a bright poppy pink.

Eve led with: "I'm sorry for your loss, Ms. Nance."

"Oh!" She pressed a hand, where diamonds flashed on fingers with nails of the same pink, to her heart. It beat under breasts as full as her lips and as perky as a teenager's.

"I can't comprehend it," she said in a voice that hadn't quite lost its roots in the Bronx. "My sweet little boy! I'm devastated."

"Of course."

"Have you found the person who did this terrible thing, who's left my life shattered?"

"We're working on it. If I could ask you some questions—"

"What could I tell you? My husband and I are spending the month on Corfu. He has business here. And I was on a short spiritual retreat when Joy contacted me."

She covered her mouth with her hand a moment, as if overcome.

"I wasn't there when Nathan needed me most. I'm going, of course, cutting off the last two days of my retreat."

"That must be difficult and inconvenient."

The sarcasm sailed over Tina's head. "Yes, very, but what else can be done? My maid's packing for me even as we speak so I can return home and prepare for the trip to New York. I'm going to say my final goodbye to my baby boy."

Reaching under the enormous sunshades, she flicked a tear away with a pink-tipped finger.

"This should never be! But I need to be strong, to offer what comfort I can to . . ."

"Aileen? Nathan's wife."

"Yes, yes. I haven't been able to think straight since Joy called to tell me the awful news. I have to do what I can for her and her children."

"I'm sure you will. You're aware that your son was killed during a burglary."

"Yes, yes. Joy gave me the ugly details."

"Did you know about the vault in his office?"

"No, I didn't. Will I say it surprised me?" Her voice lost that choked-up flavor. "Not if I'm honest. Henry, may he rest in peace, was a man of secrets. That was part of his appeal. I was so young, a child really, and he was so mysterious and romantic. I loved him with all my young heart. The man simply swept me off my feet."

"You were married about ten years." The longest, Eve thought, of the four.

"Yes, you could say I grew up as a young wife, then a mother. I gave Henry what no one else had. I gave him two children. He was grateful for that. And even though our marriage faded, we remained civil, even friendly, for the children."

The hand went back to her heart as she looked out to the sea, as if in grief.

"It's a blessing, I suppose, that Henry didn't live to see this terrible thing happen. As a father, he saw to it Nathan and Joy had every advantage. The finest education, extensive travel as part of that. When we couldn't hold our marriage together, he bought me a penthouse nearby so the children would be close to both of us."

"Regarding the vault."

Tina waved that aside. "I stayed out of Henry's business."

"In ten years, you never went into his office at Barrister House?"

"Well, of course I did. As a young, devoted wife, I might go in to urge him not to work so hard, or take him a drink. Or . . ."

Smiling now, she tipped down her sunshades. Eve decided violet-blue was accurate, and those striking eyes showed no signs of weeping.

"Henry and I made love in that office. He liked me to play sexy secretary, and then—"

"Okay. Got that. He never mentioned the vault or its contents?"

"A man of secrets," she repeated, and tapped the sunshades back in place. "Was it really full of treasures? My husband heard Henry had the Blue Moon in there."

"I really can't tell you, ma'am."

"Oh, don't call me ma'am." She laughed gayly. "Why, we're practically the same age. I'm saying if Henry really had something like the Blue Moon in there, I would've loved to see it all. Try a few things on, just for fun."

Her lips moved back to their pout. "But he never told me. Something like that? Just behind the wall? And I never knew."

"Would you have any idea who he might have told?"

"He never told me, his wife, the mother of his children. Maybe one of his dalliances." She shrugged. "He had plenty of those. I realized, after I gained some distance and experience, that Henry was addicted to sex. And the younger the . . . partner, the better."

"Anyone specific?"

The shoulders shrugged. "I hardly remember names, but you might look at the one he married years after our marriage dissolved. Nothing but a gold digger."

After the conversation, such as it was, Eve put her head down on the desk for a minute. She needed to have one more of these with wife number four. Leading nowhere, she thought, but to the conclusion that Henry Barrister had lousy taste in wives—and a definite type.

But she had to check off that last box.

At least Abernathy had come through. Though tempted to switch it up, dive into those investigators' reports, she copied them to Roarke. Comforting herself with more coffee, she contacted wife number four.

Lacey Jones Barrister O'Ryan surprised her. The mixed-race woman in her early forties hadn't bothered with makeup, had her dark hair bundled carelessly back under a floppy straw hat.

"Just doing some gardening," she said. "I heard about Nathan. I'm so sorry. I can't say we were close, but he was a nice man, had a nice family."

"You were married to Henry Barrister."

"That's right. Nathan would've been . . . well, in his late twenties or early thirties. I was about ten years younger, but we got along fine."

"Henry Barrister would have been about . . ."

"Yeah." She adjusted her hat, and set down what looked like a wicked pair of scissors. "Eighty. I was doing some modeling at the time, and caught his eye. I went out with him a couple of times. Why not? He was sweet to me, attentive. When he asked me to marry him, I was . . ." She laughed. "'What?' But he told me he was tired of playing the field—that's how he phrased it. He laid it out. He wanted a marriage partner. He wanted someone beautiful, trustworthy, someone on his arm, someone to help host his dinner parties, travel with him, share his bed. And he'd make it worth my while—his phrase again."

"Which meant?"

"A lump sum payment once it was official, a kind of annual salary for every year of marriage—as long as I didn't cheat. He didn't want any more kids. I'd have a generous stipend, I guess you'd call it, for wardrobe and other personal expenses."

"So it was basically a business arrangement."

"On one level, yes. He was offering me millions and a lifestyle that was way beyond mine. I was never going to be a supermodel. I could have all that if I wore a ring, slept with him, and stayed faithful. We didn't love each other, but we liked each other."

She paused a moment, clipped some dead-looking flower off at the head, and tossed it in a bucket with other dead-looking flowers.

"Honestly, I really liked him. He was so interesting, and powerful, really. And for a few years, it was pretty damn good. Henry showed me the world, and the kind of world I'd only seen in vids or read about."

She lifted her shoulders. "Anyway, he started looking around. Jesus, the man's cruising toward ninety, and it wasn't enough he had a wife who hadn't hit thirty. We didn't fight about it, but I told him it wasn't right. I'd been faithful, and he wasn't being faithful, and that wasn't right."

She sat, picked up a shiny red cylinder, and sipped from it.

"He said that's the way it was, and I said it broke the deal. We didn't argue about it, it was a kind of no-hard-feelings deal, it's been nice, now it's done. He gave me a settlement, and I have to say, it was more than

I'd have asked for. The thing is, we still liked each other, so there just weren't any hard feelings.

"Henry even came to my wedding. I met Liam a couple years after the divorce, and that was love. Still is. But I came into that, thanks to Henry, with my own. Liam's a successful man, but I had my own this time. We've got a really good life, a couple of terrific kids who drive us both crazy about half the time. And now that they're both in school, I'm going to start my own business. Gardening and landscaping. I like being a wife, a mom, and I'm going to like having my own business. I have all that because of Henry."

"You were married almost seven years. Did you know about the vault?"

"It's true about that?" Blowing out a breath, she shoved back the brim of her hat. "I thought that part was crazy bullshit."

"There is a vault in his home office at Barrister House, and it contained over forty stolen items. Art, jewelry."

"I didn't want to believe it. I never saw that side of him. That's not really true, is it?" she murmured. "Henry liked things. I mean to say he . . . *coveted* isn't the right word because he could get them. Important things, things most people couldn't begin to afford to have. He'd buy me jewelry because he liked me wearing something that would pop your eyes out when we went to events or hosted a party. I knew that, didn't mind that. It was part of the deal."

"Ms. O'Ryan, my impression is you and Henry Barrister had and maintained an intimacy—not sexual, but in a friendship."

"We did. We'd talk now and then. When the kids came along, he'd send presents for their birthdays, for Christmas. I appreciated that."

"As a friend, he never mentioned the vault or its contents."

"No, he . . ."

"What?"

"I don't know if it means anything. The last few years, before he died, he seemed more frail—his mind, I mean. We'd talk on occasion during the year, and I noticed that. He did say, a couple of times, that he had things put away he wished he'd given me. That I was the only one who'd been his true friend as well as his lover, and he was going to arrange something."

"Did he?"

"No. Honestly, I think he forgot, or was just rambling some."

"Any idea who he might have told?"

"He trusted me, so I really think I'd have been the first choice there. But the one he was looking around at when we were married? Well, she wasn't the only one, but she sticks in my mind. There was something off about her, something too smooth. I even told him to watch out for her. 'You watch out for that one, Henry. You want to be really careful there.' But he didn't listen."

"Do you have a name?"

"No, I'm sorry. I probably knew it at some point. I think we were in France, maybe Italy, and hosting a party. A big one. I think—I can't be positive—but I think that's the first time I saw her. Gorgeous blonde, young. Several years younger than I was. I doubt she was more than about twenty, but she'd been around."

She winced. "That sounds catty."

"No, it's an impression." And Eve wanted just that. "Do you have more?"

"I don't know who she came with. I do know she flirted with Henry, and he flirted back. Not just the way you might at a party, but more, and it hurt my feelings. He had that look in his eye, the one he had when he looked around at me when I was twenty."

With a half laugh, she set the water cylinder down again. "It still hurts a little. I saw her a few more times. But as I said, she wasn't the only one. She was just sort of the straw, you know? The last straw. Whatever that means."

"Right? What does that mean?"

Lacey laughed again, and meant it. "Who the hell knows? She wasn't the only one. The last few months, he fooled around plenty, but this one stuck in my head. In fact, a while back, I was in New York—the whole family—and I actually saw her coming out of a shop. She saw me, too. And she gave me this look."

Lacey hissed between her teeth. "Excuse my language, she fucking smirked at me, then strolled away. I wanted to punch her one."

"When was that?"

"Last December. We took the kids to New York for a week."

"Do you think this woman might have spent time with Henry?"

"Yeah, wouldn't surprise me a bit. It was that look. He didn't marry her. He told me when we split he was done with marriage. He had to be because he couldn't stop looking around. At least he figured that one out. I guess the things in the vault are like the women. He just couldn't stop wanting what he didn't have."

"Could you give me some names, other people at that party?"

"It was so long ago, but . . . I remember some. A few I keep in touch with. I could send those to you."

"I'd appreciate that. Thank you for your time and cooperation, Ms. O'Ryan."

"It's no problem. Look, could you, when you find out who did this, could you let me know? We're sending flowers to Aileen and her kids. It feels like it would be awkward to go to any memorial, but I'd really like to know the person who killed Henry's son is behind bars for it."

"I can do that. If you think of anything else—maybe the name of this particular woman will come back to you—please get in touch."

"Absolutely."

If she had it right, Eve thought, they—whoever—said the third time was the charm. Which made no sense. But she believed, in this case, the fourth time hit it.

She wrote her conversations up. It always helped to read as well as hear them. Then she walked back to Roarke's office.

"Why is it a straw? Why is it the last straw?"

"It broke the camel's back."

"What's a camel have to do with it?"

"That's the expression." He swiveled in his chair to face her. "The straw that broke the camel's back."

"Some straw isn't going to do that. They've got those big, humpy backs."

"That's why it's the last straw. It finally adds too much weight."

"That's stupid. Never mind. I think I hit on something with wife number four. Who also seems to be the most normal of Henry's series of wives. How are you doing with the Interpol data?"

"I hope you can understand that I've found it very flattering to see how often I was investigated with no adverse results."

"Should there have been?"

"Well, that depends on your point of view, doesn't it then?"

"Right. Are you in a good place to stop?"

"I could be."

"Maybe we could take that walk. It stopped raining, and I need to think. I sometimes think better when I run it by you, or somebody. And you're here."

"And I take it this applies to last straws."

"Looks like it."

"The bench by the pond is likely still wet. Let's fetch a waterproof blanket and some wine."

The sun sparkled now, and the grass, the leaves sparkled with it. The air felt light, felt clean, yet they'd talk of murder, deception, betrayal.

"For starters, he cheated on all of them. The first, and we're talking about events from last century, is still bitter. Admits it. The second claims they had a fiery passion, but the flame died, blah blah. The third—"

"The victim's mother."

"So to speak. She said her maid was packing for her to go home—after she cut her spiritual retreat short—then the trip to New York. She couldn't even remember her son's wife's name. It was all about her. The first mentioned a redheaded slut."

"Ah." As they came to the pond, he spread the blanket over the bench. "That's where that came from."

"Yeah, she's the dancing-at-his-funeral ex. The second tossed out a 'blond bitch,' which may or may not have been wife number three. Number three lasted the longest, by the way. Almost a decade. He bought her a penthouse in the settlement, which she sold right after Nathan, the youngest, hit eighteen. She remarried that year, moved to Europe."

"I suspect something in the settlement discouraged her from doing either until both children reached legal age."

"You think?" Her snicker held no humor. "Yeah, me, too. Anyway, she's lazing around in Corfu at the moment while somebody packs her black outfit for her son's funeral. She termed wife number four as a gold digger."

"And is or was she?"

"Not in the traditional sense, no."

She took the wine Roarke poured for her, and ran it through for him in detail.

"She sounds like an interesting and practical woman, and one who appears to have been genuinely fond of her first husband."

"Came across that way to me. She credits him for giving her the opportunity to have the life she has. When she says they liked each other, I buy it. She says they talked a few times a year, and he sent gifts to her kids on birthdays, for Christmas.

"It's easy enough to check that. But some other things rang bells."

He tapped his glass to hers. "Ring them for me."

"She said in the last couple years, when they talked, she could tell his mind was shaky. And he told her he had some things put away he wished he'd shown her, given her."

"Yes, that's a bell."

"More, he was going to arrange to send her something. She says he didn't, and I'm believing that, as the log on the tablet and the items in the vault check out. Unless EDD finds something taken off instead of added, I'll buy that. Plus, she comes off truthful. He told her she'd been his only true friend who'd been a lover, and he wanted to give her something he had put away."

"Some part of him might have known he approached the end of his life."

"Maybe. The third called him a man of secrets, and that's clearly true. I believe her when she says she didn't know about the vault, but she also said she wasn't surprised. The second said this was all some mix-up, which is bullshit. But the last? She said that he had a need to possess things, and she thought . . . This is the Mira territory I was already going into. She thought the things in the vault were like the women. He needed to have what he didn't."

"I understand that. I certainly needed to have what I didn't. But there comes a time, when you've more than even you could once imagine, it has to stop. The need should be satisfied. I think, Eve, he was never happy. Sporadically, yes, in the moment, perhaps. But if you're never content with what is, if you have no real balance in life, if you can't love in a way that fills you, how can you be happy?"

She looked over the little pond to the tree they'd planted together.

"So he looked for those moments in other women, younger and younger, in possessing shiny things that weren't his to have."

"I find it sad. And I wonder: Would I have ended up somewhat like that without you?"

"Not a chance. You stole—you didn't pay somebody else to do it. You did it yourself."

"And suddenly that's a mark in my favor?" With a laugh, he put an arm around her shoulders. "I do adore you."

"Also a mark in your favor. You don't cheat."

"Perhaps I fear the cha-cha, or the tango, or whatever dance you'd do on my mangled body when you'd be done with it."

"You should." She leaned against him. "But you don't cheat, not just on me, but anyone. He couldn't stop himself. One more bell, and this one keeps ringing."

As it circled in her head, she sipped some wine. "The fourth wife said there was a woman—a blonde, very young. About twenty. It's clear she thought old Henry started banging her. She said there were others, but this is the one that stuck in her head, or her craw."

"The last straw."

"She said there were others, but yeah, I think this one broke the humps."

When he laughed, she frowned at him. "What?"

"Camel's back, darling."

"Are humps. To continue, she said there was something too smooth about this one, something off."

"Well, clearly an operator. No woman—all but a girl—of twenty would find a man seventy years her senior attractive on a physical level. I suppose it's remotely possible, but highly unlikely."

"So add in the billions, and a well-known weakness for the type. If she'd aimed to be the fifth wife, she missed there, but Henry's also got a rep for generosity with his side pieces."

"Do you have a name?"

"No. I'll try digging there. Number four said she'd seen the blonde a couple more times, and the kicker? Last December—when Henry was, according to statements, showing a lot of mental decline—she saw the same woman in New York. The blonde even smirked at her."

"So you're thinking it may be they continued to have a relationship, even if only now and again."

"Of the four wives, he maintained a civil, even friendly relationship with all but the first. But here, if I'm hearing the bell right, comes an operator. Operators have an agenda. And she's in New York when the mark, if he was one, and he damn well was, is going downhill."

"He talked to his last wife about having things put away. So, your thought is he talked to this one."

"Maybe showed her. But why not help yourself to something when he did? Distract the old man, help yourself to something shiny."

"That's easy enough. He might tell someone just that. He's losing his grip a bit. He might tell someone, name names. Then you're in the pot for accessory after the fact, aren't you? Maybe theft as well. When you've only to wait. You're young, he's not. Add? If you recognized anything inside that vault, or managed to record it, did any research, you'd know very well you couldn't just sell it off, or wear it around. You'd need a client or a plan to find one."

"Huh. That's what you'd have done?"

"Oh, absolutely. And I'd be certain I could prove—true or not—I was somewhere else entirely when something went missing. How do I know for certain who else he's shown, or told? He might say no one, but he's old and forgetful."

"I want to find her. How the hell do I find a nameless blonde?"

"An operator, who may not have used her actual name."

"Shit, that's true, too. And she may have just been in it for whatever she could squeeze out of him. Cash here, sparkles there, a trip wherever. But she's the first serious maybe I've got."

She drank more wine, considered. "I'll run her by the staff, by the wife, the sister. And the estate lawyer. Maybe she squeezed enough to get something out of the will. Or something on the side of that. He'd have had prenups, wouldn't he?"

"Of course."

"I wouldn't mind getting some details there."

"I can let Garrett know you're ready to speak with him."

"Yeah, if he can fit me in tomorrow, that'd be good. I'm going to have Peabody meet me back at Barrister House in the morning. Add the lawyer, if possible, a consult with Mira. If Lacey O'Ryan gets me those names of the partygoers, I can start trying to dig up the blonde."

"Another busy day."

"That's the job. I'd take double that. Triple it if I didn't have to do the goddamn fucking shithell of a media conference."

"There, there."

When she rolled her eyes darkly in his direction, he kissed her cheek.

"What else can I say? It's also the job."

"I hate that part." She held out her glass. "Top this off."

"Happy to. I might have a name or two for you."

"Yeah?"

"Starting at the end was the way. So, a couple names. Younger, brought in for questioning a time or two, but slipped out of the nick. I haven't dipped into their finances as yet. No violence showing on either, so it's difficult for me to see the cosh that ended Nathan Barrister."

"Where are they based?"

"They roam. The one uses the front of a freelance blogger—has a blog as well. It's not bad at all. Travel blog. The other? She's a security consultant, has her own business and does well enough with it. Both travel, and neither show travel to New York within the last month."

"But they wouldn't."

"Not if they had a brain in their heads, no. A job like this? The client or broker would arrange a private shuttle. You'd have another set of identification.

"The basic moves match well enough. Jam security, slip in a window or door, take what's been commissioned and only that. But the cosh, Eve. It doesn't fit."

"I need to look at them anyway."

"I'll send them to you. I need to look at their financials. If they're smart, and they appear to be, any payments for this would be well buried."

"Then you'll dig them up. But not tonight. We're watching a vid tonight."

"Are we?"

"With popcorn. I guess we have to have some sort of dinner first." She dropped her head on his shoulder. "The leaves on that tree we planted are going sort of red, sort of."

"They are a bit. It should be a nice little show when it goes fully red."

"Then they'll all drop off so it stands there naked. It's the opposite."

"Of what?"

"People put on more clothes when it gets cold, trees go naked. It'll stand there naked through the winter, then it'll start the whole cycle again."

"We'll enjoy that, you and I, sitting here, watching it through its cycles."

"Yeah. It's kind of weird, sitting here, watching a tree get naked, then dressed again. But yeah, we like it."

He sat a moment, in wonder that this fascinating, often frustrating, equally flabbergasting woman had come to be his.

"I love you, beyond reason."

Her lips curved as she turned them up to his. "We've got reasons."

She settled back, studying the tree. "Like I wouldn't have thought of the blanket, so I'd be sitting here with a wet ass. There's a reason. Since it's not wet, let's sit here a little while longer. Then we'll go back. I'll tag Peabody, you set things up with the lawyer.

"Then." She sipped more wine. "We'll feed the cat, unless he's sticking with Summerset. We'll eat something before popcorn and a vid."

She tipped her head up to him. "How about something with aliens that threaten the survival of the human race, but we kick their slimy asses?"

He brushed a finger down the dent in her chin. "I have just the thing."

Chapter Twelve

When she woke, Roarke sat with cat and tablet, with the screen on mute, with stock figures scrolling. He wore one of his richer-than-the-gods suits, this one smoky gray and matched with a shirt that was pale-as-a-pearl gray and a tie that slashed both tones with a deep maroon.

On the left lapel he wore the little petunia pin she'd given him.

Monday, and the traditional workweek, had arrived.

"You'll have a bright day to chase the dark," he said without looking up. "A warm one as well."

"How's the weather in Big Deal-a-stan?"

Those blue eyes flicked to hers with a smile in them. "Spring's coming on in Brisbane."

"I don't understand that. It's unnatural. Let me ask you something. How do you keep the times straight? Is there like a global clock running in your head?"

Now the smile touched his lips. "It's just math."

She sat up, shoved at her hair. "Not everybody's good at math. Wouldn't it make more sense to have everybody running on the same time, the same season? No confusion that way."

"And that would be New York time and season?"

With a shrug, she got out of bed. "It'd be simpler."

"You realize that would have large areas of the planet going to work, going to school, opening businesses, and so on through the dark of night."

Another shrug as she programmed coffee. "Then they wouldn't be stuck inside during the daylight." She took a gulp of coffee. "Seems like a good trade-off."

When she took her coffee into the bathroom, Roarke glanced down at the cat. "It's not Earth logic, but Eve logic. Strangely, it works for her."

In the shower, Eve ran through her plan for the morning. She'd hit the Barristers early, see if she could get any more details—and wouldn't a name be nice?—on the blonde. If she got more, she could push more.

At Central, she needed to check on the status of the cold one Baxter and Trueheart had picked up, and any hot ones that may have come in over the weekend.

She needed to take a closer, deeper look at the files Abernathy had sent her, at the names Roarke had culled out of those—so far. At the finances he'd scoped.

Touch base with Feeney and Detective Willowby on any underground chatter about the emeralds.

The thief, she thought as she stood in the swirling air of the drying tube, had already turned over the take, and unless they were a complete idiot, had the fat fee.

Sitting on a beach somewhere, she imagined, slurping down umbrella drinks, admiring the view.

Before she was done, they'd be admiring the view in a concrete cage.

She stepped out to breakfast waiting under domes and the cat sulking on the floor a few feet away.

"You own resorts with bars and beaches and pools."

"I do."

"So why do they put those little umbrellas in drinks at the bars?"

"I suppose to symbolize celebration."

"Why not little balloons then? You pull out an umbrella when it's raining. For some reason people like to blow up balloons at a party."

"I'll be sure to run that by the bar managers. Tiny balloons, weighted, of course, so they don't just float away." He took the domes off omelets. "Your mind's busy this morning."

"Whoever took the emeralds and killed Barrister probably has an umbrella in their drink right now. Probably lazing around on some beach down where spring's coming on."

"And there's the connection."

"Maybe Fiji. That's down there, right?"

"It is indeed down there."

She cut into the omelet; fragrant steam rose. "I guess it burns my ass thinking they're soaking up rays in Fiji or wherever, kicked back in a lounge chair with an umbrella drink and a fat fee."

"Would you like a quick trip to Fiji to check the beaches and bars for suspicious characters?"

"What I want is to drag their ass back to New York, toss them in the box, and make them cry."

She ate some omelet. Yes, it held spinach, but it also held cheese and chunks of ham.

"I want to find the blonde and pull her smirky ass into the box. The timing with her . . ." Shaking her head, Eve picked up the coffee he'd poured her. "It feels like something."

"Your feel-like-somethings are usually accurate."

"I still need a name, a face. Maybe I'll have one this morning. And I'm hoping by now EDD's caught some chatter about the emeralds.

Unless whoever stole them—or more likely paid for the theft—wants to do just what Henry Barrister did. Lock them away."

"So, your mysterious and smirking blonde."

"Yeah. Somebody knew the emeralds were there, somebody wanted them. I can mostly believe no one in the household's involved there. Nothing shows otherwise."

"But."

"Mostly isn't a hundred percent, and I have to factor in just letting it slip to the wrong person. Now you're either afraid to say so, or you just don't think whoever you told could possibly be part of this."

"Or, less likely but possibly, something you said months ago hasn't clicked for you now."

"Less likely, yeah. But the blonde? Going after an old man like seventy years her senior? That screams con artist, gold digger, opportunist—take your pick."

"Possibly all three."

"Right. And the timing with her in New York when the old man's starting to slide? When you look at the whole thing, who was most likely to slip and say something about the vault?"

"Henry."

"Yeah, and you've got this blond operator right there. Wife four, and wife at the time of that party, didn't have a name, didn't know who she'd come with."

"You think party crasher."

"When I put it together, that's where I'm leaning. Make the connection. Barrister's rolling in it, and he likes them young. Flatter, flirt, fuel up that old libido. The fourth ex says she saw the blonde a couple more times, so that says she, the blonde, kept the connection going. Then she's on tap again, just a couple months before he dies. I'm thinking they stayed in touch, and maybe somebody in the household remembers her."

After finishing off the omelet, she shifted to him. "You wouldn't fall for it."

"Obviously, I prefer brunettes."

"Not that. You wouldn't fall for the play. You've been on the grift, and you wouldn't fall for it. Like Mavis wouldn't. You'd cop to the tells. Plus, women come on to you all the time."

"Do they?"

"Jesus, Roarke, I'm often standing right there. You know when it's a play."

"Add I love my wife, and want to avoid her cha-cha."

She laughed, kissed him, rose. "The point? Henry Barrister either didn't care or had a wide-ass blind spot when it came to being played by a woman. Since, by all accounts, he was a player himself, I think the first. It didn't matter as long as he got the young, hot sex."

"Worth the cost to him. Yes, I agree with that. But not just the sex, Eve, at least to my thinking. The flattery, the attention, the shine of having something young, beautiful that others would envy on his arm. In his hands."

"I'm going to agree there."

She walked into her closet and tried not to think too hard about what always struck her as acres of clothes.

She'd just go with Roarke's theme of the day. Gray.

She grabbed dark gray trousers, considered a shirt.

She couldn't go with the maroon—too close to red, and red struck her as flashy. She went with a non-flashy blue. He'd probably have pulled out a blue belt, but she stuck with gray for the belt, for the boots.

She dressed, then because she had a weakness, went with a gray jacket in buttery leather. Coming out, she tossed the jacket on the arm of the sofa as she walked over to hook on her weapon harness.

"I have some things to see to today."

She glanced back at him as she filled her pockets. "Imagine that."

"But I should have a bit of time this afternoon for the investigators' reports. I'll check in with Feeney myself, as I'm curious there."

"Okay." She swung on the jacket, then frowned. "You know, maybe the fourth wife would work with a police artist. She really hates the blonde, so she might be willing. I'm betting that face is stuck in her brain."

"Where is she?"

"Montana. Bozeman. They have to have police artists. I might try that. I've gotta go."

"You could send Yancy," he said as he rose.

"Not enough solid for that."

"If there's something there, you'll solidify it." He drew her in. "While you're about it, take care of my cop."

"I think since I'm reinterviewing and digging through files, I won't have to work hard at that one."

She kissed him. "You don't own Fiji, right?"

"The island? No. Just a few spots on it."

"It'd be funny if it turns out the killer thief ended up getting busted in one of them."

"While holding an umbrella drink."

"Even funnier. See you tonight. Cat's making his move."

It amused her the way Roarke turned, aimed those blue eyes at the cat, and the way the cat stopped his casual saunter toward the breakfast plates.

It amused her more, as she headed out, imagining Roarke would end up giving the cat a few of those little treats Galahad pounced on like a junkie on his fix.

Her car was waiting for her. She slid inside and started the short trip across town.

Dog walkers—one woman had two that looked like mops with legs prancing along. Joggers aiming for the great park. Kids in uniforms heading to their private school or being led there by a parent or nanny. A liveried doorman opening the door for a woman breezing out of her building. She carried a gold briefcase that matched her shoes, her sunshades.

The doorman hotfooted it to a black sedan to open the rear door for her before the driver could.

Eve caught a red light, watched pedestrians, a mix of business clothes and day laborer attire, stream across. A few, fresh from the subway, picked up their pace to try to make the light.

Since Peabody was one of them, Eve angled toward the curb, tapped the horn.

The tap kicked off a blast of a dozen horns Eve ignored as Peabody jumped in.

"Hey, nice timing." Peabody strapped in as the light changed. "We ran into Summerset at the street fair."

"So I heard."

"He was with Ivanna and some other people. Anyway, he and Ivanna came to the house. We ran into Trina, too."

Since Eve had already noted Peabody's hair sported more red streaks, she'd deduced that.

"So she and the guy she was with—Ben, it's not serious."

"I was worried about that."

"Ha. They came over, too. We made a ginormous pot of chili." She let out a sigh. "We had so much fun."

Before Eve could say something snarky, Peabody finished with, "I really appreciate you giving me the time. I went in yesterday."

"You went into Central?"

"Yeah. McNab went in to give Feeney a break, so I went with him. I didn't hit anything but a wall, but I read your reports, the interviews. All those ex-wives. And maybe a blonde."

"We're going to push on the blonde."

Eve turned to the gates of Barrister House. She pulled out her badge, held it up for the scan.

"NYPSD, Lieutenant Dallas, Detective Peabody."

"It'd be a handy break if she's connected, and we can identify her. McNab said there's some chatter, but right now it's gossip, speculation, anticipation. Willowby says if they're going for an auction, they're letting it brew, getting buyers revved up."

"And waiting to see where the wind's blowing," Eve added as the gates opened. "If it's blowing too warm, they might sit on the emeralds awhile. It's not like they'll be worth less in a month. In six fricking months."

"So we'll hope the blonde's a link, and we connect her."

"There are a couple possibles we pulled out from the investigators' reports. The kind who might get hired for a high-profile job like this. I tossed them to Interpol."

"Oh."

"That doesn't mean we don't look, too."

She pulled up, parked. "Abernathy can have the shine of the emeralds, as long as we get the killer."

Peabody's voice turned wistful. "Be nice to get both."

"We won't toss it aside."

The butler opened the door as they walked toward the portico. His eyes, deeply shadowed, looked exhausted.

"Lieutenant, Detective. Do you have— Pardon me. Do you wish to see Ms. Carville?"

"I'm sorry, Mr. Tyler, we don't have anything new to report. We do have a few more questions. I'm sorry to disturb the family again. Are they available?"

"Of course. The family is in the dining room. Should I have them come to the parlor?"

"We can go to them. We'd also like to speak with you, Ms. Acker, and Ms. Fortigue."

"Ms. Acker is upstairs with Trisha, the day maid."

"Day maid."

"Trisha assists Ms. Acker on Mondays and Thursdays."

"If we could also speak with her? Peabody, why don't you take Trisha in the parlor?"

"Could I bring you coffee, Detective?"

"If it's no trouble."

"Not at all. Please, come this way."

Tyler showed Peabody into the parlor, then escorted Eve toward the dining room.

"The family's just finished breakfast. Divine urged Ms. Carville to eat. She told her the girls wouldn't if she didn't."

"That did the trick?"

His lips curved slightly. "It did."

The family sat together at one end of a dining room table that would have sat, comfortably, thirty. Though the day promised warm, a low fire simmered, surrounded by pink-grained white marble. A trio of chandeliers, their crystals winking with light, spanned the ceiling.

Both girls wore sweatpants, the older with a Harvard sweatshirt, the younger, a T-shirt where Mavis Freestone grinned. While Joy Barrister wore a business suit, the widow hit between her daughters and sister-in-law with black pants, black sweater.

And all looked at her with anticipation.

"I can't give you much new information," Eve began, "but I can assure you we're working diligently on identifying the person responsible for Mr. Barrister's death."

"He'll still be gone."

Eve looked at the younger daughter. "Yes, he will. But your father deserves justice. You all deserve justice."

"Please, sit down, Lieutenant."

As Aileen spoke, Divine bustled in with coffee.

"Can I offer you some breakfast?"

"No, thanks. I would like to speak to everyone in the household. My partner is speaking to your day maid, but if I could speak to everyone else?"

"Ms. Acker is on her way down," Tyler said. "I'll take the detective her coffee, and come right back."

"I'll see to that." Divine patted his arm before she started out.

"Lieutenant." Joy took a long breath. "To say this is a difficult time doesn't begin to cover it. We've had to screen our calls—even the girls. The media, they're relentless."

"We'll conduct a media conference later today. I hope that will take some of the weight off that area."

"You have to tell them Dad didn't take those things." Chloe gripped her hands together on the table. "You have to tell them he didn't even know until . . ."

"As the primary in this investigation, I will tell them we have evidence Nathan Barrister was not responsible for the contents of the vault. And when he learned of them, began the process, along with his wife and sister, to expedite their return."

"You believe us," Aileen murmured.

"I believe you, but with your cooperation, EDD has searched your electronics, and in them found your considerable research on the contents—starting last July—your additional research on how best to facilitate their return, which corroborates your statements. I'll be meeting with your estate lawyer as well, and trust he will further corroborate."

"Thank you. I couldn't stand for Nate's reputation to be smeared by this."

"I have to go in shortly." Joy pressed her lips together, then lifted the back of her hand against them. "I have to speak to key staff, key accounts. The business has to . . . billions of people depend on Zip."

"Understood. I'll try not to keep you long."

When Divine and Uma joined them, Eve looked back at Aileen. "Could everyone sit?"

"Oh yes, of course. I'm sorry. Please, everyone, sit down. I'd like to say something first. I want to say how much I, the girls, Joy appreciate and value everything you've done."

"Ms. Carville—"

As Uma started to speak, Aileen held up a finger. "Please let me say this, let me thank you. Yesterday, while the girls and I had to spend hours making arrangements, contacting friends, relatives, while Joy had to handle business and the media, you all tended to us, looked after us. Uma, I know what you did in the office."

She put a hand to her throat, steadied herself. "I'm forever grateful. Tyler, when the girls decided to take this semester off, you arranged for their things to be packed and shipped so we wouldn't have to deal with it. Divine, you put food on the table, managed to convince us to eat. And I heard you give that reporter a very colorful piece of your mind when they managed to get your personal 'link number."

"I enjoyed that, missus, maybe more than I should have."

"I did, too. For myself, for Joy, for my beautiful girls, for Nate, thank you for taking care of us."

She took a breath, turned to Eve. "You must have more questions."

"We're following a line of inquiry. Henry Barrister's fourth wife mentioned a blond woman at a party held in Europe during her marriage."

"There was always a woman," Joy said dryly. "Not necessarily a blonde, but there was always a woman."

"She was very young at that time, possibly about twenty, which would make her mid-thirties now."

"He liked them young."

When Aileen shot a sharp look at her youngest, Anya just shrugged. "Like Chloe and I didn't know? Come on, Mom."

"According to my information," Eve continued, "this woman, whom the former Ms. Barrister couldn't identify, made a play for—I'm using first names—for Henry. Lacey also states that she saw this woman a few more times, and believed she and Henry were involved."

"This isn't surprising information." Aileen held up her hands. "I couldn't count the number of women Henry was involved with, one way or the other, since Nate and I were together."

"After speaking with his ex-wives, it became clear Henry had declined in the months before his death, as you and Joy have stated. Lacey further states that she saw this woman in New York during that time period. I'd like to know if she visited Henry here, at Barrister House."

"A blonde in her mid-thirties." Once again Aileen lifted her hands. "I couldn't begin. And I'm not sure why she's important, considering."

"Ms. Carville—"

"First names."

"Great. Aileen, if everyone in this room has spoken the truth, if no one in this room told anyone—excepting the lawyer—about the vault and what was in it, that leads me to believe Henry did. Whoever broke in, whoever stole the emeralds, whoever killed your husband knew the location of that vault, and came for the emeralds."

"He might have. Joy! He might have."

"He'd kept that secret for so long, half his life from what we can tell. Why would he talk about it to some blonde?"

"He wasn't himself the last few months." Chloe spoke up. "The last year or so really. He got me and Anya mixed up a few times, and remember, Mom, we were having dinner and he called you Lacey."

"Those are just slips, and he was slipping, but to tell someone, some woman about the vault?" Joy shook her head. "It doesn't make sense."

"I'd like to identify her, if possible. Maybe you remember someone like that who attended one of his dinner parties toward the end of his life. Or was a houseguest. Possibly last December."

"That narrows down the timing, but I honestly don't remember."

"Ms. Carville, I think I might." Uma glanced at Tyler. "Ms. Fancy."

As he nodded, Divine let out an *Ohhh*.

"That one," she continued. "Breakfast in bed at nine sharp. Greek yogurt—one-half cup exactly—with fresh berries. One slice of whole wheat toasted lightly, cut on the diagonal. Six ounces of freshly squeezed orange juice—no pulp—and coffee with cream, no sugar or sweetener."

"That's specific," Eve commented.

"I've got a good food memory." She started to rise when Peabody stepped in. "Let me get you some more coffee."

"No, thanks. I'm fine."

"Sit," Eve told her. "We may have an identification on the blonde. Ms. Fancy, you said?"

"Yes. In fact, Mr. Barrister called her that—Fancy or Ms. Fancy—in kind of an affectionate way. She was a guest here, I believe it was December, as we had the decorations up, the December before Mr. Barrister passed. She had the Peacock guest room, which . . . hmm, adjoins to the main suite. She was in residence, I believe, for several days, perhaps up to a week."

"Do you have a first name?"

"I'm sorry, I don't."

"I think she was here a time or two before. For a dinner party," Tyler added, and cleared his throat. "I believe she may have remained overnight, but, ah, not in a guest room on those occasions."

"One of those breakfast in bed for twos?" Divine pointed at Tyler. "Mr. Henry always came down for breakfast unless he had company of that nature. That was usually eggs Benedict and mimosas. And you'd take the tray up."

"Yes. While you learn to do your job without seeing certain details, I can recall a young blond woman. But again, there were others."

"Tell me what you know or remember about this particular one. About Ms. Fancy."

"I called her Ms. Fakey." At Uma's wince, Divine just shook a finger. "I'm going to say what I think."

"I wish you would. Why Fakey?" Eve asked.

"'Cause she was. Fake, and snooty with it. Didn't you say how she told you she wanted you to hand-wash and press her panties, and said she expected her bed turned down every night at ten o'clock—no sooner, no later—and to leave a tray with a cup of jasmine tea?" Divine closed her eyes a moment. "Yes, jasmine, lightly steeped, no cream, no sugar, and two macaroons, baked fresh."

"I'd forgotten the macaroons."

"I make it, I remember it. And didn't she go out every blessed afternoon? Sometimes Mr. Henry went with her, and even when he didn't, she'd have a car and driver. And wouldn't she come back loaded with shopping bags? She'd order you, John, to unload them and take them up to her room, and you, Uma, to unpack them and put everything away. Like she was queen of the place."

"Can you describe her?"

"I didn't see her much myself. Never once came back to the kitchen."

"Very beautiful," Uma offered. "I suppose mid-thirties, but it's difficult to tell. Or I'm not particularly good at that. Long blond hair." She waved her hands down to her shoulders. "I think blue eyes, but I'm not sure. Not brown."

"Height, weight, race, accent?"

"Ah, five-four or -five, I suppose. She wore heels, even around the house. Slim, but curvy. Stylish, in a sophisticated way rather than trendy? No accent that I can recall."

"Did she spend any time in the office?"

"As John said, you learn to do your job and not see. But yes, I believe they spent some time in there together."

"They did," Tyler confirmed.

"Would you work with a police artist?"

"Please." Aileen reached out. "It could be important."

"Yes, of course. I'm just afraid I might not be able to describe her well enough."

"I'm going to arrange for a police artist to come to you. He's very good."

"Do you think she killed my father?" Chloe asked.

"I'd like to know if she has any connection to the break-in. Someone knew about the vault. If she did, I'd like to have a conversation with her. You had personal contact with her, too."

Tyler nodded. "Yes."

"He'll work with both of you."

"This is exciting. Oh, missus!" Divine hugged herself. "I didn't mean—"

"I know what you meant. And it is exciting. Because it may be a step in finding out who did this to Nate. Who did this to all of us."

"I hope it is. I pray it is." Joy rose. "And not just a waste of time and effort."

"You weren't aware he had this houseguest during this time period?"

"I'd be the last he'd tell. He knew I didn't approve of his predilection for young, grasping women. Nathan was more tactful about it, but Dad knew he and Aileen didn't approve, either. I have to go in. I really need to handle things."

Eve rose as well. "We appreciate the time. The police artist, Detective Yancy, will be in touch, arrange a time that's convenient."

Tyler stood from the table. "I'll see you out."

As they left, Eve heard Joy say, "Aileen, if you or the girls need anything while I'm gone, tag me. I don't know how long I'll be."

"I didn't pay attention," Tyler murmured. "She made him happy, and I didn't pay enough attention. She was demanding and borderline rude, but she made him laugh. He was failing, and she brightened him up.

I have no doubt who paid for the contents of all those shopping bags, but—"

"She made him happy. If you remember any more about her—something Henry or she said that might add something, where she comes from, where she was going—you know how to reach me or Detective Peabody."

"Yes. Uma and I will make ourselves available for Detective Yancy."

As they got into the car, Peabody looked at Eve. "Fancy Blonde's in it."

"If she's not, it's a big, fat coincidence. What do I think about coincidences, Peabody?"

"That they're bollocks. *Bollocks*, it's a good word. I should use it more."

"If anyone can get a face, it's Yancy."

"And that's no bollocks."

"See when we can get him on this. I need to go back to Central. I've got to check in with EDD, then meet with Mira, and there's that goddamn fucking media conference, and we need to talk to the estate lawyer."

Peabody pulled out her 'link to contact Yancy. "Why do you figure men go after women half their age—or in this case about a quarter of his age?"

"Because, no matter how old a man is, he thinks with his dick."

"Oh yeah. There's that. Well . . ." She paused before making the contact. "I think it's more the penis often has, especially in this case, undue influence over the cerebral cortex."

"Not as pithy but more accurate. Actually, I think, especially after a certain age, being with someone half or more of that stops them from thinking about their mortality. She made him happy," Eve repeated. "So he wasn't thinking about death."

"Okay, that hits, and it's worth some high-end shopping bags. But not the rest."

"No. And if she's involved in the rest, and my gut's saying she sure as hell is, we'll get her for it."

Chapter Thirteen

On the way to Central, she got two tags. She found them a nice distraction from the ad blimps telling her to *Fall into Style*.

As she took them, Peabody eyed the in-dash AC. Eve held up two fingers.

"Okay, Mira has clear time at ten, and that gives me space to check with Feeney, update. Roarke says the lawyer will make time for me at my convenience."

Peabody passed Eve her coffee. "What kind of lawyer works on a cop's convenience?"

"He's Roarke's estate lawyer, too. And I guess he's mine, sort of."

"That explains that. It'll make it easier to get information. I mean, the family gave him the go to talk to us, but this'll make it easier."

"I guess we'll find out. Ms. Fancy."

Pausing at a light, she drummed her fingers on the wheel, watched a woman, sleek in black skin pants, jog with a golden-haired dog across the intersection. A man in a business suit talked on his earpiece, briefcase in hand, as he strode after her. Coming the opposite way, a sidewalk sleeper pushed his cart of belongings and talked to himself while a uniformed nanny hauled up her toddler charge to her hip and gave him a wide berth.

New York had it all.

"Ms. Fancy," Eve repeated as the light changed. "Is that an actual name or one Henry just hooked on her? Even if it was the name she went by, that doesn't mean it was her real name."

She pulled into the garage, parked. "I'm tossing the name at Abernathy. Maybe they have a file on that name."

"He's in the media deal, right?"

"Yeah, I'll toss it then. Yancy?"

"He's in the field now." Together, they walked to the elevator. "He's got another ahead of us at one, but he'll plug them in after that."

"Good enough." Eve stepped in, stuck her hands in her pockets, jiggled loose change. "Here's how I see it. Fancy Blonde's kept in touch. He's a prime mark, so she keeps a hand in. She realizes he's slipping some, mentally. An even better mark now."

Eve shuffled back as the elevator stopped and cops shuffled on.

"Gets herself the invite to stay a few days. Maybe she's just in it for whatever she can charm him out of. Shopping, macaroons, pressed panties."

A uniform glanced back at her. "Pressed panties? Is that a dessert or something?"

"Or something." Since the doors opened again, Eve got off for the glides. "Maybe she figures she can snag something in his will, or get a quick marriage out of him. How bad could it be when he's over a hundred and losing it? And frail—they've all said frail. But."

"He shows her the vault. I can see that," Peabody agreed. "But if she's on the grift, why doesn't she just slip a couple things into her shopping bags, then book it?"

"Can't do that. He might notice. He's losing it, but these are big fucking deals, and if he sees something's gone, it points at her. He's got a lot of money, Peabody, a lot of contacts. Maybe they even have some mutual acquaintances. He could find her. It's better, smarter, to wait. How long has he got? If you've got any talent, or know somebody who does, you hack into his medicals."

"Why didn't she talk him into marrying her?"

"Maybe he wouldn't bite. Or maybe she didn't want the attention. She'd get plenty as number five, seven decades younger and to an obviously sliding man. This way?"

She paused at the top of the glide on their level. "You take what you've squeezed out of him, wait, and plan. Maybe you know how to get into the vault, maybe you don't. But you want the big prize. So you wait, and you plan. He dies pretty quickly after your visit, so best to wait a little more, and get that plan firmed up good. The staff lives in, and with the estate deal going on, there's probably people in and out."

"Then the son and his family move in."

"Gotta wait, pick your time. Does Fancy Blonde know how to jam security and so on? Maybe, maybe not. If not, you need someone who does. And you need a way to get the payoff from the big prize."

"Auction."

"If she's the operator I think she is, she knows she can't flaunt those emeralds. She can't keep them, but she can pocket a hell of a lot selling them."

"It sounds right."

"It's the best line we've got, so we keep tugging."

She walked into Homicide, into a full bullpen, and Jenkinson's tie.

Today's had bananas, dozens of screaming-yellow bananas clutched in the grips of dozens of grinning, pop-eyed monkeys.

"Jesus Christ" was all she could manage.

"My guy got a new shipment in for the fall." When her detective sergeant lifted the tie, wagged it, the pop eyes jiggled.

"Socks, too." Reineke, his partner, hiked up a pants leg to reveal grinning, pop-eyed monkeys and bananas.

"It's a sickness. I swear to God, a sickness."

"Heard you caught a big one, LT."

"Yeah." She pressed her fingers to her eyes, then aimed them over the tie into Jenkinson's face. "So I don't have time to—ha—monkey around. Baxter, cold case?"

He smacked his hands together. "Closed."

"Sew it up for me."

"Coworker, been stalking her, convinced they were soul mates. But he kept it chill—says how he was shy. He's watching her place, so he sees her come out, take a walk. She does some window-shopping, even goes into a couple places, but doesn't buy anything. Then when he sees she's heading back, he runs into her."

"Imagine that."

"Right? He's: 'Oh hey, how's it going?' He likes to think she's coming on to him, says how he'll walk her home. And how he thinks she lives just down the block from a friend of his who's having a party. That's where he was heading anyway. Because she's with someone, she's fine with cutting through the park. He makes his move, and she rejects that. He's upset, shoves her. She slips, cracks her head. So he grabs her purse, the earrings and such, takes off."

"He did have a friend down her block," Trueheart added. "That's another reason he knew they were soul mates. He takes her stuff to that building, dumps it in the recycler, goes up to the party for a while, then goes home."

"He puked all that out after eight years?"

"Credit my boy." Baxter jerked a thumb at Trueheart. "He's kind of doe-eyed, all sympathetic. We had a good whiff, but Trueheart played him good. How he knows what it's like to love someone, to know they belong together."

"Guilt all over him, Loo," Trueheart said. "We have to figure they didn't catch that the first time around because he wasn't guilty, didn't feel it. And where they worked? Nobody paid much attention to him. Plus, the friend vouched he was at the party. Nobody knew he had a thing for the vic, not then."

"Good work, both of you. Peabody, I need ten in my office, then I'm heading up to EDD. I'll probably go straight to Mira after. See if you can dig up anything on the blonde in New York. Try Fancy as legit or alias. Use the basic description. Could get lucky."

In her office, wired from coffee, Eve wrote up the interviews, included her focus to identify the blonde. She copied her commander and Mira before turning her attention to her board.

A cop's mind was a suspicious mind, and she accepted that.

So the question nagged. If Fancy Blonde had stayed in Barrister House for several days, and during a period of time when Henry Barrister was slipping, cognitively, physically, why didn't any of the family know about her?

Had the victim? And if he had, given the impression of their relationship, wouldn't he have mentioned it to his wife? Due to their professional and personal relationship, wouldn't he have said something to his sister?

It just hit wrong that three adults, with their lives so closely entwined, with a multibillion-dollar business as part of that twining, wouldn't keep better tabs on a failing father—and titular head of that business.

Possible—more than, she admitted—they'd left him to his own devices in the female companion area, at least. Maybe they'd checked in, maybe he'd told them he had company, and they'd given him space.

She made him happy, Tyler had said. And maybe that was enough for them.

And maybe, just to cover it, she'd ask Roarke to do another dive into the survivors' finances. Just to make sure they hadn't pulled out a nice lump sum that could cover hiring a thief.

"Just feels off," she muttered, then put it aside to head out to EDD.

Though they were busy, she took the glides. Elevators not only closed her in, it made it harder for her to think when a bunch of other cops breathed her air.

Nobody breaks into a vault and takes one thing among many unless they're under orders. Strict ones. So much there for the taking? A reason everything else stayed put.

She agreed with Roarke. Nobody steals something as recognizable, as valuable, as unfenceable as the Royal Suite unless they have a plan for it.

Unless stupid. But stupid would have grabbed a lot more.

Young, maybe still on the green side. Roarke termed the job basic, so why hire—if it had been a hire—someone who'd demand a bigger cut?

But you get what you pay for. So a little green takes too long. Maybe dazzled by all those treasures. Maybe has to touch a few. So tempting. Nathan Barrister comes along. Panic. Grab a handy weapon and take him down. Take him out.

Run. Leave the vault open and run.

Not Fancy Blonde, if that's how it played. Eve's impression there? Not green. But she was in it. Every instinct told Eve the blonde was in it neck-deep.

Since she figured Feeney for the lab, she walked past the center ring of the EDD circus. And still, the color, the movement, the chatter poured out. Rainbows and sunbursts, hip bopping, ass twitching. As she walked by, someone sang out.

She didn't know the tune, but had to appreciate, from a cop standpoint, the lyrics.

"I got you now, fucker. In my sights and going down, down, down."

With that earwormed in her head, she aimed for the lab.

Through the glass walls, she spotted Feeney, his dirt-brown suit a calm contrast to the three with him.

McNab in a multicolored polka-dot shirt tucked into explosive red baggies, which only confirmed her red's-flashy stance. He wore the tartan airboots she and Roarke had given him for Christmas the year before.

Callendar, her hair sporting a purple haze over black, ticktocked her hips in baggies striped in red, green, yellow—all three in what Eve considered the screaming range of their particular hue. She paired it with a white shirt that had a cartoon boomer with a lit fuse centered. Beneath, it warned: ANY MINUTE NOW!

Down the long counter stood Detective Zela Willowby. Though assigned to Special Victims, she knew the dark reaches of the underground, and usually hunted them for those others bought and sold like candy.

Small, compact, she looked about sixteen, with her golden brown skin, amber eyes, sharp features. She added to that impression with platform combat boots, purple baggies that matched the heavy fringe on her otherwise black wedge of hair, and a black shirt covered with neon stars.

When she stepped in, music blasted Eve's ears.

"Jesus, how do you think with the noise?"

Feeney turned. With the weekend's work, the bags under his eyes looked like they'd hold a week's wardrobe. His hair stood up and out like a man's who'd barely survived an electric shock.

"Cut the music." In the blessed quiet, he shrugged. "Tedious work, kid. Gotta keep revved."

"The cap goes for the classical." Willowby blew a bright pink bubble with her gum, snapped it. "Seriously iced playlist."

"Got the Stones, the Boss, Fab Four, a little Heart, Bon Jovi, Gaga. Mixed in Avenue A, Mavis for more contemp."

"Keeps us juiced." Callendar sucked up some of her fizzy through a straw.

"You just missed Abernathy," Feeney told her.

"Aw, that's a shame."

He grinned at that. "He'll be back. We're running pretty smooth with Interpol."

"He's a neck-breather." McNab rolled his shoulders. "You know, breathes down your neck."

"I got it. What have you got for me?"

"Take it, Willowby."

She gave Feeney a quick salute. "Lots of chatter how something big's coming. Most of that's on dark sites where whatever it is, they can't afford it. Cough up a few hundred thou for a slave, maybe up to a mil or two for a solid sex trade or something nice and shiny, but not the big guns."

"That's it?"

"Uh-uh." She picked up her own drink, gestured with it, gulped some down. "We're starting to see more teasers. You know, like you see at the vids? Previews of coming attractions, and just on the major money sites. Like sheikhs and shit. The mega-extreme rich. They're setting the opening bid at three hundred mil, invite only. And there's nothing we've scratched up yet that says what's going up for bid."

"Can you trace any of it back?"

"Catch," Willowby said, and mimed tossing a ball to McNab.

"We're working on it, but it's slow going. The tedious deal? They bounce, add twisties, redirect, lights out. We got an off-planet ping, but that tapped out."

Eve held up a hand. "Don't talk geek to me."

Callendar picked it up. "Easiest to say they'd know we'd be looking, so they've set up a really slick system for, like, obfuscating. They didn't set this up yesterday, you get me? Took a lot of time and skill. They've got money and e-talent plenty for this."

"We'll dig them up," Willowby said. "It's going to take time, but we'll get them."

Eve looked at Feeney. "Would you bid three hundred mil on something you saw on the web? Something you didn't see in person, your own eyes, with your own expert authenticating?"

He grinned at her. "Well, hell no, even if I had Roarke's money. And so say we all."

"Gotta figure they'd go low-tech." Callendar slurped more fizzy. "Cap says invites, in the hand, private messenger."

"Going to be a select group," McNab added.

"Like the guy who had it in the vault." Willowby blew another bubble. Puff it out, snap, pull it back in. "Fancy invite."

"Fancy," Eve murmured.

"Sure. All gold, engraved, all that shit. Time, date, location. Location's probably fancy, too."

"Château, villa, mansion, castle." McNab shrugged. "And one of those black-tie deals. Gotta set the stage. But you also gotta know who'd buy in."

"Not just the ones rolling in it," Feeney put in. "But you curate, right?"

"You have to know who'd pay—maybe has before—for something they couldn't wear in public, couldn't brag about having." Eve nodded. "I've got that."

"There's where we whittle it down." Feeney picked up cold cop coffee, frowned into it.

"How about I get you a fizzy, Cap?"

"Yeah." Nodding at McNab, Feeney set the coffee down. "Lemon. I'm feeling sour. We put watches on those who fit the bill. Interpol's a big hand up on that. Auction's going to want cash or direct wire. Something like this, you probably have to lay down a deposit before the auction. Like an entrance fee, you know? Cover charge."

"Proof you're a serious buyer. Okay. You watch accounts."

"Means you've got to find the ones that aren't on the up-and-up. I don't suppose Roarke has any free time."

"Mmm. Sizzle." Willowby just wiggled her eyebrows at Eve's stony stare.

"Ask him. Meanwhile, I'm looking for a blonde. A looker, mid-thirties. Has gone by Ms. Fancy. I don't know if that's her name, an alias, a nickname. She was cozying up to Henry Barrister before he died."

"You figure she found out about the vault."

"I figure just that. She's an operator. She started working him when she was about twenty, so she knows how to play the long game. I think she's in this."

"If we find anybody who fits, you'll be the first. Thanks," he added as McNab brought him a fizzy. "I gotta tell you, when we pin this down, it's most likely going to lead to a bust at the auction. If it ain't happening in New York, it's going to be Interpol's bust."

"I want who bashed Nathan Barrister's head in. Interpol or the locals wherever can have the shiny."

"They're putting the time and brains in, too." Willowby sighed. "But it's a wheeze deal. Some of these assholes would've maybe bought from the sex slave ring we busted up. I'd like a shot at them."

"Interpol busts them for this, you give that a push."

"That's the plan. How's Dorian?"

"Good. Safe, in school, and by all accounts taking this chance at a decent life seriously. You could go by An Didean sometime, see for yourself. You're part of what gave her that chance."

"Yeah. I wanted to give her some time to settle in first. I think I'll go by there. I'm going to drop by Homicide when I take a break here. Check out the sizzle of Trueheart."

"Jesus, why do you tell me this?" Eve pressed fingers to her twitching eye. "I've got a meet with Mira. Keep me up on this, and don't forget the blonde."

Before the doors closed behind her, music blasted.

She took the glides to Mira.

Private auction, she thought. The only thing that made sense. In person, with a bunch of morally empty rich people. The private, personal messenger–delivered invitations worked, too. Classy.

She could imagine it. Black tie and sleek gowns. Champagne and caviar in a location that also reeked of money.

And wouldn't that atmosphere, the competition between the morally empty rich, kick the bidding up?

Damn right it would, so the ones running the show could afford to shell out a big pile of money to make it all work. Invest, say, a hundred million, rake in triple that if not more.

And no one involved, not a one, would give a single thought to the murder. Just another cost of doing business.

It boiled in her blood, kept her moving quickly so she arrived at Mira's a few minutes early.

"You're prompt today, Lieutenant."

Mira's guardian of the gates gave her one cool stare.

"I can wait if she's not ready for me."

"I'll just check." She tapped her earpiece. "Dr. Mira, Lieutenant Dallas is here. Yes, of course."

Another tap. "You can go right in. Dr. Mira has a ten-forty-five and has yet to have a break this morning."

"I won't keep her any longer than I have to."

She walked into the office, where Mira sat at her desk in a silky-looking suit the color of crushed raspberries. But it didn't, to Eve's eye, come off flashy.

She had her hair, with its subtle blond streaks over mink, in a kind of roll today. She'd added a single string of pearls and had pearl studs at her ears.

No, not flashy. Classy.

"Have a seat. Just let me . . ." Mira tapped keys, nodded. "There, done." She looked up. The crushed-raspberry lips curved, the soft blue eyes smiled with it. "I love that jacket."

"Oh, yeah. Thanks."

Mira rose, walked to her AutoChef on raspberry-colored shoes with high, pearl-colored heels.

Eve always found it amazing.

"You've been busy," Mira said as she programmed tea. "And all weekend."

"Killers just don't take weekends off."

"No, they don't. And the Royal Suite."

"You've heard of it?"

"Yes. I remember when it was stolen—it has to be nearly twenty years ago. International news. A very daring heist. If I recall, the speculation was a gang of jewel thieves had planned it for months, if not years."

Eve only said, "Mmm," as Mira brought her the flowery tea.

"And only to be locked away for one man's pleasure. Then stolen again. You believe the victim, and the family, and the staff, were unaware of the vault, what it held until after Henry Barrister's death."

"Evidence weighs on that side of the scale. I'll talk to the estate lawyer later today. The family—wife, sister, two daughters—all state the victim contacted him. Not right away. They spent most of the summer researching every piece, and working out how best to protect themselves and the business. Not the best way to handle it, but it's plausible."

Mira crossed her legs, and in a way that also always amazed, balanced the delicate saucer on one knee.

"He was their father, their grandfather. And yes, the founder of the highly successful family business. If they truly didn't know, it would've been an enormous shock."

"I buy that. Why did he do it? Why risk everything, your reputation, your freedom, the business you built from the ground up, just to shove things into a vault?"

Leaning back in one of her scoop chairs, Mira sipped her tea. "A need to possess. The validation of it. He did build Zip from the ground up, taking substantial financial risks. He wasn't born wealthy. He risked and pushed and worked to attain that wealth."

"But it wasn't enough."

"No, and never would be. He could look in that vault and see what he felt he deserved, and it wouldn't have been enough. The same with women. Having one, however beautiful, wasn't enough. He needed more. He was a magpie."

"A what?"

"A magpie. 'Oh, look at that! So shiny, so bright and beautiful. I want that. I want it for my nest even if I have to lose what I already have.'"

"What he already has? He gets tired of it, bored with it. Needs the new. The next piece of art that belongs to someone else, the next shiny jewel. For women, the new again, the younger."

"Yes. A constant need to possess. I doubt he was ever fully happy for any length of time. He couldn't love, not deeply, not for the long term. But he could, and did, desire."

"The vic wasn't like that. One marriage, and solid. The work they'd done so far on Barrister House makes it more . . . homey? More like a family lives there."

Eve set the tea aside, pushed up. She needed to move. "The thief knew about the vault. They didn't just stumble on it."

"No."

"The family, the staff—and they come off devoted and pretty damn straight—all state they told no one outside the lawyer—and that was only a few days before the break-in. I have a hard time swallowing that, but they're all sticking. But there's Henry."

She made herself sit again. "By all accounts he'd gone into decline, mentally, physically, too, but it's the mental deterioration that applies.

He'd gotten forgetful. The last wife told me he let her know he had something important put away for her."

"They stayed on good terms?"

"Good enough—I'll come back to that. They talked now and again, and he told her this not long before he died. He'd started to mix things up—like calling his daughter-in-law by the name of one of his exes. Mixing up his granddaughters' names, forgetting what he did, where he put things."

Eve leaned forward. "And during this period, he had a houseguest. A much younger blonde, someone he met when she was about twenty. Someone his fourth and final wife said was her last straw."

"I see. Has this woman been involved with him in the intervening years?"

"According to the staff, she'd been an overnight guest a time or two over those years. Slept with him. This last time, she had her own, adjoining room. They spent some time in his office when she wasn't out shopping on what's going to prove to be his credit."

"I see. You think he showed this woman the vault."

"He never told his family—so they say. If I hold that as true, would he have told this woman?"

Taking a moment, Mira sipped more tea. "I'd like to look at his medical records, and I'll see if I can arrange that. If he was suffering from cognitive decline, sundowning, the early stages of dementia? It's certainly possible. With his need to possess, he might have shown this woman as a way of keeping her, at least impressing her."

"But she didn't stay."

"She may have promised to come back. Just needed to tie some things up, arrange the move. And he may have forgotten he showed her in the meantime. I'll push on those medical records."

"Let me move to the thief. You read the report. It all went smooth, until."

"Which tells me completing the job—and it was a job or else why not load up, why take only the most priceless and most recognizable pieces? Completing it took priority over a human life. Ruthless, self-preservation above all, mission complete."

"Not just panic."

"Panic, yes. That may have played a part, but—"

"They only had to get away from a man who almost certainly looked weak, sick, maybe even a little dopey from cold meds."

"According to the autopsy, he would have been all of that, and," Mira added, "not much of an obstacle to escape."

"Possible he bashed Barrister before he evaluated that, but that still tells me it's not just get the hell out. He'd been in there long enough to take the goods, and the timing . . . The wife heard Barrister fall. So it was bash, then run. Fast enough he left the vault open—but still closed the window to cover his escape route."

Eve rose again, paced again. "She called out. He could've given her a bash, too, but this time he runs. He runs, leaving the vault open, closing the window, and he flips the security back on after he's clear."

She puffed out a breath. "Too much of a rush to close things up. Possibly just knee-jerk on the security. I don't like it."

Now Mira set her own tea aside. "He may have had a partner."

"Yeah, I'm toying with that. A lookout, or somebody waiting in a vehicle handling the jammer. It could work that way."

"But you don't like it."

"It doesn't sit firm." Hands in pockets, Eve shook her head. "None of it does, really. They're a family. I look at the wife because you have to, and don't see it. Where's the motive? Same with the sister. Where's the motive? They're stupid rich, not that it stops anybody, but the ties? They come off tight and true. I get the same from the staff."

"So the mysterious blonde."

"Yeah. She's in this. I need to find out how. But first I need to find her. I appreciate you looking into those medical records. You'll be able to give me a better picture of how she played him."

"Your report includes Detective Yancy working with the staff on a face."

"Yeah, later today."

"We can hope you'll be able to ask her yourself just how she played him."

"I'm counting on it. He was a player, a thief, and should've lived out his last years in a cage. But going after an old man whose mind's slipped a few cogs? It's just . . . slimy."

"When you find her, I'd love to observe your interview."

"I'll let you know. Thanks for the time."

Chapter Fourteen

She made her way back to Homicide, and noted Jenkinson and his tie, Reineke and his socks weren't at their desks.

"They caught one right after you left," Baxter told her. "DB in a dumpster, Alphabet City."

"Okay. Peabody?"

"No luck yet. Still looking."

"Keep at it. We've got about an hour before the media conference."

In her office, she got coffee, sat. She put her boots on the desk and studied her board. A minute later, she got up, added a sheet that said simply: *Fancy Blonde*.

"You're in it."

She sat, boots up again.

Must've tapped him off and on over the years. Such an easy mark.

The marriage, or lack of it, bugged her a little. He'd already gone there four times. Why not lure him into five? Big potential payday there.

Reasons why not? Couldn't quite stomach sexing it up with a man old enough to be her great-grandfather. Whatever marriage paid out, it also cut down on some freedom. A good attorney, which he'd have, is going to put a rock-solid prenup in place.

She'd check on that.

Other fish to fry, lambs to fleece. Harder to do that when you're married. Not impossible, just harder. And if he catches you there, you get the boot, and the well runs dry.

"You didn't want to be the fifth Ms. Henry Barrister. Just wanted whatever you could squeeze out of him when you felt like squeezing. Or needed to."

Because it nagged at her, she contacted Lacey O'Ryan again.

"Lieutenant. Is this important? It's my morning to make breakfast. I'm a very nervous cook."

"I'll make it quick. I wondered if you could pinpoint where you first saw the young blonde—your last straw, you said."

"As it happens. Damn it! This just looks like goo! I'm trying to make pancakes from scratch."

"Why?"

"Because I've lost my mind. It's not cooperating. I'm stepping away for a minute. I need more coffee. I mentioned your call to a friend—we've been friends for years. And she remembered. Lake Como. We took a villa there for a month. It was glorious. Until that party, and that blonde."

"Lake Como, and when, exactly?"

"It would've been sometime in June—what year was that? I don't remember. The June before I filed for divorce."

She pulled a large mug of coffee out of the AutoChef and took a long sip.

"Better. I should never cook without extra caffeine or completely sober."

"You said you saw her a couple more times between then and when you saw her in New York more recently."

"Yes, in the village near the villa. At an outdoor restaurant. Later, another friend said she'd seen Henry with her. We had some words about that, Henry and I. When we got back to New York, I talked to a lawyer, but I didn't file until I saw her again, in the early fall, I think."

"In New York."

"No, we'd gone to . . . where was it? Maine. To see the foliage, and I thought, potentially, to patch things up. And there she was, sitting in the bar of our hotel. I walked over, told her she could have him. She just smiled at me. I went back up to the room. I'd been going out to do some early Christmas shopping. Henry enjoyed that, but he'd made an excuse to stay back. For obvious reasons."

She gulped coffee, hissed out a breath.

"I told him I was done, that since he couldn't be faithful, I was done. He said he was sorry he couldn't be. And I swear he meant it. So I came back to New York, moved my things out, filed for divorce."

She let out a long, long sigh. "He offered, over and above the settlement, to buy me a house wherever I wanted. And I realized I didn't want to live in a home he'd bought for me. Even though the money I had to buy my own had come from him."

"There's a difference."

The annoyed look faded into appreciation.

"Yes, thanks. There's a difference. We split on remarkably easy terms, but my heart wasn't broken. Pride dented, ego bruised, that's all."

"I appreciate this."

"It actually felt good to spurt it out. I really don't harbor hard feelings. I told you that before. But that smirk—it's stuck too long."

"Since last December."

"Yes. We brought the kids over to see Christmas in New York. Ice-skating, roasted chestnuts, Radio City's holiday show, the works."

"Thank you. This is helpful."

"Okay. Well, I'm going to try this pancake thing again."

"Good luck with that."

December, Eve thought as she sat back again. And Henry died in February. Allegedly, and she believed it, Nathan and Aileen learned of the vault in July. Then the break-in, theft, murder came in September.

Nine months between the blonde's visit and the break-in. Seven if you counted from Henry's death to the theft. Less than three from the discovery of the vault to the break-in.

She checked the time, argued with herself. Then contacted Roarke.

When he came on-screen, she led with, "I'm sorry, but I've got a question."

"It's not a problem at the moment. I'm between meetings."

"Yeah, me, too. Okay, so you're going to steal the Royal Suite."

When he smiled, she all but heard him think: Been there, done that.

"How long between finding the location, in the current circumstances, and the grab?"

"That would entirely depend on a multitude of factors. You might say anywhere from straightaway—which is risky and reckless. But there are many in a cage or the grave who try that route. And up to a year."

"A year? I don't get it."

"Which is why you're not and never have been a successful and high-level thief, Lieutenant. You'd want authentication. Why take the trouble if they're fake? You'd need time to assess the security and so on—the rhythm of the house and occupants in this case. Unless you plan to work solo, you'd need the broker, the thief, the client. If it's an auction you're after, that takes time to set up carefully. The accounts you'd need, the location that serves, the invitation list. If you don't have the ready yourself or financial backing, you'd need to find it."

"Because it all costs."

"An investment of seventy-five, a hundred million wouldn't be out of bounds here. Unless, again, you're the risky and reckless sort. Then you might make the grab well enough, you might have the Suite in hand. But now what the bloody hell do you do with it?"

"So the smart way is to set it all up first."

"And go over every tiny, minute detail, with contingencies, alternates. This is no quick snatch of a handful of baubles. Six months to that year, though I'd consider the year on the long side."

"How about eight, nine months?"

"It fits right in there, doesn't it now? Would this relate to your unknown blonde with the smirk?"

"Yeah. Confirmed she visited Henry, stayed at Barrister House last December. She's stayed there before, shared the bedroom with the man old enough to be her great-grandfather on those stops. Yancy's going to work with the staff on a picture later today."

"I'd say this one knows how to play the long game, and would take the smart and careful route. For the time, the investment, she could walk away with up to four hundred million in profit. And more."

"There's more?"

"A reputation that would afford her an exceptional life and lifestyle. That's my time, darling. I'll be giving Feeney a hand later, but from the home lab so I can juggle in my own work."

"Appreciated. I'm talking to the lawyer later, and may work at home after that. I'll see you."

"Good luck with the media."

"Yeah, right."

She gave herself thirty seconds to sulk over that, and might have taken thirty more, but she heard the click of high-fashioned heels coming toward her office.

It didn't surprise her when Nadine walked in on those heels.

"I brought you a brownie, and potentially some information."

She could smell the damn chocolate, and chocolate would equal a boost either before or after the media. Even so, the potential information gave Nadine more of an entry.

"Give it."

Nadine set the little bakery box on Eve's desk, and her sharp reporter's eyes arrowed toward the board. "Fancy Blonde?"

"You're here to give info, not get it. I'm talking to your type in a little while."

"And I'll be there. What fancy blonde?"

"What info?"

"Fine. Can I get you coffee?"

Eve leaned back in her chair. "Fine."

In her fashionable pumpkin-colored heels that matched the fashionable pumpkin-colored dress under a short suede jacket that reminded Eve of the vegetable strangely known as eggplant, Nadine programmed two coffees.

"I've been looking into the Royal Suite—on my own," she added as she handed Eve her coffee. "That made one hell of a splash when it was stolen from the Tate."

"I'm aware."

"Every report I've dug up attributes it to a well-organized group. An e-man, security expert, someone on the inside, though they never pinned anyone there, the jewel thief, and so on."

"Is that right?"

"Since it's out there, I pushed on some sources, leaving the emeralds out of it. Clearly, from the list I have from the vault, that was the most valuable item. Well, items."

"You have a content list from the vault at Barrister House?"

Those foxy eyes smiled at Eve as Nadine sipped her coffee. "I'm a very clever woman. One of my sources was part of several of the investigations into the thefts. He strongly believes Henry Barrister worked through a broker. I'm assuming you know about how that works, and have drawn that conclusion as you're also a very clever woman."

"You're not giving me anything but a brownie so far."

"He also strongly believes that this theft—" Nadine held up a hand. "He didn't mention the emeralds, either, though he likely knows, as he's still active. Anyway, he strongly believes one of the original thieves targeted Barrister House. Assessing who bought them, where they were kept, and after the original client died, hey, why not take them back, resell them?"

"And how did this thief access the information? As a very clever woman, you'd have learned how that whole broker deal works."

"Henry Barrister was slipping more than a little. The original theft was in, what, 2042? A lot could've happened to the broker in that amount of time. Maybe he died, left files, retired, passed his clients to a replacement."

She waved that off. "In any case, this has all pumped up the investigative work on the original theft."

"Suspects?"

"He was cagey, but they're looking hard at a couple of people they believe were part of a team responsible for at least three of the thefts."

Her eyes flicked back to the board. "And one of the people they're looking hard at is a woman. In addition, Inspector Abernathy of Interpol is coordinating with that new investigative task force."

"Is that right? He failed to mention it."

"I sensed that. Meanwhile, excepting the Tate, for obvious reasons, the museums, private owners, or heirs of same are pretty damn happy about getting their items back. Once they do, that closes it down for them. They're not particularly interested in spending the time, effort, making the investment to pin down the person or persons responsible for the original thefts."

This time Nadine gestured toward the board. "Tell me about Fancy Blonde. It's under wraps until you give me the go."

"Someone who played Henry Barrister for the last fifteen years or so. I don't have a name or a face, yet. She visited him for several days last December."

"And he died in . . ." A quick flip through a reporter's mental files. "February. You think she knew or found out about the vault."

"I think I want a name, a face, then a conversation. Look, Nadine, I've got to prep for this media thing."

"You really don't. You're good at it. Hating it the way you do makes you really good at it."

"So if I liked it, I'd be crap at it?"

"Yeah, or a lot less good at it."

"That makes no sense."

Nadine set down her empty cup. "Toss this into the prep you really don't need. Nathan Barrister's murder is your priority. It has to be, and it should be. But the story, Dallas? The big shiny object is the vault, what was in it. What, if anything, was taken from it. You won't get a focus on your victim, except questions about him as a suspect."

"Another reason to hate doing this."

"I get that because I get you." She touched a hand briefly to Eve's shoulder. "My team, and they're excellent, researched Nathan Barrister thoroughly. He was a good man, a family man with a solid talent for the business his father started. I'll give that as much weight as I can in my reports."

She would, Eve thought as Nadine left. She would do exactly that.

She sat, ate a little of the brownie while she sat, and stewed. Nadine had given her a hell of a lot more than Abernathy. A task force, pushing on the original thefts. And they'd damn well push hardest at the emeralds.

She needed to find and return them. It would weaken that push when she did. Meanwhile she had to hope, had to trust, had to believe that Roarke had covered his tracks.

She ate a little more brownie, and took comfort this fresh push aimed for a group, not an individual.

EDD: Find the auction and the person or persons holding it.

She rubbed at the headache climbing up from the back of her neck, and looked at her board. At where she'd written *Fancy Blonde*.

Yancy: Get a face, a face that leads to a name.

Put those together, she'd find the killer, the thief, and the fucking emeralds.

She needed to bring justice to Nathan Barrister and his family. And goddamn it, she needed to protect the man she loved. Her badge prioritized the first; the ring on her finger symbolized the second.

She couldn't live with herself if she didn't find a way to do both.

When she heard Peabody's cowgirl boots, she rose.

"Sorry, Dallas, nothing on the blonde yet. And it's time to get down to the media center."

"Yeah."

When they walked out, she paused in the bullpen.

"There's half a brownie on my desk. If it's not there when I get back, I'm writing up the whole damn bunch of you. Check it."

"Nadine brought enough for the whole class," Peabody told her when they strode to the elevator.

"Like that would stop them."

"Point taken. Did Nadine have anything to get or give?"

"Abernathy's coordinating with a task force that's looking into the original thefts."

"Yeah?" Peabody's voice went flinty. "I guess he didn't think the NYPSD needed to worry about that."

"He's about to find out otherwise."

She tolerated the stops and starts of the elevator, of the people getting on, getting off, even the chatter inside the car that added fresh blooms to her headache.

She wanted time, just a little more of it, to settle. She needed to talk to Roarke alone, in private. She needed his reassurance no investigation would turn up anything on him.

Did she know she'd get it? Yes. But she needed it anyway.

Kyung waited for them. Tall, lean, smooth dark skin, slate-gray suit, perfectly knotted deep blue tie, he looked the part of media liaison.

"Just this way, Lieutenant, Detective. Chief Tibble and Commander Whitney have just arrived. Inspector Abernathy is on his way. I'd like to be able to tell you we can keep this brief. I understand you have important work to do, but I want to be honest with you."

And that, Eve thought, was why in addition to looking the part, Kyung wasn't an asshole.

"How long?"

"I'd judge an hour, minimum. Chief Tibble will give a statement, as will Commander Whitney. The commander will introduce the inspector, who will also give a brief statement on Interpol's involvement and the coordination with the NYPSD. If you'd also like to give a statement—"

"No."

"I thought not. We will open for questions. You can expect the majority of them to deal with the contents of the vault."

"Right."

"All investigative parties have agreed that no details on what, if anything, was taken from the vault or the home will be disclosed at this time."

"Understood."

He opened a door, ushered them into the area where Tibble and Whitney waited.

Tibble, tall, built, with his air of authority, stepped over. "Lieutenant,

Detective." He shook their hands. "Are there any further details since your last report?"

"Nothing to disclose to the media, sir. Chief, Commander, I would ask that there's no mention of the unidentified woman Detective Peabody and I are looking for. Or any mention of Detective Yancy working with the staff at Barrister House on a possible artist's rendering. I include Inspector Abernathy in that request. I would prefer to update him there personally following the media conference."

"Are there reasons for leaving Interpol out of this loop at this time? Reasons," Whitney continued, "you didn't copy the inspector on the report with that information?"

"I intended to inform him, as I will, after this is over. I kept it in my pocket for the simple reason I wasn't altogether confident the inspector was sharing with the NYPSD. I've confirmed that, as a reputable source has informed me Abernathy is coordinating with a task force formed to further investigate the original thefts, most prominently the Royal Suite.

"It's possible he, and they, are holding back information that could help in our investigation of Nathan Barrister's murder."

Whitney's lips thinned as he nodded. "So" was all he said.

"Handle that as you see fit, Lieutenant," Tibble told her. "I want a report of the outcome as soon as possible. When I have your report, I'll have a conversation with the inspector's superiors."

"I'm not looking to jam him up, sir. He's good at the job, and he's been helpful and cooperative in the past."

"Such as when you handed him an escaped prisoner, a terrorist from the Urbans?"

"I put him onto the accomplice in that escape, but he did the work. I'm not looking to jam him up with his boss."

After a moment, Tibble nodded. "Handle it your way, and get back to me."

"Yes, sir."

Moments later, Kyung escorted in Abernathy.

He'd gone with a black suit, a red tie—there's the flash.

When he stepped over to shake hands, she saw clearly he enjoyed all this. It didn't make him a bad cop; she knew he wasn't. But it did make him at least a little bit of an asshole.

She already knew he was.

"Your EDD and their counterparts at Interpol feel a strong level of confidence they'll have solid data on an auction within twenty-four hours."

He turned to Eve, and the faintest hint of sarcasm came out in that high-toned Brit voice. "I'm informed Roarke will be assisting in his capacity of expert consultant."

"That's Feeney's call."

"Of course."

"None of that is information we want to share with the media at this time." Whitney kept his voice, and his gaze, flat and level. "It could compromise their work."

"Oh, absolutely understood. Our priority is the recovery of the Royal Suite. In doing so, we're laser focused on identifying and apprehending all those responsible for its theft and this resulting auction."

He glanced at Eve again. "And, of course, assisting you and the NYPSD in apprehending Nathan Barrister's killer."

"If you're ready?" Kyung gestured.

"I want to talk to you after this," Eve told Abernathy as they started toward the media center. "Some updates."

"Excellent. I'm at your disposal."

She stood between Abernathy and Peabody, in front of a packed room where cameras and recorders already ran, and the light hit just bright enough to add yet more blooms to her headache.

Kyung introduced everyone, by rank, explained questions were to be held until after the statements.

Tibble gave his, brief, concise, emphasizing the NYPSD's determination to identify and apprehend Nathan Barrister's killer. He spoke of coordinated efforts between the NYPSD and the international police, assurances that all items found had been securely transferred and authenticated, and the process of returning them was well underway.

Naturally, any number of reporters shouted out questions when he turned it over to Whitney.

Whitney merely stood, silent, until the shouting stopped.

Like Tibble, his statement held brief and concise, focusing first on the victim, the victim's family before moving to the cooperation and coordination of law enforcement in various jurisdictions and countries.

That segued smoothly into Abernathy. Not as brief, but Eve had to give him fairly concise. Did he like the attention, like knowing he'd be on screens around the globe, have his statement translated into a dozen languages?

Oh yeah, but he kept it professional.

When he stepped back, Kyung stepped up.

"We'll take questions now. Please wait until you're called on," he said even as the shouting started.

Like having a couple hundred baseballs pitched at you, Eve thought, and picking the one ball you could hit solidly.

Tibble hit a couple, and Whitney, Abernathy managed a few singles.

All about the treasures, she thought. Those shiny objects.

Then one pitched a fastball about the victim and his potential culpability.

She stepped up.

"Nathan Barrister's family has stated he and they were unaware of the vault and its contents during Henry Barrister's lifetime. It was discovered several months after his death during some remodeling."

Plenty more flew then, and like Whitney, she waited.

"All evidence gathered by myself, Detective Peabody, and our EDD confirms this. At the time of his murder, Mr. Barrister and his family were in the process of determining the correct way to return all said items."

Before she could step back, someone shouted: "Do you have any suspects? Are any of the family or staff under suspicion?"

"If we had suspects, you look old enough to know I wouldn't tell you. I can tell you Nathan Barrister's family, and the staff of Barrister House, are not suspects at this time. Our evidence strongly indicates a planned break-in. Mr. Barrister was attacked from behind during the burglary, at which time his attacker fled."

Someone pitched one regarding EDD's findings, and Eve threw the ball to Peabody.

"Detective Peabody can answer that more adeptly than I can."

Peabody's eyes shouted "Oh, shit" at Eve, but she stepped up.

She handled it.

So it went, and it did bleed past an hour.

Plenty tried various ways to dig out if anything had been removed from the vault, what had been taken if so, what was the estimated worth.

They got nowhere.

Others wanted the combined value of all items assessed, more information on them.

Those got a "soon to be forthcoming," but Abernathy let them know they considered it the most valuable recovery of stolen items at one time, with an estimated combined value of more than four billion USD.

That caused more salivation until Kyung shut it down.

"That went very well," Abernathy said the moment they were out of the conference area.

"Yeah, peachy. Did you have to give them an amount?"

"I was authorized to."

"Great. Let's talk in my office."

Chapter Fifteen

This time she chose the glides, and only half listened to Abernathy's small talk chatter as they wound their way back to Homicide. In the bullpen, she turned to Peabody.

"Contact the estate lawyer and let him know we'll be there within the hour."

Then she gestured and led Abernathy into her office.

"The victim's estate lawyer, I presume."

"That's right."

"So you do suspect one of the family."

"At this time, I'm just gathering or confirming information. Coffee?"

"Tea, actually, thank you."

He moved to her board as she programmed the drinks.

"'Fancy Blonde'?"

"A line of inquiry. An as-yet-unidentified woman who may have been a guest in Barrister House during Henry Barrister's final months."

"And you think due to his mental and physical decline, he may have shown or told her about the vault?"

"It's a possibility." She handed him the tea. Took her own coffee. "He liked women, much younger women. It's possible he met her some years before in Europe, and they had an affair. I wanted Interpol to be aware we're pursuing this line."

She shrugged. "Could be nothing." But she didn't think so. "But Nathan Barrister's killer knew about the vault. Targeted a specific set of items in the vault. We have no evidence to contradict the statements the family didn't know it existed until last July, and no motive for arranging a break-in."

"If they'd wanted the emeralds, they could simply have removed them at any time."

"Exactly. Unless they wanted the big, juicy scandal. Another possibility," she said when Abernathy's eyebrows quirked. "Then you toss murder in the mix, which seems extreme. Unless someone in the household wanted Nathan Barrister dead."

"So you *do* suspect someone in-house?"

"Abernathy, all evidence points to the break-in, and the murder as a result of the theft. But when I have a dead body, I suspect everyone. The estate lawyer may give me a reason to pin that down, or cross it off. Meanwhile, as you know, whoever has the emeralds is starting to hype an auction. Our take is the invite list will be relatively small and very exclusive, entry will require a significant deposit. As anyone willing to shell out that kind of money will want their own authentication, we're looking at an in-person event. Swank. High-class venue."

"We would agree with that probability."

"Good. It won't be a one-person operation. Thief, broker, coordinator, their own authenticator, an e-man, possibly a researcher, security. So, a team. Fancy Blonde may be part of that team."

He nodded along with her summation.

"If you'll give me whatever you have on her, I can help coordinate the identity search."

"I hope to have some information to pass along within another twenty-four. Now, why don't you tell me how long you've been coordinating with the task force looking into the original thefts, and why you haven't chosen to share that information with the NYPSD?"

His mouth tightened, barely a fraction; his eyes flicked, barely an instant. But she saw both.

"The original thefts don't apply to your case."

"And you know that how, exactly?"

"Clearly, it's extremely unlikely."

"Unlikely, however extreme, doesn't shut it off. Some of the original thefts go back decades."

"Which is my point."

"And if you're willing to split your time, cut the NYPSD out of the loop to pursue that line, you've got a reason. I don't give a flying fuck if there's a half a percent probability it ties into my investigation, the NYPSD should be informed, and you know it. Murder trumps all, Abernathy. You're looking for teams—and a team is behind this current case."

"You appear to be well-informed."

"Not by you."

He sipped his tea, then set it down. "There's more than a half a percent probability the NYPSD may have a conflict with the goals of the task force."

"Is that so? How do you figure?"

"Seriously, Lieutenant, do you want me to spell it out?"

"Yeah, I do."

"You're perfectly aware Roarke has been suspected in any number of high-level thefts in the past, which makes him a suspect in the original thefts that constituted items recovered from the vault, and the items stolen from it."

Watching him, she sipped her coffee, eased a hip down on her desk. "You're thinking he maybe broke into the Tate and took the emeralds? Wasn't that back in like '42 or thereabouts? He'd have been like eighteen, nineteen?"

She shook her head on a laugh, drank more coffee. "If a teenager managed that, I hope they beefed up their security after."

"A team," Abernathy said stiffly. "The original theft, as well as many others, would have been the work of a team. It's been proposed Roarke may have been a kind of apprentice."

"You're reaching, and you know it. And you're not stupid enough to think Roarke broke into Barrister House, killed Nathan Barrister, in order to snatch back what he snatched before he could buy a legal drink."

"No, I do not, but—"

"Add the owners of the recovered property don't give a good damn who stole them way back whenever. They want their property returned. That includes the Royal Suite, and pushing on who stole a painting of rocks and trees or a naked woman statue twenty or thirty years ago isn't going to get them back."

"Crimes were committed."

"Yeah, they were, and good luck digging back in the freezer to thaw those out. But my priority is Nathan Barrister. I brought you and Interpol in, and quickly, because my victim's father had a vault full of items of considerable worth stolen, at various times, from around the fricking world. The NYPSD has cooperated and coordinated with you, down the line."

She pushed off the desk. "You held back. I get the emeralds are your priority, and I've got no problem with that. But you held back because you want the shine of bagging the original thieves, maybe a nice promotion."

"And you don't want the shine or the promotion? Captain Dallas?"

"I turned down the bars because I belong right where I am. But that's me. I don't blame you for wanting otherwise. When we get the emeralds, and we goddamn will because they're linked to my victim, you take all the shine you want. You won't trace them or anything else in that vault back to Roarke. Because even if, in your alternate universe, he helped himself to any of it, he's too fucking smart to have left a trace.

"Push there, you'll get nowhere. Push there to the detriment of my investigation? You'll stand on the wrong side, Abernathy. And you don't want me as an enemy."

"We have different approaches, but I assume we both work diligently to apprehend criminals and pursue justice."

"There you go. Let's do those things. The NYPSD will continue to cooperate fully with Interpol on these matters. They expect the same cooperation from you and your side of it."

He inclined his head. "Understood."

"Then we're clear. Now I've got to go talk to a lawyer."

He started to step out, then stopped. He nodded to her board. "The task force is looking at a handful of females. You might do a run of a Jenna Lynn Delaney from, ah . . . Savannah, Georgia, whereabouts unknown."

"Thanks. I'll do that."

When he left, she took her coffee to stand at her window for a few minutes, just to settle herself.

He'd look, she decided. He couldn't help himself. But he'd look in the wrong direction assuming Roarke had been part of a team.

Still, the sooner she found the goddamn emeralds, the sooner Abernathy and the rest would move on.

She finished her coffee, went out for Peabody.

"With me. Run a Jenna Lynn Delaney out of Savannah, Georgia. The task force is looking at her."

"You got something out of him?"

"Yeah. We had a meeting of the minds." She headed for the glides.

"Okay, got her. Jenna Lynn Delaney, Savannah, Caucasian female, age thirty. Blond and blue, Dallas. A looker."

Peabody angled the screen so Eve could see the face,

Short blond hair, heavy fringe over big ocean-blue eyes, heart-shaped face, wide mouth, slight overbite.

Yeah, a looker. And one of the thieves Roarke had spoken of.

"Five-seven," Peabody continued, "one-twenty. Father unknown, mother, Constance Delaney, deceased, no sibs. Ah, mother died at thirty-nine, and Delaney went into the foster system. Got a juvie record. Shoplifting, truancy, got a B and E, all before she hit eighteen. Nothing since."

"She got better at it."

"She's got an address in Savannah. No marriages, cohabs, offspring. Lists her occupation as security consultant."

Roarke had hit one. "Well, that fits."

"She could be Fancy Blonde. Younger than we thought, but maybe."

"Yeah. Dig for travel to New York, aliases, client list, all of it."

They jogged down the metal steps of the garage. "Send the ID shot to Barrister House, see if any of the staff recognize her."

She got behind the wheel, plugged in the lawyer's address in the Financial District.

"Abernathy gave me enough to start. Probably the task force has more on her. But we can dig, too. She's a thief," Eve said as she pulled out of the garage. "Probably works cons. Looks-wise, yeah, she'd have been the type Henry Barrister would go for."

"I'm getting v-mail all around, Dallas. I'll send the photo."

"Send her data, so far, to EDD. They could check her through the underground."

"Got that. I have to say her data's really clean after the juvie bounces, and there's not much of it. Her security deal—by appointment or referral only, no address listed. Travel, travel . . . Nothing recent to New

York. Checking on the time frame she'd have been at Barrister House. Nothing."

"Does she own a vehicle?"

"Yeah, two. An all-terrain and a Road Star convertible. That's a nice one. Back to travel. She came to New York three years ago, first-class shuttle, round trip, eight-day stay."

"Find where."

"That's going to take a while."

"She may have a place she likes to stay. We find it, we trace her. Or she may do the stay-with-rich-old-men thing."

"I'll dig, but it won't be quick. At least we have a name, we have a face."

"Doesn't mean it's the name or face, but we've got something." And maybe Roarke could find more. "Odds are she's a professional thief—it's a very neat fit—and this task force wouldn't look at her unless she fit."

She passed Garrett Beyer's office building in a hunt for parking. Two blocks later, she stopped Peabody's heart by hitting vertical, zooming across the street, and dropping into a slot with very few inches to spare.

"I'm okay, I'm okay. Just need to reboot my entire system."

"Do it while we walk. I want this tied up, then we push on the blonde, whether it's this Delaney or somebody else."

She got out, headed for the crosswalk.

"But you don't think it's somebody else."

"I think it's a real neat fit. But. Data says she's thirty—which she could have adjusted. But if that's correct, she'd be even younger than the twenty the fourth wife estimated. Not impossible, either, when you figure she'd glammed herself up for this party she crashed."

"She's got a really nice place in the Historic District. Two vehicles, and her income's one-point-six a year. That's pretty smooth for a security consultant who only works by appointment. I can't find, yet, a client list."

"She can explain that by claiming client privacy. She probably does some security work. Gotta cover the bases. Roarke can dig deeper into the finances."

They moved with the flood of pedestrians at the intersection, kept going. Eve checked the time.

"Yancy's probably working with the Barristers now. I'd tag him, but why interrupt? They've shut down the 'links either for that or just to avoid the media."

"I could maybe reach the sister, if she's still at work."

"We'll let it ride."

They turned into the building with its big glass doors and important lobby. All dignity, Eve thought.

"The law firm has five fricking floors. Beyer's on fifty."

They waited at the silver doors for the bank of elevators that served twenty-five to fifty.

"Top floor's always the most important."

Eve just rolled her shoulders. "Why is that? Then you've got to ride up, ride down. Important should be easier. Like main level."

"It's all about the view."

They stepped in with half a dozen others who called out half a dozen stops.

Eve decided that made her case.

Business suits rather than uniforms, but it worked just as frustratingly as at Central. People on, people off. Stop and go.

At fifty, they stepped out into the plush and dignified lobby area of Beyer, Lance, and Goldberg, crossed the black tiles to the reception desk and the woman who manned it.

She wore her ruby-red hair in a razor-sharp wedge around an angular face.

"Lieutenant Dallas and Detective Peabody to see Garrett Beyer."

"Yes, of course. I'll inform Mr. Beyer's office. Please have a seat."

She didn't want a seat, but to get this done. Cross it off, move on.

A couple sat in a pair of cream-colored chairs, holding hands, making moon eyes at each other. She pegged them as easily seventy-five. Apparently moon eyes had no age limit.

A single male, mid-twenties, dressed like a street rat until you noticed his designer boots and wrist unit, sat in another area, looking bored as he scrolled on his 'link.

She pegged him as a trust fund baby here to push for an advance.

A woman came out of a set of doors—fiftyish, shining brown hair swept in a complicated twist, black suit, black heels, polite smile.

"Lieutenant, Detective. I'm Opal Richmond, Mr. Beyer's admin. I'll take you back to his office."

They went through, past office doors—closed—a break room that looked like an upscale lounge, what she assumed was a law library, and to the double doors of the corner office.

Opal knocked, then opened the right door. "Lieutenant Dallas and Detective Peabody."

"Come in, come in." Beyer rose from his massive desk in front of a wall of floor-to-ceiling windows that made Eve's stomach want to pitch.

He gestured them toward a seating area at least ten feet from that glass wall.

He offered a firm handshake. "So nice to see you again, Lieutenant, and to meet you, Detective. We'll have coffee, Opal, and some of those sugar cookies if you don't tell my better half."

"I'm the soul of discretion."

"Milton's on a health kick, and he's dragged me along."

He sat comfortably, a man lean in his pin-striped suit, his golden brown face pleasant. His hair had a waving white streak through the black on the left side.

"So," he began, "Henry had a secret vault."

"A secret from you?"

"Yes, until a few days ago when Nathan contacted me. I'm very sorry about what happened to him. I liked him very much, and his family. I want to say, so I will, he was not his father's son in many ways."

"In what ways?"

"We're all flawed, aren't we? But one of Henry's flaws was women. He simply couldn't be without a variety of women. Nathan and Aileen were devoted to each other. I can say that professionally and personally. As far as the vault?"

He paused as Opal brought in a tray.

"Thank you. You'll hold everything, won't you?"

"Yes, of course."

She poured the coffee, then went out, closed the door behind her.

"The vault," Beyer continued. "Yes, I was stunned to learn about it, but when I thought it through, it didn't shock me. Henry needed to possess. He worked hard, and as far as I can tell you was scrupulously honest in his business dealings. Zip was his pride and joy. Nathan simply didn't have the same needs."

"When he told you about the vault?"

"It took him some time to tell it all. He was upset, worried. I got no more than bits and pieces at first. He wanted to protect his father's legacy, his own family, the business, so he wanted to proceed carefully. His hope was to return everything anonymously. It's not a simple process."

"No, it wouldn't be."

"I was working on it. We'd hoped to have the process firmly in place in another week or so. Now, of course, all of that's moot. I can only assure you the family had no intention of keeping any of it. It made him sad. Nathan. It made him sad to know his father had done this."

"And his wife, his sister, his daughters were fully on board with this process?"

"No one objected. In fact, Aileen had done considerable research on the items, where they'd been taken, and into the process of return. She's very good at her work."

"Who benefits most from Nathan Barrister's death?"

"Aileen. The house will go to her now. Nathan inherited sixty percent of the company in his father's will. Aileen will inherit eighty percent of Nathan's share. His daughters will each get ten percent. The girls already have ten percent through their grandfather's will, so they'll have twenty now. Joy has twenty, through her father."

"So Aileen now has the largest slice of the pie."

"Correct."

"Why such a disparity between his children for Henry?"

"He didn't see it that way. He intended for Nathan to run the business, and to take over Barrister House. He left Joy very well provided for. Beyond the interest in the company, there's real estate, financial accounts, jewelry, art."

"From what I've learned, Aileen Carville has no interest in running Zip."

"No, I believe that will fall to Joy and the girls. Chloe's aimed there since childhood. She's worked there, she's studying to step into her father's shoes." He paused to sample one of the cookies. "I believe Anya intends to join Zip's legal team when the time comes."

He held out the tray of cookies. "Please, take one. Then I can tell myself I took one to be polite."

When they both took one, he sat back with his.

"Surely you don't suspect Nathan's family in his death."

"There was a break-in, but we have to close off all the avenues. Do you know the name Jenna Lynn Delaney?"

He pursed his lips, then slowly shook his head. "It's not familiar."

"She may have been involved with Henry Barrister."

"Ah well. I certainly didn't know all the names of Henry's women, but I don't recall that name."

"Peabody."

"If you'd look at this." Peabody offered her PPC. "Do you recognize her?"

He looked, and Eve knew he looked carefully. "She's his type, I'd say—any lovely young woman was. But I don't recognize her. Milton and I did, on occasion, attend dinner parties, cocktail parties at Barrister House during Henry's reign. He loved entertaining up until a few months before his death. But she doesn't pop out for me. I'm sorry."

"Not at all. What about the staff? Your opinion."

"Henry trusted them implicitly, as did Nathan and the family. I never saw any reason to question that trust. In fact, I quite like them. I'll add Henry was generous in his will to his staff at Barrister House. A year's salary for every year of their employment, plus certain items he felt showed his affection."

"And Nathan?"

"Adjusted his will when he decided they'd move into Barrister House, began the same. A year's salary for every year of employment under him. You could say, from their point of view, the longer he lived, the more they'd benefit."

"You could. Henry left Nathan the house, and its contents. Those would include the vault. Why didn't he tell Nathan?"

"My opinion, again?" He let out a sigh, smiled just a little. "Henry simply refused to believe he could die. And while he lived, what was in the vault was his. Only his. While I believe he loved his children, in his way, he also knew them. He would have known Nathan would never go along with what was in that vault."

He paused again. "I have a list of the contents, and I've spoken with Aileen, so I know what was taken. I also believe Henry would never have wanted his son to die for them. I'm more sorry than I can say that it came to that. Anything I or this office can do to help you find who's responsible, consider it done."

"Did anyone in this office besides you know about the vault?"

"No, not even Opal. No, not my partners, not my husband, not our children. Though Nathan and I became friends, he came to me as a client. And one in distress. I only wish he'd come to me sooner, and I had been able to act more quickly."

"I appreciate the time, the information, and the discretion."

"Whatever we can do." He rose as Eve and Peabody did, extended his hand again.

Eve kept silent as they were escorted out, as they rode down to the lobby level.

"He's telling it straight."

"I agree with that. He does that stuff for you guys, too, right?"

"Yeah."

"I don't guess he'd take on small potatoes like McNab and me. We have stuff now. I mean, not like buckets of it. But stuff, and we should take care of all of that. I liked how he was focused and real, you know?"

"Ask Roarke to set it up." Eve pushed through the glass doors. "Nobody says no to Roarke."

"He wouldn't mind?"

"Why would he mind?"

"Then I'll talk to McNab. I'll start digging deeper on Delaney when we get back to Central."

Eve checked the time. "Do that. I'm going to drop you off there, work some of this from home. Pull Roarke in as soon as I can. She's going to be part of this. I want to—"

She broke off when she felt the punch in the back. If he hadn't brushed past her, hadn't glanced back, then started to run, she might've put it down to a street bump, even a quick pickpocket attempt.

But as he ran, she saw him retract the switchblade in his right hand.

"Son of a bitch. Record on!"

She took off after him.

"Male, mid-twenties, brown hair," she shouted back to Peabody. "Five-ten, one-seventy. He's got a blade, and he just tried to stab me with it."

"Holy shit!"

"Call it in, call it in!"

She had to dodge a group of four who decided they owned the sidewalk, then the table and its contents from a pop-up vendor the man she pursued heaved over.

She could hear people scream as he shoved or knocked them out of his way, and into hers.

But she started gaining, dodging cars through the intersection as he did.

"Police!" she shouted, and jumped over a kid who'd taken a spill on his airboard.

By the middle of the next block she was ten feet back and reaching for her weapon.

He veered for the street in the middle of the block. He looked back, and she could see he was winded. And looking back, he tripped, lost his footing. Arms pinwheeling, he fell into the street.

The oncoming Rapid Cab hit the brakes, but not soon enough.

More screams now as the wheels ran right over him.

"Police! Stay back, stay back!"

As she rushed over, the cabbie leaped out of the cab. "He came outta nowhere. I swear to God!"

"Call for medicals. Stay by your cab. Call for medical assistance."

"I tried to stop, I tried. Oh my God. Is he dead?"

She got down, couldn't find a pulse. And though she could see it wouldn't matter, started CPR.

"Dallas!"

"Control the crowd, call it in. I want medicals, I want uniforms. Talk to the cabbie."

She finally sat back on her heels beside the mangled mess. Swiped some of the blood on her hands onto her pants. "Shit. Shit. He's gone.

"Peabody, get a field kit from the car as soon as we have crowd control."

"Beat droids two minutes out, ambulance one."

"He needs the morgue."

"Did he cut you? Dallas, I can't tell."

She shook her head. "No."

She stayed where she was, listening to the approaching sirens.

Not a street bump, not a street thief. He hadn't wanted her wallet, but her life.

Chapter Sixteen

Eve didn't need the MTs to pronounce him. Dead was dead.
 With the beat droids dealing with the crowd, Peabody brought her a field kit.

"Talk to the cabbie, and shit, the fare."

The fare, she noted, comprised two middle-aged women who clung to each other and wailed.

"See if you can arrange transpo to take those two screamers wherever they need to go. And have the morgue pick up what's left of this guy."

"You're not hurt."

"I'm not hurt." Eve pulled the switchblade out of the right pocket of the dead man's bloody trench coat. She flipped the trigger, snapped out the lethal blade. "Not for lack of trying."

"Jesus. Let's hear it for Thin Shield."

"Yeah, let's."

Eve bagged the weapon, dug out the would-be assassin's wallet. She flipped through his ID, including a driver's license, both in the name of Timothy Kruger. Age twenty-six.

"Twenty-seven next week. Well, happy fucking birthday."

She verified his ID with her pad.

"Identity confirmed as Kruger, Timothy, age twenty-six. Mixed-race male, resides at 512 West Twenty-Sixth. Occupation listed as business consultant.

"Yeah, I bet you were. Had some bumps before this last one. Grand theft auto, illegals distribution, fraud, assault. A short and varied career."

She bagged the wallet, then pulled out his 'link. Since she found it locked and passcoded, she bagged it for EDD.

"Who hired you, Kruger? You didn't decide to stab me in the back on a whim."

Thinking ahead, she called for a search warrant for Kruger's apartment.

She scanned traffic. Uniforms had come to barricade off the scene, routing traffic around the bloody mess of it. The two women got into another cab. With his fares on their way, the cabbie bent over from the waist and puked.

And Peabody, being Peabody, patted his back until he'd emptied his guts.

Eve straightened, stepped back when the morgue wagon pulled up. Peabody crossed to her.

"Cabdriver's shaken up. Been driving eight years, not even a scraped bumper."

"Wasn't a thing he could do."

"I told him just that. I got his statement, his fares' statements, names, and contacts. We're taking the cab in, processing it. Uniforms are taking him home."

"All right. Timothy Kruger." She passed the bagged 'link to Peabody. "Have someone take this in to EDD. We'll go take a look at his place, see what the hell. Next of kin's his mother, address a few blocks from his, so we'll notify."

"You know I can deal with that. You could go home. You got a lot of his blood on you."

"I need to see his place. He had to be a hire."

"If he was, they didn't get what they paid for. Dallas, maybe his mom doesn't need to see his blood all over you."

Eve looked down at the blood on her shirt, her jacket, her pants, her damn boots. "Yeah, that's a point. I'll take his place, you'll notify. You'll need to log the rest into evidence. Write up your separate report."

Since the uniforms had things under control, she walked the rest of the way to her car.

"He tailed me, goddamn it, and I missed it. Distracted, not paying enough attention." She gave the steering wheel a sharp smack with the heel of her hand. "No vehicle registered under his name or the mother's, but he had one. Parked along here, you bet your ass. Maybe boosted, maybe borrowed, but it's close by. Tailed me, parked, waited for us to come out of the lawyer's."

With a low level of fury simmering, she pulled out into a break in traffic.

"If that's how it went, and my arrows are pointing there, too, somebody's worried we're getting too close. This Kruger, Dallas, they had to hire him for this hit pretty damn quick. Maybe the media conference set it off. Alternatively—"

Peabody gripped the chicken stick as Eve wove in and out of traffic like the car was a thread in a loom.

"Ah, alternately, maybe he's connected to the thief. Or is the thief."

"We won't discount it. He's got plenty of bumps, but none are for burglary. Maybe he's better at that than the rest."

"If you hadn't had protection, you'd be the one bleeding on the pavement, so he wasn't all that bad."

"Maybe it wouldn't have killed me, but it sure as hell would've ruined my day. And slowed me, and the investigation, down. Taking out a cop, and taking out a cop on the street? Ballsy."

"Risk taker."

"Yeah, and he panicked when I didn't go down. Fast on his feet, but he panicked. Potentially, so did the thief. So maybe. The mother's Marcella Kruger, that building," Eve said as she pulled over. "Apartment 404. If she's not in, her employment's just down the block. Server at Mama's Diner. Take the field bag from the trunk so she doesn't see the weapon or the rest. Take a cab back to Central. You got the fare?"

"Yeah, I got it."

"Expense it."

They both ignored the honks and shouts as Peabody turned to her. "If you find anything, need me, tag me. Either way, go home after and have a big drink."

She slid out, retrieved the bag. "Glad you're not stabbed."

"Pretty happy about that myself," Eve said, and pulled out again.

This time she didn't hunt for parking, but slid into a loading zone, flipped on her On Duty light.

And sat a moment.

The attempted murder didn't bother her overmuch. People had tried to kill her or do her harm before, and would again. That was the job.

But she'd missed the damn tail, and she was good at spotting one. Distracted, she admitted. And with a worry she couldn't quite shake.

The damn emeralds. Why the hell had they come into Roarke's clever hands all those years ago, into that specific vault, then those emeralds in that vault become a target?

Add a dead man, and that dumps it all right in her lap. And just for fun, toss in an Interpol agent who continues to see Roarke as a big catch.

So with all that circling in her brain, she'd missed the damn tail, and someone else was dead.

She shoved her hands through her hair, breathed out.

"Fuck it. Work the case."

She got out, crossed to the building. Decent building, street-level restaurant where it remained warm enough for some early diners to sit outside.

And more than one gave her a wary eye as she walked to the side street door and mastered in.

Blood on her clothes, she thought again. She wasn't going to think about what Summerset would have to say about it. Instead, she climbed two flights of stairs, then turned her recorder back on.

"Dallas, Lieutenant Eve, mastering into DOS Timothy Kruger's apartment for warranted search."

She stepped in.

Small, neat, decent street view, decent furniture. Black, fake leather sofa, wall screen twice as big as anyone needed one to be. Framed posters—mostly sports—for art.

Gaming consoles, two-person table for eating, closet-sized kitchen alcove. Hall bath, small, surprisingly shiny.

The bedroom doubled as an office with the workstation and bed taking up about the same amount of space. With a high-end comp system on the desk.

She tried that first, found it locked, passcoded.

He'd made his bed that morning, she noted, even fluffed the pillows. No kicked-off shoes, no tossed-off shirt.

He'd been a careful guy.

She moved to the closet. All-male wardrobe, so he lived alone. Sportswear, trendy guy gear, a couple of higher-end suits.

And every pocket empty.

Nothing in the shoes—good kicks, good boots, good dress shoes.

She tried the dresser, found his underwear neatly folded, his socks the same. T-shirts, sweatshirts, sweaters.

And the bottom drawer was locked.

"Now, that's interesting."

She went back to the car, got the set of lockpicks she kept in the glove box. Back upstairs, she sat on the floor and got to work.

She didn't have Roarke's skill and never hoped to, but he'd taught her well. When she pulled the drawer open, she decided it deserved an *Aha*.

"Lookie here, would you? We got more switchblades, hunting and combat knives, three stilettos, a couple of garrotes, two stunners, a handgun—I bet that cost you, Tim—I think it's a 9mm, which would jibe with the ammo box. We've got a silencer in case you want to kill quietly. And I'm pretty sure this is a bone saw for dismembering your kill."

Shaking her head, she made sure to get it all on record. "You were a very bad boy, or you sure as hell wanted to be. Plenty of Seal-It in here, a couple of clone 'links, and a case full of vials. Handily labeled. We've got your poisons, knock-out drugs, hallucinogens.

"And I've got a feeling, when I toss this place, I'll find more of your tools. I don't believe you were in business consulting, Tim, but I bet you could be bought. So who paid you to do me?"

She did find more—two more stunners, a ghost gun. More knives, and five thousand in cash. Crisp, fresh bills, banded together.

He'd have more than five, she thought. Anyone that well supplied would charge more than that to take out a cop, to take one out right on the street in broad daylight.

She tagged Feeney. He said, "Yo."

"I need someone to sweep up the electronics at 512 West Twenty-Sixth, apartment 203."

"You've got blood on your shirt."

"It's not mine. Some asshole, from the looks of it a hire, tried to put a hole in me. He's dead. I'm not."

"Okay then. You figure it's connected."

"Yeah, I figure."

"We're getting more chatter, no names yet, but we're closer. They're calling it the Royal Event, and keeping the doors shut tight. We're picking at the locks. I'll send somebody for the e's."

"Appreciate it."

"How'd he get dead?"

"Run over by a cab."

"Tough way to go. We'll get back to you."

She tagged Whitney next, gave him a full update.

His face was stone. "On the goddamn street, and in the back. Go home, Dallas. I'll send a team to confiscate the weapons and the cash."

"Yes, sir. Commander, I toyed with the idea Kruger might have been part of Barrister's murder. Clearly, that doesn't fit. There's nothing here to indicate he doubled as a thief, and if he'd been in Barrister House, he'd have been armed."

"Agreed. Go home. That was a very nice jacket," he added.

"Yeah. Well."

She went out, locked and sealed the door. As she started down the stairs, Peabody tagged her.

"I'm on my way to the lab. The mother took it hard, but she wasn't surprised. She said he liked violent games, violent vids, violent sports."

"Hey, so do I, but I don't go around stabbing people in the back. He had a big drawer full of illegal weapons. He liked a variety. Whitney's sending a team to pick them up."

"On the vehicle? He didn't have one, but his uncle did, and his mom said he asked his uncle if he could borrow it. How he had a job."

"When?"

"Today, this morning. She said she thought about ten or eleven."

"Before the media conference."

"Affirmative. I got the make, model, license plate. And just got tagged they located it under two blocks from where we parked."

"I missed the tail."

"Give yourself a break on that."

"After seeing his cache, I'm not too sorry about the way he went out, but dead means I can't get any more out of him. I'm going home. Anything pops, I'll let you know."

"Have that drink."

She went out, ignored the double takes.

And drove home.

As she went through the gates, she tried to think of something pithy to toss at Summerset. Came up blank.

She could go in another way, grab an elevator, bag up the clothes, dispose of them elsewhere in the morning.

The hell with it, she decided, and went in the front.

He waited, of course, in his stiff-necked black suit with the cat sitting at his feet.

Instead of the expected, his tone came out shocked. "You're injured."

"It's not my blood. And it's not my fault Roarke puts stuff like this in my closet."

He held out a hand. "Give me the jacket."

"What?"

"Give me the jacket. I'll see what I can do. Put the rest, including the boots, in the elevator and send them down to me. I'll deal with it."

She stripped off the jacket, and he took it with two skinny fingers. "I'll see what I can do," he repeated. "Take the elevator straight to the bedroom. Roarke's in the lab."

"Shit! I forgot. I'm not on my game."

"He wasn't yet twenty when he took those emeralds. I worried then, but never thought I would worry now. As you are."

"He covered his tracks."

"I have no doubt. And yet. You'll tell him about this, of course, but he doesn't have to see you covered in blood. Take the elevator."

The cat, scenting the blood, wound around her legs and meowed in a way that seemed both concerned and pissed off.

He went with her into the elevator, where she just leaned back against the wall. She thought she'd take Peabody's advice on that big drink.

Then she stepped out, into the bedroom, just as Roarke came in.

"It's not my blood. None of it's mine. I'm not hurt."

He was across the room before the first words came out, and his hands searched her for wounds.

"I'm not hurt. I swear. Let me clean up and I'll—"

But he caught her against him. She felt him shudder once, then pull her closer yet.

"You'll get it on you. Let me—"

"Shut up. Just shut up." He took care of that by covering her mouth with his. "I need this," he murmured. "Give me this."

"Okay." Running her hands over his hair, she repeated, "Okay. It's okay. I'm okay."

"You'll tell me what happened."

"Yes. I just want to get out of these clothes, shower it all off."

"All right." He unhooked her weapon harness himself. "Do you need to go back out?"

"I hope to hell not."

"Then I'll get you a change and take your clothes down to Summerset."

"He said to put them in the elevator, send them down." She stripped off the shirt, saw the blood had soaked through and onto her support tank. "He didn't want you to see before I could explain. Neither did I."

"The sentiment's appreciated, but I don't need protection."

"I wasn't hurt." She pulled off her boots, her belt, emptied her pockets. "I wanted you to know that first."

When she'd stripped down, he handed her a sweater and lounge pants so light and soft they might have been woven from vapor.

"I'll send the rest down."

"Roarke, I'm—"

"Don't say you're sorry to me." The words snapped out. Then he touched a hand to her cheek and softened the tone. "Don't even think it."

She just nodded, but she did think it. "Give me five minutes. Maybe you could wait in the office. I've got to update and write this all up after I tell you. And I could really use a drink."

"So could I. I'll wait for you."

He picked up her bloody clothes, retrieved the belt that carried more blood, and sent them down. Then he thanked whatever deity might listen for bringing her home to him again, safe.

When she came into the office, he had the fire on low and a glass of wine waiting.

"Thanks." She took one long, slow sip. Then a second. "I'm going to start about why the blood. I can backtrack after to the rest of the day. We went to see the lawyer," she began, and took him through it, step-by-step.

When she told him about feeling the punch in the back, he turned her around, pulled up the sweater.

"You've the faintest of bruises, nothing more."

"I told you I wasn't hurt. He ran, I ran after him. I nearly had him. He kept looking behind, and he tried a jump toward the street. Lost his footing, went flying out. A cab ran over him—driver couldn't have stopped. I couldn't get a pulse. I knew he was gone, but I had to try."

"And ended up with his blood all over you."

"Yeah. Someone hired him, Roarke."

"That's more than possible, and probably connected to the emeralds and Barrister's murder."

"Not possible. It's a fact. He borrowed a car this morning, said he had a job. He tailed me and I fucking missed the tail." She drank again. "After, I tossed his place. He's got a drawer—locked. I picked it—"

"Congratulations."

"Right. It was loaded with weapons. Knives, stunners, handguns, garrotes, poisons, name it. He was a pro, maybe still a little green, but a pro. It threw him when I didn't go down, and it scared him when he saw I was going to catch him. But I really don't think this was his first time out. Somebody hired him."

"What time was your media conference? This afternoon, wasn't it? I wasn't able to watch."

"After the hire, so that didn't set this off. Unless somebody got wind. Abernathy's talking to people. They've got a task force looking into the original thefts."

"Is that so?"

"Don't brush it off."

But she saw, in his eyes, he did just that.

"Darling Eve, I've been looked at for that and more over the years. Yet here I stand with you. But this has you worried, distracted, and you missed a tail. So I'm telling you to put the worry aside. I'd be the one in the nick, after all, and I've no worries about it."

"Abernathy and I had a discussion."

Now he smiled. "Did you really?"

"They think the emerald heist was a group."

"Correct, and they always have."

"He thinks maybe you were involved as a kind of apprentice."

This got a laugh, easy and delighted. "Sometimes it pays to be underestimated. And all that should reassure you."

"It should." Maybe it would. Eventually. "He also gave me a name, a possibility for Fancy Blonde, a thief. Jenna Lynn Delaney."

He frowned over his wine. "The one who rang a faint and distant bell for me, in my hunt. That name wasn't on the list he gave us."

"No. He's ambitious, tried to skirt around us with this task force. But he gave it to me after our discussion. She needs a deeper look, and so does Timothy Kruger. Because—"

"Whoever hired the thief hired the failed assassin. That clicks nicely."

"I have to update, write up the attempted stabbing."

"I'll see if I can make that distant bell ring louder. Then we'll have a meal." He touched his lips to hers. "Considering the stab in the back, bloody coward, it can be pizza."

She'd never argue with pizza.

She updated her board first, then took the rest of her wine—why the hell not—to her command center.

She wrote up the interview with the lawyer first. And just as she thought about tagging Yancy before she started the rest, he tagged her.

"Did you get me a face?"

"We got one. Sorry for the delay. First, I was delayed, then when you've got two people, they tend to remember things differently. I can tell you right off, the picture you sent—Delaney—that's a no. Some similarities, but both wits said too young right off. But they both also agreed on the final sketch. Do you want me to run it through face rec for you?"

He was walking, she noted, on a nice fall evening, and after putting in extra time for her case.

"No, I'll do it. Send it to me, then go have a beer."

"I hear that. I've got a pizza date coming up."

"Funny, so do I. Thanks, Yancy."

"Not every day I get to work on a case with a secret vault full of the mega-dollar fancy. I want to say, Dallas, they're a really nice family, including the staff. Divine offered to make me dinner, and when I told her I had a date, told me to come back when I didn't. She meant it."

"I liked them, too. Go have that pizza and beer."

So not Delaney, but she could have been the thief, the murderer. Just not what Eve thought might be the conduit.

So she'd look for two blondes.

She switched over from her report to take Yancy's incoming, and waited for the face to come on-screen.

When it did, she felt the blood drain out of her own.

Coincidences, she thought. How many times had she said they were bollocks? Should she have seen this coming? Should she have put it together?

Hard to say. Really hard to say.

And hard right now, she admitted, to think.

She pushed up, walked over to her balcony doors, threw them open. And let the cool evening air wash over her.

She didn't hear Roarke come in—he moved like the air itself—but he spoke from behind her.

"The bell rings more clearly. I've been out of the game awhile now, so had to refresh a bit. Jenna Lynn Delaney has a reputation in certain circles for being a clever and discerning thief. Started young—and not so successfully. But got considerably better."

"The blonde's not Delaney."

"No?"

"No. Yancy sent the face."

She turned then, and seeing her stand so pale, so stiff, he lowered the glass he'd brought to his lips.

"What is it?"

"Look for yourself. The sketch is on my desk screen."

He went over, and when he saw the sketch, stood very still.

Regret came first so when he turned to Eve his eyes were full of apology. "Magdelana. I'm sorry, Eve."

"I don't need 'I'm sorry.' Did you tell her? Did she know you took the emeralds?"

"I don't . . . I might have done."

"Yes or no?"

"Don't interrogate me, Lieutenant. Let me think. I might have done. It would've been some years after, as I hadn't met her when I took them. But I trusted her, which was my very big mistake."

"You told her. At some point you told her. Or enough she understood."

"Enough," he agreed. "I think enough. Something about traveling to London, then holding my future in my hands, and being foolish enough to say I wish I'd kept some of it, as she'd look brilliant in emeralds."

"That would be enough for her. It's all deliberate. You have to see that."

"We hadn't met when she targeted Henry Barrister. You said she was twenty."

"Sometimes fate bites you in the ass. That's something you'd say."

She made herself breathe, reminded herself to think like a cop.

"She used him, then fate bit you in the ass and he gave her a direct line to you with those fucking emeralds. All this is deliberate."

"How?"

She pulled at her hair. "How can you be so goddamn smart and still have a blind spot for her?"

"I don't. I know what she is. I took steps to keep her out of our lives. I'm gobsmacked she had the bloody nerve to come to New York after I sent her off."

"I'm the one who punched her in the face."

"And me as well, as I recall very clearly. That was after I'd told her to leave New York, that she'd be hauled out if she tried to stay at any of my properties in this world or any other. I simply don't follow you on this as deliberate."

"For fuck's sake. You stole the emeralds. I punched her and you gave her the boot. She finds out where they are. What better way to tie you up, to pay you back than to take them—only them—and make a splash out of it?"

She began to pace. "She'd know Interpol looks at you, probably knows about Abernathy. She'd make it her fucking mission to know. She waits until Henry's dead—nobody, in her mind, can link her to the theft. After she rakes in her share, she'll give Abernathy or someone like him a big fat hint to the original."

"Why would anyone believe her?"

She spun around to him. "Why did you? Ever?"

Chapter Seventeen

Even understanding her anger, he felt his own rise.
"Bugger it, Eve, I was besotted. That was the beginning and end of it. She wasn't just another beautiful woman I could enjoy, but someone I could work with, talk to about the work because she wanted what I did."

"Which was?"

"More." He threw up his hands. "I trusted her, and she betrayed me for that more. For whatever good it did her. It was a period of my life that's over and done. We didn't come to each other as children. I can't tell you she meant nothing to me, because she did. But I can tell you that whatever she meant is less than nothing compared to you."

"I don't need your reassurance."

"Don't you?"

"No." She struggled for calm, then repeated, "No. I've never understood why you wanted me, why you love me. But I know you do. I don't need you to tell me what we have is more important, more real, more everything than whatever you had with her. Because I know it is. She's also everything I'm not, and that can be a hard swallow."

"She's cold, careless with people, incapable of putting anyone above herself, without a single ounce of loyalty. Yes, everything you're not."

It struck him, amazed him. "Here you are, such a sharp cop, with instincts and insights that often seem preternatural. And you think she wanted to hurt you because you were less than she is? Christ Jesus, Eve, she wanted to hurt you because she knew you're so much more."

"I don't care about any of that."

"You do. Yes, of course you do."

"It can't be top of the list right now. She played you back then. She played you when she came to New York, and played me, too. Don't let her play you now."

"I won't. She hurt you, deliberately, cruelly, and I don't forgive it." The rage bubbled up again, so this time, he walked to the open doors. "The bloody, buggering nerve of her to come back here. She's been careful to avoid what's mine. Only last year she mistakenly booked a room in one of my hotels—I'd only recently acquired it, so it's doubtful she knew. And was escorted out by security."

"Where?"

"Ah . . ." He pressed fingers to his temple. "London? Yes, London. A favorite hotel of hers, it seems—which I was unaware of when I took it over."

"When?"

"I can't say precisely, sometime last fall, I think, or late summer."

"She'd have come to New York, to Barrister House not long after."

He turned, slowly. "Well now, of course."

"You didn't let it go. You embarrassed her, took a place she wanted away from her. She thinks she found a way to pull in a few hundred million and pay you back at the same time."

"All right." Calmer now, or stonier, he nodded. "I see how it could be."

"She'd have contacts. Brokers, thieves, whatever she'd need."

"She would, and if she didn't, she'd make them. She's good at it. We'll talk this out. We'll sit down, eat, and talk this out."

"I don't want food, I want—"

"Eve, you need food. You're still pale. Can I tell you how it twists in me to see you pale, and know, somehow, I'm the cause of it?"

"It's not you."

"However unwilling, unknowingly, I brought her into our lives. At eighteen I took what has now cost a man his life. She's a part of that, so we need to sit, eat, talk, and bloody well think. Please."

"All right. Fine."

"Close the doors, will you? It's too cool now."

But she took another moment in that cool air while he went to program the pizza.

She heard him talking to the cat, and had to blink the sting of tears from her eyes. She would not cry. Would not give that conniving bitch a single tear.

"You're still angry," he said when he came back. "So am I. The anger may grow in different directions, but it comes from the same root."

She sat and didn't object when he topped off her wine.

"Who would she work with?"

"It's difficult to say. I think it's unlikely she'd work with people I'd know or have had dealings with back in my time. It's less likely I'd pin that down straight off, you see."

"Yes, I see. What about this Delaney?"

"She's good, good and careful, and keeps a low profile. From what I can gather, so far, she doesn't take just any job, and if working solo, is discerning there as well. I'll need to dig more. I could see her taking such a basic job—the break-in—due to the emeralds. Her fee would be substantial. And it's the thrill of it that's worth as much to such as we."

"A man's dead."

"And there I lean against her—again from what I have so far. Careful, I said. Young, but experienced. The kill? Sloppy, and you risk an off-planet cage for decades and more. The window right there, and out you go, empty-handed or not, but you go if you want to live to steal another day."

"Would Magdelana try it herself? The theft?"

He took a moment to think it through.

"Not impossible, but unlikely. Climbing in windows, not her style. And I can't see her taking only the Suite. The temptation for more would have been too much to resist."

"Best guess on her part in it."

"Coordinate. Find the right broker, one willing to take this on, find the right thief, the right venue for the auction, design the event. Take the lion's share, of course. It's most likely she had all she needed, the location of the vault, very likely the combination. Where the Suite would be taken for authentication and to whom, how it would be transported to the location of the auction, and so on. It's delicate and complicated."

"Eat." Reaching out, he rubbed a hand over hers.

Because he looked at her with his heart in his eyes, she picked up a slice.

When she bit in, her system thanked her. She wouldn't cry, Eve reminded herself, and she'd eat.

"I need to write up my report. I'm not giving Interpol Magdelana yet. I will. I have to, but I want something solid down first. I need you to dig in on Delaney and Kruger's finances. Recent payments, substantial. Would she have that kind of money?"

"Doubtful. But she'd have financing. The broker would finance the job, and they'll take in considerably more than the, at a guess, ten to twenty million for the heist. As for Kruger, I couldn't say the going rate for killing a cop, and I . . ."

He set down his own slice, stared at her. "You think she hired him to kill you?"

"Duh," Eve said, and took another bite. "Kill me, take me out or just down so she buys time to finish up the auction. Who else?"

He had to get up, had to walk away as the fury all but burned him from the inside out.

"There's nowhere she can hide I won't find her." In contrast to the burn, his voice was ice-cold. "Nothing she can do to spare herself for the payment I'll exact for this."

"She's going in a cage." Eve spoke flatly, waited for him to turn. She knew that look, that Scary Roarke look. And sent him one of her own. "In a cage, Roarke, and potentially for the rest of her life. That's what's going to happen, has to happen. That's what I want, and what you'll give me."

"There are times you ask for the impossible."

"No, I don't. The hard, sure. You're pissed."

"That's a small word for what's in me."

"I'm pissed. And I trust us both to do what's right. What I can live with and keep my badge. Don't let her take that from me."

"Ah Christ, you know the buttons to push." He turned away, turned back. "I need her to pay."

"Let's make sure she does. A man's dead. Well, two men now. Whatever part she played in that? She'll be in that cage a very long time. She won't like it."

"How long?"

"Twenty-five to life, depending on her involvement with the theft, which includes Barrister's murder. Add to that, if she hired the assassin? Conspiracy to murder a police officer. Life—that's two life sentences, most likely off-planet."

"If you make that happen, I'll be very grateful."

"We'll make it happen. Now you sit and eat."

He came back to the table. "I never thought of her for this. I don't think of her, so I never thought of her for this."

"Neither did I. And when we close the door on her cage? We won't think of her again."

"All right, Lieutenant. How do we make this happen in a way you can live with?"

She polished off her first slice. "I'm hungry. That's good." So reached for another. "My part, to start, I put her in New York, with Henry Barrister. I make that connection, and find out how she traveled. My bet, one of Barrister's private shuttles. Then I trace back where she traveled from. Maybe London, since you handed me the info she was there. I track all her aliases, including Ms. Fancy, and start digging for the broker."

She picked up her wine, gestured. "Meanwhile, EDD finds the data on the auction."

"It'll be soon. If she moved on you like this, it has to be soon."

"That's exactly right. You get me those finances—the suspected thief's, the dead assassin's. We track the payments back."

"They'll be well covered on the other end, but aye, I'll bloody well track them."

"I know you will."

"You've still a worry in there."

"A couple." But she ate. Not just because she was hungry, but because she needed and wanted the fuel. "She wants to break you. She wants the big pile of money, yeah, but she really wants to hurt you along with it. How much does she know about your . . . former profession?"

"Well, she certainly knows details about any jobs we pulled while together. But together puts her in a very bad light as well. In any case, I don't leave a trail. Add she tried that once, and it didn't work for her."

"Can she put you at Filthy Rich Estate when oops, the Duchess of Filthy Rich's solid gold underwear goes missing?"

"First, the market's too narrow to steal gold underwear, but had I done so, she might try to claim I was there. But again, had I done so, I would have already put myself, and solidly, elsewhere."

He reached over for her hand. "Put that worry away. She was good. I was better."

Not away, Eve thought, but she could—for now—put it aside.

"The other thing. I have to update EDD, Whitney, Peabody, and that's going to bring in my bullpen, Tibble. I have to update them on Magdelana."

"And her connection to me."

"That's right. I have to do that without saying the two of you pulled jobs together in the before. They'll know it, but I can't clarify or confirm it without putting them in a squeeze."

"I do cause you problems," he murmured.

"Yeah, like inventing, designing, manufacturing the magic lining that spared me a stab in the back. I think we can call it a wash. I know my people, Roarke. There's not one of them who'd turn on you."

"I know that. I'm honored by that. But."

"But. I need to approach your connection to her as strictly personal, romantic. She's the old classic. The woman dumped."

"It's scorned, but comes to the same."

"You dumped her, she tried to jam you up, failed. Some years later, she tries to sex you up—"

He couldn't stop the smile. "Really?"

"She was wrapped around you like ivy before I punched the pair of you."

"I'll remind you I was not wrapped around her."

"Regardless, she tried, failed. Now—if this comes up at all—she'd like to jam you up again. More, she's tried to have me killed. Get me out of the way on two levels—personal and over the investigation."

"That would be true. All of that's largely truth, except she left me, looking for a bigger payday. And the sex me up? Deliberately insulting on your part."

"You think?" Now she smiled, sipped. "Anyway, I'll handle it. So will you."

"I need to be there, be part of it when you take her down. And I know you will."

"I want you there, I need you to be part of it. That's personal and professional."

"All right then. Where do you want me? In the lab working with EDD, or in my office, working on the finances?"

"Maybe check in with EDD, with whoever's working it overtime. But the finances are key." She sat back. "Let's get to work."

Eve decided the hell with Earth rotation and contacted wife number four yet again.

Hair wild, eyes a little crazed, Lacey answered.

"I'm sorry to disturb you again," Eve began.

"Whose idea was it we'd each take a day to cook? Mine. What was I thinking? Why did I think I could or should make a pot roast? The kids'd be happy with canned spaghetti, but I'm cooking this huge slab of cow."

"Are you trying it sober?"

On a laugh, Lacey shoved at her wild hair. "Not anymore, thanks for the reminder. What is it?"

"I'm sending you a police artist sketch. I'd like you to tell me if you recognize this woman."

Lacey reached for a bottle of wine, and her jaw snapped shut, her eyes narrowed when Eve sent the sketch. "That's the bitch. The smirking, slithering bitch."

"Could you be more specific on how you recognize her?"

"That's the smirking, slithering bitch who went after Henry when we were married—younger then, but that's her. And the smirking, slithering bitch I saw in New York last December."

Pouring herself a generous glass, she let out a half laugh. "I'm a seriously happily married woman and mother, and that still pisses me off."

"Why wouldn't it?"

"Enough I actually talked to another friend of mine who was at that party way back. She remembered her, too. She thought her name was Sabrina. Anyway, what's the interest?"

"She's a person of interest in an investigation."

"Yeah?" Now she smiled. "Are you going to arrest her?"

Eve started to brush that off with a standard cop answer, then changed her mind. She understood the still-pissed-off very well.

"Yes, I am, as soon as I find her."

"That absolutely makes up for cooking day. Do me a favor and let me know when that happens. I swear to God, I'm popping champagne. Henry was a hound, but I know a snake when I see one."

"I'll do that. Thanks for your help."

"In this case, my pleasure."

Satisfied, Eve wrote her report. She held off sending a copy to Abernathy. She wanted a little more time, just a little more time before she put him on the scent.

Instead, she started on Henry Barrister and/or Zip company private shuttles from London to New York the previous December. Expecting a slog, she programmed coffee, prepared to dig in.

Within twenty minutes, she shocked herself.

"Son of a bitch! Son of a bitch, there you are. Sabrina Fancy, single passenger, London to New York, December 12."

She called for an ID shot, got nothing.

"Fake passport, fake ID, only activate and use it for Henry maybe. When did you leave, where did you go?"

She hunted, and found Henry had provided her transportation again. This time New York to Sorrento, Italy.

"And what was there for you?"

She sat back, studied the board.

"Another man. Another rich man, that's my guess. Close to Christmas now, big, fancy holiday parties, cons to run, people to filch. And plans to make."

She rose, paced.

There had to be a reason to go to that place, at that time. After Henry showed her the vault, because he damn well did. Or she stumbled on it. Either way, she knew. Plans to make, she thought again.

Need help with that. What came first? The broker or the thief?

Broker.

No one small-time, and very likely someone already known. A relationship? Maybe personal and professional.

She glanced at Roarke's office, then shook her head. No, let him do what he did. She'd handle this.

Sitting again, she pored through the Interpol files for something that clicked. Broker, thief with connections in Sorrento. Empty, she widened it to Italy.

"Okay, try another way." She searched for more travel for Sabrina Fancy, and found nothing. Restarted, trying privates from Savannah, Georgia, to Sorrento. She went through January, February, March.

Programmed more coffee.

April, May, June. Goddamn it.

And hit in July.

"Delaney Lynn, single passenger, Savannah to Sorrento—Sorrento's it—July 15, return flight, bam, New York City, July 20. Flight from New York to Savannah, July 25."

She sat back, closed her eyes. "That's a big-ass bang. Needed to have a look at the setup, spend a few days watching, casing, making sure about the security system. Who paid the freight? Luxe Travel private. Anybody with enough money can book from them."

She contacted Luxe Travel, and got what she'd expected. No one authorized to get or give that information. Contact during regular business hours, with a warrant.

"Fine, fine, fine."

She accepted that, and got another boost when she found Delaney Lynn's September travel to New York. Two days before the break-in. Return flight canceled.

"Huh."

That had her up and pacing again.

"Why aren't you gone? Did you decide to stay for the auction? Because I really think it's here. Magdelana needs it to be here, in Roarke's adopted city.

"Maybe, maybe. Or shit, we're going to find your body floating in the East River. Maybe she had Kruger take care of you. Let's find out where you stayed. High-end hotels. Nobody's going to pinch dollars on this job."

She started with the Roarke Palace. Definitely highest of high-end, plus, they wouldn't give her the brush-off.

"I'm sorry, Lieutenant, we have no one registered under the name of Delaney Lynn."

"Try Jenna Lynn Delaney, and variations of that name."

"Give me a moment, please."

On hold, Eve paced.

"Lieutenant."

"Right here."

"I did find a Della Lane who checked in on the date you wanted. She checked out on Saturday evening—requested late checkout. She had a one-bedroom suite on the Premium level."

"I'm going to send you a picture. I need you to show it to anyone who might have had contact with her. Maid service, room service, check-in or -out."

"Of course."

"What was your name again?"

"Pilar Vincenti."

"Ms. Vincenti, I'd like you to contact me if anyone recognizes this woman."

"Oh. Well, actually, I do. I was on Saturday evening. I checked her out myself."

"This woman?" Sometimes fate didn't bite you in the ass, Eve thought, but gave it a nice, sweet kiss. "The one in the photo?"

"Yes. She was in a hurry, seemed upset."

"Did you arrange for transportation?"

"Ah . . . no. She said someone was picking her up, but she wanted a printout of her bill. I remember, as she seemed upset. I asked if there was anything I could do to help."

"She said?"

"No, thank you—polite—but she was taking care of that herself. Is that helpful?"

"It's very helpful. There would've been a doorman on duty."

"Of course."

"Is he or she on tonight?"

"I'm not sure, but I can check."

"If you could, and show the photo. It would also help if I know what car service picked her up."

"Just give me another minute."

More coffee, more pacing, more thinking.

"Lieutenant, Allen was on, and did see her leave. He believes she got into a private car, a sedan. Not a car service, but a private car, a late-model Mercedes sedan. He didn't notice the driver."

"That's fine, that's good. You've been a tremendous help, thank you."

"You're more than welcome."

She headed to Roarke's office.

He sat, fingers flying over keys, his hair tied back, sleeves rolled up. And muttering to himself, mostly curses that spanned both English and Irish.

He said, "What?" And didn't sound pleased.

"I wouldn't interrupt, but I have stuff that may be helpful."

"All right then." He stopped, shoved at his hair. "Be helpful then."

"I've confirmed Magdelana as the last straw on Henry's last marriage, and as the smirker in New York last December. She went by Sabrina Fancy. Henry flew her in on one of his personal privates from London. Then, after her stay, flew her out to Sorrento, Italy."

"Sorrento." He picked up his coffee and looked more interested.

"Does that pop anything for you?"

"Not right off, but I'll push there."

"I don't have anything, yet, on further travel under that name. But I do have a Delaney Lynn, on a Luxe Travel private, from Savannah to Sorrento in July."

"Ah, well then, that's a lovely connection, isn't it now?"

"Yeah, it is. She stayed a few days, then flew to New York."

"To look over the job, of course. You may find she made her way onto the grounds. Floral delivery, messenger service, or the like."

"Okay. She came back, same way, a couple days before the break-in, and under Della Lane, stayed at your hotel. The Palace. That's confirmed by Pilar Vincenti at the desk, who was really helpful. You should toss her a bonus. She checked out Saturday evening—seemed upset. Someone in a Mercedes sedan picked her up. I can't find any travel for her out of New York."

"It would be foolish of her to stay for the auction, and she doesn't strike as foolish. Upset, you said? Maybe she copped to a double cross or worse. She's gone to ground."

"That's possible. They could have put Kruger on her."

"I don't think so. I've got his not-well-hidden business accounts."

"That would've been helpful information for me."

"I haven't unwound the source of the payment for you. Which appears to be only made this morning. Seventeen-five."

"Huh, I figured I was worth a little more."

"That would be the deposit, darling. A standard thirty-five percent. He won't see the rest, of course, and had only withdrawn five thousand of that, in cash. But as for Jenna? There's no transfers for several weeks before yours. It appears he's been for hire for about two years. Yours would've been his biggest score by far."

He held up a hand before she could speak.

"And yes, EDD will be able to trace the other payments, the other victims well enough. As for Jenna again, her accounts are well hidden, but I've unearthed a couple. There are three deposits I believe apply here. From different sources. One from July, which would jibe, wouldn't it? One from the time of the break-in, and one made a little later in the early hours of Saturday morning—which would be after authentication. All told, she earned fifty million."

"She's alive then."

"You thought otherwise?"

"Considered it, but they wouldn't have wired the last payment if they intended to kill her. Double cross doesn't fit, either. Except maybe it does."

"In what way?"

"Need to think about it. I have to get this all down, written out. Think."

"An hour more."

"Two."

"Two then."

She wrote it all up, studied her own notes, made calculations, read over previous data and notes.

"Double cross," she muttered. "Yeah, it could fit."

And thinking how, she put her feet on the desk, sat back, and studied the board. As she ran other scenarios in her mind, she dropped into sleep.

Chapter Eighteen

She stirred when Roarke lifted her out of the chair.

"Shit, I dropped out."

"As well you should."

He carried her to the elevator as she tried to work her way out of the sleep fog.

"Different kind of double cross. I've got a couple of what-ifs."

"Good for you. Sleep on them. I've made some headway on the sources. Not quite pinned—someone knows what they're doing, and well. More than Magdelana. She's good at it, but not this good. So I'll sleep on that while the search continues on auto."

"Magdelana. Is she good at working both ends?"

"Excels there. What's the other end?"

"Not sure."

"Here now." He set her on the bed, where the cat had already made himself comfortable. He took off her shoes, then fetched her a nightshirt while she pulled off her sweater.

After dropping the shirt over her head, he began to undress.

"A favor? I'd like it if we've given her enough time and attention until tomorrow."

"No problem with that." She finished undressing, slid into bed.

Tired, she thought, in her mind, in her body. But the need was stronger than the fatigue. And because she knew him—she did know him—she understood he'd have that same need.

So when he lay beside her, holding her as he always did for sleep, she tipped her face up to find his mouth.

"Be with me," she murmured. "I need you to be with me."

"Always."

Tender, so tender, each touch, each taste.

The cat gave a kind of sigh before he jumped off the bed.

Soothing each other, she thought, this quiet, gentle mating that brought warmth instead of heat, and comfort more than passion.

She gave herself to it as she gave to him. Love, just love, with no questions, no doubts. He murmured to her as his hands skimmed and glided. In Irish, words she knew now, others she didn't. But all from his heart.

The sound of them, soft in the dark, made her feel cherished.

She gave them back, the words she knew, and added her own.

And the sound of them, soft in the dark, made him feel cherished.

His fingers skimmed over that faint bruise on her back as if to erase it, and for a moment, he held her tighter as the thought of losing her destroyed him.

"Don't think about it," she whispered—because she knew him. "Don't think about it now. I'm here. Be with me here. I love you. Roarke. I love you."

And took his mouth again so he could taste the words.

Be with me, she thought again and drew him into her.

They moved together, slow, drawing out each moment, living in the shimmering pleasure love offered.

My love, my heart, my all, he told her with his words, with his body. He felt her long, slow release, heard it in her throaty sigh. As she melted under him, he took his own.

When she woke in the morning, she saw him on the sofa with the cat. He wore a black sweater and pants and worked on a portable. On the wall screen it looked like maps, various routes highlighted, and bunches of numbers.

"Did I sleep through to Saturday again?"

"You didn't, no. I've cleared my schedule for the day."

"Countries may crumble. You don't have to do that."

"They won't, and I do. You'll want coffee to wake up that busy brain."

"You've got something."

"Very nearly. Wake yourself up, Lieutenant. I'm more than ready for breakfast."

She got coffee, a quick shower to unmuddle her brain. When she came out, he had plates under domes, had the cat busy with his own breakfast as he stood at the window.

"It's back on auto. Just a few more layers."

"On which source?"

"I've focused more, for obvious reasons, on the source for Timothy Kruger's payment, I'll get you the other, but that's my priority."

"I don't have a problem with that. I'm going to get dressed while it's running. It's going to source at Magdelana or connect to Joy Barrister."

He turned. "The sister?"

"It's what works. It's not the wife. She benefits most financially, but she loved her husband, and it's not about money."

"Then what?"

She went into the closet. "Ego, power, anger, insult, greed. Pick one, maybe all. Would Magdelana work with someone in the house, the family?"

He came to the closet door. "Absolutely."

"I can't figure out how they linked up for this, but it's a strong possibility. Hell, pick something." She gestured to the clothes. "I don't care. I just want to get started."

"Will you confront her today, if she's the source?"

"I'm going to find a way to confront whoever the source is."

With a nod, he chose black trousers, a black leather jacket that would skim to her hips and had buttons of dull gold. A black vest with metallic gold pinstripes.

That worried her.

"Those stripes are shiny."

"You said you didn't care. Trust me."

He chose a crisp white shirt, a black belt with a buckle in that same dull gold. Sturdy black boots with a side buckle.

Then, because he knew the cat, Roarke stepped out again to guard breakfast.

"The double-cross theory makes you think of the sister."

"The data we have on Delaney has no mention of violence. Ever. She comes off smooth, and all the things you said before. Careful, professional in her questionable profession. She's just collected the last payment on fifty million. Why's she upset when she checks out of the hotel?"

He followed. "Because she's heard the media reports. A murder at Barrister House."

"And who's going to be prime suspect? The thief. Now, she could've been upset because she killed a guy, but why does she stay after that final payment? Why does she get some sleep in New York instead of poofing?"

Oh yes, he followed very well.

"Because when she went to bed to get that sleep, she didn't know there'd been a murder."

Eve came out for her weapon harness. "That's how I see it. And I looked back over the notes. There was a quick bump on the security. Like it flicks off, then on again. So my what-if? She does the job, out the window, and gone, unjams the security."

"And someone else jams it again." It played like music. "There was that quick, almost indecipherable blip on the system."

"Right." She sat, lifted a dome, and saw he'd gone with the all-American style. Bacon, eggs, toast, butter and jam, berries.

"You gave me a basic time frame for the job. But if you take out the time to open the vault—because she had the combo—that would put her back out a solid twenty minutes, and maybe more because, by all accounts, Delaney's good. She'd be quick and clean. The glitch or bump came about thirteen minutes before TOD."

"The sister." Roarke sat beside her. "For the house, the business?"

"She doesn't get the house, or more of the business. And that's the thing. I'm wondering if it sticks in her craw that the son got the house, everything in it, a bigger share of the business. She's the oldest, but he's got the penis. Sure, she got plenty, but you look at the big picture. He got more. Was valued more."

She shrugged as she ate. "Maybe she wanted to keep the stuff in the vault, got overruled. Maybe she didn't. But all that, and the time they took to try to figure how to get it back? Gives her plenty of room to plan this out. Or to hook up with someone who can pull it off, leave her in the clear."

"They keep the money, which she doesn't need, it lets her remove her brother and stand as head of the company—more shares or not. It takes a slap at her father, exposes what he did, and puts her and the rest in the light of trying to make it right."

"It plays a tune for me. Financially, yeah, the wife, the daughters, but in every other way, the sister benefits most."

"What a mind you have."

Scooping up eggs, Eve corrected him. "It's her mind. She has to lure him downstairs. It only helps that he wasn't feeling well, but she had a way around that. Tells him he had to come down, no, don't wake Aileen. He goes down, sees the vault open, sees the emeralds gone.

"Shock, worry. Move to contact the police. He hears his wife, probably, and before he can answer, bash. Aileen walks in. All she sees is him. Joy just has to ease out, wait a couple minutes, then rush in, take over."

Eve crunched into bacon. "It's a pretty solid plan. You've got to go with the bungled burglary because it's all laid out nice and neat."

"I'll wager that bothered you all along. The nice and neat."

"Some, but you have to go with the evidence. As we got more, it bothered me more. And there's the timing of the hire for the hit on me. Morning, after I went to Barrister House and got the Fancy Blonde information, arranged for Yancy, and before the media conference. Still, if Joy Barrister arranged for the hit, she got the hit man's name from somewhere. And fast."

"Magdelana."

"She'd know people in low places."

"She would, yes."

"And somebody hungry enough to take on a cop, and basically right away. So that's how I see it right now. That could change, depending."

"I don't think it will," he considered as he topped off her coffee. "As I sit here with my very clever cop, it all fits very well. How will you handle it?"

"We need the auction location, the time. If we take Barrister before that, they'll delay. Go under and delay. If I'm right and Joy Barrister and Magdelana started turning this wheel, she knew Barrister was going to take out her brother. Maybe the broker knew, maybe not. But that doesn't let him off the hook. The thief, either, or anyone else connected. It's murder during the commission of a crime, and they're all in the soup."

Nodding at the screen, she drank more coffee. "How much longer, do you think?"

"It's painstaking, but I'd say under an hour now. Well under."

"If she's working with Barrister, Magdelana knows we've ID'd her. She'd like that. She wants us to know it's her because she thinks she can get clear."

"She would, yes."

"She'll be sorry for it. I need to get going. I need to run this by Whitney, update Peabody, Feeney. I'm going to brief my detectives and officers to prepare for an op. We'll get that location, and we need to be ready to go."

He rose with her. "I'll stick with this, then I'll come into Central, work in EDD on the rest."

"In case we go sooner than later. I won't leave you out."

"And I won't hold you up. If it's in New York as we think, if it's that important for her to shove my face in it, I can help with blueprints and security. If it's not, I can help with transportation."

"She didn't know you. I wonder if you understand that."

"You didn't know me then."

"People change, sure, but their underlayment doesn't. It just doesn't. She never knew you." She kissed him. "I do."

He pulled her in, held on. "Take good care of my cop."

"I was distracted yesterday, but you took care of me. I won't be distracted today."

As she stepped back, her 'link signaled.

"Robert J. Wenn. I know that name."

"As you should. Very successful criminal defense attorney."

"So what the hell does he want?" She answered. "Dallas."

"Lieutenant, good morning."

He looked like a very successful criminal attorney, with his silvered dark hair perfectly styled, electric green eyes hooded under ink-black brows. Somewhere around sixty, he'd worked skillfully for decades to, in her opinion, undo the knots people like her had tied around defendants.

"Mr. Wenn, what can I do for you?"

"I believe there's something we can do for each other. I have a client who, for certain considerations, has detailed information to offer you regarding your current investigation."

"And what considerations might those be?"

"My client requires immunity for any charges pertaining to the theft of the Royal Suite."

"Is that all? As the item or items taken from Barrister House have not yet been made public, I have to assume your client was involved in the break-in, the burglary, during which a man was killed."

"Not by my client. Lieutenant, my client contends, and has convinced me, to have taken no part in the death of Nathan Barrister. But has information that will lead you to those responsible, and possibly lead to the recovery of the Royal Suite."

"Would your client be Jenna Lynn Delaney of Savannah, Georgia?"

His gaze stayed steady—she gave him credit for it. "You're very good at your job. So am I. I believe part of the skill required in our work is separating truth from lies. My client asks for a meeting, at a neutral location, with you and a representative from the prosecutor's office.

"She could have fled, Lieutenant. She didn't. She's in a position, has chosen to be in a position, to assist you in finding Nathan Barrister's killer. We have yet to face each other in a courtroom, but I know your reputation. I believe this would be your priority. It's also hers."

"I have to talk to my boss, and the prosecutor's office."

"Of course. Let me add that she is not willing, at this time, to talk to any law enforcement officers but yourself."

"My partner will attend this meeting if it happens."

"That's agreeable. No other agencies, for now. At that time, if we can come to an agreement, I'll give you an address. I appreciate your consideration."

Eve looked at Roarke. "Well, well, fucking well."

"Will you give it to her? Immunity?"

"That's not up to me."

"We both know you'd have influence there."

"She didn't kill Barrister, and I can make that case to Whitney and the PA. Immunity for the theft, that's sticky for me."

"But you have a priority."

"Yeah."

"I want to be at the meeting. There's a language we can speak, Ms. Delaney and I, that won't necessarily require words."

"I got that. Whitney first." She made the contact.

He watched her, pacing, pausing, pacing, as she made her case to her commander. It didn't surprise him when she pushed for Cher Reo; Eve and the APA had a rhythm.

When she finished, she turned to him again. "Okay, one down. He'll talk to the PA. I'm going to bring Reo up to speed. Then get Peabody on board."

"I'll just go down, speak to Summerset. He can continue on the financials until I can get back to them. He can handle it," he said as she started to object. "He has the skill, and he'll use that skill with discretion. You know that."

"Shit. Are we going to have to make him an NYPSD consultant now?"

Roarke smiled. "I believe he would be appalled at the offer. I'll be downstairs."

She found it both endearing and amusing that the richest man on- or off-world gathered up the breakfast dishes and carried them out so the cat wouldn't lap at them.

As she contacted Reo, she made her way to her office so she could pace there. So she could study her board yet again as she and Reo talked.

She got more coffee, circled her board, contacted Peabody.

They'd want this meeting quickly, in her judgment. Get those wheels turning. While she waited for the go from command, she tagged Jenkinson.

> In the field, eta unknown. Cover things.

His reply came quickly, and was as colorful as one of his ties.

> Some fucked-up fucker tried to stab you in the fucking back? Tried to put a fucking hole in you on the fucking street?

> I don't have any extra holes in me, and they had to shovel up what was left of him off that fucking street. Cover things, Detective Sergeant. Briefing, full available squad, when I'm back in the house.

> Fuck the fucking all. You got it, Loo.

Imagining Whitney and the prosecuting attorney hammering out some details, she headed downstairs as Summerset headed up.

"I understand you may have some issues with my active participation in this matter. I would like to say something. You once asked me to remove that woman from this house."

"After I knocked her ass out."

"Yes. I was more than pleased to do so. She hurt him, and that would have been enough for me. Whether or not he deserved your fist in his face at that time is debatable, though I can certainly see your side of it. But we're now, now, where she's doing all she can to hurt him again. More, she'd destroy him if she could. She would have if the attempt on your life had succeeded. If anything I do helps you put her away, I'll find that very satisfying."

"And that has to be enough for me."

"Good." He looked down at the cat. "Now Galahad and I have work to do." He started up again, paused. "At that time you told me to get that trash out of your house. Now I'm saying to you, get that trash out of our lives."

"That's exactly what I'm going to do."

She went down to where Roarke waited. He'd tossed on the black leather jacket, and she imagined he'd tucked in a weapon somewhere.

She wouldn't ask.

"We should have more data on the finances shortly."

"Every bit helps." Her 'link signaled. "Commander."

"You're go for the meeting. Reo is speaking to Wenn now. She'll give you the location."

"Yes, sir. We're getting closer on the sources for the payments to Delaney. We'll see if she confirms."

"And for the payments to Timothy Kruger?"

"Also close. Commander, I'll brief my division on my return, and begin preparations for a raid operation on the auction if, as I believe, it will take place in New York."

"I'll attend. Keep me updated."

She pocketed her 'link. "Now we wait."

"We'll wait outside. It's a lovely morning."

As they stepped out, he took her hand. They stood a moment, looking out over the lawn, at the leaves fluttering in the light breeze.

"You want to get moving, I know, get this done. But since we have to wait, we may as well enjoy where we are, what we have."

He kissed her fingers. "The family's coming for Thanksgiving, and Brian as well. I thought we might ask Crack and Ro again this year, Louise and Charles."

"Yeah, sure."

"And Richard and Catherine, the children. It means quite a bit to Nixie to have that time with you."

"She tags me once in a while."

"Yes, I know. You're a hero to her. Doing your job, yes," he said before Eve could, "but you kept your word to her, and put the people who slaughtered her family in prison. Even a young girl knows not everyone keeps their word."

Both their 'links signaled.

"Summerset," Roarke said.

"Reo."

Eve moved off a few paces.

When she turned back, Roarke slid his 'link in his pocket.

"You have an address."

"Yeah, Wenn's son's penthouse on the Upper East. I'll program it, you drive. Summerset?"

"Since you won't want all the tech, I'll bottom line it."

He got behind the wheel.

"It's clear someone else is good at their work. Though she covered it very well, and very quickly, an inactive Zip account was activated, then shut down again yesterday. A deposit of exactly fifty thousand was made in cash."

"Cash."

"Cash, yes, into this inactive account, then wired to various other financial institutions in various locations. It bounced around over the course of a few hours. The seventeen-five was wired to Timothy Kruger's account, and the remainder moved about a bit more, and now sits in that temporary account, where, I suspect, it will be withdrawn, in cash, when the bank opens today."

"You've got the bank?"

"That's right."

"I need it. I'm going to have a couple of soft-clothes detectives surveil. I want her going in—or her rep going in—pulling it out. It'll be a nice bump when we bust her."

"Why wouldn't she simply hand Kruger the cash?"

"She'd have had to deal with him directly. A lowlife."

As they'd spoken, she'd done a run on Wenn's son.

"Stephen Wenn, age thirty-three, an associate in his father's firm. Got a twin sister, Rachel, who lives in Savannah, where she relocated six years ago and lives, with her husband and their two kids, right next-fucking-door to Delaney."

"The world can be very small."

"The sister practices law down there through Legal Aid, the husband's a doctor. Internist. So Delaney meets the son on one of his visits, maybe Wenn, too. She's in trouble, that's who she taps. If that's who picked her up from the hotel Saturday, they waited to pull this lever."

"You'll find out why."

"Did she contact Magdelana, the broker, Joy Barrister? Any of them?"

"If I were in her position," Roarke told her, "that would be a firm no."

He pulled into the underground parking at a tower of silver and shimmering blue and straight into a reserved slot.

"It's yours, isn't it? This place."

"The younger Wenn's penthouse has some stunning views."

He took her hand again as they walked to the elevator. Inside the car, he swiped a card.

"Express," he told her. "We'll go straight to the penthouse foyer."

"You leave me nothing to bitch about."

"My fondest wish come true."

The car ran smooth and quiet, had silvered walls, and carried a scent both pleasant and fragile.

It opened into a foyer with a black-on-white mural of the New York skyline running over the walls and doors that gave the feeling of standing in the center of the island of Manhattan. The occupant had added floating benches on either side, which worked, Eve thought, as they did their floating over the East River and the Hudson.

Eve pressed the buzzer.

The younger Wenn answered promptly. Though he wore it longer, just over the collar of his navy pin-striped suit jacket, he had his father's dark hair, minus the silvering. His eyes were of a quieter green.

He extended a hand to Eve, then to Roarke.

"Stephen Wenn. Thank you for coming."

He led them into a huge living area with one of the stunning views. Through another floor-to-ceiling wall of glass, a generous terrace spread.

He'd furnished it to suit the size, including a baby grand in glossy black, low-slung sofas, high-backed chairs in shades and patterns of gray and black. In contrast, his art ran to the big, bold, and splashy.

Two people rose from one of the sofas, the lawyer and the client. Wenn had gone all dignity in slate gray, navy-and-maroon-striped tie, polished wingtips. His client wore a Yale sweatshirt that dwarfed her, and Eve deduced she'd borrowed it from her host.

She'd paired it with black jeans and kicks—which Eve assumed she'd wear in the course of her work.

She had her hands—ringless, slim, long-fingered—clasped together. That was nerves, but the look she shot Roarke was pure, naked admiration.

"Lieutenant Dallas, Robert Wenn." He walked over to shake her hand. "Roarke, isn't it?"

"It is."

"As consultant," Eve put in.

"Sorry, excuse me." Coastal Georgia glided slow and easy through the words. "Steve, Rob, could I have a minute? Could I have the room for just a minute?"

"Jenna."

"I know." She held up both her hands to her lawyer. "You don't have to worry. I'd just like a minute."

"Would you like coffee?" Stephen put a hand on Jenna's shoulder—protective, affectionate—as he spoke to Roarke and Eve. "Dad, give me a hand with the coffee."

He nodded, gave Jenna a warning look, then walked out of the living area with his son.

"First, I want to thank you, Lieutenant Dallas, for giving me a chance to explain things. But I have to—" She took Roarke's hand in both of hers. "You're the best that ever was."

"If that were true, you'd have no reason to say so."

She just beamed at him. "You hear things, and we have some mutual acquaintances. I . . . You gave it up. This has me seriously thinking it's time for me to do that. But how did you do it? How did you just walk away?"

"If I were to walk away from something I could be considered the best at, it would be because I no longer needed it in the same way, and needed something else more. And then, I fell for a cop. A good, smart cop with integrity and compassion."

She glanced at Eve. "That's what I hear."

"Even the what I needed more paled next to that. She knows my truth. Tell her yours."

"I'm going to." She looked at Eve with direct blue eyes. "I swear by all the gods and goddesses, I'm going to."

The buzzer sounded again.

"Looks like you're about to get started on that," Eve said.

Chapter Nineteen

Reo and Peabody arrived together. Hands were shaken, introductions made, seats taken, and coffee served.

Reo, in her no-nonsense gunmetal-gray suit, her fluff of blond hair tamed in a roll, took a tablet out of her briefcase, then glanced at Eve.

"Record on. Reo, APA Cher, Dallas, Lieutenant Eve, Peabody, Detective Delia, expert consultant Roarke meeting with Delaney, Jenna Lynn, and her counsels Wenn, Robert, Wenn Stephen."

"Ms. Delaney—"

"Jenna, please. Just Jenna. I can hear we're from the same part of the world."

"Yes. Jenna, your counsel and I have spoken, and I'm aware he has given you the terms of this agreement. But we are now on record, and I will explain those terms for you again, on the record. If you have information that can and does lead to the identification of the person or persons responsible for the murder of Nathan Barrister, if you have information that can and does lead to the recovery of the items taken from

Barrister House, I'm authorized to offer you immunity for any charges related to the theft of those items. If you're not truthful, if your information proves false, the immunity will be invalidated."

"I understand."

"Do you also understand that when a death occurs during the commission of a felony, those who participated in the commission of that crime can be held responsible for that death?"

"Yes. It's why I'm here."

Reo took a tablet out of her briefcase, handed it to Wenn. "You'll want to read the agreement before instructing your client to sign it."

"I'm going to sign it. I'm going to tell you everything I know."

"You'll just wait on that, Jenna," Wenn said, and read. He nodded as he read, then handed it to Jenna.

"Thank God," she murmured as she swiped her signature.

Wenn took it back, signed, handed it to Reo. Once she'd signed, she tapped. "I'm sending you a copy, Mr. Wenn, and a second for your client."

Once done, Reo set the tablet aside. "At this point I'd like Lieutenant Dallas to read you your rights and start the interview."

"Jenna Lynn Delaney, you have the right to remain silent."

After reciting the Revised Miranda, Eve asked Jenna if she understood her rights, and further understood waiving certain rights in conjunction with the agreement she'd just signed.

"Yes."

"Did you kill Nathan Barrister?"

"No, I did not."

"Did you enter Barrister House last Friday evening after circumventing the security system?"

"Yes."

"Did you enter by a window, access the vault in the room Nathan Barrister used as a home office?"

"Yes."

"Did you remove anything from that vault?"

"I removed the Royal Suite, which included a necklace, a bracelet, a ring, a pair of earrings, and a tiara, emeralds, diamonds set in platinum."

"Why did you only remove those items?"

"Those were my instructions."

"Who instructed you?"

"James Mulligan—someone I knew by reputation—and she went by Genevieve Delecroix, and spoke flawless French and Italian. But as I'm not an idiot, and no matter how much money someone waves at me, I don't go in blind, I took time to find out who she was. Magdelana Percell. He's a broker—retired—a kind of liaison between people who want something that's not theirs and people who can get it."

She paused, reached for the soft drink Stephen had brought her in lieu of coffee. "Can I go to the start, work forward?"

"All right."

"Mulligan contacted me, offered to fly me to Italy—Sorrento—to discuss a major job with a major payoff. Either way I'd get a few days in Italy on his dime. It was his villa—I checked that, too. Really lovely spot, and that's where I met her."

"Magdelana Percell."

"Yes. She was clearly in charge. That's my opinion, but I'm a good judge. He's smitten, you know? But regardless, they offered the job. An in-and-out, no muss, no fuss. I probably wouldn't have taken it, but then they told me the target. It's legendary. Whoever took it the first time? A genius. I was sort of disappointed I wouldn't have to be, but the prospect of holding all that? I couldn't say no."

"Why wouldn't you have to be a genius?"

"They already had the security system, the location of the vault. They had the damn combination."

She blew out a breath. "You know how they say don't look a gift horse in the mouth?"

"Why do they say that? Who wants to look in a horse's mouth?"

"I don't know, but I should have. It was too good to be true. They offered me twenty, and I pushed for fifty and got it. Fifty million dollars and a chance to hold the Royal Suite. Fifteen when I take the job, another fifteen when I open the vault, send them a photo, and the rest on authentication. I make a good living, but nothing like fifty for one job, and one I barely have to prep for."

She rubbed her hands on the thighs of her jeans. "Palms are sweaty." She blew out air. "Anyway. I went from the villa to New York, to look things over. The security system? Old, needed updates. I bought some fancy flowers, boosted a delivery truck, and got access to the grounds, got a look at the entrance and the butler guy. Everything was just the way they'd said it would be."

She shrugged, drank some more. "So I hung out with Steve." Her eyes widened. "He didn't know. None of it. About this, about what I do. He didn't know, or Rob or Rachel and her family. I swear."

"I'm not interested in jamming them up."

"Okay, good. I went home, did my prep, waited for the go. I really didn't need much time. Honestly, I could probably have gotten in before I left New York, but I like to take time, practice, consider contingencies, Plans B, C, and D."

"Give me an example of Plan B."

"Run like hell. Lieutenant—everybody—I steal things. That makes me a bad guy, but I've never hurt anyone. I don't carry a weapon, and nothing I take is worth more than a person. Not to me. Not ever."

Closing her eyes, she took a breath.

"I got the go, so they flew me back to New York. I was set to proceed, Saturday night."

"Friday," Eve corrected.

"No, see, I was supposed to move on Saturday, but they bumped it up a day to Friday night, last minute. I was kind of irked because there was a big gala at the hotel I was going to crash, but a job's a job."

"Who bumped it up?"

"She did, Magdelana. So I went in a night early."

"At what time did you jam the security?"

"Twelve-seventeen. Then you take a solid minute to be sure, then through the gates. I had the window open in a couple minutes, maybe less. Then you take a minute again, you listen, you feel. When I knew I was clear, I opened the panel, as instructed, opened the vault. An old beauty. I'd have liked to crack it my way, but as instructed. And holy Jesus, all that inside. Just beyond."

For a moment, in memory, Eve supposed, her eyes shined like stars.

"I might've swayed for a minute because wow. I probably drooled some. Then I held that necklace in my hands."

She glanced at Roarke. Eve knew something passed between them, but it didn't show.

"Then the earrings, the bracelet, the ring, the tiara. I bagged each piece up, and I was out and gone."

"You left the vault open, but closed the window."

"As instructed. It bothered me to be sloppy, but those were my instructions."

"What time did you reengage the security?"

"Twelve-forty-two. In and out, and in and out clean. I swear it. I don't know why they killed that man. I don't know why they set me up for it. But I got out clean. I was to meet the authenticator at one-thirty."

"Where?"

"Some warehouse downtown. I've got the address. I went back to my hotel and changed out of my work clothes, then I left my room, walked a few blocks, took a cab downtown. I met the authenticator and the security. Security guy let me in. The authenticator went over each piece, gem by gem. Careful, thorough. Took about an hour. A little more, I guess."

"Name."

"He didn't give it, I didn't ask. Look, he was an old guy, probably has great-grandkids. I don't want to put him in the sling. The security guy? I didn't get a good feeling, so I'll draw you a picture—or I'll describe him so somebody can. He's the one who locked them up in a case and took them away. It was about three-thirty, I guess, when I got back to my hotel. I had to come down some, settle, so maybe five before I could get to sleep. I slept most of Saturday. I got up, ordered some food—including a bottle of champagne. I took a shower, and I turned on the screen while I ate. Watched some silly vid, relaxed.

"Then I switched to check the media reports, and that's when I found out about Nathan Barrister. I panicked. I don't panic, but I panicked. I was going to run, but . . . I couldn't. Finally, I called Steve. I just told him I was in trouble, I needed a place to lie low, to think. And he came and picked me up."

She looked down at her hands. "I can be sorry I waited so long, and I am. But I was scared, really scared. Too scared to think straight, then I was angry, so fucking angry at what they'd done—I looked him up, Nathan Barrister. A wife, kids, a good life. I thought about that, and about how they wanted to hang that on me even if I poofed. And I couldn't live with it.

"I told Steve everything, and then Rob when he came, when Steve asked him to come."

She looked up again. "I don't want to go in a cage, and I'm not sorry for doing whatever I can not to. But if I do, it won't be for something I didn't do. Would never do. I didn't kill Nathan Barrister."

"I know that," Eve said simply.

"You believe me?"

"I already knew you didn't kill him. You've now verified. We've already gathered most of the information you've just given."

"But . . . It's good info, and I gave it willingly. I don't—"

"There are a couple of pieces we didn't have, and some of the verification helps considerably." She shifted to Reo. "It's good information and corroboration."

"So the immunity holds?"

At Reo's nod, Eve said, "It holds. My advice, since you got this free pass? Find another line of work, because you won't get another one."

"Yeah, that's what I've been thinking."

"Think harder. Now, let's go over a few points."

"First? Ah, the Interpol thing."

"I'll handle it. It'll be easier to handle if you know anything about the auction."

Now Jenna smiled. "I'm not supposed to. Being as I'm not a trusting sort of person, I laid a couple of bugs in the villa. There had to be an auction if they wanted to make anything, and let me tell you, the woman, she's all about making it. I didn't like her one bit."

Points for you, Eve thought.

"New York, that's the plan. I can't tell you where, don't know if they'd decided at that point, but she insisted on New York. He wanted Europe, but she's the type most men don't say no to. I can sure as hell describe her for you."

"No need."

"I heard you were good. Anyway, big splash. She wanted that. Elegant, luxurious, plenty of security, but discreet so it doesn't bump too hard against the elegance. She wanted to have it all planned out before the heist, so they could turn it over fast. I know she wanted to set an entrance fee. A cool five mil just to attend. Keep it small, exclusive. Top it off at two dozen at the most.

"She ran that show, too. 'Leave it to me, lover.' She talked on the 'link to somebody a few times. Not a man—different tone. More businesslike. Ah, she wanted the next payment, said things were falling into place, and she'd certainly make sure that it was absolutely clear so the person on the 'link could do what she needed to do."

"Did she say what that was?"

"Not exactly, but I heard her say something, sort of annoyed, about him not being her problem when they'd done their part. That the other woman would have what she wanted. I think now? The 'him' was Nathan Barrister. I didn't know, I swear it. I'd never have taken the job if I'd known. Somebody wanted him dead, Lieutenant. The bitch in Sorrento? She wouldn't give a shit one way or the other. She just wanted the emeralds, and what they'd bring her. I heard her talking to the broker once, and she said something like joy was an easy mark, and now she'd have payback and a payday in one big, shiny package."

"'Joy was an easy mark'?"

"Yeah, like I said, all she wants is the money—that's what makes her happy. You know, brings the joy."

"Right." Eve took out her 'link, scrolled, then turned it to Jenna. "Do you recognize this woman?"

"That's her! That's the bitch."

"Can you be more specific?"

"The Magdelana bitch in Sorrento who called herself Genevieve, and orchestrated this whole fucked-up mess."

"All right. The terms of the agreement require you to remain in New York. I'd advise you to stay right here."

"I'm not going anywhere. I want you to bag her. I want to know when you do."

"A few details. You used a jammer to shut down Barrister House security."

"Yeah. I figure she probably had the way in without that, but wanted the cops to see it different."

"Let's have it. And the device used on the electronic window lock."

Jenna slumped a little, let out a sigh. "Yeah. Fine. I'll go get them."

When she left the room, Wenn turned to Eve. "I assume you're satisfied Jenna has been truthful and forthcoming, as your investigation had already unearthed some of the details she's given you."

"That's correct."

"And she has provided more details as well as confirmed what you'd learned in the course of your investigation."

"Also correct."

"The PA's office is satisfied," Reo said.

Jenna brought in her tools, handed them to Eve. "It was such loose security, I only needed a mini. I want to say something. If I hadn't wanted to get some sleep, I'd have taken a red-eye back to Savannah. But I'd have heard about the murder at some point, and I'd have come back. I'd have come back to do just what I've done."

Eve passed the devices to Peabody. "I believe you."

"When you bag her, she'll roll on whoever did the murder."

"Yes, she will."

After a long, probing look, Jenna nodded. "But you won't give her immunity."

"Not in a thousand years. You played this smart, Jenna. Keep doing that. Stay put."

Peabody waited until they all rode down in the elevator.

"Whoa and a wow, and a bang, bang, boom!"

"Save the boom until we have the auction location."

"Dallas, Willowby says today for that. McNab's on board, and says Feeney says the same. They just need a few more nibbles."

Eve looked at Roarke.

"Yes."

"The immunity's going to hold," Reo put in, "whether or not you recover the emeralds. Wenn will make sure of it, but my boss is going to be a lot happier if you get them back, take down the rest."

"Then happiness is coming because that's just what we're going to do. And we're going to hand you Nathan Barrister's killer. Magdelana wasn't talking about happiness when she said Joy's an easy mark. Joy Barrister."

"Give me a motive."

"He'd been in her way all her life, taken first place. She wanted him gone."

Eve moved quickly through the garage.

"She didn't care about the vault, what was in it. She cared that their father left it all to her brother. All of it. She cared he left his son the bulk of his business, put him in charge. Not her, never her."

"Take the front, Peabody," Roarke said as Eve got behind the wheel.

"Killing him doesn't change any of that," Reo pointed out.

"The widow isn't going to take charge of Zip. She'll lean on her sister-in-law there. And all that stuff her father collected over the years? Her brother's not getting the credit for turning it in. Hell no. She'll get it."

"She must've hated him," Peabody murmured. "To do what she did, how she did it."

"That's exactly right."

Eve bulled her way through traffic as a way to vent her anger. "She hated him because her father favored him. Hated him because he had a solid marriage, a loving family. Hated him for living his happy life in the house where she'd grown up."

"She was an easy mark," Roarke agreed. "Magdelana would play on that hate, scrape the masking layers off it. And give her a way to take what she wanted."

"They met up, right here in New York last December. That's when it started."

"If so, we're talking premeditated on Joy Barrister and conspiracy to commit for Magdelana Percell."

"That's what I'm going to drop in your lap. And I meant that thousand years, Reo."

"I heard you. I'll update my boss from Central because I want to see how close you are to dropping this into our lap, and adding a whole bunch of emeralds along with it."

"Peabody, book a conference room. I need about an hour prior, then we're doing a full briefing. I'd like ten minutes with Mira in my office if she's free. I'll work around her schedule."

She flicked a glance in the rearview, saw that Roarke appeared absorbed in whatever he did on his PPC.

"All your detectives?" Peabody asked as she got to work.

"If someone's on a hot, they can skip and read the record. Have Uniform Carmichael pick half a dozen officers. Inform the commander. Put Lowenbaum on tap.

"When we get the time, date, location, we'll have an op in place, which we'll then refine to suit the venue. Bunch of filthy rich people bidding on these emeralds? They'll have their own security. The venue will have more security."

"And Abernathy?"

"Yeah, bring him in. Feeney pulls in who he wants from EDD."

"You don't think Joy Barrister will be at the auction."

"No, Reo, I don't. I just need to work out how and when we take her so I can drop her in your lap."

"She'll have the best legal team billions can buy."

"She's going to tell me how and why she killed her brother. I know how to play an easy mark, too. And she's going to roll right over on the others involved in the theft. I need a warrant for her condo. Search and seizure."

"How about some solid probable cause?"

"They moved up the break-in. Aileen Carville was due to leave for a weekend girls' trip at some spa with a couple of friends. They planned to go in on Saturday when she was gone, pretty much do what was done. But Nathan gets sick—and his wife would've canceled her plans. Move it up a night, when they're not sharing a bed."

"Solid speculation, but—"

"She paid an assassin to kill Eve," Roarke said it mildly as he worked. "I have the particulars on that. It seems that's enough to hang a warrant on."

"Give me those particulars and it's done."

"I'm betting she got the contact for the asshole who tried to stick me from Magdelana. I prove that? It puts Joy Barrister in for the hire, and Magdelana in for conspiracy to murder a police office."

"That is correct."

"I'm willing to use that as a lever, deal with them on it if—"

"The hell you say." Roarke snapped it out. "You bloody well won't."

"Neither of them are going to see the outside again, so—"

"No, bollocks to that."

"I find myself in agreement with the bollocks," Reo said, and Peabody chimed in.

"Add me to that. You could maybe deal with the fact a man died— their hire—in the commission of a felony, which they conspired to set up. So they don't do another twenty-five to life on that one.

"Anyway," she said before Eve could speak. "We've got the conference room, all are so informed. And Mira can actually give you that ten in about fifteen minutes, and will come to you."

"Good. Excellent fast work, Peabody." Eve pulled into Central's garage. "And a solid take on the rest. I can work with that."

She got out, moved fast again toward the elevator. "I can set you up with a desk, Reo."

"I have my spots."

"Peabody, set up the basics in the conference room. Roarke—"

"I'm for EDD, yes."

When the doors opened, she let out a huff of breath. "I know you can do it, and we're going to look the other way so you can do it. I don't want this damn elevator stopping on every floor."

Reo didn't bother to look away when Roarke swiped a card and the car started its upward climb.

"That's really handy. I end up taking the stairs and the glides about half the time. I'll be in the briefing," she told Eve. "And you'll have your search-and-seizure warrant shortly."

"Counting on it." When the elevator opened, she turned to Roarke. "Location, time."

"You'll have them. New York, likely somewhere on Long Island, and tonight."

"What?"

"A few more layers cleaned off on the drive downtown. We'll have exact before long, but plan around that."

She held the door open. "Tonight?"

"Tonight, yes. Give us that hour. I think we may have a great deal more to add to your briefing."

"Why didn't you— Never mind. Go."

She stepped out, let the doors close.

"Get us set up, Peabody."

"Check it."

"Get me that warrant, Reo."

She walked into the bullpen, deliberately turned away before she could so much as glimpse Jenkinson's tie.

"Unless we're under attack, I need an hour. Send Mira in whenever she gets here."

She went in, got coffee. Then she stood at her skinny window and started working in her head on logistics—needed the venue, the security, the blueprints—but the basics she could outline.

And timing.

She took a long drink. Somewhere, likely within the next twelve to eighteen hours, she'd have Magdelana in the box.

She didn't have the words to express just how much she looked forward to that.

Until then, Eve reminded herself, she needed to put that immense satisfaction aside. Because she needed to get her there first.

And she needed to bring Nathan Barrister's killer to justice.

She turned back to her board.

"Got a pretty good idea how to do it, all of it. Just need to refine it some."

Meanwhile.

She added Magdelana's sketch and her official ID shot to her board.

Stepped back, smiled.

She added James Mulligan, and had a glimmer of satisfaction.

Then she sat at her desk and started refining her pretty good idea.

Chapter Twenty

When Mira came in, wearing a deep green sheath and matching, sort of swingy jacket, Eve asked her to close the door.

"Of course."

"Take a seat. I have that tea you like."

"Something tells me I might want coffee for this."

"Take the desk chair. As you can see from the board, I have names and faces of the prime suspects in the murder, the collusion re the theft, the attempt to kill me."

Mira's soft blue eyes did a quick and thorough study. "You weren't hurt."

"No." She handed Mira coffee. "Primarily, I want to discuss the murder. Joy Barrister. We have linked her to a payment to the murder for hire, so we've got her there. No reason to try to take me out other than trying to screw with the investigation into her brother's murder and the theft."

"No reason to do that unless she was involved."

"Correct. For immunity, the thief has provided us with considerable information. She did so after she learned Barrister had been killed."

"And she's not responsible for his murder. That's something you believe."

"Yes, as does Reo. One of the keys? She was scheduled to break in on Saturday, when Aileen Carville would have been out of town. They moved it up to Friday, rescheduling after Nathan Barrister left work ill."

Mira scanned the board again, studying, Eve knew, both Joy and Nathan Barrister.

"A better plan," Mira concluded, "with Aileen Carville still in the house. A better plan, as it worked out that she, rather than his sister, discovered the body."

"A nice extra bonus for them. Joy Barrister knew her brother was unwell, and Aileen would be sleeping in the guest room. The opportunity to kill him, using the break-in as cover, was better that way. He's weak, groggy with cold meds, and yeah, the wife is still there."

"Yes. I read your report after you spoke to the estate attorney. She was, and likely had been, firmly in second place from the moment her brother was born. Add he gets the house and everything in it."

"Which includes the vault."

"Yes. He takes charge of the company, and with the majority share."

"Which, although she won't have a majority share even now, is going to be in her hands, under her control. It's not the money. She's always had money. It's the insult. It's never quite measuring up to her brother in her father's eyes. Add he had a long, happy, successful marriage. Two college-age daughters who loved him and have done well."

"The only way she could have what she felt entitled to, what had been denied her, was to remove her brother. From what we know of him, he was most likely kind to her, inclusive both personally and regarding the business."

"The way I see it, that just burned her ass even more."

Mira smiled a little. "I wouldn't disagree."

"She had the opportunity and the means, and sure didn't quibble about hiring a kill on a cop. I think she had motive."

"Clearly. With her brother gone, she's in charge, in control. His widow has her own business, his daughters are still in college. She will be Zip Global now. In addition, Eve, by killing his son, she not only pays her brother back, but their father."

"Kills the favorite, smears the old man's rep, and comes off the savior."

"And in her fear you were close to identifying her cohorts, she attempts to have you killed or severely injured." Mira finished her coffee. "While foolish, it also demonstrates her mindset. 'I've come this far, done this much, I won't be stopped now.'"

"If she thinks that, she's got a surprise coming."

"While I'm very glad you weren't hurt, the foolishness comes from her thinking removing you would have stopped the investigation. When, in fact, it would have accelerated it.

"In any case, I'm happy to observe when you bring her in for interview."

Mira set the mug aside, recrossed her legs.

"Let me add, I have read over Henry Barrister's medical records. He had progressive mixed dementia, and was moving from stage three to stage four. Misplacing things, forgetting names, confusion, increased difficulty completing tasks. He would have benefitted from memory care, but refused it."

"That fits with his behavior toward the end."

"But that's not really why you asked me to meet with you here, with the door shut."

"No. I'm asking if I can speak to you now as doctor/patient, or whatever it takes for what's said to stay in this room."

"You've only to ask. It's about the blonde. I know who she is. You're concerned about Roarke."

"She knows things. I need to, and I will, convince her she'll get nowhere with that. I believe I can, and I will, twist that around on her and away from him, if I need to. Hell, I'm going to need to. I need to take her down, but I'm not going to let Interpol or anyone use her to go after Roarke. I can't."

The thought of it burned in her belly like acid, twisted her heart into painful knots.

"I have to take her down or I don't deserve the badge. I can't let her take him with her, or I don't deserve him."

Mira's gaze stayed calm and steady. "Do you value my opinion?"

"Of course I do."

"You've proven time and again you deserve both. The fact it weighs on you cements that fact even more. She thinks she's a very clever woman. I see her as more cagey than clever. How did you end this with her last time?"

"I punched her in the face and had her tossed out of the house."

"Good for you. How did Roarke end it with her last time?"

"He banned her from any of his properties. Also had her tossed out of one in London. That's right before she came here this time, to Henry Barrister."

"Ah, see, cagey, but not so very clever. Do you believe in redemption?"

Eve hedged. "Specifically or in general?"

"A cop to the bone," Mira murmured. "Let's say specific in this case, because clearly you do. Roarke has more than redeemed himself for any past transgressions. There's no one who knows him who thinks otherwise. She doesn't know him. She knows a ghost, a shadow from the past. You'll do what you need to do. She won't best you. She didn't the last time, either."

"I fell apart for a while."

"And this time you won't." Mira rose, took Eve's face in her hands.

"She wants to shake you, so don't let her. Take control, and don't let it go. Hold on to your power, as a cop and as the woman Roarke loves. Make damn sure she sees it."

"Okay. Okay. Sorry to pull you up here, but—"

"Stop. Whatever conflict you're dealing with inside that complicated head of yours, stop that, too. You know what to do and how to do it."

"Yeah." She stuck her hands in her pockets. "I guess I do, and better get started on doing it."

"It should also remain in this room that I'm going to feel a great deal of personal satisfaction when you've done it. Let me know when you have them."

"I will. Thanks. Really."

"You're welcome. Really."

When Mira left, Eve turned back to her board. She looked at Magdelana, then at Joy Barrister. On the surface, she thought, the two women couldn't be more different.

But under the skin, so much the same.

"Yeah, I know what to do so both of you end up in cages."

When she'd worked out what she could with what she had, she went back out into the bullpen.

Today's tie was flaming red with a bunch of little black-suited ninjas in various martial arts poses. Some had nunchucks. Some had swords.

And she worried about her mental health, as she almost liked this one.

"I got something to say."

"Yeah, Jenkinson, I figured that."

He got to his feet, nodded to the bullpen at large. "Whoever hired that fucker to stick you? He's going fucking down."

"I believe you're using the wrong pronoun."

"Yeah?" Eyes sparking, he nodded again. "She's going fucking down."

"So say we all," Baxter called out from the other side of the bullpen.

So say we all echoed around the room.

"Appreciated. Briefing in ten on taking her, and those she conspired with to kill Nathan Barrister and put a hole in me, the fuck down."

"It should hurt," Santiago put in.

"When I brief you on who's going down, you'll understand it'll hurt. A lot."

When she turned to leave, the EDD team walked in with Callendar and McNab adding a shock of color even Jenkinson's tie couldn't compete with.

One glance at Feeney's face told the story.

"You got it."

"We got it."

"Cochran Estates, Long Island." As Willowby spoke, she sent the flirt eye in Trueheart's direction. Eve could feel his blush from ten feet away.

"Big wedding and event venue," Callendar put in. "If you've got pockets as deep as the Grand Canyon. Private shuttle strip's a convenient two-minute drive away."

"The shuttle strip and the estate are in blackout since yesterday, and through tomorrow."

"You figure it's tonight."

"Tonight, cocktails and hors d'oeuvres, musical entertainment at half-seven. Black-tie," Roarke continued. "There will be swag bags."

"Swag bags?"

"Attendees will receive a gift bag containing an exclusive, designed-for-the-event perfume, a pair of champagne flutes with emerald-green stems, and a bottle of Château Lafitte champagne."

"That's his brew." Feeney jerked a thumb at Roarke.

"It is, yes. The auction begins at nine, where they'll seed with a selection of other items. The main event's scheduled for eleven, following a short break where desserts are offered and the Royal Suite can be viewed through a shockproof glass case. The bidding floor is three hundred."

"That's million," McNab added.

"How the hell did you get all this? Swag bags?"

Roarke shrugged. "A bit of luck."

"Consultant Dreamcake calls it luck. I call it genius." Willowby beamed at him. "We were close, right on the edge of it. He tipped it over."

"Genius luck then. Conference room." She turned to Jenkinson. "Whitney, Lieutenant Lowenbaum, Reo. Contact and tell them we're starting in five."

She started out. "I need to see the venue, inside and out. Blueprints, security schematics. A rough idea of the number of attendees would be helpful."

"They sent out two dozen invites," Feeney told her as they walked. "Twenty-two said hell yeah. And they can bring the plus-one thing, and their own security—that's limited to two."

"That's maximum eighty-eight," Roarke said to save her the math. "You can expect half that many again including the auction holders' security, the servers—unless they're using droids there—musicians, and so on."

"This Cochran Estates. Wouldn't it have its own people?"

"They've been paid twelve million to turn over the estate for three days. The Royal Group—a handy shell company—booked it with a fifty percent deposit in March."

Eve frowned at Roarke. "I take it that's more than they'd usually make on an event."

"Midweek, yes. Their major take comes Friday to Sunday, though they do quite well otherwise. But for this, they had no outlay but the venue itself."

She paused at the conference room door. "Just curious. About how much are the bad guys shelling out to pull this off?"

"A hundred, a hundred and fifty million, and that already recouped, or nearly, with the entrance fees. Take you and your team out of the mix? They could expect to make a profit of triple their outlay. Likely more."

"Add bragging rights," Willowby said. "Pull it off? You've got a rep for doing the mega, doing it classy. Hey, Peabody. Whoa, mama! Cinnamon buns!"

"Jacko's. Roarke had them brought in. And I already had one. I couldn't help it."

"Who could, who would?" And Willowby aimed straight for them, with McNab and Callendar on her heels.

"Seriously?"

"Already well-earned," Roarke said.

"I ain't complaining." Feeney walked over and helped himself.

"How did you get lucky, genius?"

"I know someone—Brian—who knows someone who knows someone else who wasn't averse to a bribe, and who happened to have the means to send us a scan of the invitation. It's quite elegant."

"That works. That works really well."

"So we thought. Have a cinnamon roll."

She had half a cinnamon roll because Willowby had it right. Who could or would say no? But she wanted to keep herself light and ready.

As she ate, she studied the images of the venue easily found on the website. An elegant two-story brick with thick white columns flanking the entrance. Lots of tall windows.

Inside, the entrance hall, the ballroom—main event space—the anterooms, the bar area, main-level johns.

Up a sweep of stairs to the bedrooms, sitting rooms, bathrooms. She took note of entrances, exits, the grounds—a good-sized pond, plenty of trees, lots of parking, gardens, walkways.

An outdoor swimming pool, and pool house. Large patio area, several terraces. All of it gated—with a gatehouse at the main entrance to the estate.

As the team filtered in and descended like locusts on the rolls, on the coffee, she studied the blueprints.

Kitchen area, office areas, storage, security station, all below the main.

"Big place," she muttered.

"Yeah, about fifteen thousand square feet." Feeney took another hefty bite of his roll. "Was some bigwig's place back last century. They turned it into the fancy, high-dollar event space about fifty years ago."

He took a swig of coffee. "You know, kid, these people are arrogant sons of bitches, throwing a damn party with your cocktails and your canapés."

"Arrogance is part of the reason. Arrogance, ego, greed, and payback."

"You got who hired the one tried to put a hole in you?"

"Yeah, or I will. She's the easy part."

Abernathy arrived, shot Eve a hard look. "So much for cooperation."

"That's why we're here. I got the blonde's face and ID last night, got the call from the lawyer first thing this morning. Specifically for me and the prosecutor's office or no meet. I called for this briefing as soon as I had the information."

"And your prosecutor has tied Interpol's hands regarding the thief."

"Do you want the thief or the emeralds?"

"Both."

"She could've poofed, Abernathy. We might not have ever laid a finger on her. She learned about Barrister's murder, and she stood up. These people set her up for it, and she's helped us, in ways I'll soon relate, pinpoint who ran the show, who killed Barrister, and who hired some asshole to kill me on the street."

"I only heard about that attempt on you shortly ago. I'm very glad he didn't succeed, but—"

"There's no but. Everyone's going to get what they need. We've got the venue—and that's as of ten minutes ago."

"You have it?"

"Just, and we know it's tonight. Since I don't want to go over this a half dozen times, grab a pastry and take a seat."

"I know the blonde, Magdelana Percell, is a former associate of Roarke's."

She ignored the headache brewing at the base of her skull, and kept her gaze steady on his.

"That'll be part of this briefing. We're going to get the emeralds back, Inspector. You'll want to take the win."

"We'll see."

"Kind of a dick," Feeney commented.

"Yeah. A good cop, but kind of a dick."

Reo came in. "You've got your warrant. I'm getting one of those buns. Whitney and Tibble are right behind me."

Eve stepped toward the door. "Chief, Commander."

Tibble glanced past her to the conference table and the trays of rapidly depleted rolls. "You know how to hold a briefing, Lieutenant."

"Roarke's contribution. Please, help yourself. We're waiting on Lieutenant Lowenbaum."

"I eat one of those," Whitney speculated, "Anna's going to sniff it out. But I'm risking it." Then his eyes narrowed. "That's Cochran Estates."

"Yes, sir. That's the auction venue."

"I've been to events there. It's massive and it's well secured." He turned, scanned the room. "If you need more cops, you'll have them. Ryan, I assume you and your team can and will deal with that security."

"Happens it's one of Roarke's systems. Place like that pays for the best. We're working on it."

"Cochran Estates," Whitney muttered. "Arrogant sons of bitches."

Feeney just grinned into his coffee as Whitney walked away.

"And who likes taking down arrogant sons of bitches?"

"Oh," Eve said, "we do. We really fucking do."

Lowenbaum came at a fast clip. "Sorry, I got held up with . . . I know those buns. Those are Jacko's. Hot damn."

"Grab and sit. We're about ready."

She waited another minute, then stepped to the front of the room. "McNab, wipe the icing off your fingers and work the screen. Everybody sit, settle down. This will be a major operation, and the people we're taking down will have armed security. It's highly probable they'll be armed with illegal weapons. That means body armor and helmets.

"Before I lay out the op, backstory details. On Friday night, the Barrister House security was compromised, the vault in the home office opened, and the Royal Suite—McNab, bring it up—was removed."

"Pretty damn sweet," Baxter commented.

"The thief hired Robert Wenn, attorney, and arranged for immunity in exchange for pertinent information."

She held up a hand when the grumbles began.

"The thief did not kill Nathan Barrister during the break-in, something I'd already concluded, and the information provided confirmed my conclusion, and added details. My conclusion, supported by the evidence, the timing, the statements, is that these three people conspired to steal the Royal Suite, Magdelana Percell as coordinator, James Mulligan as broker, and Joy Barrister, the victim's sister, who provided the ways and means. And who used the cover of the break-in and theft to murder her brother, Nathan Barrister."

She noted Abernathy shifted in his seat, sat up even straighter now.

"Motive. I'll start with the blonde. Obviously primary motive is gaining a jewelry collection worth half a billion or more. But she has a side motive. Several years ago, she had a . . . romantic relationship with Roarke that didn't end well. About a year and a half ago, she came to New York and attempted to restart that relationship and was rebuffed. That didn't end well for her.

"For a number of years, she had a relationship with Henry Barrister, and returned to New York last December, stayed at Barrister House, during which time Henry Barrister is reported by numerous sources to have gone into cognitive decline. Mira has confirmed, through access to his medical records, that he had dementia.

"We believe, during that period, he showed Percell the vault and its contents. She had the combination, which she provided to the thief she and her partner hired. She targeted the Royal Suite specifically, and only that. And with her conspirators, set up the thief to take the rap for the murder."

She went through it all, point by point so even Abernathy looked mollified and intrigued.

"As for the attempt on me, the payment for that unsuccessful hit has been traced back to Joy Barrister."

"Bitch'll fucking pay."

"Yes, Detective Sergeant, she will. We have a search-and-seizure warrant for her condo, and will move on that at the appropriate time. We will then make an arrest, at the appropriate time. EDD, with Detective Willowby and Roarke's assistance, has worked around the clock to ascertain the time, date, and location of the auction to turn the emeralds. Without their efforts and skill, we wouldn't have that information, certainly not in time to move on it.

"Bring up the venue, Detective."

As he did, Eve turned to the screen.

"Cochran Estates, Long Island. There's a purpose here, too, as the coordinator wants it in New York, where it pulls me in, and Roarke. Regardless, the festivities, and they're elaborate, start tonight at seven-thirty with cocktails and hors d'oeuvres."

"Cocky, aren't they?" Detective Carmichael commented.

"Yeah, they are. Blueprints, McNab. And here's how we're going to castrate them."

Abernathy raised his hand. "I can have half a dozen agents experienced in this sort of situation brought in by four, latest."

"We'll take them, we'll use them."

"I'll add that once the operation is successfully completed, we will take possession of the Royal Suite, and take responsibility for its security and its return."

"All yours."

"Give me a moment to speak to my superior and have that process begun."

When he stepped out, she scanned the room. "Any comments, questions, remarks before I lay this out?"

"I got one for Reo. Are you going to step on these assholes, and hard, for taking the stab at the lieutenant?"

"Yes, Detective Sergeant, I am." With a wide, humorless smile, Reo put down one fashionable heel and ground it into the floor.

"Okay then." Now he glanced over at Roarke. "Can't much blame you for the blonde. She's a looker."

"She is, but can't begin to measure up to the lanky brunette who holds my heart."

"Man." Willowby fanned herself, then patted her heart. "Dreamcake express."

"Enough of that." Eve shoved her hands into her pockets. "Enough."

Abernathy came back—and none too soon—gave Eve the nod.

"Let's get started."

It took more than an hour to lay it out, assign teams, perfect the timing.

Then she took questions, considered some suggestions, some options, worked some of them in.

"That's it. Twenty-one hundred, in the garage for transportation. Anyone without Thin Shield, you're vested. Everyone wears a helmet. Dismissed. Peabody, hold a minute."

McNab pranced over on his rainbow airboots. "I know this is to-the-top important, and dangerous, but man, it's going to be fun."

"How do you figure the fun?"

"Dallas, come on. We're busting in on a bunch of mega rich in their fanciest duds. The type who've gotta think that money can buy them in or out of anything. And we're taking them down, the NYPSD's taking them down on Long freaking Island."

"A man died in the mix of this."

His green eyes hardened. "Yeah, and none of them give a rat's ass. We do. And taking down those rich assholes? Yeah, I'm getting some jollies out of it."

"Get them after. Peabody, find out—discreetly—Joy Barrister's location. I want to move on her place, but I'd rather she wasn't there when we do."

Despite the tie, she turned to Jenkinson. "You and Reineke, on the search with us."

"I'll tag along," Roarke said as he wandered over. "To deal with any e's as needed."

"Take the boy here to help with that," Feeney decided. "The rest of us will monitor for any change in the auction plans. And yeah." He nodded at Roarke. "Shuttle arrivals."

"Expect high-level legal team for Barrister." Reo stepped up. "Likely high-level sleazy for the other two. I'm on tap whenever you want to put them in Interview."

"I'll let you know."

"She's at work," Peabody told Eve, "but is about to leave for Barrister House. She plans to stay there for several more days. I said I contacted her, as we didn't want to disturb the vic's wife, but wanted any details on the memorial. It's day after tomorrow, and they're still working on those details."

"Good. Perfect. She's got a crew working on the place, but we can deal with that, if necessary. Let's get this done. I want to be back here to go over the whole thing again with Abernathy's team."

When they arrived at the lovely five-story building that had escaped the ravages of the Urban Wars, lobby security walked over.

Jenkinson grinned. "Hailey, you old bastard. Is this where you ended up?"

"Sure is. Sweet gig. I heard you made DS. They'll promote anybody these days."

"This is my lieutenant. Dallas, this is Detective Hailey, retired from the six-three."

"Loo. How's it going?"

"Not bad. Detective, we have a search warrant for Joy Barrister's apartment."

"Is that so?" His eyes changed, and she saw the cop in them. "I heard her brother got murdered. He was a nice guy. I gotta figure this pertains to that."

"You don't appear surprised it would."

"She's got a hard shell."

"Is anybody up there?"

"Like a beehive most days. Cabinet guys were here since about eight, doing the last of the kitchen install. They just left a couple minutes ago. Closet designer types later today. Got kitchen counters coming in, but that's tomorrow. Place is clear right now, as the other guys went for their lunch break. You can count on about an hour and a half. They take their time."

"Makes it easy. Maybe you could give us a heads-up if she decides to drop by and review the work."

"Count on it. I'm going to swipe the elevator for you, take you straight up. She's got the whole frigging fifth floor."

"Appreciate it."

They rode up in an elevator Eve assumed had been refitted and updated, though it maintained the look of old and classy.

They came out on five into what Eve supposed could be called the foyer area, though it stretched across the building from north to south with windows letting the light in on either side.

A trio of tall plants scooped up the light on the south side. A few chairs, a couple of long tables allowed someone to sit, though she couldn't think why they would.

A huge vase with an Asian pattern stood on one of the tables and held a mass of white flowers and spilling greenery.

"Record on. Lieutenant Dallas. Everybody, state your name for the record." When they had, she took out her master. "Entering the apartment of Joy Barrister on a search-and-seizure warrant. All records on," she ordered, and mastered in.

Jenkinson let out a low whistle.

Given the age of the building, she'd obviously had walls taken down to achieve the wide-open living area. More likely, Eve thought, the space had, at one time, been more than one unit.

While currently empty, the floors gleamed in a gray that nearly hit black, and the scent of fresh paint came off the white, white walls.

A chandelier made a waterfall of sparkling crystals.

"If the rest is like this," McNab commented, "this is going to be quick."

"Look for e's. Jenkinson, you and Reineke start that way. Peabody and I'll start this way."

She found a powder room, obviously remodeled, the main suite, empty. It had a large closet/dressing room still being finished, and a large bathroom.

"Still tiling in here," Peabody observed. "It's a lot of tile. I guess it's elegant, but strikes me as cold."

"It takes cold to bash your own brother's head in. Where's her closet safe? She'd have one."

"Maybe in storage like the rest of her stuff. It looks, to my eye, like they gutted this closet and started up a new design."

"You've got the eye."

Eve moved on, then angled her head at a locked door.

"Can't master through that kind of interior lock," Peabody pointed out.

"No, but I can pick it." She'd brought her lockpicks, as she'd thought she might want them.

She was still working on the lock when Roarke started toward her. She hissed at him.

"I've got this."

"I should hope so. We found the security hub. McNab's having a look at it."

"Any safe?"

"Not so far. The other side of the apartment is well under construction. They're doing a good job of it. There's a kitchen, a kind of morning room, formal dining, another powder room. A guest room with en suite. As there's no home office on that side, I'm assuming you're unlocking one."

"Yeah, that's my bet. And yes!"

She opened the door. Unlike the rest, Joy had kept it furnished, and had obviously decided not to include it in the remodel.

"Plenty of space. You can hit that desk unit, Roarke, and, Peabody, take the drawers in the desk. Little sitting area, but it looks like business in here. No fuss, no frills."

She opened a door. Storage and a mini-AC and friggie. Across the room, she tried a second door. Locked.

She turned to see Roarke smile at her, said, "No." And got out her picks again. It took her longer, she accepted that, but she damn well wanted to do it herself.

"Got a locked drawer here, too," Peabody told her.

"A lot of locks for a home office. Roarke, take care of that one."

She tried to ignore the fact he took care of that one while she still struggled.

"Clone 'link, locked," Peabody told her. "A small disc file, some cash, and how about a police-issue stunner?"

"How about that? Bag it all. We'll take it in."

And finally, she heard the lock give.

And there she found the safe. Floor to ceiling, as wide as the standard door.

"It's another vault."

"Not at all. A large safe," Roarke said from behind her. "But given the spacing, only about eighteen inches deep. That's a Crown safe, and that model? Hmm, twelve to fifteen years old."

"After her brother moved to Brooklyn. It's hers. Always been hers. Open it."

"Happy to."

McNab came in. "It's solid security and overkill for a building with— Hey, that's an old Crown."

"Not very old, really."

It took him less time to open the safe than it had for her to pick a lock. Deflating.

When he had, when he pulled the heavy door open, she let out a breath.

Chapter Twenty-One

Peabody said, "Gosh!"

"Is that real?" McNab asked. "Is that real money?"

"I don't think she'd lock up play money." Eve took out a stack. Hundreds, banded. "Two thousand."

"It's just full of stacks of money. And are those actually gold bars?" Peabody walked over to peer in. "Gold bars stacked up on the floor of the safe."

Jenkinson and Reineke came in. "Sorry, LT," Reineke began. "There's nothing— Holy shit! Talk about payday."

"That's a fucking lot of fucking money. This broad never heard of banks?"

"Banks keep records. Maybe she earned some of this," Eve considered. "But I'm betting she's been skimming for a few decades. Dipping her hands in the company till. CFO. It's an open field. Maybe her father kept some cash around. He's losing it, so why not take some, sock it away?"

"They're much the same, aren't they? Father and daughter." Crouching down, Roarke lifted one of the gold bars. "I'll wager this is real enough. He never appreciated how much she took after him, did he? Money being her weakness rather than women."

"How much do you figure's in there?" McNab wondered.

"I'd be surprised if it's less than a hundred million. Mixed denominations on the cash, but a lorry load of it."

"She could've just handed Kruger the cash," Eve said. "No record, no trail. But she didn't want to do it all face-to-face. I guess that was beneath her."

She stepped back. "Peabody, we're going to need to tap a forensic accountant to go over her books, Zip's books. Make that a team of accountants.

"We'll take what e's there are in so you can go through them at Central. We lock it all back up."

"Do you take her now?"

"No. We can't risk her finding a way to warn Magdelana, or Magdelana hearing about the arrest and going rabbit." Eve shoved her hands in her pockets. "As much as I'd love to bust her myself, the arrest and the auction op go off at the same time. I'll talk to Whitney about setting that up."

"Bring her in," Jenkinson said, "let her call her big-shot lawyer, let her stew till you're ready for her." He shot out a toothy smile. "She spends the night in holding."

"Yeah, that part's a real shame. Peabody, contact the commander's office, tell them I need a few minutes." Eve shoved the safe door shut. "Lock it up."

Back at Central, Eve went directly to Whitney's office, where the admin waved her straight through. He sat at his desk, and spoke into his 'link. "I'll get back to you. Lieutenant."

"I'm sorry to interrupt, but wanted to update you immediately on the results of the Joy Barrister search."

When he gestured to a chair, she resisted.

"It won't take long, sir. The apartment is largely empty as the remodeling's going on. However, her home office—securely locked—is not. We confiscated her desk unit, and the clone 'link, discs, police-issue stunner, and cash found in a locked desk drawer."

"EDD on the 'link and desk unit?"

"Yes, sir. The big one, Commander? Another locked door within the office concealed a large safe. We were able to open the safe. It's filled with cash, Commander. At a visual, we estimate about a hundred million, along with sixty-three one-kilo gold bars. Valued, the expert consultant estimates, between nine and ten million."

Whitney sat back. "You always think you've heard it all, but you never have and never will. She has over a hundred million in cash and gold in her home office safe?"

"Well, sir, it's a big safe. We'll need a forensic accountant team to go over her personal books and the business books."

"The expert consultant can't handle that? Joking, Dallas." He held up a hand. "All that wealth at her fingertips, and she skims and hoards. I'll start that process."

"After the arrest, sir."

"When are you picking her up?"

"I feel the risk, however small, of word of her arrest getting to Long Island isn't worth taking. I'd like her picked up at the same time we raid the auction. I'd request a pair of experienced detectives, as she will resist. I can brief them on the situation."

"You could do that. But I'll take care of it myself."

"Yes, sir. If I could have the names of the arresting officers when you select them."

"I said I'd take care of it. I'll make the bust personally."

For a second, maybe two, her mind went blank. "Sir?"

"Joy Barrister hired a hit on one of my cops. I'll make the collar, and I'll enjoy it. I believe Chief Tibble might enjoy going with me."

He sat forward again. "Joy Barrister murdered her brother, and her motive appears to be Daddy liked him best. She helped set up the break-in and theft to cover that murder. Over and above all of that? She hired a street thug to stab you in the back. You're valued, Lieutenant. The chief of police and I will make this arrest when you signal you're a go on the auction."

"Yes, sir. She'll lawyer up immediately."

His eyebrows lifted, with those dark cop's eyes beneath showing a hint of amusement. "Do you think I've forgotten how it's done, Lieutenant?"

"No, sir. I apologize for giving that impression. I want to say Aileen Carville won't believe it, but her oldest daughter, Chloe, will. If you drop some of the details during the arrest."

"And she'll help her mother deal with the shock, likely stop her from offering assistance, as in contacting the lawyer for her sister-in-law. All right."

"Buys just a little more time."

"Leave it to me. And you can leave it to me with some confidence."

"Complete confidence. I'll signal when it's a go. Thank you, Commander."

"In this case, I'm thanking you, Lieutenant. Like I said, I'm going to enjoy it."

As she left, she admitted, she'd have enjoyed it, too. But she had plenty to do before the op—and busting Magdelana? That went beyond enjoyment. It might even hit orgasmic.

While approaching the glides, Feeney tagged her.

"You want to come up to the lab."

"I've got to—"

"Come up to the lab," he said, and clicked off.

"Fine, fine, fine. But since I'm up here, it's down to the damn lab."

So she took the glides down to EDD, strode straight to the lab and in. Everything smelled like a fizzy. Candy sweet.

She noted they'd even dragged Roarke onto the fizzy team.

"We got into the clone out of the locked drawer. Conversations on it," Feeney added.

"It's pretty common to have conversations on a 'link."

"Conversations between Barrister and the blonde."

"Okay." Eve flicked a glance at Roarke, who stood silent, but she saw the ice in his eyes.

"We just started at the last convos. We'll work our way back, but you want to hear this one. Callendar, give us the playback when she contacts the blonde the first time yesterday."

And Magdelana's voice filled the room.

"Joy, sweetheart, you know you shouldn't contact me at this point."

"I'm on the clone, and I'm alone. She knows something, that Dallas creature. She was at Barrister House again, and those idiot servants told her about you."

"About me?"

"Enough about you—a young blonde he called Ms. Fancy—your visits to my father, so she's having a police artist come, work with them. And I don't like the way she looks at me. It's falling apart!"

"Calm down." Now Magdelana's voice turned hard, hard and cold. "Everything's going to be fine. It's gone exactly as we planned, hasn't it? You're now in charge of your family business, aren't you, and the thief's on the hook for your brother's tragic demise. She has no reason to look at you. Why is she looking for me, or a blond woman?"

"I don't know! How could I know? She has this idea my father told someone about the vault. And he did! He told you. And one of them might have seen us together when you were here. She's relentless, this policewoman. You need to call everything off and go away."

"I'm not going to do that, Joy. We've come too far. You got what you wanted, and I intend to get what I want and what I've invested in. There's a simple solution. I know someone in New York who can take care of this."

"Who? How?"

"Timothy Kruger, a professional. I'll give you his contact information. For a fee, he'll eliminate her."

"Elim—kill her?"

"She's a thorn in your side, isn't she? Pull out the thorn, Joy. With her out of the way, the entire thing bogs down. I'll get what I want, and the rest won't matter. No one will have any reason to look at you for your brother's death. Delaney will go into the wind, or, if necessary, we'll take care of her. It won't matter if anyone saw you with me. I was simply visiting Henry, that's all. And they'll never find me once this is done."

"I'll give you Tim Kruger's contact information."

"No. No, you set it up. You do that. I'm not speaking to a hired killer. You tell me his fee, where to wire the money, but I won't speak to him or meet with him."

Magdelana sighed. "Joy, you're so delicate. All right. I'll take care of it and get back to you. It shouldn't take long."

"That ties it all up nice and neat, doesn't it?" Eve said when the call ended.

"They both had video blocked, so we don't have that. But?" McNab lifted his fizzy like a champagne toast. "The voiceprints do the job."

"The blonde got back to her. Deposit of seventeen-five on fifty K, gave her where to wire it." Feeney pursed his lips. "No contact since."

"Magdelana's busy with auction prep. She did her part on it, and has other potatoes to fry."

"Fish," Roarke said, despite himself. "Fish to fry."

"Make it fish and chips. She's not listening for reports on some guy getting splatted by a cab. As for Barrister? She's probably waiting to hear the job's done."

"You could pick her up now, on this." McNab gestured again. "Hold on the murder."

"No, still a risk. Plus, it would spoil Whitney's fun. He plans to arrest her tonight, with Tibble."

Feeney let out a snort. "He'll get a charge out of that one. Okay, what we'll do is get you a transcript of the convos."

"Get me the audio, too. I want to hear it. Thanks."

She walked to the glass doors, looked at Roarke. "Walk and talk a minute."

When he stepped out with her, she started toward EDD. "You had a fizzy."

"They're oddly energizing."

She turned into the circus, then immediately into Feeney's office, and shut the door.

"I understand what you're feeling."

"Do you?"

"I understand what I'd be feeling if I heard a conversation involving plans to have you murdered, so yeah."

"She planted the seed. I expected she'd watered it, but not that she'd planted it. And not just to protect herself. There are other ways to throw a spanner in the works, and in the end she wanted us—or me—to know she'd done all this. She simply decided it was easier to have you killed, to have Joy Barrister pay for it. Gives her another one over on a wealthy woman and removes you all at once."

He lifted his hands, let them fall. "She didn't have this when I was with her. I know there are things about her I didn't see or want to. But not this, Eve. I wouldn't have missed or ignored this."

"People evolve or devolve. Stuff in them can, you know, calcify. She's focused on the emeralds and turning them in a big, splashy, billion-dollar way. Taking a slap at you? Big personal bonus. She planted that seed as much to get Barrister off her back and add a new lever as to take me out. Right now? She's not thinking about me. You, you're still in there, but she's not thinking about me."

"She will be."

"Oh, she will be. You good?"

"I'll be better when it's done."

"We'll get it done. I've got to get back. Don't OD on the fizzies."

"You can trust me there. Eve." He took both her hands, brought them to his lips. "I'm with you on this, and in your way. But I need something. I need, when it's done, to speak with her. I need to see her in a cage and speak with her. Only speak with her. Privately."

"All right. Let's go make it all happen." Because she felt he needed it, she leaned in, kissed him. "Go finish your fizzy and play with the geeks."

She went down, and when she turned into the bullpen, Jenkinson hailed her.

"Anybody gets dead the rest of the day, Whitney's got it covered."

"Okay. If and when Abernathy's team gets here, I want them in the conference room. I'll brief them. Anyone here needs a refresh, they can join in."

"We got it, boss."

Knowing the truth of that, she went into her office. Energizing or not, she went with coffee over a fizzy, then went over every step and stage, every action—expected or unexpected—every reaction, planned or unplanned.

Shut down the shuttle strip. Eyes and ears on the estate, circumvent security—alarms, cams, locks. Box them in. No way out. Deal with the guards, armed security.

Round them up, take them out.

The emeralds? Interpol's deal.

She studied the blueprints on her wall screen, hunting for any area she hadn't covered.

Then she contacted Nadine.

"You need to be alone so no one can hear me."

"One second. Hey, Shelley, give me a few minutes. Shut the door, would you? Thanks. What's going down?"

"I'm telling you because I know you'll hold it, hot as it is, until I say otherwise."

"Yes, you can know that."

"The NYPSD and Interpol, in a joint operation, will raid Cochran Estates on Long Island tonight, where the underground auction of the Royal Suite is taking place."

"Well, slap my ass and call me Sally."

"I'll get to your ass later, Sally. Our intel indicates twenty-two invitees, with or without plus-ones, will be in attendance. Heading the auction and responsible for the theft are James Mulligan, Irish national now based in Sorrento, and Magdelana Percell, also currently based, with Mulligan, in Sorrento. The joint operation expects to arrest all attendees and organizers. Interpol will take possession of the Royal Suite and expedite its return to the Tate in London."

"Give me a time."

"We expect to move in between twenty-three hundred and twenty-three-thirty. I'm not finished."

"Don't let me stop you."

"At the time of this joint operation on Long Island, other NYPSD officials will arrive at Barrister House and arrest Joy Barrister for the murder of Nathan Barrister, her brother—"

"Holy crap!"

"Not done. For accessory to the theft of the Royal Suite, and for conspiracy in murder for hire of a police officer. She is also under suspicion for embezzlement from Zip Global, the business her father founded and where she currently serves as CFO."

Nadine waited a beat. "Are you done now?"

"I think that's enough. You can get the rest as it comes. Needless to say, we can't have any Channel Seventy-Five drones or copters or vans within sight of the raid."

"Needless, no problem. She killed her brother for the emeralds?"

"No, she used that as cover to kill her brother because her father apparently liked or respected him more. We'll never actually know which. Try to keep it off the widow and his kids, Nadine. They've been through enough. I've gotta go."

"You know this is going to cost you another media conference."

"Yeah. Don't get me started."

When Abernathy arrived with his team, she took them all in the conference room to go over the details, assignments, steps, and stages once again.

She was back in her office, pacing, when Roarke came in.

"I finished briefing Abernathy's team. They looked solid to me."

"No doubt. We've time yet. Haven't eaten since morning, have you now?"

"I haven't had—"

"Time, you'll say, which you do now." He went to her AutoChef. "You can have what we e-geeks had earlier."

She caught the scent of the burger before he took it out. Since she found it hard to argue with a burger and fries, she didn't.

She picked up the tube of Pepsi he'd cracked for her, drank.

"We're set. Things go wrong, but we're set for that, too."

She bit into the burger, followed it up with a couple of fries.

"We'll be there early enough to get some of the auction play on record. That's almost as tasty as these fries."

"In her element. That I would have expected. The rest? The callousness of murder?" As she often did, he walked to her skinny window, looked out. "That I wouldn't have."

He turned back to Eve. "They're much alike, aren't they? Joy and Magdelana. Wanting and taking what they want, whatever the cost to others."

"I expect Mira will label them both sociopaths."

"There's an emptiness in that, isn't there? That lack of genuine feeling. Ah well, they can both cling to that emptiness in a cage soon enough."

"She'll try to run, won't she?"

"Oh, without question."

She smiled as she ate. "Good. I'm looking forward to that."

When the time came, she stood in the garage, counted heads, counted transpo. Weapons, protective gear.

"You know where to be and what to do. We're moving out."

She got in the EDD van with Roarke, Feeney, McNab, Callendar, Peabody, Willowby, Baxter, Trueheart, and two uniforms.

She contacted Whitney.

"Sir, we're leaving Central now."

"Chief Tibble and I are ready to roll on Joy Barrister at your go. Good hunting."

E-geeks spoke their e-speak along the way. Feeney cursed traffic, Willowby flirted with Trueheart. Eve just let her mind go blank, gave it a rest.

Then she checked the time.

"ETA, Feeney?"

"Give it fifteen."

"Officer Carmichael," she said into her mic.

"Lieutenant."

"Take your team to the shuttle strip. Detain anyone there, secure any shuttles. Shut it down. No incomings, no outgoings."

"Twenty to target, Lieutenant. Will relay when it's done."

McNab shifted to the controls and monitors. "Get you heat sources as soon as we're in position."

"Willowby, Callendar," Feeney said from the driver's seat. "You're eyes and ears with McNab. Roarke, you and me take security."

"I'm working on that."

"From here?"

"Just getting it laid out. We'll want a rolling surf, not a straight charge or winding snake."

"I need it locked when we're in," Eve reminded him.

"Yes, my associates and I discussed that. We can do it by remote."

"Everyone wants in," McNab said.

"We're in, we shut down the gates," Roarke said as he worked. "When all teams are inside the building, we lock the building. If the teams assigned outside require entrance, they signal, and we open for them.

"You're nearly close enough now, Feeney. Give us another quarter mile. There we are. Can you lock on from here, Ian?"

"Locking on, and . . . three, two, locked. Wow, lots of people. Main-level area. Another six, lower level—that's the kitchen area. No one above main level at this time."

"Give me a little room, Dreamcake. We gotta get Lieutenant Kick-Ass those eyes and ears. You wanding out, Callendar?"

"Wanding now, and wrapping, little push, and whoa! Adjusting volume," she said as voices boomed out. "Ha. Got your ears."

"Eyes coming, doing the triple, Roarke."

Still working, Roarke nodded at McNab. "You've got it."

"Tricky, sticky," Willowby muttered. "There's lower, and your six. Servers, looks like."

"Let's get a count if we can," Eve said.

"Another two coming down," McNab told her. "Eight, lower level."

"Got your main. And there's the crowd. Fancy. Count 'em, McCutie. I'm tripling to upstairs."

"Looks like, jeez, lotta movement. I'm saying eighty-couple in the main—the ballroom place."

Eve scanned the main, figured eighty-five, and didn't have any trouble finding Magdelana.

She stood, her hair a cascade, sparkling with tiny diamonds. She wore red, no surprise, that shimmered down her body like scarlet rain. It dipped low in front, left her back bare to the waist.

Diamonds swung like mini chandeliers at her ears, more nestled in her cleavage, sparkled at her wrists, on her fingers.

The dress slit up the left side to expose her leg to the thigh, and a pair of high, high, needle-thin red heels.

Try running in all that, Eve thought. Please try.

See how far you get.

She found the partner, too—slim, glossy brown hair, handsome and tanned in his tux. With a diamond-shaped emerald stickpin.

Eve contacted Whitney. "We're at the target, preparing to move, circumventing security. You're a go, sir."

"Copy that. Take them down, Dallas."

"First wave complete," Roarke announced. "Gate clear. Cams will hold steady as they are, no record, for twenty. Feeney?"

"Yeah, yeah, I see where we're going."

Officer Carmichael spoke in Eve's ear. "Shuttle strip in our control, sir."

"Hold there. Lowenbaum, take the gate. Team one, move in behind SWAT."

"Second wave complete. Alarms deactivated."

"Team two, move into position."

It took minutes more, and muttering from Roarke and Feeney, before

Roarke told her the third wave was complete. "All exterior cameras on hold."

Lowenbaum reported three guards taken down, and the exterior clear. "Teams three and four, into position."

Feeney punched a fist into his palm. "Got that bitch!"

"So you did." Roarke kept his eyes on his monitor. "One more . . ."

"Ladies and gentlemen." Magdelana's voice came through the speakers. "I hope you've enjoyed the evening so far. If you'd take your seats for the main event, I'd like to give you a brief history of tonight's star. The Royal Suite!"

"Locks down, surf complete. You're a go, Lieutenant."

"Then let's go. Moving now," she said to the rest of the teams.

Out of the van, she went through the opening of the gates, stayed low, moved fast. In the mansion, lights gleamed through the windows.

Abernathy caught up with her. "Two guards inside the front entrance."

"We've got it. Stunners on full." She crouched at the door, gave Peabody the nod. "Go now! Take the doors! Now!"

She went in low, took the guard on the right down. Peabody and McNab shot streams together to take the second.

And all hell broke loose as cops poured in every door. She heard shots fired, wasn't surprised, and kept going.

She saw Lowenbaum take out an armed guard, an Interpol agent and Jenkinson yet one more amid the screams and rushing feet.

"This is the police! Hands up, stay where you are."

She knocked down the woman who swung a studded evening bag as she ran, shrieking, then dodged the fist of a man who came behind her. And came up with her left in an uppercut that took him out.

She saw a woman faint, a man dive for cover as streams flew. She felt one ping off her helmet, and kept going.

Because she saw Magdelana run toward one of the side rooms.

It took her time to follow. She cuffed a man on the floor, and kept going. Disarmed another, sucked up his rabbit punch to her ribs before she restrained him.

She used the grapple to disengage her recorder.

When she broke in, Magdelana stood, bashing a chair against the glass exterior door. She'd managed a couple of cracks.

"You're going to want to put that down, put your hands up, turn around, and get down on your knees."

Magdelana turned, her face full of fury and fear. "Let me go. Let me go now, or I'll ruin him."

Her breath heaved, but her eyes stayed hard as the diamonds she wore.

"I'll destroy him, you, and everything he's built. You know I can. You know I will."

"No, you won't, because whatever you think you can do? It won't touch him. And I'll stuff it down your throat until you choke. Hands up, and on your goddamn knees."

"I know things about him you don't."

"No, you don't. He's a hell of a lot smarter than you. I bet that burns. Now, one more time, hands up, on your knees, or I'll put you on them. Just give me a reason."

She heaved the chair and charged.

Eve sidestepped the chair. She could've stunned her, had just enough time, just enough room. But . . .

"How about an encore?"

Putting all she had into it, Eve punched her, a sharp left jab to the face. And watched Magdelana's eyes roll back as she went down.

"Okay, McNab had a point. That was fun." She let out a breath. "You're done now. You're mine now."

After reengaging her recorder, Eve restrained her, adding another zip tie to secure her to the leg of the sofa.

She stood a moment, just one indulgent moment. Then Eve went back to help clean up the rest.

Chapter Twenty-Two

In the end, they had 112 individuals restrained, some receiving medical attention from stuns and other minor injuries. She'd personally used more than half the zip ties on her belt and both pairs of handcuffs she'd brought with her.

Since she'd come out of it with a handful of bruises, she counted it a very good trade.

She counted five officers—three of hers, two of Abernathy's—under medical for minor injuries, so yes, a good trade.

"Jenkinson, how's Reineke's foot?"

"He'll limp some a day or two, but the medic says no breaks. Lowenbaum's guy's good, and Trueheart? Well, he'll have a shiner and a sore jaw."

"Good. The blonde's in that room there. She should be conscious by now. I want her and the broker in separate vehicles for transport."

"We've got it. Willowby took a hit, illegal handgun from one of the security fuckers."

"What?" Willowby wasn't in her count. "Where is she?"

"Outside with the medicals. Just a graze, LT. Said she didn't even know it till the party was over."

"Start getting them loaded up. Coordinate with Abernathy on the foreign nationals. Peabody! Work with Jenkinson on the transport. Load the servers and catering staff separately. Baxter, work with Lowenbaum to secure the weapons for transport."

She went straight out, waving off questions. She scanned the medical vans and spotted Willowby sitting in the doorway of one, the left leg of her black baggies hiked up.

Roarke stood beside her while the MT tended to her wound.

"Hey, Dallas, I got shot! With a genuine freaking bullet. How often does that happen?"

"To me personally, twice. Three times, I guess, but that one hit the magic lining so it doesn't count."

"Sure it does, and wow! I'm going to let you hold that personal record between us. Shit! Stings."

"You didn't want the shot," the medical reminded her.

"Makes me goofy, and I'm feeling fine. Juiced! I might not toss these baggies. Could wear them as a fashion statement."

When she hissed again, Roarke took her hand.

"Take a blocker," Eve advised. "Avoid the goofy, cut the sting."

"Yeah, I can go with that. Anyway, we got them good."

"We sure as hell did. Take the blocker." She flicked a glance at Roarke. "We'll be a while. Any injuries?"

"Nothing to speak of."

"Me, either."

She stepped away to contact Whitney. "Commander, situation controlled. We have one hundred and twelve individuals for transport to Central. No fatalities, twenty minor injuries, including six officers, being treated on-site. Interpol has possession of the Royal Suite, as well as a few other items believed to be stolen goods."

"Good work, Lieutenant. Joy Barrister has been arrested, booked, and is in holding awaiting her legal representatives."

"Good work, Commander. It's going to take a few hours to mop this up, sort things out. I'd like to begin interviews with Barrister, the broker, and the blonde—in that order—in the morning."

"An excellent lineup."

The way he grinned, Eve deduced he was still riding on the arrest.

"You're in charge," he told her.

Since she was, she went back in to start mopping and sorting. Abernathy hailed her.

"How are your injured?" she asked him.

"Treated, and good to go. Yours?"

"Same."

"The Royal Suite is secured. We need you to open the shuttle strip. We'll transport it back to London from there."

"I'll take care of it."

"Lieutenant, the attendees, we'll call them. You can charge them."

"And I will."

"These are extremely wealthy individuals with connections in high places. It won't stick. Deportation, yes, criminal charges, no."

"It'll leave a smear. The international media's going to go batshit."

His lips twitched into a smile. "You have a good point on that."

"And anyone who deployed a weapon against your officers or mine, I'll make it stick."

"I applaud you for it, and for the success of this operation. You'll have our full cooperation. The catering staff?"

"I've got Carmichael and Santiago interviewing them now. Most likely, they'll be released. I need to bat cleanup here, Abernathy." At his blank look she translated. "Finish this up. I'll clear the shuttle strip. You deal with the paperwork on the emeralds."

Long before she returned to Central, Channel Seventy-Five broke the story of the raid, the recovery, and the arrest of Joy Barrister.

It didn't surprise her to find Kyung waiting in the bullpen, and wearing one of his well-tailored liaison suits even at that hour of the morning.

"Lieutenant, congratulations. Major congratulations."

"And my reward is a media conference."

"I'm afraid so. The list of those arrested at Cochran Estates has leaked. Many are well-known names. So is, of course, Joy Barrister. You deserve better than addressing the media, and at eight A.M. I realize that only gives you a few hours at best. I doubt it's necessary, given your connections, but I'd be happy to arrange a hotel."

"I've got work. I'll take a booster. Don't worry about it," she said before he could speak. "But I'm out by nine. I'm interviewing the main players, so I'm out by nine."

"If not before. I'll make sure of it."

She nodded, stepped back as those not already in the bullpen filtered in.

"Listen up! We're going to interview the rich assholes we collared tonight. Teams of two. Make it sweaty. None of them are getting more than a slap on the wrist, if that, but make it sweaty. The DOJ will take it from there. We're going to interview those with illegal weapons, any who deployed weapons of any kind, any who obstructed officers. Make that sweatier.

"Trueheart, get an ice pack on that eye, and everyone's cleared for a departmentally approved booster. You did damn good work tonight. Commendations will be forthcoming." She paused. "So will pizza."

She went into her office, where Roarke waited with coffee, a candy bar, and a booster. "Take the booster first, since you won't be leaving this morning."

She popped the booster, gulped coffee. "I can't. This is going to take hours, plus media deal at oh-eight hundred. You've done more than your share. Go home, get some sleep."

"What I will do is have Summerset send or bring us both a change of clothes. I'm in this until it's done."

"All right, but you could catch a couple hours in the crib."

"Not in this lifetime. I've seen the crib. I'll be in EDD, helping close this down."

"In that case, I just promised pizza."

He smiled, kissed the faint bruise on her jaw. "I'll take care of that."

"Thanks. You ought to know, I punched her in the face again."

He lifted his brows, brushed a finger over the bruise. "Did she give you that?"

"Give me a break. She threw a chair at me. Missed. She won't get anywhere trying to tangle you up. You have to trust me there."

"I trust no one more. You trust me when I promise you, she's nothing to tangle me in. Do what you need to do to put her away."

"I will. Before you go, do you know any of those fuckers we collared tonight?"

"I do, yes, know a few of those fuckers. Know of all."

"Then give me a quick rundown."

When he had, she passed the information to her team.

She did her interviews, and left it to her chief and her commander to deal with the attorney general and the lawyers from the Department of Justice.

She ate some pizza, and thought longingly about a shower, a long, hot shower.

Then Summerset came into her office.

"Your change of clothes, Lieutenant. Roarke was very specific."

"Yeah, I bet. Appreciate it."

"Congratulations on what you accomplished. Is it appropriate to tell me if you've dealt with her yet?"

She figured, in this case, he had a right.

"I punched her in the face again, mainly because I wanted to, and it'll hurt longer than a quick stun."

"I'm pleased to hear it."

"But her interview is later this morning. If you're worried, don't be. She's going away, and she won't take Roarke down."

"I hope her cage is small and cold and dark."

With that, he walked out.

She grabbed a shower, and felt human. Roarke had gone with leather—charcoal-gray trousers and jacket, slate-gray vest with some navy running through it—she supposed that explained the short-sleeved navy tee. Thick soled, above the ankle charcoal boots with navy laces.

She pulled out a memo cube, listened to Summerset's voice.

Roarke suggests dispensing with the jacket for the primary interviews, and wearing the Giant's Tear outside your shirt.

He would, she thought, but she saw the purpose in it.

She dressed, dealt with the media conference. And as the volley of questions never stopped, gave full credit to Kyung when he stepped up and announced Lieutenant Dallas had duties.

As she left, she pulled out her comm. "Bring Barrister to Interview. I have A booked."

Abernathy rushed after her. "Lieutenant, I need a moment, in your office."

"Make it quick. Start now."

"Then I'll begin by asking if your duties include interviewing Magdelana Percell."

"They do. Barrister, the broker, then her."

"As she was very likely the instigator of it all, I assumed you'd take her first. I realize you have personal interests you would want to protect—"

Still on the glide, she whipped toward him.

"Don't start that bullshit with me. Barrister is my priority because she murdered her brother in my city. And when I break her, she'll add weight, she'll add details I can use against the broker and the blonde. I take the broker next because when I break him, I get more."

She turned into Homicide, waved off Baxter, and strode into her office. Shut the door.

"I take her last because I'll have everything I can squeeze out of the other two, because yes, she started this ball rolling. I know what the fuck I'm doing."

He held up both hands. "I apologize. I apologize," he repeated. "What you say makes good sense. I only brought it up because I want to assure you, you'll have no issues from me. Roarke will have no issues from me now or in the future. I believe he saved my life last night."

"Is that so? He didn't mention it."

"He called out a warning, and even before I could turn, he fired on the man who intended to fire on me. I don't and won't forget that. And I've seen, clearly, he has given his time, his skills, taken considerable personal risk as consultant for this department. The file on him is closed. I give you my word on it."

"I'll take your word on it."

"Let me also add, we'll file charges against the three you're about to interview. Should they ever be released from your system, they'll find themselves in ours."

"Good to know. But they won't get out."

"If we don't speak again before I leave, it's been, as always, an experience working with you."

"Same," she said, and shook his extended hand.

When he left, she realized the weight that dropped off her had been heavier than she'd admitted.

She rolled her shoulders clear, then walked out to meet Peabody and Reo.

"Busy, busy," Reo said. "Barrister's got Jefferson Pinkney as her primary attorney. She actually tried for Robert Wenn." Reo grinned. "Refused. Not that Pinkney's easy."

"It won't matter. We've got her. No deals, Reo."

"Even if I wanted to, I couldn't. The media would swallow the PA whole after all this. No deals other than on- or off-planet. We won't offer on unless we need that push."

"You won't. You up for it, Peabody?"

"Got a twenty-minute catnap at my desk, popped my boost, had pizza and two tubes of Pepsi. I'm way up for it."

Eve opened the door to Interview A.

"Record on. Dallas, Lieutenant Eve, Peabody, Detective Delia, Reo, APA Cher, entering Interview with Joy Barrister and her legal counsel Jefferson Pinkney."

Pinkney had let his hair go snow-white. It was a good look against his deep brown skin. His eyes were a cool blue, his suit a perfectly cut gray worn with a tie of navy and maroon.

"For the record," he began, "we object strenuously to this absurdity. To my client being dragged from her family home in the middle of the night and incarcerated. Her brother, whom she grieves for, was clearly murdered during a burglary. It appears—"

"Before you roll out any more and waste all of our time, Detective Peabody has something for you and your client to listen to. Playback, Detective."

"Playback from the clone 'link taken from the desk in Joy Barrister's home office. Time stamp included."

Magdelana's voice came through.

> *Joy, sweetheart, you know you shouldn't contact me at this point.*

And when Joy's voice came through, she turned to her lawyer. "How can they do this? Go into my home! Make this stop."

"Duly executed warrant." Reo opened a file, took out a hard copy. "Search and seizure."

"This was a private conversation."

"Not anymore," Eve said even as Pinkney warned Joy not to speak.

"I'm not going to listen to this. I refuse. Do what I'm paying you to do and stop this."

Eve paused the playback. "You're not in charge here. You're never going to be in charge of anything again, unless it's the prison laundry. This is one of several private conversations you had with Magdelana Percell, who is now charged with conspiracy to murder, with conspiracy in murder for hire of a police officer, with conspiracy to steal roughly half a billion in jewels from the vault in the office of Barrister House, among other things. All of which you were part of and had knowledge of before and after the fact."

She glanced at Pinkney. "I'm sure your client hasn't informed you of all this."

"Voiceprints on clone 'links are hardly one hundred percent accurate."

"Accurate enough, and she admitted to the private conversation, on the record, before you could stop her. Let's finish this playback where your client and Magdelana consult on hiring a Timothy Kruger to kill me, and the subsequent conversation where your client agrees to wire the down payment for the hit. Then we can backtrack to the earlier ones where they conspired to hire a thief to take the jewels, discussed your client's wish to eliminate her brother and use that burglary as cover to do so—and set up the thief for the murder."

She shifted to Joy. "We've got it all, and to add a nice flourish, there's the hundred million or so, and the gold bars, in your home office safe. We'll be going over your books, and taking a hard look at where you skimmed from the company your father founded and left in your brother's hands instead of yours."

"I'd like to consult with my client."

"Consult!" Joy turned on him. "I'm not paying you to consult. You assured me you would handle this quickly."

"We'll give you a minute." Eve rose. "Dallas, Peabody, and Reo exiting Interview for attorney-client consultation. Record off.

"She's going to fire him," Eve said when they stepped out.

"That or he withdraws as counsel." Reo shook her head. "She didn't tell him a damn thing. He'd have been prepared for some of this if she'd told him. He'd have worked out a strategy to counter some of it. He'd already have a deal in mind to propose after we went a few rounds."

"She's scared," Peabody put in. "But she's more mad and insulted."

"She's already said too much on record. Admitting the 'link's hers, private conversation." Reo shrugged. "He knows even if he can get her off on the murder, she's cooked on the murder for hire."

Minutes later, Pinkney stepped out. "I'm no longer attorney of record on this matter. Ms. Barrister believes, against advice, she is more capable of handling this interview and its results."

After a nod, he walked to the elevator.

"I'm going in hard," Eve said. "She'll break. The scared and the mad and yeah, the insult. No nice cop, Peabody. Any opening you see, you go hard."

"Yippee!"

They stepped back in, Eve restarted the record.

"Let the record show Ms. Barrister has released her attorney. Do you waive legal representation?"

"What good is it? Idiots." She tried to fold her arms, looked shocked to find them restrained.

"I won't be treated this way, dragged from my home, thrown in a cell, forced to wear this hideous thing, accused of horrid crimes. Have you forgotten who I am?"

"No." Eve slapped her hands on the table, leaned in. "You're the woman who's been stealing from her own company because she wanted more than she'd been given. You're the woman who plotted for months to murder her own brother because your father favored him."

"How dare—"

"Shut up. You're the woman, the coward, who lured her sick brother out of bed on the pretext of a break-in, and when he stood at his desk, preparing to report it, you're the woman who struck him from behind."

"You can't prove any of that. You—"

"Oh, bitch, please." Eve rounded the table. "You're the woman who, when she heard her sister-in-law coming, hid, and when Aileen saw the husband she loved bleeding on the floor, slipped away. I bet you counted off the seconds until you rushed in, all shocked."

"That's ridiculous!"

But Eve saw the fear growing.

"There was a break-in, there was a burglary! You said so yourself. The Royal Suite was taken from the vault."

"Yeah. You and Magdelana had several conversations about it. We've got them from your 'link."

"It's not my 'link."

"Jesus, Joy, you already said it was. Plus, it's got your prints. Not just voiceprints." Eve wiggled her fingers. "Fingerprints."

"Her father takes some of the blame," Peabody put in. "Always putting her in second place, her brother first. She just couldn't settle for being stupid rich, for having everything handed to her. She wanted what he had, too, and killed him to get more of it."

"What do you know about it?"

"I know a jealous, conniving, murderous bitch when I'm looking at one. You tried to have my lieutenant killed, because you're afraid of her. Your money doesn't mean shit here. You're going down."

"And hard," Eve added. "He got the house, everything in it—that's the vault, too. You couldn't take that! Why the hell should you? You're the firstborn, for God's sake.

"He got the bulk of the business, why should you accept that? The old man wanted a son, and he got one. You? You're an afterthought."

"He had no right! No right to cut me out that way! I wanted what I deserved, what I'd earned!"

"So you took it. You killed your brother so you could take it."

"He was always in the goddamn way! Placating me. 'Oh, you know how he is, Joy. But it's a family business, and yours as much as mine.' Lies! And he finds that vault, and all he can think about is how to give it all back, how to do that without ruining that old bastard's reputation and legacy?"

"So you got him out of the way, and opened a way for you to take control, to spin the vault so you'd look like the good guy. You moved the break-in from Saturday night to Friday because he wasn't well."

"Easier that way," Peabody put in, then clutched her hands together. "'Oh, Nathan, I think someone's downstairs. Please go down and see.'"

"As if I couldn't handle it myself." Joy's chin jutted. "Typical male, typical, typical."

"You came up behind him. You took that amethyst club, and you struck him with it. You killed him with it."

"Nathan was always fond of that piece. Then Aileen's calling him, coming toward the office. I nearly had to kill her, too. Idiot. But she didn't see anything but Nathan, so I left her to it, left her to scream like a lunatic."

She looked at Eve. "I paid good money to have you dealt with. I wouldn't be here if it had been money well spent."

"Tough luck. You know, you don't strike me as a woman who wants to go down alone. You weren't in this alone. You're going to take some hard lumps, Joy. Don't you want the others to take theirs? Come on, Joy, pay them back."

Joy took a deep breath. Folded her hands on the table.

"It was all her idea. That blond bitch. All of it. She's the one who should be in here. She lured me into it."

"How?"

"I stopped by to see my father, doing my duty by him, as always. I saw the office door locked. I have a key. I thought, I actually worried he might be in there hurt or even dead, so I unlocked it and went in.

"She was in there, in the vault I didn't even know existed. He'd told her. He hadn't told his own daughter, but he'd told her. It all started there. It all started in that room. It all started with her."

When it was done, Eve stepped out.

"I'll take her down, Dallas, and write it up."

"Write it up later. Get her down there and have them send the broker up. We'll keep it moving."

"I can't take any more coffee, but I still need caffeine." Reo pointed to Vending. "I'm getting a Coke. Do you want?"

"Pepsi."

Mira stepped out of Observation. "She has no remorse. She regrets being caught, regrets what consequences she'll face, but she doesn't regret killing her brother, attempting to have you killed, embezzling. She doesn't regret leaving her two nieces without a father, or her sister-in-law without her husband."

"Because she's the center of her own world."

"That's exactly right. You did good work in there, all of you, and she certainly gave you more than enough to see the other two share her fate."

Eve cracked the tube Reo offered. "Broker next. I don't know the extent of his feelings for Magdelana. If he has them, he might try to protect her. He can't, and we'll make that clear. I wouldn't snarl at a deal on this one, as long as he does plenty of time."

"He's got a good lawyer, slightly on the sleazy side but decent enough in litigation. She—Edie French—is repping them both."

As she drank, Eve smiled. "Good to know."

"I'd like to continue to observe."

"That's always welcome."

She waited until the broker and the lawyer—wearing a dark pink skirted suit, her streaked brown hair in a fancy braid—settled in Interview.

"Next round," she said, and pitched the empty tube into a recycler.

Chapter Twenty-Three

Eve walked in, started the record, read off the necessary. She sat.

French started the ball rolling.

"My client and his partner, whom I'm also representing, contend that Joy Barrister requested they hold an exclusive auction for several pieces, including the Royal Suite. With the request she offered proof of purchase for all items."

Eve let out a quick laugh. "Are you seriously trying that? Anyone in your client's line of work is well aware the Royal Suite was stolen from the Tate in London a number of years ago, and has been missing since that time."

"My client is a retired businessman who has lived in Sorrento, Italy, quietly, for a number of years."

"Your client is a broker for thieves, fences, and those who covet what doesn't belong to them, a business he inherited from his grandfather.

Just save it. We have the evidence, and we have Joy Barrister's statement, which coincides with said evidence."

She looked directly at the broker. "You and Magdelana conspired with Joy Barrister to steal the Royal Suite from the vault where Henry Barrister had it locked away, after he paid to have it stolen. This theft was used as cover for the murder of Nathan Barrister. Not by the thief, but by Joy Barrister. She has confessed.

"She has further confessed to conspiring with you and Magdelana Percell in the hiring of a hit man to kill me."

"Wait a bloody minute." Shock covered Mulligan's face. "I know nothing about such a thing. Nothing."

He had plenty of Irish in his voice, but it didn't make her feel sentimental.

"Playback, Peabody."

Once again, Peabody played back the conversation between Magdelana and Joy.

"Jesus, fecking Jesus Christ. That's madness."

"My client is not on that playback, nor is his name mentioned."

"He's been sharing a villa and a bed with your other client, whose voice is."

"Regardless—"

"No regardless." Mulligan held up a hand. "I'm saying this clear. I knew nothing of this. She went around me, behind me. She'd know I wouldn't go for it. You don't go for cops. You don't."

"You want us to believe that."

"I do, as it's God's truth. Killing isn't what I do, or have ever done. You said Joy Barrister did her brother. I believed it was the thief in some sort of panic. I was prepared to give you the name of her in exchange for a deal."

"We have her name. We have her statement. We have Joy Barrister's confession."

He lifted both hands to his face as his head drooped.

"And I've been played for a bloody fool. No, I'll speak," he said when his lawyer tried to interrupt. "I was retired, and content. I had a wife, I had a family, and then she came along. I lost it all for her. So bewitched was I, so entranced by her. And she played me for a bloody fool. Did murder or had it done."

He turned to the lawyer. "I'm the one paying you. And you won't be representing Magdelana. What money she has, I expect they've frozen up. I have the funds that have nothing to do with any of this, so I'm the one paying you. And not for her."

"All right."

"I know I'm on the hook here, but I'll swear, take any test you have to prove the truth of it. I knew nothing of this paid hit, knew nothing of plans to kill anyone. I broker deals, or did."

Reo nodded. "If what you tell us proves to be true, if you had no knowledge, did not conspire in the murder for hire of a police officer, if you had no prior knowledge of the plans to murder Nathan Barrister, we can take two life terms, consecutive, off the table."

"In exchange for one? Bugger it."

"In exchange for twenty to twenty-five, on-planet. If every single word you say on record proves true. One lie, it's life."

"Take the deal." He put a hand on his lawyer's arm. "I want the deal."

"In writing," French said.

"It will be. This is on record. I've offered a deal, you've accepted. Both on record."

"Start talking," Eve said.

"I first met Magdelana a year ago. Only a year ago, and everything's changed."

Nearly ninety minutes later, Eve stepped into her office. And again, Roarke waited.

"I came down when you were finishing with him. You'll eat something now."

"I had pizza."

"Before dawn." He programmed the AutoChef. "He had a lot to say in the few minutes I was observing with Mira."

"He spilled enough guts for five people. I just came in for five to clear my head before we take her in."

"You believe he didn't know about the Barrister murder, about you?"

"Yeah, I do. Do you?"

"Aye." He took out a bowl. "Here, sit now. It's the tortilla soup you like. Fuel up for her."

"Yeah, okay. How about you?"

"I tapped your AC for the group in the lab. I expected you to look tired."

She ate. "Nope. Not tired. I haven't had a fizzy, but I'm energized. You need to be okay with what's coming."

"I am. I find myself with some sympathy for Mulligan. He'll spend two decades behind bars because he couldn't or didn't resist her. She'd have done the same to me. In fact tried that once."

She ate more, sat back. "Abernathy's grateful for you seeing he didn't get dead last night."

"I'd hardly stand idle while anyone took a hit in the back."

"He wants you to know your file's closed. You won't have any problem with him."

Now he smiled a little. "I didn't have a problem with him, but I appreciate the gesture. And I know it eases you, so for that, I'm more than grateful."

"It does. And when I'm done with her, I'm done with her."

"We are."

"We are. I'm going to have her brought up now, finish this off."

"I'll be in Observation." He leaned down, kissed her. "I'm in there with you. I stand with you."

"I know it."

When she went back into the bullpen, Jenkinson stood up. "You taking her now, boss?"

"Yeah. I told you to go home. Whitney's got us covered for the rest of the shift."

"You think any of us are going home before you finish? Not a chance. FYI, Trueheart's not the only one with a shiner."

And that added another dose of the energized.

"Peabody."

"I'm with you. I'll tag Reo. She wants to observe unless we need her in there."

"Not this time."

Once again, she opened the door to Interview A.

Magdelana did have a shiner, and a bruised cheekbone. Wanded, Eve assumed. Seeing her in the orange jumpsuit added one more bounce.

Before she could call for the record, Magdelana held up a hand.

"I want five minutes with Dallas, off record and without eyes and ears behind that glass." She rattled her restraints. "I can hardly hurt you."

"Yeah, that's my concern. Take down Observation. Peabody, step out. It's okay. Step out."

When she had, Eve sat. Saw Magdelana's eyes land, and hold a moment, on the Giant's Tear.

And the quick flash of fury laced with envy.

Yeah, Roarke knew it would burn.

"Say what you want to say."

"If you don't find a way to get me out of this, I'll make sure Roarke pays the price. I know he stole the Royal Suite from the Tate. I know details about every job we worked on together. He probably stole that rock you're wearing around your neck."

Eve lifted it by the chain. "This little thing?"

"You think you're smart? You're nothing, and nothing to him but a kind of shield."

Eve yawned. "Sorry. Long night. Done yet?"

"I'll spill it all. I'll get a deal or he goes down. Now cut me loose."

"No."

"I thought you cared about him."

"You'll never understand what we have together. Stop trying. You can claim Roarke broke into the Tate as a teenager and took those emeralds. And not only won't anyone believe it, but I'll turn it so you were part of that heist. Part of the team."

"There wasn't a team."

"Interpol and Scotland Yard think otherwise. Anything you accuse him of, I'll hang on you." She leaned in. "You should believe me, you should know I'm really good at this, and I'll make sure decades are added to what you'll already pay."

She sat back. "You really never knew him. Do you think he left a single bread crumb? Anywhere, anytime?"

"You'd risk that?"

"It's not a risk because I do know him."

"I'll dredge it all up anyway."

"Go ahead, and I'll make it my mission in life to see you're the one who pays the price. I'll make it hurt, Magdelana. Beyond even what you're afraid of right now."

Before Magdelana looked away, Eve saw what she needed to see. Fear and despair with it.

"I warned you."

"Yeah, back at you. Observation up." Eve rose, opened the door.

"Record on," she said.

She waited until Peabody took her seat.

"You've been read your rights, on record, and are aware of the charges against you."

"It's all a mistake. I was duped, used."

"Yeah, we've heard that one before, right, Peabody?"

"If I had a dollar for every time, I'd be rich."

"You are presently without legal counsel. If you can't afford counsel, counsel will be provided for you."

"Access to my funds has been cut off, and I'm well aware how useless public defenders are. I'm an innocent woman, and have nothing to hide. I trusted the wrong man. I gave him my heart, and he used and betrayed me."

"You're speaking of James Mulligan?"

"That's correct. He swept me off my feet." A little tear slid out of her good eye. "He promised me everything. I thought we were happy. I thought he loved me."

"You were so happy you came to New York last December and stayed several days at Barrister House with Henry Barrister and shopped your ass off on his accounts."

"Henry was a dear friend. I knew he didn't have long to live, so wanted to spend some time with him. He was always generous."

"You went by the name Sabrina Fancy."

"His nickname for me."

"No, the name on the false identification you used to pass through Customs. You flew on Barrister's private, but you still had to pass through Customs on your return, considering the shopping haul. It was on that visit that Henry, suffering from cognitive decline, showed you the vault in his home office and the contents therein."

"I don't know what you're talking about."

"Do you think the staff didn't notice the time you spent in there? With and without him. The time you spent in there with Joy Barrister?"

Magdelana let out a quick, frustrated sound. "Of course I spent time in there with him, but he never showed me a vault. And I've never actually met his daughter."

"Really? That's strange."

"Playback time, Lieutenant?"

"Yeah, let's roll that. You know where to start."

Joy, sweetheart, you know you shouldn't contact me at this point.

Magdelana's lips trembled open, shut again firmly as the playback continued.

"The two of you seem chummy enough, for people who never met, to conspire to hire a paid assassin to take me, a police officer, out. To kill me."

"That's certainly not me on that recording."

"Jesus, dumbass, do you think we haven't traced it back to the clone 'link in the luggage in the freaking bridal suite in the Cochran Estates?"

"I don't have a clone 'link."

"Not anymore you don't. It was tucked away up there with your fancy underwear, and it has your prints. Voice and finger. We have the conversations on that 'link and Joy Barrister's."

Eve rose, strolled around the table, leaned down. "You're going down for that one, bitch. No getting around it. You're cooked there."

"I want a deal."

"Yeah? I want a nice big glass of wine. In a few hours I'll actually get my want. You never will."

"I have information, and plenty of it, on James Mulligan and on Joy Barrister. They used me, they colluded and used me. I was in love, and that made me foolish, vulnerable. I didn't know what they planned, then I was in too deep. I want immunity, and I'll tell you everything."

"Gee, what do you think, Peabody?"

Peabody made a buzzing sound. "Too late."

"You know, that's right. Barrister's already confessed to everything, and given us just a big shiny treasure trove on you. And we made a deal with Mulligan already. He added to that shiny."

"They're lying!"

"So Joy Barrister didn't kill Nathan Barrister and pay a hit man to kill me?"

"No. Yes, yes, she did all that, but they're lying about the rest."

"Selectively lying, all while confessing—in Joy's case—to murder and more so she'll spend the rest of her life in a cage. Man, she must have something against you."

"She does! She hates me. She and James were lovers. She loves him, and wants to punish me for being with him, for taking him from her."

"Here I thought you took him from his wife."

"I was blinded by my feelings for him, and he . . . he twisted them. Used them. And she hated me for being with him, for my close friendship with her father."

"How did she know you were friends with her father if you never met? You're tripping over yourself here, Magdelana. I bet you're a lot better at this if you have some time to think."

She rounded the table again. "Listen, stupid! We have the 'link conversations. The lab verifies it's your voice. And none of those conversations support what you're making up here on the spot. You ran the show, start to fucking finish. You're nobody's dupe, and you're not capable of love."

Magdelana's breath came too fast now, and her fingers twisted together. "You'll be sorry," she murmured.

Eve got down, pushed her face close. "No, I won't, but you will be."

She saw that fear again, and the belief with it.

"I can give you others, plenty of others."

"Not interested."

"Thieves, murderers, hired killers, weapons runners."

"Don't care, got you. But it does cause me to wonder what kind of pool you swim in. Last December, Joy Barrister caught you in Henry's office, vault open. And you drew her in, you offered her what she wanted most. Control, more, her brother out of the picture, and she traded that for what you wanted. The Royal Suite."

"If any of that were true, why only that if there was so much more?"

"Biggest prize. Get your hands on that, your rep's made. You'll be rolling in it. You can be whoever you want wherever you want."

"An innocent man and a cop have to die," Peabody added. "You don't care about that, as long as you get that big prize, that big rep, throw that big party."

"Interpol and the locals are going through that villa in Sorrento, inch by inch. They're going to find plenty."

"I want a deal. I'll confess to arranging the theft, but that's all. I want a deal."

"You hired someone to break into Barrister House. You gave them the security system, the combination of the vault, and you instructed them to take only the Royal Suite. To leave the vault open and the window closed."

"That's right. That's all I did. The thief I hired is Jenna Delaney."

"We already have her name, and she has immunity."

More shock. "How could she—"

"She has a moral compass. And she's one more person, it turns out, who's smarter than you. Hiring her's not all you did. Jesus, have you forgotten the conversations, on record, with Joy Barrister?"

"I'll give you more." Another tear spilled, and struck Eve as genuine. "I want a deal."

"You get nothing. Two men are dead, six officers were injured at your big show last night. A family's lost a husband and father."

This time when Eve slapped a hand on the table, Magdelana jumped.

"You get nothing. You've confessed, on record, for arranging the break-in and theft at Barrister House, a felony. A death resulting from the commission of a felony makes you just as responsible as the person who bashed in his skull."

"I didn't kill anyone!"

"You planted the seed, you watered it, fertilized it with your particular brand of bullshit. Now reap the harvest. You are on record conspiring to hire an assassin to murder a police officer."

"You won't give me a deal like the others because you're jealous. You're burned up with jealousy because Roarke loved me, because he had the best sex of his life with me."

The laugh just burst out. "Yeah, right, that's it." She lifted her left hand. "Didn't put one of these on your finger, did he?"

"He just wanted a cop in his pocket."

"The lieutenant's in no one's pocket."

"It's fine, Peabody. She can try to convince herself to believe that. She'll have the rest of her life to try to convince herself to believe that. You gotta have something to hold on to when you're doing a couple of lifetimes in an off-planet cage."

"I'm not going to prison."

"Oh yeah, you are." Once more she leaned down, leaned in. "For Nathan Barrister, you're going to prison. For arranging the theft of the Royal Suite, you're going to prison—you've confessed, on record, of your own volition."

She stared into Eve's eyes now with pure hate.

"I should've found a better hit man."

"That's right. Why didn't you?"

"We were in a hurry. Tim was handy."

"Your mistake. And since he's dead, killed in his attempt to kill me, you're also on the hook there. You're going over, Magdelana, and you're never coming back."

"I'll get out, and I'll do you myself. I'll kill you myself."

"No and no, but you can hold on to that, too."

"I'm adding threatening a police officer with bodily harm to the charges, Dallas."

"Oh hell, Peabody, give her that one."

"No, sir. I won't."

Eve shrugged. "Anyway. Interview End."

"He stole the Royal Suite."

Eve paused at the door. "He who?"

"Roarke, you know damn well. He stole it from the Tate."

"Really? He'd have been, what, about eighteen? Nice try."

"He told me!"

"Uh-huh. You buy that one, Peabody? That some kid from Dublin went to London, broke through the security of the Tate Gallery, then through the security around the Royal Suite, and walked away with it?"

She could see Peabody did, at least sort of. "Nope. It was a team. No other way." She rolled her eyes at Magdelana. "I'm saying she's the one who's jealous. Kind of pathetic. I'll take her back down."

"Thanks."

Eve stepped out, breathed out. And every cop in her division, including her commander, stepped out of Observation.

And, obviously preplanned, every one of them gave her a golf clap.

"Cute. Go the hell home."

"I'm writing it up."

"Detective Sergeant, go home."

"No, sir, boss, I'm writing up the interviews, filing them." Jenkinson jabbed a finger at her. "You go the hell home."

"I've got a couple of personal matters to see to first," she said when Roarke and Mira stepped out with Reo.

"You go on and do that. We got you covered here. I hear you've got a cop bar opening up soon. When you do, first round's on me."

"That it's not." Roarke laid a hand on Jenkinson's shoulder. "Drinks on the house opening night for everyone here."

"Who's going to argue with that?" And Jenkinson strolled off with the others.

Whitney stepped up. "Exceptional work, Lieutenant. Relay the same to Detective Peabody."

"I will, sir, thank you."

"I enjoyed this. Damn if I didn't enjoy this."

When he left, Mira moved up. "As classic a sociopath as I've ever seen. The planet will be the better with her off it. You handled her perfectly."

"In the end, she turned out to be an easy mark."

"She underestimated you, that's my take," Reo said. "If she's smart, she'll get a lawyer, even if it's a PD. Won't do her any good. Like you said. She's cooked. I'll go write up my end of it. Get some sleep."

Then she stood alone with Roarke.

"There are darker places in her than there were, I think. Or they've spread to smother any of the light she had."

"Do you still want to see her?"

"I do. It can wait if you'd rather be done with this today."

"No, let's close the book all the way, then toss it in a fire. I'll take you down, give you the time and space."

She took him down, down past the more hospitable holding cells where unfortunates waited for bail or lawyers, down farther to the much less hospitable where more waited for transport to other cages.

A guard opened a security door to let them through.

"Who you going for, LT?"

"Magdelana Percell. Quick visit."

"Down four, on the left. That one offered me a bang if I let her out."

"Did she?"

"Yeah. Even if I weren't gay? I mean, step back."

"Write it up."

"You know, it happens."

"I know, but for this one, write it up."

She walked Roarke back to where Magdelana sat on the cot in the cell. And stood slowly when she saw them.

Eve stepped back, nodded to the guard.

The electronic bars slid open. Roarke stepped in and heard them close behind him.

Magdelana leaped toward him, threw her arms around him.

"I knew you'd come. Oh God, Roarke, thank God for you. What they've done to me! I was a fool, I admit I was a fool, but I trusted . . ."

She pressed her face against his chest, trembled, wept.

"You'll get me out, I know you will. Pay whatever needs to be paid. That woman." She lifted her face now, tears delicately spilling. "She attacked me! Again. Look at me, look what she did. She struck me. Help me get out. Help me get away from her. I think she's going to kill me."

"Take your hands off me, Magdelana, or I'll take them off, and you won't like it."

"Roarke." Stepping back, she pressed her fingers to her lips, brought out more tears. "You can't blame me for what happened between us before. I love you. I only wanted—"

"Be quiet, and listen to me. Listen very carefully to me. You'll get no help from me. Not now, not in any lifetime. Be grateful you have a life to spend in prison. You tried to kill my wife."

"No, no, no. It's a lie. I never—"

"Be quiet!"

It wasn't the sharp, commanding tone that silenced her, but the look in his eyes.

And that brought a kind of visible terror.

"I know what you did, all you did. You helped kill a man who leaves a wife and children behind him. For that, I'd never help you. You set a hit man on my wife, and for that, but for her asking it of me, you wouldn't draw the next breath.

"No," he murmured. "No, not true. You live because she's shown me there's a right way, a just way, and a wrong and selfish way."

"You can't mean—"

"I do. Know I do. I never loved you any more than you me. But I cared for the woman I thought you were. I warned you before to stay away. You chose otherwise. Here's the price you pay for it."

"I could've ruined you. I didn't."

"You tried. Some of the eyes and ears behind the glass were mine. You failed, and you always will there. I owe you pain, Magdelana, and I'll hold that in reserve should you try to come at me, and twice that and more pain if you try to come at her.

"Sit on the cot."

"No, I—"

He spoke, very softly. "Do you want me to put you there?"

She stepped back, sat. And he stepped up to the bars.

"Eve."

She'd given him privacy, and trust, keeping clear so he could say what he needed to say without her listening.

Now she moved up again. "On the gate," she called to the guard.

When the door opened, he came out. Once more he heard them close behind him as he walked to Eve.

Magdelana rushed to the bars. "You can't leave me here! I'll die in prison. I can't live that way. You can't leave me here."

He kept walking, never looked back. When they were through the security door, Eve took his hand. Because he needed it.

"Okay?"

"I am, yes."

"So we close the book?"

"We do, but burning a book, even this one? I can't do it. So we'll lock it away."

"That'll work. Want to go have a lot of wine, get a little drunk, maybe have some crazy monkey sex?"

He let out a laugh, an easy one that relieved her. Then lifted her hand, pressed her knuckles to his lips.

"I honestly can't think of anything I could want more."

"Then let's go the hell home."

KEEP READING FOR AN EXCLUSIVE IN DEATH Q&A WITH J. D. ROBB!

Overview

When did you first meet Eve Dallas?

Well, I can't even remember exactly when, but I know my children were still in school. I had been working and I got tired. I had about 15 minutes before they got home from school, so I decided to lie down.

And that's when it happened – while lying down, I started thinking about this woman: Difficult ... Homicide Lieutenant ... Ooh, wouldn't it be cool if it was in the future? ... a dark past and hard-bitten, cynical, sarcastic, with this difficult background.

Then I thought, well, there's nothing I can do with her. I didn't see how I could fold that kind of a character into a Nora Roberts book.

So, she just had to wait.

When I was finally convinced to do some books with a pseudonym, I thought, "Okay, I'll agree to do it if I can do something different." And that's what she was. She was something different for me, the futuristic setting was different for me.

And they (publisher, editor, agent) said, "Okay, give that a shot."

What was it like to create a world in the near future?

I could make my own world. That was a lot of freedom.

Societal changes, technology, all of it – I didn't have to answer to reality. It was speculative and it was *my* speculation of how I would like to see the world with – as you know – licensed companions and the gun ban and the Autochef (that was the coolest thing for me) and how the police operated. The fact that everything changes, everything stays the same. You still have people who are going to go out and kill other people, and you still have to have investigators and the rule of law and the courts and all of that. That has to be stable.

But I could just make up everything else, traveling, space travel. The link that I had – well before the iPhone and the smartphone. It was kind of cool to see all of the things I imagined actually happen after I'd written about them in the 90s.

How did you envision the Personal Portable Computer when you first wrote about one in 1994?

I absolutely envisioned that as being a computer you could hold in your hand.

What I didn't know (and I can't change it because I built the world and you have to stick to the rules) is what do we need a link for? So the characters have to have these two devices now because I didn't quite foresee the future like Steve Jobs. I didn't see that you could just have everything, the communication, the search engine, cameras, all of it, in something you could hold in your hand. So I had two.

Roarke

When Roarke walked onto the page, what was your first impression?

When Roarke walked on the page, I knew he was much more than a suspect. This was going to be the guy, because he was perfect for it.

I didn't know *everything* about his background. You just don't until you get to know the characters and they evolve.

But I knew that, like Eve, he'd come from different, difficult beginnings, horrific beginnings, just like she did. (They don't know that about each other either.) But the attraction is there. They get each other, whether they really understand that or not. And then they learn more about each other. He was someone, he was much too interesting to be a one-off, just a suspect and then we move ahead.

Was it important to you that Roarke and Summerset learn that there are good cops in the world?

I think it was really important to show Roarke and

Summerset that not all cops are bad, not all cops are careless. And certainly that not all cops are like the ones they dealt with during the end of the Urban Wars, who were full of corruption and violence.

That there are some cops – and Eve's got that inner squad – who not only respect the rule of law but the spirit of it and again stand for the victim. The victim comes first.

Summerset

What was your vision of Summerset?

I saw Summerset as very formal and – as Roarke's *major domo* – someone who takes care of a big-ass house. Very responsible, very formal, very snooty, is how I saw him. We don't know right away that he's basically raised Roarke and saved him, but he takes his responsibilities (for the house) and his responsibility for Roarke on a personal level very seriously. He's a very serious man.

Why does Summerset still see to the day-to-day running of the house?

I think he loves running the house. He's Roarke's father and what a wonderful situation for him to have his grown son to be a part of his daily life.

He likes to cook, he likes to bake, he likes to organize, and he can certainly take all the time off he wants. He has another life, but this is something he wants. He wouldn't do it so well if he didn't want to do it.

Could you explain Summerset's initial reaction to Eve Dallas?

I think when he first meets Eve, he's appalled, seriously appalled. He sees the street cop — kind of crude and light on manners and she doesn't dress well. She doesn't take care of her hair.

He sees the surface because that's all she lets anybody see at that point and he is sincerely appalled: What? What is this? How can Roarke — who has such culture and such taste and style — be attracted to this person who has none of those things?

Plus: a cop.

Do Eve and Summerset have a loving relationship at this point in the series?

I know that a lot of readers think they love each other like a father and daughter. No, I don't think so. I think they have affection — and some of it *reluctant* affection.

I think Somerset would look after her. She has been hurt to save him from being hurt. That's her nature.

They certainly don't hate each other as they did. I mean, they just despised each other initially. They've evolved because they both love Roarke. They have come to understand that they *both* love Roarke. That, again, makes a foundation. It makes a kind of bond. And I do think the insults and that sort of thing are habitual. I wouldn't call it their love language, but that's just how they talk to each other.

Expanding the series

Initially, you planned In Deaths as a trilogy.
Yes, the In Death series was conceived as a trilogy.

Each case stood on its own, but the overarching theme was Eve learning about her past.
Yes, Eve learning about where she'd come from. And also the evolving relationship with Roarke. All of that I would thread through three books.

That was the initial plan. So I kind of had all of that in mind, even when I wrote the first book, the pacing and the timing and how it's all going to come around and be wrapped up in book three.

What made you decide to expand beyond a trilogy?
I decided to write more because I'd really fallen for the characters and the world, all of it.

I didn't think I would like to write books under another name. I was very resistant. If I write it, I want my name on it.

And then I got that first book.

I had written the second by then, but when I got the first actual book, it was the coolest thing ever.

So there was that. And I thought, well, I will continue. I could look at the relationship again, now that they're married. But, they're still learning about each other.

They haven't settled into each other yet because they really didn't know each other that well when they got married. They loved each other, but they still had so much to learn. Eve had a ton to learn about marriage.

And then I took the series case by case, the case being the focus with subplots and subtext about whatever was going on outside the investigation.

Then you have more characters popping in and that kind of thing.

And that evolution of Eve as cop and as boss, all of that, I could grow it, instead of having that limited to three and now it's done.

I had all the time in the world to make changes that made sense in her evolution as well as adding characters that made sense.

Urban Wars

When you started* Naked in Death, *did you see the Urban Wars as a potentially real event?

It seemed to me that if things didn't change, if they got worse, we could be heading toward something very like the Urban Wars.

I put them in Eve's past for the books because that wasn't the story I wanted to write.

I wanted to see how people had come out of the Urban Wars. How things had changed. How they looked at what had happened before. And how to avoid letting it happen again.

Because when you just have cities burning and people killing each other whether it's for ideology or it's because "you have that and I want that" or whatever the reason, society isn't going to last very long. I wanted to hope that people have more common sense. Like I said, you still have terrible murders and bullshit things happen, but let's not do that again.

What it's like to write an In Death

Is writing an In Death like visiting friends?

It very much is. The world is familiar, the people are familiar. You can't get too comfortable or you're able to coast through the book and that's not going to be any good.

So you have to come up with something that challenges yourself as a writer and the characters and will appeal to the readership.

You have to – every time – repeat it's 2061 because somebody might have just picked up that book as the first. You have to give at least a brief overview of the main characters and who they are and what they do.

You have to come up with something that either you haven't done before or you do it again but in a different way.

And the books are really so interesting to write. I still really love writing them. If I didn't, I would wrap it up.

Code name

If Eve lived through the Urban Wars, what would've been her code name?

What would her code name be?

I don't know – Badger maybe. It would have to be something animal. I would have to think about it. It wouldn't come to me like that [snaps fingers] because it would have to be right. Could be Fox [nods], could be somebody that's smart and determined.

So, smart and determined. I used code names [in Bonded], so one occurs to me, but I gave that to a character, so it couldn't be hers.

If you lived in the Urban Wars, what would your code name be?

What would my code name be? I don't know, what's an introverted animal that just wants to be left alone?
Voice off-screen: Armadillo.
Nora: There you go. I could be an armadillo.

NORA ROBERTS

For the latest news, exclusive extracts
and unmissable competitions, visit

 /NoraRobertsJDRobb
www.fallintothestory.com